"Although he was nominated for the Nobel Prize in literature four times, Stefan Żeromski's work is not as widely known outside Poland as it should be. Thus this elegant translation is most welcome. Set in Paris, Warsaw, and the spa town of Cisy, the novel is surprisingly modern. At its heart is the story of Tomasz Judym, a young doctor torn between his dedication to bettering the situation of those in the poverty he had escaped and the seduction of working for those who live comfortable, seemingly sophisticated lives. When he meets a young woman who shares his views, he must make a decision about his future. Throughout the novel, descriptions of nature echo the struggle of life at the turn of the century as Judym recognizes that what is sickening his patients is sickening the earth as well. A beautiful, prescient story."

    —Celia Jeffries, author of *Blue Desert*

"A much welcome—indeed, superb—translation of a Polish classic, *The Homeless* follows a young idealistic doctor making his way in a world in need of change. Moved by the plight of both the lower classes and the natural environment, he confronts the overweening materialism of the age of industrialization. The concerns raised by the great Polish novelist Stefan Żeromski over a century ago still resonate today."

    —Patrice M. Dabrowski, author of *Poland: The First Thousand Years,* editor, H-Poland

"Translated in all its lyricism and reverence for the natural world, *The Homeless* is formally Victorian in style, but timeless in sensibility. Żeromski was celebrated for his critique of environmental destruction and the woeful state of public health in Poland at the end of the nineteenth century, but a surprising bonus here is his proto-feminist empathy with both educated women forced by social convention into marriage or frivolous pursuits and poor women whose lives are limited to child-bearing, hunger, ignorance, and the potential heartbreak of emigration."

    —Karen Manners Smith, Emerita Professor of Women's History, Emporia State University

"For all the seeming outwardness of his mission to create hygienic living conditions for the poor, Tomasz Judym, the impassioned doctor at the center of *The Homeless*, is equally in thrall to his own porous, lush, and turbulent interiority. In a different author's hands, this high-minded romantic hero, subject to such flights and falls of emotion and sensation, could prove exhausting. Yet Judym never fails to fascinate, largely because of the marvelous poetic prose of Stefan Żeromski—so granular are his descriptions and evocations, so dense with ingenious metaphors, arresting visual imagery, and music."

—**Deborah Gorlin, author of *Open Fire* and *Life of the Garment***

"Hailed in turn as his nation's conscience and the spiritual beacon of his generation, Stefan Żeromski weaved, with *The Homeless*, a poignant story of a young doctor torn between ambition, vocation, and love—one that remains as sadly compelling and compassionate today as it was over a century ago."

—**Jeremi Szaniawski, Amesbury Professor of Polish Language and Culture, UMass Amherst**

"Dr. Judym, who comes from a poor Jewish family, is a highly dedicated doctor without a home of his own, a 'doctor without borders' who unapologetically advocates for and delivers expert medical care and humanitarian aid to those in greatest need while making the ultimate sacrifice of his own personal happiness. The detailed descriptions of nature and of the coal mine create a sense of awe but also show how nature can be raw and unforgiving."

—**Mark Poznansky, MD, PhD, Director, Vaccine and Immunotherapy Center, Massachusetts General Hospital; Professor of Medicine, Harvard Medical School**

"Żeromski describes the bleak and powerless lives of industrial workers with a pathos that elicited a wide contemporary response to the novelist's call for social reform. As the protagonist, Dr. Tomasz Judym, forces upon himself a choice about which class he will serve, Żeromski illuminates the socioeconomic matrix that precipitated many of the great conflicts and sweeping political changes of the 20th century. The novel is not an easy read, but it is worth the reader's patience."

—**Frederick Smith, MD, physician and bioethicist specializing in the care of indigent patients**

"*The Homeless* addresses the persistent challenges of infectious disease outbreaks and dangerous workplace exposures. A poignant story of the struggle of one individual to promote public health that resonates to this day."

—Lisa Chasan-Taber, Professor and Chair, Department of Biostatistics & Epidemiology, School of Public Health and Health Sciences, University of Massachusetts

THE HOMELESS

THE HOMELESS

THE HOMELESS

Stefan Żeromski

TRANSLATED BY
Stephanie Kraft

WITH AN INTRODUCTION BY
Boris Dralyuk and Jennifer Croft

PAUL DRY BOOKS
Philadelphia 2024

First Paul Dry Books Edition, 2024

Paul Dry Books, Inc.
Philadelphia, Pennsylvania
www.pauldrybooks.com

Translation copyright © 2024 Stephanie Kraft
Introduction copyright © 2024 Boris Dralyuk and Jennifer Croft

Originally published as *Ludzie Bezdomni* in 1900

Printed in the United States of America

Library of Congress Control Number: 2023952437

ISBN 978-1-58988-184-6

Contents

Introduction   vii

Volume One

CHAPTER I	*Venus de Milo*	3
CHAPTER II	In the Sweat of Their Brows	25
CHAPTER III	Dreams	48
CHAPTER IV	Sadness	66
CHAPTER VI	Practice	71
CHAPTER VI	Naughty Dyzio	84
CHAPTER VII	Cisy	96
CHAPTER VIII	A Tuberose	109
CHAPTER IX	Come!	116
CHAPTER X	Confidential	118

Volume Two

CHAPTER I	Large-hearted Provincial Ideas	177
CHAPTER II	Old Men	187
CHAPTER III	"The tear that flows from your eyes"	201
CHAPTER IV	At Dawn	207
CHAPTER V	On the Road	213
CHAPTER VI	At Dusk	231
CHAPTER VII	The Rage of a Cobbler's Son	239

CHAPTER VIII   Where the Wind Blows   244

CHAPTER IX   "Open a New Vein!"   266

CHAPTER X   A Pilgrim   276

CHAPTER XI   "Sprinkle Me, O Lord"   293

CHAPTER XII   Daimonion   300

CHAPTER XIII   The Torn Pine   303

Translator's Note   · 317

Introduction

WHO ARE the titular homeless of Stefan Żeromski's novel? The word occurs twice in this sprawling portrait of Polish society at the end of the nineteenth century. In one instance, it describes the ragtag, fractious band of youthful Polish bohemians knocking around Munich: "There were painters, students, artists of every level of talent, craftsmen and homeless waifs, called in German 'unhappy Poles.'" In the other, it refers to pregnant peasant women taking refuge in a mismanaged hospital in the fictional provincial spa town of Cisy:

> When he felt the need, the administrator of the estate deposited beets, randomly discarded barrel staves from the distillery, broken parts from the threshing machine, and other items in the hospital rooms. At other times attendants, the administrator, the bursar, the estate steward, and other functionaries borrowed beds for their guests, and dishes and utensils were stolen in impeccably careful Slavic style. Often a homeless mother-to-be on whom someone had taken pity lay there during her confinement, or a farm hand ill with colic, or a child with smallpox.

Artists and wastrels, penniless peasants—these certainly fit the bill, but surely Żeromski had others in mind as well. Is not his protagonist, Tomasz Judym, fundamentally a man without a home? An idealistic intellectual in a society only reluctantly lurching into modernity, a highly educated commoner never completely accepted by the gentry, he faces a dilemma: Should he devote himself to alleviating the plight of the poor—a grueling, uphill, perhaps even hopeless path in life—or pursue personal happiness by marrying the woman he loves? Either way, he will remain alienated, unable to experience the human condition in full. And what of his love, Joanna Podborska, an orphan with equally high ideals who works as a governess to young women well above her station? She too is a person without a home, feeling keenly and expressing clearly the precarity of her position: "A governess, as a stranger in her environment and usually socially inferior, is constantly under something like censorship. Let her only give someone reason to bandy her name about and—she is gone!"

For Żeromski's ardent admirers, of whom there were many at the turn of the century, the title of his novel suggested a far larger set, one encompassing not only the seemingly doomed idealistic youth represented by Tomasz and Joanna, but the whole of the Polish nation. Indeed, one of the earliest responses to the work in English, published anonymously in the January 1902 issue of London's *Quarterly Review*, rendered the title as *The Homeless Race*. By the time Żeromski's book appeared, the Polish people had been stateless for over a century. Between 1772 and 1795, what had once been the largest country in Europe was partitioned out of existence by the Russian Empire, the Kingdom of Prussia, and the Habsburgs. The shocking collapse of Poland's sovereignty coincided with, and fueled, a literary efflorescence. For many impressionable European readers, the rise of the Romantic movement established poets, in the words of Percy Shelley, as the "unacknowledged legislators of the world." Among Poles, poets wielded even greater influence. With no acknowledged government or borders to bind and protect them, literature came to serve as legislation; Poles lived and died by their authors' words.

From the time of Adam Mickiewicz (1798–1855), the first and still most cherished Romantic bard of the Polish people, through that of Positivist novelists like Bolesław Prus (1847–1912), who urged their readers to abandon devastatingly foolhardy national rebellion in favor of more attainable causes, down to that of the Young Poland movement, whose authors filtered their ruminations on what was to be done with Polish society through a blend of new stylistic influences ranging from Naturalism to Symbolism, generations of Poles took their cues from literature. Uncertainty as to the wisdom of a series of failed popular uprisings weighed heavily on the hearts of those whose works had driven young men into action, as did a sense of responsibility for various obstacles that stood in the way of Poland's progress: friction between classes, ethnic discrimination, the living conditions of the provincial and urban poor.

Few authorial hearts were as manifestly burdened by these pressing national questions as that of Stefan Żeromski, who was born in 1864 near the town of Kielce, in what was then the Russian partition of Poland.

Shortly before his birth, his father had been deprived of his estate for having participated in the January Uprising, the last and most disastrous of that century's insurrections against Russian rule. Having failed to earn a high school diploma, Żeromski entered a veterinary college in Warsaw, but was expelled for participating in patriotic student activities—a venerable tradition among Polish authors, going back to Mickiewicz. Thereafter, he earned a living as a private tutor and began to write. In the early 1890s, he traveled throughout Europe, storing up impressions of Austria, Germany, and Switzerland that would later find their way into his novels. The first of his novels to attract attention, *The Labors of Sisyphus* (1897), is autobiographical, focusing on Marcin Borowicz's growing rebellion against the Russification forced upon him and his classmates at a provincial high school. Although the title refers to the profitless efforts of the Russifying authorities, it also applies to the opposition; the spirit of Poles may be unbreakable, but the Russians are still in charge. Żeromski shows a certain ambivalence towards his hero's idealism. In taking on a force so much more powerful than himself, is Marcin not destined to keep rolling a boulder uphill all his life?

This ambivalence towards the possibility of progress, this honesty about the plight of his homeless people, is one of the qualities that set Żeromski's work apart from that of the Positivists who came before him. It ensured his place as "the conscience of Polish literature" until his death in November 1925, almost exactly seven years after Poland won its independence. Another quality that set him apart is evident on every page of Stephanie Kraft's deft, insightful translation of *The Homeless*. It is his distinctly modern, Naturalistic style, at one moment unsparingly direct, at another enchantingly lyrical—a style evocatively characterized by that early anonymous critic for *Quarterly Review*: "strong even to brutality, coarse even to slang, reeking of the evil smells of poor men's hovels, jarring as their hoarse voices, unlovely as the sights on which it dwells; withal incisive, picturesque and somehow artistic." A fine example is Tomasz's first glimpse of the countryside on the way to Cisy, which unexpectedly gives rise to bitter memories:

> The doctor had never seen the country—the land, soil, open space—at that time of year. A sacred primitive instinct awakened in him, a dreamlike passion to farm, to sow and tend grain. His feeling diffused and wandered in those wide perspectives.

Near a forest where green leaves had just begun to show was a place for a house on a hill surrounded by trees. Alders and poplars were still black. Only a slender, soaring birch was covered so tightly with a thin film of leaves that the bare twigs were hidden. Pale blue hepatica smiled around the trunks. Beside the forest was a glen with a stream flowing through it. A man was moving on a hillside, leaning over, doing something, working at something, planting or sowing.

"God bless you, fellow. May your grain spring up a hundredfold," Judym thought. His eyes were riveted on the place as if it were his family home. But he saw another home: a basement, a damp grave full of reeking vapors. A father forever drunk, a mother forever sick. Blight, poverty, death. What were they doing there? Why did they live in a cave underground, built deliberately to foster sickness in the body and, in the heart, hatred of the world?

Kraft has made *The Homeless* available to anglophones for the first time one year after the release of Anna Zaranko's retranslation of *The Peasants* (1904–1909), a novel by Władysław Reymont (1867–1925), Żeromski's near contemporary and the winner of the 1924 Nobel Prize in Literature. Both novels depict, with nuance and acuity, the difficult lives of the Polish lower classes at the dawn of a new era. Yet the questions that plague Tomasz and Joanna—questions about the power of the individual in opposition to society, the cost of idealism in a far-from-ideal world, and the value of personal happiness—should make *The Homeless* particularly resonant for readers in our time.

Boris Dralyuk and Jennifer Croft
Summer 2023

VOLUME ONE

· CHAPTER I ·

Venus de Milo

Tomasz Judym was on his way back along the Champs-Élysées from the Bois de Boulogne, to which he had traveled on the Belt Railway. He walked slowly, one step at a time. His hat and coat felt more and more oppressive as the glare of the sun flooded the space around him. A rosy dust hung over the distant panorama of buildings that thrust themselves into view from the Arc de Triomphe—a fine powder that was beginning to eat like rust even into the lovely pale green spring leaves, even into the empress trees. The fragrance of acacia seemed to float from all sides. Its white flowers with reddish centers lay on the gravel, around the trunks, next to the buildings, in the gutters, as if bloodied by a fatal stab. They, too, were sprinkled imperceptibly with the merciless dust.

The time when all the world took its walk was approaching, and the fields were beginning to tremble from coach traffic. A monotonous rattle like the distant noise of a large factory came from the wooden pavement. Beautiful, glistening horses were running by; harnesses, drivers' boxes, and the spokes in the wheels of light vehicles glittered in the sun. And in gleam after gleam, without a pause, women's spring couture passed in streams of pure color, the full prism of colors, creating a delightful impression, like a view of unspoiled nature. Now and then a face emerged from the flood of pedestrians—a refined, delicate face of incredible beauty that caressed the eyes and nerves. The sight of it wrung a sigh from him, like the sigh of a man longing for happiness. Then the face was lost, carried past him in the twinkling of an eye.

In the shelter of chestnut trees, Judym found a free bench. With great satisfaction he sat down near an old nanny with soft hair on her upper lip and two children in tow. He took off his hat and, fixing his eyes on the river of vehicles that rushed through the middle of the street, slowly cooled off.

More and more people were making their way along the sidewalks, elegantly dressed people in gleaming top hats and light-colored overcoats and bodices. An old woman with shifty eyes led a young goat with a snowy white coat into the well-dressed crowd. A pack of children followed the goat with adoring looks, gestures, and a thousand shouts. A big ragamuffin with a red face ran by like a madman, shouting the results of the latest horse race. Then the human river on the sidewalks resumed its flow; even, serene, and charming. In the center its current moved briskly, wreathed in a foam of light, exquisite fabrics that took on an aquamarine tint in the distance.

Every opened leaf threw a clear reflection of its shape on the round white pebbles in the gravel walks. The shadows moved slowly, like the small hand on the white face of a clock. The benches were full, and in the meantime the shade retreated from the place where Judym was sitting, to be replaced by a cascade of molten sunlight. Nowhere around him did he see another refuge, so the doctor rose willy-nilly and trudged on toward the Place de la Concorde. He waited impatiently for a chance to slip through the vortex of coaches, carriages, cabs, bicycles, and pedestrians at the bend in the main wave of traffic rushing from the boulevards in the direction of the Champs-Élysées.

At last he stopped near the obelisk, then pressed on deep into the garden of the Tuileries. It was almost empty. There were only pale children frolicking near the dull pools and a few men in their shirtsleeves playing tennis in the Grande Allée. Passing the gardens, Judym turned toward the river, intending to wander in the shade of the walls on the square in front of Saint-Germain-l'Auxerrois and slide casually into a seat on the open upper level of a bus. At that moment he thought of the empty bachelor apartment on Boulevard Voltaire, where he had spent his nights for a year now, and was repelled by the bareness of its walls, the banality of its furniture, and the overwhelming tedium, the sense of foreignness, that every corner of it exuded. He did not want to work, to go to the clinic. Not for anything in the world.

He found himself at the Quai du Louvre and, with a feeling of blissful relief in his neck and back, stopped in the shade of the first chestnut tree on the boulevard. Languidly he surveyed the dirty, almost black, water of the Seine. As he was standing there like a streetlight, a thought flashed through his mind as if it had come from somewhere outside him: "Why the devil shouldn't you go to the Louvre?"

He turned and went to the great courtyard. Immersing himself in the shade that clung like deep water to the thick wall, he made his way to the main entrance, and was soon in the cool halls on the second floor. Around him stood centuries-old statues of gods, some of extraordinary proportions, some life-size, most with hands and noses irreverently damaged. Judym paid little attention to these defacements of the rulers of the world. Now and then he stopped in front of one, usually when some amusing affront to the divine form caught his eye. What interested him above all was the chance to relax in the exquisite coolness, far from the hubbub of the Parisian street. He was not so much in search of masterpieces as of a bench to sit on. After a long tramp from hall to hall, he happened on one in a corner that adjoined two long galleries and housed the *Venus de Milo*.

In that corner, which formed a small room lighted by one window, the white torso of Venus, or Aphrodite, stood on a low pedestal. A cord wrapped in red plush kept viewers from approaching her. Judym had already seen the precious statue, but had not given it the attention he usually paid works of art.

Now, having found himself a comfortable seat in the shade next to the wall, he began to kill time by gazing at the face of the beauty in marble. Her head was turned in his direction and the dead eyes appeared to be watching him. Her inclined forehead seemed to be emerging from shadows and her brows were knit as if she were looking at something. Judym gazed back at her and only then saw a small, barely visible fold between the eyebrows—as if that head, that mass of stone, were thinking. She peered forcefully into the dusk around her, penetrating it with pale eyes. She was immersed in the mystery of life and smiling at something in that universe of secrets. Exercising her infinite, pure understanding, she possessed knowledge about everything. She saw the works and days of ages on earth; she saw nights and the tears that flowed in their dark hours. Her white forehead still reflected her wise musings, but her dreaming lips exuded great virginal joy. A look of adoration was locked into their smile: adoration of happy love. Of a sinless natural life for a free spirit, a free body. Of the keen power of sensual delight not yet blunted by work or worry, those unhappy sisters.

The smile of the goddess greets one who comes from far away. Once she fell in love with the beautiful mortal, Adonis. The miraculous dreams of first love blossomed in her bosom like the seven-branched amaryllis. Her narrow, slender, round shoulders rose; her virgin loins quivered with a sigh. The long centuries that broke off her arms, tore her chest from her lower body, and furrowed her lovely shoulders with dents never succeeded in destroying her. She stood in twilight, "emerging," the heavenly Anadyomene rising from the sea, the one who arouses love. Her bare hair was fastened in the *krobylos* style, with a beautiful knot. Her slender oval face breathed an indescribable charm.

Only as Judym looked more deeply at the brooding forehead did he understand that he had before him the visage of a goddess. It was Aphrodite herself, who was conceived from the foam of the sea. Without intending to, he recalled the indelicate legend of the cause of that foaming water, the mutilation of Uranus. But indeed this Venus was not Pandemos, or even the wife of Hephaestus or the lover of Anchises—only a bright, good symbol of life, the daughter of the sky and the day.

Judym was so absorbed in his thoughts that he did not notice the people who were moving around him. In any case, there were not many. He only became aware of them when he heard several sentences spoken in Polish in the adjoining hall. He turned his head reluctantly in that direction, certain that someone from the "colony" of Polish expatriates was approaching—someone who would sit by him and assert a right to several minutes of meditation on the beautiful Venus.

He was pleasantly surprised to see the "nonresidents of Paris." There were four of them. First came two young women—very young. The older might have been seventeen, the other perhaps two years younger. Behind them a stout woman moved forward heavily, an aging person with gray hair and a large but still pretty face. Beside the matron walked a young lady of twenty-something, a beautiful, graceful brunette with blue eyes. They all stood in front of the statue and looked at it in silence. Judym heard only the labored, muffled wheezing of the older woman, the rustle of silk with the teenagers' every movement, and the ripple of the pages of a Baedeker as the brunette turned them over.

"Everything is beautiful, my dear," the matron said to her, "but I must sit down. Not a step further! Anyway, it's worth looking at this celebrated lady. Yes, there is even a bench here."

Judym rose from his seat and slowly walked a few steps to the side, as if he wanted to look at the statue from a different angle. The ladies looked at each other inquiringly and lowered their voices. Only the oldest of the three younger women, still intent on the Baedeker, did not see Judym. The stout elderly woman sat down on the bench with an energetic air, stretched her legs to their full length, and answered some whispered remarks from her young companions in a whisper of her own, which, like that of many old ladies, carried so far that if necessary it could have substituted for a telephone.

"Oh, Pole or not, French or not, Spaniard or Turk, I don't care," she said. "May God give him health for coming away from that bench. My legs have given out altogether. Now look at that, you two, for indeed it's something out of the ordinary. I saw it once a long time ago. Somehow it seemed different to me then…"

"Because it was certainly different," said the youngest of her party.

"Don't think about whether it was different or not. Just look. They will ask later in the salon about that. Not a word out of you."

The other teenager needed no encouragement to observe the Venus in an odd way. Her hair was blond, her complexion tawny, without luster. She had a narrow forehead, a straight nose, and thin, set lips; it was impossible to say whether she was pretty or not. She created the impression that she was sleepy or daydreaming, for her eyelids were almost closed.

Her face aroused Judym's curiosity, so he stood and studied her guardedly. She was looking at the marble divinity in a perfunctory way, but with an expression that suggested that she was memorizing its features—that she was absorbing it from the corner of her eye. Now and then her flat, narrow nostrils widened slightly as if her breathing were quickening. At a certain moment Judym noticed that the eyelids that had been lowered out of reverence and maidenly modesty opened languidly, and the eyes that had been covered saw not only the statue, but him. Before he managed to see what color those eyes were, they were hidden again by her lashes.

Meanwhile, the young woman with the Baedeker read the entire chapter on the history of the statue aloud and pressed close to the plush rope. She rested her hands on it and began to gaze at the statue with curiosity, enthusiasm, and the abandon peculiar to women. One might have said that in that moment she embarked on the adventure of seeing *Venus de Milo*. Her eyes had no glance to spare for anything except the statue; they only wished and attempted to enumerate all its beauties, all the hallmarks of Scopas's chisel of which Baedeker wrote, to remember them, and to arrange them in her mind systematically, like clean linen in a traveler's trunk. Those eyes were sincere to the point of naivete. Like her whole face, they mirrored the subtlest shadows of her passing thoughts; they gave off faithful echoes of every note of her soul. They said everything with no regard for whether anyone saw their expression or not.

After a few minutes' observation of that face, Judym was convinced that even if the lovely young woman wanted to conceal her impressions, her speaking eyes would immediately give her away. He stood in the shadows to watch the play of emotions over her bright face. Here was curiosity with little knowledge. He saw the first radiance flit over her eyebrows, press her eyelids together in delight, and coax her lips into a charming smile. The same feelings he had had a few minutes earlier he saw now on the cheeks of this unknown young woman, and it caused him genuine pleasure. He would have been delighted to ask if he were right, and to hear from her beautiful lips an outpouring of her impressions. He had never felt such a wish to talk about art and listen attentively to another person's thoughts about the fleeting sensations it inspired.

Meanwhile that other person, absorbed in studying the statue, paid not the least attention either to the scrutiny or the man who was scrutinizing her.

"I remember," said the elderly lady, "another set of marble figures. It was a mythological scene. A winged divinity or cupid kissed a beautiful maiden. It is perhaps somewhat inappropriate for you, my chatterboxes, but so beautiful, so charming, so pleasing…so moving.…"

The young woman with the Baedeker raised her head, listened closely to what was said, and spoke up, turning over the pages of the book.

"I noticed something here," she said. "*L'Amour et Psyché.* Antoine Canova. Isn't this it?"

"And perhaps with Psyche. But I hesitate to show it to you," the old lady added quietly.

"In Paris! We're in Paris now! We must wet our lips in the cup of licentiousness," the brunette whispered to her so that their younger companions could not hear.

"What are you doing, outflanking me? Go ahead and look at every cupid painted and sculpted, but they—"

"You think we understand everything here, Grandma," the youngest said with a proud expression. "But I don't know why we waste so much time looking at all these corridors full of pictures when it's so heavenly on the streets. Paris! What a city!"

"But, Wanda," moaned the brunette.

"Well, you understand this, Miss, but I understand absolutely nothing! What's interesting here? All these museums and collections have something of the coffin about them, except that they are even more tiresome.

Cluny, for example. What pits, caves, pieces of peeled wall, bricks, legs, hands, bones!"

"What are you saying?"

"You don't agree? Take Carnavalet. Bones; foul, dusty cadavers; old rubbish from under the churches. And you must walk around it looking solemn and haughty, and stand by everything for fifteen minutes, pretending to look at it. Or here: pictures, pictures, pictures without end. Well, and those figures—"

"My child!" her grandmother broke in. "Those are masterpieces, I tell you—"

"I know, I know: masterpieces. But, after all, all these pictures are as alike as two drops of water, with lacquered trees and nude girls, like these."

"Wanda!" her three companions shrieked with fright, looking around them.

Judym did not know which way to move. He understood that it would be polite to leave so as not to hear what people were saying when they were not aware that he was Polish, but he did not want to. He felt not only the wish, but even the courage, to join in this conversation. He stood helplessly where he was, looking straight ahead with wide eyes.

"Well, let's go to that *Cupid and Psyche*," said the old lady, rising from the bench. "But where is it? And there's not a thing to eat…"

"Don't forget, Grandma, that today we were going to go to that shop on Tivoli Street, the 'real Louvre.'"

"Be quiet! Well, wait. Where is that Canova? I remember, we were there in January. It's gone somehow. Just a minute."

"If you ladies will allow me, I will show you the way to *Cupid*…that is, to Antonio Canova," said Dr. Tomasz, removing his hat and bowing repeatedly as he approached the group.

On hearing Polish spoken, all three young women moved involuntarily toward the elderly lady, as if a bandit had appeared and they were taking refuge under her wings.

"Ah," she said, raising her head and taking the young man's measure with a wry look. "Thank you. Thank you very much."

"Pardon me, ladies, but when one hears…hears our language in Paris, indeed, so…so very, very rarely," Judym faltered, feeling unsteady on his feet and uncertain in his speech.

"Do you live here?" she asked sharply.

"Yes. I've lived here for a year. More than a year; some fifteen months.

My name is Judym. As a doctor, I'm pursuing certain studies here. It's actually—"

"As a doctor, you say?"

"That's right," he replied, seizing this thread of conversation though it would lead to personal questions that he found difficult to tolerate. "I finished medical studies in Warsaw and at present I work in clinics here, in the field of surgery."

"I'm pleased to meet you, doctor," she said in a drawling, rather cool voice. "We travel, as you see, as a foursome, from place to place. My name is Niewadzka. These are my granddaughters—Natalia and Wanda Orszeńska, orphans—and that is their dearest friend and mine, Miss Joanna Podborska."

Judym was bowing once more, with the clumsy management of his feet that seemed an inborn trait, when Madam Niewadzka said in a tone of lively interest, "I knew—yes, that's right—someone of that name, Mr. Judym or Miss Judym, in Volhynia, I think. Yes, it seems to have been in Volhynia. Are you from that area, sir?"

Dr. Tomasz would have been overjoyed to pretend that he had not heard that question. But when Madam Niewadzka turned her gaze toward him again, he said, "I'm from Warsaw, from the city itself. I'm one of the undistinguished Judyms."

"How so?

"My father was a shoemaker, a poor shoemaker on Ciepła Street. On Ciepła Street," he repeated with a prickly satisfaction. At last he had avoided shaky ground and the polite circumlocution in which he was not fluent, and which aroused in him an exaggerated fear. The women were silent and moved slowly, side by side, their dresses rustling.

"I'm very pleased, very pleased to have the opportunity to make such a pleasant acquaintance," Madam Niewadzka said serenely. "So you have examined all the works of art here? No doubt you have, since you live in Paris. We are much obliged to you."

"*Cupid and Psyche* will surely be in another building," Miss Podborska observed.

"Yes, in another building. We will go out to the courtyard."

When they were standing there, Madam Niewadzka turned to Judym and said with a kindness that was not quite genuine, "You mentioned your father's occupation with such frankness, sir, that I'm truly humbled. Please believe that I had no intention of causing pain by asking about your connections. It's simply the habit of an old lady who has lived a long time and seen many people in the world. It's gratifying, truly, to meet with someone to whom one can speak of things, people and relations of long ago, but how much pleasanter, how much pleasanter…"

"Your father, sir, the cobbler—did he make ladies' shoes or men's?" the younger Orszeńska inquired, blinking.

"Boots, mainly boots, in his rare moments of sobriety. Most often he made drunken scenes wherever he could."

"Well, I can hardly comprehend by what miracle you became a doctor, and what's more, in Paris!"

Miss Podborska darted a look of desperate embarrassment at the speaker.

"In what you have told us," said the dowager, "I see great, very great courage. Really, I have never heard the like before. If you please, doctor, I'm old, and I've seen many different types of people. How many times I've been in contact with…people who didn't belong to society. With persons…in a word, with persons whose origins were in the layers of society that are called—whether rightly or wrongly doesn't come into it—common. Those gentlemen always tried very hard to pass over the question of their pedigrees. I've known, and this is the truth," she continued with a certain pensiveness, "those who at one time of life, usually in youth, confessed with exaggerated fervor to their status as a peasant or some such thing. Later, not only did their swaggering egalitarian candor go by the board, but it was replaced by coats of arms on the carriage doors of those so fortunate as to acquire carriages."

Judym smiled sarcastically and walked several steps in silence. Then he turned to Miss Podborska with a question.

"What sort of impression did the *Venus de Milo* make on you, madam?"

"Venus," said the brunette, as if the question had awakened her from a bad dream. A blush covered her face, then vanished and seemed to deepen the color of her lovely lips, which trembled a little.

"Her whole back is as rough as if someone had beaten her for four days in a row with an overseer's whip," Wanda said flatly.

"Lovely," Natalia said in an undertone, turning her lusterless eyes toward Judym. For the second time the doctor had his chance to look into those eyes, and again all his faculties warned him that something was amiss. Her look was like cold moonlight with no radiance, when the moon's face above the sleepy earth is hidden in a fog.

Miss Podborska grew animated. Her face instantly displayed her inner excitement.

"How beautiful she is! How real!" she exclaimed. "If I lived in Paris, I would come to her…well, not a million…but every week, to look at her as long as I liked. The Greeks in general created such a wonderful world of gods. Goethe…"

The mention of Goethe aroused Judym's distaste. He had read something of that poet's work and had enough of it some time ago.

As luck would have it, the old lady stopped in an anteroom leading to the hall where *Cupid and Psyche* was displayed, and with a wordless signal in her large, pale eyes asked Judym to show the way. When they found themselves before the figures, smoothed by the sculptor's refined finishing technique—the painting in white marble—no one spoke.

Judym was sorry to think that his role ought to be ending. He felt that since he had blurted out the information about his father from Ciepła Street, he could no longer spend time with these women or cultivate their friendship. Again he saw in his mind his room on Voltaire Street and the concierge's old hag of a wife with her eternal senseless questions. At the moment when he was most at a loss as to what to do and uncertain about how to detach from them gracefully, Madam Niewadzka seemed to divine his thoughts.

"We are going to Versailles," she announced. "We would like to see the area and, on the way, stop at Sèvres, at Saint-Cloud. Those harum-scarum little ones rush from place to place day and night, and I collapse from exhaustion. Have you been to Versailles, sir? What's the most comfortable way to travel? Train? They write here about some pneumatic tramway. Is that better than the regular train?"

"I've been in Versailles twice on that pneumatic tram and it seemed very convenient to me. Certainly it moves slowly, twice as slowly as a railroad car, but it makes it easy to observe the area and the Seine."

"So we'll take it!" Wanda said with finality.

"What time does this curiosity leave here?"

"I don't remember, madam, but it's easy to find out. The main station is just next to the Louvre. If you will allow me, ladies…"

"Oh! We wouldn't dare put you to the trouble!"

"But the gentleman will find out. What trouble will it be, grandma? He's a man of the city, a Parisian," Wanda proclaimed, parodying Judym's tone a little.

Tomasz bowed and walked away. Pleased at such an incredibly favorable development, he hurried at full speed toward the station on the Quai du Louvre. In the wink of an eye he found a conductor, crammed his memory with all the departure times and returned, straightening his back every minute and adjusting his tie.

When he had informed the ladies of the departure times and shared information about how to find their way around Versailles, Wanda fired off again. "So we are going to Versailles," she declared. "That's no great matter. We are going there on some air train, and the gentleman with us."

Before Judym could collect his thoughts, she added, "Grandma already said that in spite of everything, he can come."

"Wanda!" Madam Niewadzka almost shrieked in despair, blushing like a girl. After a moment she turned back to Judym and tried, with trembling lips, to summon a friendly smile. "You see, sir, what a horned demon we have here, though she claims the right to wear a long dress."

"Would you ladies really allow me to accompany you to Versailles?"

"I would not dare ask you since it might interrupt your work, but it would be very nice for us."

"By no means… I would be most happy…So long ago…" he mumbled.

"At ten o'clock, sir!" Wanda said to him, raising her finger and executing a series of vivid conspiratorial signals with her eyes.

The doctor had already taken a liking to this girl, as if she were a good friend with whom one could chat at length about subjects brought up in conversation, and even about other things. The three other ladies maintained an awkward silence. Judym felt that he had forced his way into association with these women. He understood that he was their social inferior, but that at the same time he, a cobbler's son but now a doctor, was an aspirant to "society." He distinguished these two aspects of himself, and he bit his lip to the quick.

After viewing the medallions of David d'Angers, several of which infused the hearts of those present with something like prayer, they withdrew from the museum to the courtyard and from there to the street.

The elderly lady called a cab and told the other women that they were going to the shops. Judym said goodbye to them with an elegance in which he was indulging for the first time in his life—and went his way. On the upper deck of the omnibus making its way toward Vincennes he fell into deep, meticulous contemplation. This was a monumental event in his life, like the moment in which he had received his license or prescribed and compounded his first medication. He had never been in close contact with women like these. He had only passed them often on the street, seen them sometimes in carriages, and dreamed of them with unassuaged longing in secret places in his soul, where there was no check on his thoughts. How often, as a schoolboy and an older student, he had envied footmen their right to look at these beings, corporeal but indeed so like miraculous flowers enclosed in an enchanting garden.

The thought of the women in his life leaped to mind: relatives, acquaintances, sweethearts, each more or less like men in their movements, their instincts, their coarseness. That thought was so repugnant that he closed his eyes and listened with the deepest joy to the rustle of gowns, which still filled his ears. Every nimble movement of these slender women's feet was like a musical trill. The glossiness of lovely mantles and gloves, of light frills around the neck, aroused in him a particular excitement, not so much sensual as aesthetic.

The next day he rose earlier than usual. He examined his wardrobe and all the possibilities it offered very critically. Around nine he left home, and since he had extra time, he decided to walk. As he squeezed through the crowd, he brooded about the talk with which he would amuse the ladies. He arranged inexpressibly graceful dialogues in his mind, and even imagined using flirtatious forms of speech that had always seemed like rubbish before.

There was no one at the tram station. Judym stopped under a tree and, full of anxiety, awaited the arrival of his friends of yesterday. Every moment he heard the roar of boats heaving in the waves of the Seine and the rattle of omnibuses boiling up on the bridge and the nearby streets. On the other side of the river a crystalline chime announced the hour of ten. To Judym that sound seemed a solemn assurance that the beautiful creatures were not coming, and that they were not coming for a particular reason, namely, that he was waiting for them. He, Tomasz Judym, Tomek Judym from Ciepła Street.

He stood that way, looking at the gray, sluggish water and whispering to himself, "Ciepła Street. Ciepła Street."

He felt too stupid for words, and somehow disgusted and bitter. On the far edge of fleeting memory an image of a squalid tenement formed.

He raised his head and shook off those thoughts. People of every sort were moving around him, among others the itinerant barker for the daily newspaper *l'Intransigeant*, who carried a tall pole with a transverse board that had a notice of the contents of the latest issue glued to it. At that moment the barker put down the pole and leaned on it, chatting with some friends. In Judym's mind the name of the newspaper linked itself to a multitude of thoughts with one bothersome, unpleasant, almost painful idea wandering through them: Ciepła Street. Ciepła Street.

At that moment he thought of his family and the conditions under which its life had passed as something immeasurably foreign, as if it were a petit bourgeois family that had eked out a poor existence during the reign of King Jan Kazimierz more than two centuries before. The ladies he had seen the previous day already seemed to him like close friends or sisters because they were refined in their persons, dress, speech, and movements. It was a grief to him that they had not come; the thought that they might not come at all was unbearable. If they did not, it was because his pedigree included those cobblers.

He decided to go to Versailles, bow to them, and avoid them. What could he care about a few women of the aristocracy, if you called it that? He would only like, just once more, to see, to get a good look at how that person—not that she was of any importance—walked, how she looked at any picture with her curious eyes.

"Of course," he thought as he gazed into the river, "of course, I'm a boor, and there's no more to say. Am I capable of enjoying leisure time, or have I ever thought about the proper ways to enjoy oneself? The Greeks spent half their lives in skilled recreational pastimes. Medieval Italians perfected the art of idleness, and these women do the same. I would enjoy myself on an outing, but with whom? With women of my own standing, with, I suppose, young working women in the city, with students—in a word, with those one calls women. But with these women? It's as if it were the nineteenth century and I were still living with great-great-grandparents in the beginning of the eighteenth. I haven't mastered the art of conversation; it's as if an estate clerk wanted to compose dialogues like Lucian because he could write with a pen. I wouldn't enjoy myself for thinking that I might do something awkward, like a cobbler. Perhaps it's better this way.

"Ah, how strange: each of these women is very interesting to a man, each one of them. Even the older one is up to date and has her imagination attuned to what we call culture. And I, what am I? A shoemaker's son—"

"Didn't I say that our doctor would already be waiting for us?" Wanda called from behind him just then.

He spun around and saw all four of his friends standing before him with cheerful faces. Amid pleasant chatter the young women climbed onto the upper deck of the train as Judym painstakingly hoisted the grandmother to a seat near them. From that elevation they could see the agitated waters of the Seine. The river drove forward between granite banks, panting, tormented, straining as if in a death struggle. The turbid, dirty, grayish-brown, almost black current through which steamboats splashed, roaring every minute, seemed sad, like a slave with slender fingers turning the heavy stones of a hand mill.

"How small, how narrow," Joanna remarked.

"Ooh! It looks like a grandchild of the Vistula."

"An absolute caricature of the Isar," said Natalia.

"That's true! Miss Joanna, you remember the Isar, our dear, bright green Isar, pure as tears," Wanda rhapsodized.

"Oh, pure as tears?" Judym put in.

"What? You don't believe it, sir? Grandma, this gentleman actually confesses that he does not believe in the purity of the Isar."

"Really, what awful water!" the aging lady said in an effort to drown out Wanda's last words as quickly as possible, since for no apparent reason they had evoked a blush like a fleeting cloud on "Miss Joanna's" face.

At the moment when Judym was about to say something statistical and scholarly about the waters of the Seine, the train gave a long bleat and moved along the bank of the dark river, bending its line of cars on the curving switches like the limbs of a long body. Branches of chestnut trees with long leaves swayed beside the passengers' faces. Soot and acrid city dust ate into the bright green, soft surfaces and slowly blanketed them as if with a red tarnish.

The day was cloudy. Every little while the deep shadows of clouds flitted over the area they were passing. The light in the somber forenoon was ashen. But no one paid any attention to that because they were attracted by the houses of rosy stone on the suburban streets.

"What kind of stone is that? What kind of stone is that, sir? Sir?" Wanda pressed him. But before he could collect his thoughts she left him in peace and, smiling, turned her head in the opposite direction. The delightful, inebriating fragrance of roses wafted up and filled all the air over the gardens that ran down a hill to the river. Here and there, breaking like flames through the cover of green trees, they could see huge borders of scarlet and yellow.

Judym watched the ladies' faces. All of them, including the grand-mother's, seemed rapt with enjoyment. They were turned involuntarily toward the source of the lovely aroma, breathing it in with closed eyes and smiling lips. Natalia's face in particular riveted his attention at that moment. Absorbed by the smell of the roses, she seemed a bright butterfly for whom the flowers were created and who alone had a mysterious right to them.

Between the gardens the blackened walls and chimneys of a factory pro-truded here and there, like the repugnant torso and dead limbs of a parasite born of dirt and living in it. By the water, far along the bank, crawled rows of poor suburban houses, small and crude. In one place a coal pile burst into view like an abyss, smearing the neighboring walls, doors, and win-dows with its black breath. Far, far away the misty Meudon forest could be seen.

"What do you like best in Paris?" Judym asked Natalia, who was sitting beside him. It was one of the questions he had prepared like a lesson the day before.

"In Paris?" she replied, drawing out the phrase with a smile on her beau-tiful lips. "What I like, what gives me pleasure, is everything. The traffic, the life…It's like a storm! For example, around St. Lazare Station—I don't know the name of the street—when you ride in a carriage and see people rushing along the sidewalks, the waves, waves…the roaring flood…Once I saw a terrible flood at my uncle's, in the mountains. The water suddenly surged and you wanted to call to it, 'Higher! Faster! Fly!' It's the same way here."

"And you, madam?" he asked Wanda.

"Me? The same," she said quickly. "And the Louvre. But not that painted one. Tssh! You know, doctor. That one. Now no doubt you will direct that question to 'Aunt' Joanna, though you should have begun with her, because she is our teacher and our sweetheart. You see, sir—a small thing, but embarrassing. Listen: I'll tell you. Miss Joanna likes, first, *The Fisherman,* second, *The Meditation,* third, *Venus,* fourth… Anyway, all of us love *The Fisherman* and *The Meditation.* Grandma—"

"What *Meditation?*"

"You don't even know it, sir! And do you know what? *The Meditation* was painted in the new town hall. Eyes closed, slender, young, and to me personally, altogether unattractive."

"Ah, in a town hall."

"In a town hall, ah! Now in which gallery is *The Fisherman*?"

"We were just wondering about that. That's what we want to know: which?" the grandmother put in.

"Just a minute. Grandma thinks that I don't know such a silly thing. Oh, with apologies to the respected audience, beyond the Seine, in that garden where there is water and those ducks with crests—"

"Luxembourg," Natalia whispered.

"In the Luxembourg Gardens!"

"Do you know Puvis de Chavannes' *Poor Fisherman*, sir?" Miss Podborska said.

"*Fisherman*? I don't recall…"

"Some connoisseur and Parisian you are," Wanda teased, pushing out her lips contemptuously.

"Connoisseur and Parisian? I'm an ordinary surgeon."

Just as he said that, he remembered the picture. He had seen it a year before and, struck by the unutterable strength of the masterpiece, had preserved it in his memory. With time everything about the painting, the particular airiness of the colors, the lines of the figures and landscape, the simplicity of means and the entire story the composition told, had been buried under other things, and all that remained was the sense of something painful beyond expression. That memory was like an obscure echo of an injury done to someone, some shame without parallel for which the viewers were not to blame, but which seemed to call to them from the earth only because they were witnesses to it.

Joanna, who had raised the question about *The Fisherman,* was sitting on the end of a bench behind the two young women and their grandmother. As she waited for an answer, she leaned out a little and gazed at Judym so attentively that he had to look into her clear, bright eyes. His excitement at the delight they revealed jogged his memory more than a thousand words of description of Puvis de Chavannes' canvas, and he began to recall even the colors, the landscape. The rapture in those eyes seemed to bring the picture back to him, to summon up impressions effaced long ago.

Yes, he remembered. A thin man, or rather not a man but a humanoid from the periphery of the great capital, with unkempt hair and beard, in a shirt so old it hung loose on him, in pants hanging on sharp hip bones, stood before him again with his fish net immersed in water. His eyes seemed to rest on the curving poles that held the net, but they saw anyone who passed by. They did not look for sympathy, of which there was none.

Neither complaint nor tears were to be seen in them. "This is the benefit that comes to you from all my strength, from my soul," their sunken sockets said.

There in the painting stood the fisherman, embodying what the culture of the world meant to him—a terrifying product of humanity. Judym even remembered the feeling of amazement that descended on him when he heard and saw the impression the painting made on other people. Clusters of great ladies formed before it, together with beautifully dressed, fragrant young women, and men in luxurious clothing. And that crowd sighed. Silent tears flowed from the eyes of those who came there laden with the spoils of their positions in society. Obedient to the command of immortal art, they were overtaken for a moment by a sense of how they were living and the order they had established in the world.

He only said, "Yes. I saw that picture by Puvis de Chavannes in the Luxembourg Gallery."

Joanna retreated toward Madam Niewadzka's arm. The doctor saw only her white forehead framed with dark hair.

"How Miss Joanna blubbered there! How she blubbered!" Wanda whispered close to Judym's ear. "Anyway, we all—I myself shed tears as big as peas with cabbage."

"I'm not in the habit," Natalia smiled.

"No?" asked the doctor, lazily taking her measure with his eyes.

"I was very sorry for that man, particularly for his children and his wife… Everything so thin, as if it were whittled from sticks like dry brushwood twigs in a pasture," she said with a blush, but at the same time smiling with closed eyes.

"That fisherman is as like the Lord Jesus as two drops of water, isn't he, Grandma?"

"The fisherman? Yes, very similar," said the elderly lady, who was preoccupied with gazing at the landscape.

The tram rolled onto a street in the village of Sèvres and stopped in front of a two-story house. The travelers could see straight through to the numbers of the rooms in the inn. The place was no sight for ladies. A drunken soldier wearing a military cap at an angle was holding a disreputable-looking girl by the waist and the two of them, leaning out of a window, made faces at the people in the train.

Fortunately, the tram moved on. It had hardly gotten beyond the last houses of the little town to a sad, empty space in an open field when the sky suddenly went dark. A hard wind blew up. The nearby forest clouded over into gloomy gray and soon a dense rain poured down in thick drops like grain.

Panic arose in the tram cars. Streaks of rain leaked in under the roofs, cutting down sideways and wetting the benches. The ladies huddled together in the most sheltered places and pulled their dresses around them as best they could. In knightly style, Judym sheltered them from the rain with his own person. As he stood with his back against the frame of a seat, he noticed a leg projecting from deep within the heap of dresses. A foot in a shallow patent leather slipper with a high heel rested against an iron railing, offering a long view of a slender leg in a black silk stocking. Judym wondered to whom to attribute this charming sight. He read it as the result of chance and inattention, so he was afraid to raise his eyes and only stole glances at it from under the shade of his eyelashes, as if he were a thief who had broken into a house.

The train moved onto the great avenue of Versailles. Luxuriant old trees gave the passengers a little cover from the rain. The women tried to shake out and smooth their clothes. The beautiful leg did not disappear. Drops of rain spattered onto the gleaming leather, pushed down light dust from the short upper part of the slipper like tapping fingers, and were lost in the soft silk. Now Judym knew to whom the leg and the slipper belonged. He raised his eyes to Natalia's face and felt cold fangs of pleasure sink into him. As usual, the young woman's eyes were lowered. From time to time her eyebrows, two thin lines ever so slightly bent, rose a little higher, as if they were two levers pulling the resistant eyelids upward. On her lips, the lower of which was slightly curled, lay a smile he could hardly have described, a smile full of venom and wantonness.

"Ah, yes," he thought, studying that peculiar face.

Natalia felt his gaze on her. Her cheeks went pale; the pallor seemed to dissolve the smile on her lips. The shadows around her lowered eyes took on a deeper blue and the line of her rather prominent nose sharpened.

The tram hurried along to the square in front of the palace of Versailles, and the travelers rushed off its upper platform, which was very wet. The doctor, clearing a way for his companions, secured a place in the small station. With so many people crowded in that it was literally difficult to move a hand, it happened that he stood behind Joanna and Natalia. The rest of the passengers, packed into this retreat from the rain, pushed Natalia against Judym's chest, with her face beside his mustache. Her pale hair, hanging in strands because of fashion and the rain, wound itself over his mouth and eyes, and he quivered. Everyone in the building was quiet; only the breathing of a heavyset asthmatic man broke the silence. Streams of rain splashed from the roof without a pause and veiled the open door like a dark curtain.

Natalia tried to move, but only rested one arm on Judym's shoulder. Then her profile was more sharply outlined to his wistful eyes. She intended to say something, but only smiled hastily. She raised her perpetually lowered eyelids and looked him in the eye for a moment, boldly, searchingly, intoxicatingly.

Madam Niewadzka stood close by the door. Though she was getting more air than any of them, she was breathing heavily, and her face was quite red.

"You know, my girls," she said in her resonant whisper, "I would rather be drenched in the rain than inhale the breath of these wine merchants."

"How do you know they are wine merchants?"

"It's easy!" Her swollen eyes flashed. "Two sour cellars are blowing straight in my face, and you ask how I know?"

She was speaking to Wanda, but Judym heard what they were saying. For his part, he had not the least desire to trade the crowded tram station for the rain. But he said to Madam Niewadzka in Polish, "We could get to the square quickly. It's not far. But you ladies will be soaked. We don't even have an umbrella."

As he spoke, he moved forward a little, as if he were going to lead the older lady out of the crowd. Then with his whole body he bumped into Natalia, who was wearing a thin, delicate dress. He looked with blazing eyes into her face: it was pale, cold, and stony. Her eyelids were lowered again.

The rain slowly stopped. Only from the gutters of a neighboring house did a stream of water flow steadily with a loud splashing, and a few men armed with umbrellas came out. Space was freed inside the station, but for an exhilarating moment, Natalia did not change her position. At last she moved toward the door, following her younger sister, who stretched out her hands to feel if rain was still falling. Before it stopped completely, the cheerful light of the sun glowed for a moment. The stones of the sloping square gleamed as if they had been sprinkled with broken glass, and the

sight lured everyone out of the cramped shelter. Judym offered the grandmother his arm, and the whole group quickly made its way to the palace.

In the long, spacious rooms, amid walls hung with historic paintings,
the tightly knit group seemed to divide. Each one looked over the inferior canvases on the lower floor in her own way. Before long, those paintings began to bore them. Judym walked as if through long, long avenues
lined with trimmed trees and worried involuntarily because there was no
end in sight. In any case, he had already been to Versailles, so neither the
royal apartments nor the Hall of Mirrors interested him very much. He
marched along to the right of the elderly lady, who stopped every few paces
to put a lorgnette with a long tortoiseshell handle to her eyes and look at
the paintings. A series of battles from the Napoleonic Wars, crowds of soldiers, leaders' theatrical faces and gestures, horses foaming wildly, moved
along before the doctor's eyes like rows of distant, juvenile dreams.

Somewhere farther on they stopped in front of a white marble bust of
the dying Corsican. When they had returned from that part of the palace
and passed the halls with the pictures of battles again, the old lady put
her arm around Joanna's waist and said, "We are far away, in the world of
heroes. We are dreaming. We are dreaming."

Joanna's face went pink, or rather red, and she blurted out, "No! Nothing like that! Not at all! I only—"

From that moment, though Judym watched her imperceptibly, she
restrained herself and tried to wipe the record of her feelings from her face.

They examined the royal apartments in detail. When Madam
Niewadzka had listened with a solemn face to all that the doorkeeper, with
exquisitely fluid movements, had told her, and when, after touring the
small salons, she was steering the group toward the exit, Wanda looked
behind her and hissed, "Miss Joanna, we're going!"

Judym followed the girl's gaze and looked closely at Joanna. She was
leaning on a little chair covered with damask of a faint blue color and
looking out the window. Her expression was so strange that Judym involuntarily restrained himself from speaking. Then he approached her and
asked, recalling what the doorkeeper had said a moment before, "Are you
thinking of Marie Antoinette, madam?"

She darted a troubled look at him, like a person who is caught red-
handed, and said hesitantly, "From here, through that window, you can
see the great courtyard and the gate. That way—the rabble burst in that
way. Drunken women, men armed with knives. Marie Antoinette saw it

from that window! I had such a strange feeling…All that dreadful crowd shouted, 'Death to the Austrian!' And that way—she fled through that door, she fled that way…"

"Miss Joanna!" the others called.

"But you mentioned a feeling…"

"A feeling…" she said, looking down and growing pale. "If you please, sir, we are very cowardly. We are afraid not only during the day, but also in what we call dreams. I'm quite afraid of that rabble I was just thinking of."

"Rabble?" Judym said.

"Yes. Of their shout, that is. I'm afraid of something of that kind. I myself don't know what."

She raised her eyes, innocent eyes with a strange expression of fear or pain. Once again she glanced back at the small chamber with a look of genuine sorrow, then quickly followed the others.

On the journey back to Paris they stopped at Saint-Cloud. As they stood on the hill behind the railway station, the young women uttered a cry. At their feet, stretching far into the countryside and vanishing in the reddish mist, lay a desert of stone: Paris. Its reddish color was slashed here and there by an odd dark sign, by the Arch of Triumph, the towers of Notre Dame Cathedral, and the Eiffel Tower. From the far edges that the eye could barely reach, the mists were streaked with blue, and smoke drifted from factory chimneys that looked like thick riding whips in the distance. Those whips drove the expansion of the desert. But the noise of its life did not reach this hill. The desert seemed to have expired and stiffened in its sprawling, stony form. A strange excitement filled the newcomers, like the excitement aroused by the sight of great natural phenomena: mountain ranges, glaciers, the sea.

In the train, Judym sat beside Natalia, but he even forgot that she was so near. His eyes were immersed in Paris. Disconnected thoughts burned in his mind, thoughts that were exclusively his, perceptions beneath the surface of awareness, impossible to confide to anyone. Then he articulated a question to himself: "What did that woman mean by saying that she was afraid when she looked out the window of Marie Antoinette's bedroom?"

He took his eyes off the city and tried to look at Joanna again. Now he studied her profile more carefully. Her chin had the classic Sarmatian or Caucasian shape. It projected out very slightly so that between the chin and the lower line of the nose a lovely parabola was formed, with a rose-colored mouth blossoming in the middle. No sooner were the features of her face lit by a sensation than her lips became a living flame. That flame altered, brightening or fading, but it always had a singular force of true expression. He could not keep from thinking that even a criminal impulse would be reflected on that face as ingenuously as joy at the sight of blooming irises, the cheerful colors of a landscape, the curious fantasies of a painter, and the sight of commonplace objects. It was clear that to those eyes, everything became something natural and good. Yet sometimes a weary reluctance was reflected in them, and an exhausted smile. Even then there was still something childlike: sincerity, alacrity, and power.

Like her facial expressions, Joanna's movements had something about them that made them unlike those of other women. If she wanted to put what she felt into words, she raised her hand, or at least her eyebrows, very quickly, spiritedly, as if she had turned off everything that could stifle the melody of her thoughts, looks, smiles, and movements.

"Whom does she remind me of?" thought the doctor, looking casually at her eyes and forehead. "Haven't I seen her somewhere in Warsaw?"

Then it came to him as if in a happy, illogical *nota bene* that indeed he had seen her only the day before, in front of that smiling white statue

He parted with the ladies at St. Lazare station. The elderly woman announced to him that the next day they were leaving with their group for Trouville, and from there for England.

Judym was effusive in his good wishes. Then he returned, a little tired, to his cramped room.

CHAPTER II

In the Sweat of Their Brows

A YEAR LATER, NEAR the end of June, Judym woke in Warsaw. It was ten in the morning. Through the open window the racket from Widok Street invaded his room, the old, familiar noise of cabs rattling over stones as big as loaves of bread. From below, from the narrow yard on which most of the windows of the furnished rented rooms looked out, heated vapors were pulled upward as if on warm wings. Judym had stayed here since the previous day. Now he got up and went to the window. Through the chinks between its panes, he saw a watchman with a brass plate on his cap who with inborn, uncultured surliness was explaining something to an old lady in a black shawl.

Youth boiled in the doctor's veins. He felt a latent strength in himself, like a man who is at the foot of a great mountain, takes the first step toward the faroff summit, and knows that he will reach it. He had not yet shaken off the fatigue of the journey from Paris to Warsaw, which he had made without a pause, but the previous day had been full of such pleasant feelings that he had completely forgotten about the coal soot that had worked its way into his clothes.

As he had looked through the window of the train car at the landscape, the villages with white cottages, the boundless fields, the ripened grain, he had felt no great difference between this country and France. Here and there the alien hulks of factories jutted up and smoke flew across a clear sky. Villagers by no means more ignorant than those in France, and sometimes so wise that it was gratifying to see, came into the car, along with craftsmen and laborers like their French counterparts. Listening to their conversations, he said to himself every moment, "And is it true that we are barbarians, half-Asians, Scythians? No! We are like everyone else. We slog forward and that's all there is to it. If you had settled the French in with the Poles here, you would have seen that, undermined as they are by their wretched constitutions, they all would still have managed."

When he was traveling back to the city, Judym had brought that agreeable, optimistic thought with him. It was like the sweet, strong smell of one's native fields. He slept wonderfully and now, with his first glance, he greeted the "old digs," Warsaw.

As he looked at the city, he thought of his family. He had to see them—not just out of duty, but because he wanted to see them, to see their faces. He went out of the hotel and walked along until he was lost in the crowd on Marszałkowska Street. He enjoyed seeing the wooden pavements, the new growth of young trees that gave some shade, the new houses that had replaced the old, dilapidated ones.

Passing the garden and the square behind Iron Gate, he felt at home. His heart went out to the part of the city he knew most intimately. By narrow alleys, among stalls, booths, and little shops, he walked to Krochmalna. The scorching heat of the sun flooded that gutter in the form of a street. From the narrow neck of ground between Ciepła Street and the square came a stench as from a cemetery. As in the past, a swarm of Jewish people filled the area.

As she had long ago, an old, ailing Jewish woman sat on the sidewalk selling boiled broad beans and other beans, peas, and pumpkin seeds. Here and there, peddlers of soda water shuffled along with containers at their sides and glasses in their hands. Judym felt nausea at the very sight of those glasses, sticky with dried syrup, that dirty paupers were holding.

One of the peddlers was standing by a wall. She was so ragged that she was almost naked; her face was yellow and lifeless. She was waiting in the sun, for people going that way were most likely to be thirsty. She held two bottles of red liquid that looked like juice. Her grayish lips were whispering something, perhaps urging passersby to drink. Perhaps pronouncing the name of God, Adonai, which was not supposed to be spoken by mortals. Perhaps uttering a curse, spawned like a worm in dirt and poverty, at the sun and at life.

On his right and left stood open shops, shallow shops that reached not far inward from their thresholds and looked like papered drawers standing upright. On the wooden shelves in stores like these lay cigarettes for three rubles, and nearer the door passersby were lured by boiled eggs, smoked herring, chocolate bars, attractively displayed candies, slices of cheese, white carrots, garlic, onions, little cakes, radishes, peas in pods, buckets of kosher sausage, and jars of raspberry juice to be mixed with water.

In each of these shops heaps of mud were blackening, preserving their cooling moisture even in the heat. Dirty children in dirty rags crept over this filth. Each of these caves was home to several people who spent their lives there in idleness and chitchat. Usually some father of a family sat inside—a greenish, melancholy man who did not move from his place from dawn till dark but looked at the street, squandering time on dreams of ways to make fast money.

A step farther on, closed windows gave a view of the interior of a workshop where men or women bent over under low ceilings, shortening their lives, Judym thought. He could see that this was a shoemaking workshop, a dark cave with a palpable stench issuing from it, and close beside it was a factory where wigs worn by pious Jewish women were made. There were more than a dozen such wig-makers' establishments standing in a row. Pale, sallow, haggard girls, unwashed and uncombed, were industriously dividing hair. From yards, doorways, even rows of garret windows under old roofs covered with tin or brick, faces leaned out: sick faces, gaunt, long-nosed, greenish, grimy faces. Bloodshot eyes looked around—some weeping, some in their misery unresponsive to anything—perpetually sad eyes that dreamed of death.

At one gate Judym stumbled over a peddler woman carrying heavy baskets of vegetables in both hands. She was disheveled from head to foot. Her wig had slipped backward like a cap and the shaven crown of her head gleamed white as the head of a bald old man. Her bulging eyes looked out with an expression of torment transformed into peace, without any life, like eggshells. In the swollen veins of her forehead and neck the blood seemed to be tapping audibly. On the threshold of one shop sat an old, hunchbacked porter, chewing on a raw cucumber which together with a hunk of bread made up his lunch. He had carried two cabinets bound together with cord there on his back and left them in the middle of the street.

Judym walked quickly, murmuring something to himself. Dusty green or rusty red walls like mottled, muddy rags passed before his eyes. Ciepła…The sidewalks were as broken as ever, the pavement as full of ruts. Here there was not one passerby in a top hat, and rarely a lady in a hat. In general, the people on the street looked like the walls. They wore what manual laborers wore, most often without collars. If a cab passed by, everyone looked at it.

From a distance Judym saw the gate of the building where his family lived. He approached it with a depressing feeling of unwarranted shame. He was going to have to greet people of low condition, and now that he was returning from abroad, that was more painful to him than ever. He made his way rapidly to the gate, intending, though he himself was hardly aware of it, to avoid strangers.

The yard branched out in three directions. A noisy factory that was new to Judym rose over one neck of it; an old coal yard took up another; and a third led to a building a few stories high. It was to that building that Judym directed his steps. When he was standing in a hellishly dirty hall, he heard a familiar jangle in the basement: "neighbor" Dąbrowski, a locksmith, was plying his trade. Judym went downstairs and glanced into another hall that led off to the left from the locksmith's door. There he saw a great open space and, beyond it, the subterranean home that had been his family's. He felt a sour coolness that pushed him away.

A small, grimy boy emerged from the locksmith's workshop and looked closely at the visitor. Judym hurried upstairs, passing the second and third floors, only slowing down as he neared the attic. There was a window without a pane in front of him, a patch of wall with a loophole for a gun. The brick that filled the bottom of that opening had been so smoothed by the hands of children who played there that it had taken on an oval shape. How many times he, Judym, had crawled through that opening to the outside of the wall and hung in the air! In a corner, the waterpipe for the building loomed black, moistening the entire wall. Above the pipe, a sooty stain from a kerosene lamp reached to the ceiling. The walls were full of shadows and sadness, like the boards that make a coffin.

The last flight of stairs led to a dark hall that ran along the attic. Judym stood in front of a doorway in that hall and knocked once, twice, three times. No one answered. When he rattled the door handle one more time, a thirteen-year-old girl came out and looked him over with the eyes of a mature coquette. Without being asked, she queried, "Who are you looking for, sir?"

"Wiktor Judym's apartment is here?"

"Yes."

"Do you know if anyone is home, miss?"

"Only the aunt must be there. She may have gone down to the yard with the children."

She leaned closer and looked Judym in the eye with the directness of city people. At that moment, he heard a terrible clamor deep in that apartment—a torrent of vituperation, of incoherent vulgar cursing, spilling out like the lowing of a cow. He was amazed. He listened keenly and then quietly asked the girl what it meant. She smiled roguishly and said, "That's my grandmother. She's mad."

"Mad? And you keep her at home?"

"Certainly. Where else could we keep her?"

He moved the girl aside and glanced into the room. In a corner by the stove sat a human specter, fastened by her hands and legs to a hook protruding from the floor. Her head and shoulders were covered with shaggy gray hair, the rest of her body with frayed rags. Now and then horrible eyes like two flashing, flaming swords appeared from under her hair and her lips fired off a volley of appalling expressions. With an instinctive movement Judym withdrew into the hall and began to question the girl.

"Why don't you put her into a hospital?"

"Why? That's a good one! It isn't possible."

"Why not?"

"There's no room. And where would we get the money to pay for her?"

"Why do you keep her shackled like that?"

"Why? Because she'd take an axe, a knife, a cleaver, and kill the children, Papa, and Mama. What a devil she is! My God!"

"Has she been sick for long?"

"Her, sick? Mad, not sick. I should be as healthy as she is! When father has to fasten her down, what a tug of war it is! Father's no weakling, but he can hardly get the better of that hellcat."

Judym waved to her and escaped down the stairs. When he stopped in the yard, he glanced down the road by the factory wall and saw a crowd of children running, jumping, and playing. On a pile of beams heated by the sun sat his Aunt Pelagia, an elderly woman who had been given a home with Judym's brother Wiktor for many years. She was thin, sickly, and peevish. She rarely had a good word for anyone, and she cuffed the children right and left.

Judym walked toward her slowly, grimacing under his mustache and wrestling with himself. He found it painful to be greeted in an open space within eyeshot of tenants and gawkers. He felt an irritation brought to the fore by the peculiar pity that is the marrow of family feeling.

Aunt Pelagia turned her head and noticed him, but she did not budge from where she was sitting. When he approached and touched her soiled sleeve with his nose in an attempt to kiss her hand, she leaned forward hastily and smacked her lips impassively in his hair.

"When did Tomek come? We knew nothing about it," she said, speaking obliquely in the third person and with her characteristic dryness.

"Just yesterday evening. Are you well, Aunt?"

"Eh, my health… I'm boiling. It's warm now. I sit down here. Winter will come and maybe this will finally end."

"Ah, I don't like all this either."

"I know…"

"You're looking pretty well, Aunt. What's new with Wiktor and his family? How is he?"

"What…How is Wiktor…"

"Well?"

"He's at that factory."

"At Miler's?"

"Pfft! No. In the iron works by the steel mill."

"By the steel mill!"

"And in the steel mill."

"Why on earth?"

"He switched. He says he likes it better. Well, and it will be easier for him. But it's Tomek's fault, nobody else's," she said indifferently, straightening the folds of her skirt.

"It's my fault that Wiktor changed jobs?"

"That he switched is Tomek's fault. When he was a stupid lout, he did whatever he found to do. Tomek took him and put knowledge into his head and now he doesn't like to work. He took to things that weren't like him. He reads books. And how! He's a scholar!" She smiled sardonically, baring white teeth.

Judym listened numbly. "Does he earn much?" he asked.

"No, not much. She had to go to work because they couldn't make ends meet anymore."

"Where does she work?"

"In a cigar factory. They leave in the morning and I must watch the children, cook the food, and tend to the house. Where will Tomek settle down? Here or somewhere out in the world?" she asked, pretending to be indifferent.

"I don't know yet. I've just come back."

The conversation broke off. Judym looked sideways at the scrap of asphalt pavement that seemed to wander around this place, lying amid the stone buildings as if someone had thrown it there absentmindedly. He saw a little tree that grew straight up from the asphalt crust. Near the trunk, a grating lay over a drain that held offscourings of every description.

The sun was getting hotter. A pack of children were playing in the shade of the high factory wall. Some were so emaciated that he could see the webs of blue veins in their transparent faces. Others not only had cheeks, necks, and hands tanned in the sun, but also the skin on knees that protruded through huge holes. Among the waving, kicking crew, some small ones with rickets crept about with shockingly crooked legs and traces of smallpox on bare, shriveled limbs. The entire band looked like yard litter or dry leaves the wind was sweeping from place to place.

The leader of the noisy gang was an eight-year-old boy, very thin, without a cap, dressed in his father's underwear and his mother's shoes. This cavalier yelled at the top of his voice, which he was authorized to do as commander of the others and leader of a battalion. When he bounded like a deer toward the center of the yard, Judym recognized him.

"Why, that's Franek!"

"Yes. Franek," said his aunt.

Dr. Tomasz stopped his nephew and an expression of clear displeasure appeared on the boy's face. A girl younger than Franek stepped out of the crowd and moved close to their aunt. It was Karolina, Judym's niece. She had large eyes in a gray, shriveled face. They glowed like coals from under a mane of hair that covered her eyebrows and ended at her nose. Her face was cunning and prematurely aged, her look obstinate and searching, like the look of a man who has lived through the bitterness of a hundred disappointments and has no illusions left.

Judym pulled her to him and kissed her. She did not resist. She only gazed into his eyes with her grave look, as if asking what might be in it for her. Franek punched "Uncle" lightly on his shirt cuff and mumbled something vapid in answer to a few questions, then moved away toward his crowd of friends.

Judym's chat with their aunt was reaching a dead end. As often happens in such cases, his mind was filling with his own thoughts, new thoughts that had no place at all in that conversation. These children running around this stuffy alley, enclosed by huge bare walls, reminded him, without his knowing why, of squirrels shut into a cage. With their lively movements and constant jumping, they needed open space, trees, grass, water.

"Surely Tomek would like to see Wiktor as soon as possible," said his aunt, who never liked to feign tenderness she didn't feel.

"Well, of course."

"It's hard to catch up with him anymore. Sometimes he's not home for three days… three nights…"

"And where is he?"

"Bah! Who knows? Anyway, he might come today."

"I'll drop by in the evening, and now I'd like to say hello to my sister-in-law. Can I go to the factory where she works? Will they let me in there?"

"Sometimes they let people in. Tomek could try. It will be easier for you gentlemen doctors than for us common folk."

"Where is that factory?" Judym asked. The conversation was becoming burdensome to him.

His aunt gave him the address and directions. He left the house with downcast eyes and walked along the streets leading to the periphery of the city, looking absently for the cigar factory. There was no uniform row of apartment buildings here, and rarely a house of more than one story. Low, ramshackle wooden structures sprawled as far as he could see. They resembled neither palaces nor country cottages, but brought both to mind. They were hung with gaudy signs and spattered with mud. The dirt blocked the passerby from seeing into them as effectively as blinds. The fronts of these buildings most often housed small shops. In one, kielbasa of poor quality was sold; in another, even shabbier store, cheap coffins.

Among these urban holding pens, covered with old brick tile or tar paper on which mold showed here and there, a new tenement shot up in one place or another, erected hastily, as if by a sandstorm. Such an object, with an invisible roof, with three blind walls and one fitted out with a row of windows, stood out among the old, almost medieval structures like a directional sign announcing a new order of things. With its ruthless, austere line, its pavement and its stark, rugged, prison-like wall, it foreshadowed the annexation of these areas to advance the development of a great city. Even more often, the view of the low buildings was disrupted by the enormous torso of a factory with strong walls, a wide gate, and an array of smokestacks. Among the roofs in the distance, he saw these smokestacks everywhere.

In the middle of the street, wagons loaded with brick dragged along over the broken pavement, spewing rose-colored dust in every direction. The drivers who delivered it were sprinkled with that dust from their heads to their heels, and their faces were as void of expression as the bricks themselves. Now and then a large freight wagon loaded with crates wrapped in mats rumbled by. Atop each of these ships of the road a strapping Jewish man in a red caftan of mixed cotton and linen usually sat, brandishing a whip and shouting at a pair of horses for whom every step was unimaginably toilsome. One of the wagons blocked Judym's way at a gate before a large building.

The number on the building was the one he was looking for. A sickening odor of tobacco that surrounded the building and pervaded the air on the street confirmed that he had reached the right factory. He walked in through the gate, went over to the porter, and asked if he might see a worker, a woman named Judym. The man would listen to nothing until he felt forty zlotys in his hand. That sensation jolted his thought process into action. He disappeared for a bit, then brought over a poor drudge covered with dust. After much discussion, that worker wagged a finger at Judym and led him into a wing of the building.

Inside, tobacco dust invaded his nose, throat, and lungs and forced him to breathe twice as rapidly as usual. On the second floor, a large hall was filled with a crowd of perhaps a hundred women bent over long, narrow tables. These women, dressed as simply and lightly as possible, were rolling cigars with nimble movements that appeared at first glance to be painful spasms. Some lowered their heads and shook their arms like cooks kneading dough. They were busy wrapping coarsely cut tobacco into leaves that had already been quickly and expertly trimmed. Others were putting the rolled cigars into wooden presses. The stifling air, full of the odor of bodies working in hot weather in a low, cramped place, laden with the dust of aged tobacco, seemed to tear tissues, eat away at throats and eyes. Beyond the first hall was a far larger one where at least three hundred women were engaged in similar work.

Judym's guide did not allow him to stop there, but led him on by narrow stairs and hallways past machines for drying leaves, past a mill that was grinding snuff and a shredder that cut various types of tobacco, to a large room where the finished product was packed. That room was seething with activity. As they passed it, Judym noticed a girl who was sticking excise labels on packets of cigars. Her hands moved with such speed that he was astounded. It was as if she were pulling an unbroken white tape off her table and winding it through her fingers. The finished packets flew out of her hands into the basket under the table as quickly as if a machine had thrown them out. To comprehend what she was doing, one had to look closely and watch for the beginning of the fastening of each packet.

Beyond that room was another room, dimly lit. There, according to Judym's guide, his brother's wife was working. The windows were fitted with wire screens; their tiny holes, thickly sprinkled with red dust from the city, let in little light and kept the miasma inside from escaping. Bins of coarsely cut tobacco lay in the corners. In the center were several work stations with four people to a table, packing cigars. Long tongues of flaming gas shot horizontally, hissing, out of curving pipes that ran from each table.

Judym saw his sister-in-law at the first table, sitting at a corner beside the gas flame. On the other side, a tall man with the face and complexion of a cadaver stood, or rather swayed on his feet. Farther on, at the opposite end of the table, sat an elderly Jewish man with a cap so low over his eyes that only his long beard and his sunken lips could be seen. To Judym's sister-in-law's left stood a young woman who, without a pause, reached into a pile of coarse tobacco and took out a handful at a time, threw it onto a scale, weighed out a quarter of a pound, and gave it to the man who was rocking on his feet. The doctor stopped in the doorway and stood there for a long time, once again trying to understand the four workers' patterns of movement. He saw people fidgeting convulsively as if they were having seizures, yet their motions were full of unbroken symmetry, method, and rhythm.

On the table two empty metal containers, each a long square tube widened at the top into the shape of an oblong glass, moved constantly between Judym's sister-in-law and the man next to her. Every few seconds she seized one of them in her left hand, turned its wide opening down, and rested it on her knee. In her right hand she took a piece of paper from a pile of papers with the factory label printed on them, put it around the end of the metal form, folded the corners of the paper onto the form, and sealed them with wax. Then with a movement quick as lightning she dipped the wax in the gas flame.

She had hardly touched the wrapped corners with her finger when her neighbor took the container from her hand, while she took the one standing in front of him to perform the same operation. The man turned the container so that the opening was up and put the end with the label affixed into a hole of corresponding size in the table. Then he received the scale from the young woman who was weighing out tobacco, sprinkled a quarter of a pound into the opening, and pressed it down with a tamper that fit the shape of the container. Having executed that with two rhythmic inclinations of his body, he took the container out of the small paper bag filled with tobacco and reached for the new container that Judym's sister-in-law had just labeled. A third worker took the filled packet he had left in the hole and labeled it from the other end, dipping the wax in the fire as his companion on the opposite end of the bench had done.

During the course of one work day those workers at one table loaded a thousand pounds of tobacco into quarter-pound packets, filling four thousand packets in no more time than ten seconds each. Their motions were harmonious, with rapid, tireless movements of hands always flying like flashes of light to certain points, then jumping back with the resiliency of elastic bodies.

There Judym saw, clear as day, what working people call "the way": *usus,* or standard practice, the series of odd measures, proven by blood, sweat, and tears, that constitute the shortest, easiest, most essential lines between two end points of work. As he thought of his own "standard practice" in the clinic, in the operating room, his attention became even more deeply engaged with the toilsome labor of the people he saw before him. Far into the room stood a table like the first one he had seen; a Jewish woman with a red scarf on her head was working beside the flame. The scarf completely covered her hair; her large forehead bulged from under it. The veins in her neck and temples were swollen. Her eyes were closed, but they opened after every monkey-like movement of her head, when it became necessary to seal the paper cone with wax. Then the eyes, watching the gas flame, flickered monotonously.

Her face was gaunt and sallow, like all the faces in this factory. On her parched, unattractive lips a wordless smile like a sob appeared from time to time. In it the doctor saw the effort to breathe, and the forced dwindling of the breath—the sigh of the hollow consumptive chest perpetually starving for air. The flash of the diligent eyes and that smile, together with all the motions she made, reminded him of the mad movement of a machine wheel on the edge of which something flickered like a small, radiant flame.

When Judym's sister-in-law saw him, her hands trembled and she did not touch the wax to the flame. Two big tears rolled quickly from her eyes before a joyful word of greeting escaped her lips. She stopped working and looked at him, weeping.

The man who pushed the tobacco into the packets did not see the doctor. When he did not receive the container at the proper moment, he looked at her as one cogwheel would look at another if the other stopped moving.

Judym went over to his sister-in-law, nodded to her, and told her he would wait for her in the factory yard at noon. It was only a quarter of an hour until that time, so he went out of the cigar packing room and waited in the hall next to the entrance. Old women sat there in small, dark rooms, sorting tobacco leaves in silence. Sprinkled with tobacco dust, thin, shabby, and gray—forbidding creatures with bloodshot eyes—they were like the Fates officiating at their secret rites. As Judym stood in the doorway waiting for his sister-in-law, they looked at him from deep in their eye sockets with expressions so bitter and vengeful that he was force to turn his back and avoid them.

As soon as the lunch hour struck, Judym's sister-in-law was first to hurry downstairs. A crowd of women were scattered behind her. She was more than a little pleased that she could show off her brother-in-law, the doctor, to all of them. "When did you arrive, brother? What's new with you? Have you been to our place on Ciepła Street?" she asked loudly, over and over.

Her worn, soiled face beamed with pride and satisfaction. Her lips, parted in a smile of genuine happiness, showed sparse, greenish teeth. Her eyes shone like coals. She walked through the factory gate with Judym and, out of habit, hurried down the street for the midday meal. The doctor did not restrain her but walked rapidly himself. Only when they were at the gate of the tenement on Ciepła Street did she stop and slap herself in the face.

"Christ! Why am I running like a jennyass? I've led you on quite a chase."

"Not at all. We'll have more time to talk. Will Wiktor be here?"

Her face fell.

"Oh, no. He eats at the Wajses' with some of the people from the factory. They live on Czerniakowska Street."

"And so he should. You can hardly ask him to walk so far for lunch."

"That's what he says," she said hastily.

As they started up the stairs, Judym caught the smell of meat fried in grease that he knew well from his childhood. The kitchen door was open to the corridor. Hot air burst from it, and a stuffiness that seemed unbearable.

Wiktor was not home. The aunt was cooking lunch. She hardly noticed the doctor's presence. He, for his part, did not try to attract her attention but went quickly through the first room, which doubled as kitchen and apartment for their aunt, to the second, which was the Judyms' bedroom. It was a low garret; his head reached the ceiling. Two beds stood there, piled with linen, and between them a chest of drawers covered with a crocheted scarf. There were photographs of relatives in frock coats, in the center a photograph of the doctor in his student uniform, all in frames cut with fretsaws. Somewhere in a corner, a clock with long weights jingled. The doctor's glance took in all this furniture, some of which was familiar to him: it had been in his parents' basement.

His brother Wiktor did not come, and it was hellishly hot in the flat, so Judym left, promising to come back in the evening. Wishing to find relief from the heat, he went into the Saxon Gardens, sat by a side path, and, with no one to notice, fell into a reverie. From long ago, from the time he had begun to study science for himself as a boy in school, certain half-realized ideas in the realms of chemistry and physiology had spun themselves out in his mind. His thoughts always turned to some powerful light, a thousand times stronger than electric light, which could enable a doctor to see the inside of a consumptive's lungs. In his imagination he made colossal discoveries in tuberculosis therapy and built hospitals such as the world had never seen.

The second dream that haunted him was the possibility of utilizing the refuse of large cities. The third was the invention of a new means of locomotion that would halt the force that drove the growth of factory towns and disperse those hives of bricks and people throughout the country. His schoolboy dreams were transformed into strong latent passions. How many hours he had spent on his new engine! In his student quarters he had had a corner fitted out with bottles and retorts, which, it seemed, contained miraculous secrets. With time that great light of aspiration, illuminating the early years of a poor young student like an aureole, died down under the breath of criticism, but cast its mystical glow on every circumstance.

The place that would be happier because of these great inventions was always Warsaw, the "old digs." Development hitherto unknown would date from the introduction of new railways, the Judym railways. Warsaw would be massive, would extend for miles, with parks full of pines, drowning in trees. Warsaw, where there would be no more basements or garrets, where tuberculosis, smallpox, and typhoid would be eradicated.

Now the old visions came again. Ideas that eluded him, clues to the nature of the engine he longed to invent, insinuated themselves into the dusk like long lines of luminosity and showed the shapes of mysterious things that lay there.

The park was filled with people. Judym had not looked around him before the afternoon was gone. Toward evening, crowds of Jews began to arrive; a human flood filled the main promenade, the side paths, and all the walks. There was no place to walk, so whole groups spilled over onto the streets or moved a few steps to the right or left.

The crowd was garishly dressed. The women wore fashionable colors. They formed a shimmering mass with their scarlet or bright blue bodices, their violet or red hats adorned with flowers or birds' feathers that bobbed above their heads with every movement. Men pushed stylish dress to the point of vulgarity, exaggeration, and absurdity. It was stuffy in the beautiful park. The leaves that hung from the trees seemed to fade and the grass to wither. The good smell of stocks seemed faint, unable to drown out the scent of bodies.

At twilight, Judym left the park and went toward Theatre Square. By the time the streetlights were lit, he was at Bank Square. The harsh glare of a street lamp fell on the sidewalk that led toward Elektoralna Street. In that light, waves of people could be seen flowing ceaselessly to the dark shape of the bank as if into the neck of a bottle. Judym stopped. That black mass of heads and bodies, moving quickly as ants, aroused a physical antipathy in him. They looked like surging swarms of maggots. To mingle with the rabble living there, behind this square—never! Never!

He turned on the spot, full of determination to see his brother some other time—and went into an elegant restaurant.

The next day he got up at five in the morning and went to his brother's apartment. When he entered through the gate, the sun had lit up the upper part of the wing of the building and lent the charm of its dawning to those shabby walls with their dingy rose tint. Even the dilapidated windows behind which poverty hid—those tired eyes of an ailing house eaten away inside by indigence, perpetually deprived of the glow of cheer—seemed at this one moment to open, to look at the sky and pray to the sun. When the doctor knocked on his brother's door, Wiktor was standing in it, already dressed. He was a tall man with a somewhat unkempt beard, large as a spade, that framed his features. His face was pale, not tanned, and the skin seemed to be soaked in something black. When he looked at his brother his eyes laughed like a child, though he greeted him in a cool, businesslike tone.

"How are you, Tomek?"

"What's new with you?" the doctor asked in a tone equally free of sentimentality.

"Well... it is as it is."

"You know, I'll go with you."

"Good," Wiktor said, taking his lunchbox.

When they found themselves on the street, they walked for some time in silence, simply not knowing what to say first. Finally, Wiktor said, "You were in Paris?"

"I was."

"Will you stay here now?"

"Certainly. I must settle here in Poland. I'll see; I still don't know anything. I'd like to be in Warsaw if I can make a living."

"After all those years of study, you still can't make a living!" His brother smiled incredulously, but with a hint of irony.

"That's the way you see it?"

"That's the way I see it. But what can I know?"

Judym noticed that "can" and began to chafe. They walked in silence again. The streets were almost empty. Now and then a cart loaded with vegetables or bread went by. An exceptionally noisy cab darted past, carrying a sleepy arrival from some early train. The pounding of feet reverberated against the walls of buildings as people walked to work with lunch pails in their hands.

An elderly Jewish man passed them, carrying two large sides of cured meat in a huge basket on his back. Down the whole length of the street, watchmen with brooms beat away yesterday's dry dust and dirt.

"Aunt told me that you changed jobs again," Judym ventured.

"Oh, yes. I fell out with Raczek, one of the foremen there. I hope I showed him!"

"Showed him what?"

"We couldn't stand him. We'd had enough. He said I didn't look like a worker because I wear gaiters, a jacket and a tie. That, he said, wasn't the way it should be. What are my gaiters to that swine? I go to work like any other fellow, in the same shirt and pants."

"Of course, but why get into a row about just anything?"

"Oh, about just anything! We knew what we got into a row about," Wiktor said, spitting. "He was only picking on me, the rascal, I know. What is he to me? I could put a big Tartar hat made of paper on my head and go into town and walk around the streets on a holiday and that would be none of his business, the dogsbody. I took it, I fired back at him once and again—well, I had to get out of that hole."

"And how are things with you now?"

"At first it was rough. But once they brought in the Bessemer converter, the 'pear' or whatever they call it, the work went very well for me. It's hard work and it burns the eyes, but I prefer it here."

"You see—I want to tell you something. You may prefer it there, but Teosia had to go to work. Yesterday I was in that cave she goes to."

"I didn't force her."

"You didn't force her, but being poor forced her. I tell you, she shouldn't work for long around that tobacco. The work is too hard."

"There's not much light work in the world just now," Wiktor said indifferently. "What was I going to do? I'm not idle myself, after all."

"I'm not reproaching you. I'm just sorry about your wife."

"So am I, but what's to be done about it?" Wiktor said sardonically, throwing his brother a sideways glance. "You went away from home, and we stayed as we were. You're sorry about my wife; so am I. But you can be as sorry as you want and it's no use. As long as I'm in there pitching, there's no need for anyone to leave home."

"You think that what somebody like Raczek says hurts your self-respect!"

"It doesn't hurt my self-respect! I'd make you wear thick boots, rough rags, denim, like any fellow from the country who comes hanging around and works in the sewers. We'd see—"

"Clothes don't make the man," said the doctor, thinking even as he spoke that that was a trite maxim quite unrelated to Wiktor's complaint.

Wiktor walked a dozen steps or so without a word. Suddenly he turned to Tomasz and said gruffly, "You see, this is the way it is. You're a gentleman now, and I'm a fellow hardly better dressed than our dead father. Our aunt took you away from home, brought you up, and sent you to school. Well, that's good. Very good. I'm being truthful when I tell you that makes me happy. Your life was like a rose in the garden, and mine, you think…. How you dress makes no difference to me, though you wear those clothes because, you see, our aunt took you. What would you have been if she hadn't? When I buy a jacket, I've clawed for it as if I'd dug it out of a wall. Do you understand?"

The words stabbed the doctor.

"You think my life was like a rose in a garden. If you knew…"

"What do I have to know?" Wiktor almost shouted. "You were my own brother! I remember that once our aunt came in a cab when we both were running barefoot in rags through the gutters. She took you because you were better-looking, and that was it. You came to see us sometimes for a few hours, but you were dressed up, in a uniform in those days, and you had sour looks for me, a ragged apprentice."

"What are you—"

"Well, I'm not talking through my hat! Only when you went to university did we grow closer, but that was something else, and anyway—"

"I'm grateful to our aunt," the doctor said, looking at the pavement. "If it hadn't been for her, I would have been back where we started. That's true. She helped me find my way into the world. But I went through a lot because of her."

"You went through a lot?"

"You know what our aunt was like."

"Yes, I do."

"She was said to have been an admirable girl. She made it out of the cellar and into the world quickly."

"Why should you be wrapped in cotton wool? 'She made it out into the world'; rubbish! She was, or so they said, the most popular lady of joy in Warsaw! One fellow our dead father made shoes for revealed to him that there were counts, I tell you—and not only counts—"

"Well, all right, all right," Tomasz muttered impatiently.

"Does that annoy you?" His brother gave a coarse laugh.

"I want to tell you how it was because you brought it up, and you don't know. She got together a pile of money and bought a four-room apartment on a third floor. She had lovely furniture. What didn't she have in there!"

"That was said to be the first arrangement!"

"That was still her situation when she took me. She was past her prime then, not leading her former life, but a lot of people came to see her. They played cards and drank. All kinds of people came, young women and older ones. That's where I grew 'like a rose in a garden,'" he said with a pained smile. "During the first years I ran errands, polished things, cleaned floors, washed pots and pans in the kitchen, set up samovars and flew around, flew around constantly doing shopping. I still remember that house and those kitchen stairs.

"How I suffered there! In perhaps two years, Aunt took and rented a room in a corridor with a separate entrance for one student. He didn't pay much, but it was also his duty to teach me and prepare me for secondary school. The chap taught me conscientiously and got me ready. Radek was his name. I went to school. Aunt paid my entrance fee, I can't deny it, but she also abused me for all she was worth. I found out later, when I was older, that she lost a lot at cards. At the time, I didn't understand what was happening at all.

"In my experience she was only stingier and more furious all the time. Really furious. Sometimes she was so enraged that she ran through the rooms in the apartment, from one to the other, and God forbid that you should fall into her hands just then! I always slept in the anteroom, on a straw mattress that I was only allowed to drag from the dark passageway behind her room when all the guests had left her. I lay down to sleep late at night and I had to get up earlier than everyone else. As time passed, fewer guests came, but she rented three rooms off the common corridor to subletters. Then I couldn't go to bed before the last of these poor vagabonds got back at night. And I had to get up while everyone was still asleep.

"Anyone who felt like it beat me: Aunt, the maid, the subletters. Even the guard at the gate pounced on me, if not with a fist in my back at least with words, often harder than a fist! And there was no appeal. When Radek went away after the end of his school term, I worked at my lessons in the kitchen, among potatoes and butter on a table heaped with pans. How many times Aunt chased me away for any fault at all! How many times I had to beg her on my knees to take me back into her 'house'! Sometimes in a fit of good humor she gave me her worn-out shoes and I had to wear them, to the delight of the whole school. Winter came, and I ran around in worsted slippers with high heels. There was another winter when you could see the prints of my bare feet on the snow for the whole season, even if the upper parts of my shoes covered them.

"As soon as I made it to the next-to-last year of school, I got out of there. But all my childhood, all my early youth, passed in constant indescribable anxiety, in wordless misery that I only understand now. And anyway… anyway…what's there to say?"

"That's our aunt for you," Wiktor laughed. "Our father didn't like to talk about her, but anytime he was good and soused, he cursed her right and left."

Tomasz threw up a hand and walked on in silence. The streets were full of sunshine. Fragrant violet shadows lay around houses comfortably tucked between trees.

Tomasz and Wiktor turned toward the neighborhood where the factory was located and stood on a hill, looking at it. From below the large expanse of walls the Vistula coursed into an open field, bending like a great arc of bright silver, dazzling as a white flame lit by the morning sun. The thirsty eye seized on the distant sight of that free-flowing water, the level green meadows, the bluish forests, the soft lines losing themselves in space. Nearer, on the shore of the river, it rested on dark clumps of spreading trees.

The brothers sat by a garden wall on a lawn and looked silently at the landscape in front of them. From the industrial plain below them, from the mass of blind walls, from the narrow, elongated buildings that exhaled, through thin pipes, puffs of steam that looked like miraculous hunks of floating silver in the sun, came the incessant rattle of iron. Doctor Tomasz was overtaken by an illusion that those ringing hammer blows, those moans like the jerking of chains, let off steam that exploded in all directions from tar paper roofs coated with smoke. The wild, hard, stifled roar of engines, trembling as if from some insatiable passion for speed, seemed to find a visible embodiment in the great clots of grayish-brown smoke that wheeled in constant, rapid semicircles. This smoke from a multitude of tall, round, narrow brick chimneys with metal welds was like gangrene in the expanse of clean sky. It hovered low, wandered over buildings, and spilled onto the streets like a gray fog in which the forms of houses, street lights, carriages and people grew indistinct.

Now and then the men could feel, at regular intervals, two successive blows of a steam hammer that made the earth tremble for several dozen paces from the factory. Wagons drawn by very large horses rolled over the battered pavement. Those vehicles, consisting of two connected poles that lay on thick axles, dragged their loads of iron from place to place: blocks of raw iron like hardened ridges of earth, flat iron bars, grating, rails—straight or coiled like ribbons—huge rods, parts of bridges, machines. Some of them could be heard in the neighboring streets. Two long bars of hammered iron protruded like tails behind the rear wheel of one wagon, beating against each other at each rumble of the wagon with unbearable shrieks. It seemed as though that insane rage, like a creature in chains, was hurling down the bars in diabolical fury and baying out its final sigh in torment.

As the Judym brothers were sitting and waiting with braced nerves for one of the noisiest vehicles to reach its destination, someone suddenly spoke up from the sidewalk opposite:

"Judym! Why are you sitting there? Judym!"

The brothers did not hear that voice right away. At last Wiktor glanced over and then rose from where he was sitting. A tall young man was walking across the street toward them, a blond man with a short, fair beard and blue eyes. His face was pale from time spent in the factory, but his lips were a healthy color, and smiling. He wore shabby clothes, a percale shirt, and a hat with a brim shaped like wings.

"That's our new assistant to the engineer who first installed the Bessemer converter," said Wiktor.

The young man came up to them and began to speak. Every few seconds he threw a sharp, bright, searching glance at Tomasz.

"This is my brother. He's a doctor," said Wiktor. "He just came back from Paris."

The technician held out a hand and gave his name, not pronouncing it clearly, as often happens with introductions.

The three men walked slowly down to the lower part of the street, chatting about inconsequential things. Wiktor was pleased to be able to boast about his brother, though he tried not to show it. He talked a good deal and finally, without asking Tomasz, inquired if his brother might visit the factory and particularly the steel mill. The young man hesitated for a moment, but in the end promised to take the visitor under his wing.

They went down into a narrow alley created by the bare walls of the factory and stopped in a cramped doorway. It was seven o'clock. In the factory yard they were surrounded by the barking of hammers and the dull growling of electric engines generating almost a thousand horsepower. Wiktor disappeared and the doctor was alone with the young engineer, who led him through large rooms where iron bars dozens of yards long were shaved, holes were drilled in them, and in the twinkling of an eye less powerful machines punched out large holes in flat pieces of iron two fingers thick as easily as a human finger could put holes in a piece of honeycomb. In one place grating for bridges was riveted with white-hot screws. In another, iron bars were cut with scissors, like linen. Judym passed from enormous workshops to an empty room where hardly a dozen people were working, welding rails.

Doctor Tomasz watched this work with lively interest. Machines had little to do here. These operations were only performed by muscles and hammers on very long handles. In a corner of the room a man was tinkering with something, a man with such a torso, such a mass of muscle, that Judym stared at him as if he represented an unknown species of human being. He had seen such clumps of muscle, but only in marble and in drawings. It seemed that if that arm were raised and that fist struck the wall, the wall would be shattered to bits in an instant. It was a splendid sight when the strong man took his hammer and, together with a fellow worker, began banging two burning ends of rails to join them together.

The doctor did not want to leave. He watched the man with burning curiosity, watched and catalogued to himself the muscles on his body. Moving behind the young engineer, he enjoyed from a distance the sight of this man with the physique of a blacksmith.

"There's another strong man," his companion said.

"Which one?"

"That one."

Beside the powerfully built blacksmith, a young fellow stood with his body turned sideways. He was perhaps twenty-eight years old, with a face so beautiful that Judym stood as still as if he had turned to stone. It was a slender face with sharply drawn features, regular as if sculpted from ivory. A small black mustache shadowed his upper lip. His figure was almost thin, yet somehow wonderfully shapely. His movements were not rapid, but they were sure of their mark, economical, harmonious.

"Is he a blacksmith as well?" Judym whispered. "He looks like a maybug compared to that Hercules."

"Oh, he's not so bad," his guide smiled.

Soon after that the slender man's turn came. He lifted his hammer and began to strike. Only then did Judym see what his companion meant. Bare hands flung the hammer out backward and to the right in a circular motion and hit the bar with a side blow that started from the floor, slamming into the iron with deafening force. The man's body stood as straight as if it had no part in the action. Only his hips recoiled with a sure, slight movement that reflected the power of the blows, and his shirt tightened over the muscles of his shoulders. Sheaves of sparks like blue and gold stars fluttered from under the hammer, surrounding the splendid, knightly figure like a halo befitting a person of great strength and amazing beauty. After the last blow the young blacksmith retreated to a corner of the room with a movement like music, rested his hands on the handle of his hammer, and whistled through his teeth. Drops of sweat stood on his forehead and streamed down his grimy face.

From the blacksmith shed, they entered the iron and steel foundry. Smoke from slowly charring straw, the odors of various acids, and stuffy air degraded to the last degree filled these black, grave-like workshops that belched fire. The rough, churned-up dirt floor smoked and burned the feet. The black walls seemed to be covered with wounds; they trembled as if in unrelenting pain.

In one end of the huge shed stood a pear-shaped container with a wide base. It tapered toward the top, which was finished with a small opening. This large retort turned on a level, hollow axis that let in heated air from a blower. The whole container could tilt in such a way as to pour out its contents at the proper moment.

When Judym went into the room, the "pear" stood upright, loaded with layers of pig iron and coke. A current of air heated to eight hundred degrees was let in from the bottom of the vessel, blowing with enormous force. Black soot, flashing now and then with a distended flame, began to burst from the opening at the top. Dark clouds filled the building and surged out through the great gate. Smoke shot up faster and faster, growing whiter and wispier as it rose. At intervals, billions of starry sparks flew out of it. When the coke was entirely burned, a long, enormous, vibrating fire exploded from among the sparks with a terrifying roar. It was red at first, then paler, then blue, and finally took on a blinding brightness.

Almost in the fire itself, very close to the vessel, were several people with a young technician at their head. Sparks burned his clothes and the brim of his hat as he raised his face toward the flame. His bloodshot eyes examined its color, assessing whether the iron had been converted to steel. At a certain moment he gave an order for silica to be thrown into the maw of the vessel, since silica assimilates mechanically with iron at a temperature of 1,400 degrees.

The flame went mad. Its column, narrow as a double-edged sword, gave a muffled roar and flew up. It seemed that it would tear itself from its place, surge, and explode upward. The dim room lit up with an incandescence that was unbearable to the eye.

Just then on a platform with an iron balustrade, behind the flame and about halfway to the top of it, a black figure appeared like a salamander. It seemed to be in the fire. The doctor fixed his eyes on it and studied its movements. That worker dipped a long tool, a certain kind of chimney sweep's broom, in the spitting liquid.

Then the doctor saw that the black figure on the platform was that of his brother. His heart burned as if a spark from the blazing fire had flown into it.

CHAPTER III

Dreams

To the medical world, Dr. Antoni Czernisz's return after the summer vacation was like the beginning of the year. Dr. Czernisz was a truly exceptional man, a physician of the first rank, not only in Warsaw. His name was a household word, repeated often in specialized literature and not unknown in the scientific community abroad. Indeed, it must be said that he enjoyed greater recognition in foreign countries than at home.

Dr. Czernisz came from a poor background. By his own efforts he had finished his studies and acquired a name in the world and a comfortable living. Relatively late in life—not until after age forty, when he was a wealthy man—he had married a woman of great beauty. Madam Czernisz had been the "only hope" of an impoverished family with aristocratic connections. She had probably married not for love but from conviction. In her time, she had been a spirited fighter for women's emancipation. As time passed, children were born and duties and relationships removed her from wider life but did not destroy her aspirations and beliefs. She always set her hand to a worthy cause. Those causes were not the older enterprises that had breathed the zeal for activism into her, but a measured enthusiasm persisted in her pursuit of them.

The "thinking class" gathered in the Czerniszes' salons. Their hospitality extended to every distinguished element in Warsaw. Receptions were organized so that every other Wednesday the intelligentsia of all professions attended, and on the other Wednesdays, only physicians. If someone from outside the medical circle wandered in on the wrong day, he was madam's guest.

The doctors did not waste their time in small talk at these Wednesday meetings. The group, which in the beginning was made up of the doctor's closest friends, drew in others. If someone had a completed paper, he read it there. If someone was presented with an unusual case in his practice, he shared information about it with his colleagues. Someone who had been on a scientific tour might give an account of what he had seen and noted as appropriate for medical practice in Poland.

These sessions were not pompous, but they were not overly casual. People took them seriously, and, more important, enjoyed them. With a host who was modest and wise, full of distinction and benevolence; a hostess who charmed her guests with every word and gesture; rooms with the finest appointments and more than one work of art; and an atmosphere of thought, genuine excellence, and culture—they attracted everyone.

Judym, who as a student had been acquainted with Dr. Czernisz, paid his respects to him early in September and was invited to join the circle.

In the middle of October, the first Wednesday gathering for doctors took place. Dr. Tomasz went to the gathering with a paper to give. He had hesitated for a long time, feeling fearful and then eager, but finally he had decided to present his work. He had written it some time ago, while he was still in Paris. Now he added an introduction and a few local statistics. Dr. Czernisz, who knew nothing at all about the work, asked and encouraged him strongly and eloquently to read it. He even made him feel obligated.

"How can this be?" the doctor had demanded. "You ask, friend, if you should express an idea you brought from Paris after nearly two years of studies. What should we read, then, when we come together? What we all know, what we've talked over among ourselves a thousand times?"

These arguments were even more effective in convincing Judym because it so happened that when he was abroad he had read various papers before professional societies. There was even a little ambition of a low order in this. He was only restrained by an anxiety related to the particular environment in which he would be making his debut.

On the appointed day he reviewed his manuscript once more, dressed in black, and went out at dusk. When he was about to pass through the gate of the doctor's house, he felt a tightening in his throat that altered shamefully into a strong desire to turn back. There was even a moment of utter cowardice. In spite of that he finally pressed the doorbell over which Dr. Czernisz's name appeared. Then, with a pain in his head, he heard a series of dull chimes giving out something like a stammer or a sarcastic giggle, and the rattle of the latch.

He walked up marble stairs covered with a wide, colorful runner and into a brilliantly lit front hall. He felt his host's hand on his shoulder. All around him he heard the sonorous hum of men in spirited conversation.

Stumbling over rugs, bumping into furniture, finally he came, led by Czernisz, to a sofa from which a lovely woman rose. She might have been thirty years old. She was dressed without show, but her simple gown draped her figure with such grace that Judym immediately felt the innate apprehensiveness of a cobbler's son. His greetings and his manners were no less influenced by his origins. With the lively sensitivity of noble natures, Madam Czernisz not only noticed his uneasiness but felt disconcerted and distressed herself. At that moment Dr. Tomasz remembered that, in spite of the slight confusion that passed at a certain moment, he was going to read, to speak to a group of strangers who were sure of themselves, prepared to judge, ready for conversation and the free play of ideas.

The doctor's wife chatted with him about Paris and tried, with some success, to put him at ease. He warmed to her intensely and began to speak. But another person came up from the left, and still another called her to the other end of the room.

When he was alone, Judym looked around and saw many doctors he knew by sight from the hospital and the street. There were hardly two, however, whom he could have greeted with a familiar press of the hand. He sat stiffly in his armchair, with his legs as rigid as logs on the soft carpet, and endured the torment of waiting. The doorbell sounded every minute and another person appeared in the bright light. When the salon and the adjoining smaller rooms were filled completely, Dr. Czernisz announced in his soft, quiet voice that their colleague Dr. Judym, newly arrived from Paris, would read a work entitled "A few notes" or "A word on the subject of hygiene."

Judym heard this announcement with genuine fright. But when the collective eyes were turned on him, he grew calm, approached a small table, and took his manuscript from the side pocket of his jacket. Slowly, as if reluctantly, the buzz of talk turned to an undertone in which the name "Judym"…"Judym" could barely be made out, like a chord fading away in space.

He began to read. The introduction he had hammered out like a blacksmith with erudite words and sentences was a speech on the contemporary state of hygiene. Not only the sentences, in which the same noun was repeated more than a dozen times, but the ideas were rigid and trite. As he lectured, Judym felt and saw, as if through a fog, that he was the target of cold, harsh glances tinged with mockery. But that had a salutary effect on him.

He read with redoubled effort about disinfectants that were used in hospitals he had visited, about new remedies and treatments—about quinosol, for example, and about various applications of corrosive sublimate—in a word, about everything he had culled from foreign books and journals. His hearers began to show an interest, and their curiosity grew as he described new disinfectants for private houses, such as unpolymerized formaldehyde and others. That subject filled the first part of his paper.

At the beginning of the second part, Judym raised the question of what science, which in general took an interest in the issue of health, had undertaken to promote hygiene for the disadvantaged classes. In order to explore this question from every angle, he began to talk about things he had seen in Paris and elsewhere. He spoke of the style of life of the so-called reserve army of industry, of bands of people, drunk on absinthe, encamped and dancing in the ballroom of Vieux-Chêne on Mouffetard Street, or in a room at la Guillotine and in other places.

It was a long account. His audience listened attentively. He turned from that subject to a description of the lodging house Château Rouge.

"I went there often," he said, "and even, I must confess, spent a whole day in that den. That nightmare will never be expunged from my memory. One enters from a small street, Galande, in the neighborhood of Notre Dame, the oldest quarter of Paris. In the vicinity, the famous tavern Père-Lunette flourishes. The clientele of the Château, the old palace of 'La Belle Gabrielle' d'Estrées, the mistress of King Henry the Fourth, is of two sorts. The first are sightseers. The second are the poor, who find cheap absinthe there and a place to be comfortable for a few hours. The cover charge is fifteen centimes, for which the customer has the right to sit at a table and rest two hands and a head on the edge of it until two in the morning. On frosty or rainy evenings the customers, of whom not one, obviously, has his own home, simply lie on each other.

"After one o'clock passes and they are thrown out, they scatter in every direction. Some go to sleep under bridges, to the fortifications, to the Bois de Boulogne, to Vincennes. Others with a dozen pennies in their pockets look for some cheap lodging. Most of them spend the night at the Château; then some go to les Halles Centrales to eat soup with rice for two sous, and during the course of the day to assist the porters on duty for a dozen or so centimes, sometimes for thirty or so. Others gather cigarette butts and partly smoked cigars and shake the tobacco out of them. Then they wait by the monument to Etienne Dolet on Place Maubert at six in the morning and sell little bags of that tobacco for ten centimes each to workers on their way to the factories.

"Château Rouge can accommodate several hundred people. On winter nights there are five hundred. Predominantly women and children gather in the first hall, where there is a buffet, because a metal stove is smoking away there. In the next room, the old bedroom of *'La Belle* Gabrielle,' men lie on the bare floor. The owner charges each one ten centimes for the right to sleep until two in the morning. In the third room, which is decorated with frescoes and which they call the Senate, people sleep on tables and on the floor. There the ones who gather unsmoked cigars and cigarettes blow their merchandise out of its wrappers and put it into small bags. There the pimps wait patiently for their street girls, night workers who support them. Tired street acrobats, often tattooed, sleep there, and petty artisans, people whose occupation is bathing dogs in the river, opening cabs at the railway stations, removing dead cats, and other professions not fit to be mentioned publicly.

"On the left side of the 'Senate' is the 'parlor of the dead,' where the drunk, the sick, and persons in the host's good graces lie side by side. Finally, there is the so-called 'salon,' with frescoes depicting the exploits of the criminal Gamahut, the murderer of Madam Ballerich. Usually some poor devil elucidates these mysterious daubings to sightseers, or sings for them, in Parisian street language, songs that express the misery of the human race, like this one, for example, which begins:

> *C'est de la prison que j't'écris;*
> *Mon pauv' Polyte,*
> *Hier je n'sais pas c'qui m'a pris,*
> *A la visite;*
> *C'est des maladi's qui s'voient pas,*
> *Quand ça s'déclare,*
> *N'empêch' qu'aujourd'hui j'suis dans l'tas*
> *À Saint-Lazare!*

"When I went to Château Rouge for the first time, I was wearing a top hat, so the courteous owner took me for an Englishman out to see the city's distinguished sights, and with lamp in hand conducted me around his place. It was late at night. Our conversation and his light awoke some guests. A ragged street girl rose from beside one of the walls. Her face was swollen, parched by some inner fire, and for several minutes she looked at me with large eyes. This sight was so disturbing, so indescribable, that if I may borrow the words of the poet, 'until now my soul burns.'"

This lyrical departure surprised his hearers. They saw it as a rhetorical turn and overlooked the unfortunate few notes on the pipe of sentimentality. But Judym felt a true fire burning his soul. He spoke of the Cité Jeanne d'Arc in the vicinity of the Salpêtriére hospital, where thirty or forty or more laborers' families were housed. Each family had its own quarters there, but through the flimsy walls they heard each others' quarrels. Whole bands of children loitered around on the stairs and in the gutters and streets, infecting each other with sicknesses and inclinations to bad behavior. The women were loose, the men caroused.

"Even those traces of domesticity are nowhere to be found among the inhabitants of Cité Doré, Cité des Kroumirs, and Cité de la Femme en Culotte, beyond the northwest fortifications," he continued. "One of those camps comprises avenues of shacks surrounded with refuse dumps. The owner of the land, a former garbagewoman, used to traipse around them a long time ago dressed in men's clothes—no one knew why—collecting the rent. Another of these agglomerations of humanity consists of actual pigsties on free ground, where children sleep on heaps of rags and dirt; where the writer Haussonville saw an elderly woman scraping shreds of meat off an old bone from a rubbish dump onto a crust of blackened bread; and a pair of old men whose home was a shack on wheels in which they moved from one of those slums to another.

"But let's not be sad about this. We have our own Paris, Parysowski Square, outside the wall of Powązkowska, and a Jewish quarter not at all less shocking than the Cité des Kroumirs. It's worth it, if only once in one's life, to walk through the teeming streets leading to the Jewish cemetery. There one can see inside ateliers, factories, workshops, and homes of which philosophers never dreamed. Whole families can be seen sleeping in spaces under the ceilings of shops, where there is neither light nor air. Where several families share the same nest, piles of groceries lie, and businesses, industries, family affairs, love and vice are carried on, food scorches on stinking grease, consumptives cough and spit, children are born, and the incurably sick of every sort moan as they drag along the shackles of life: these repugnant places sigh as one passes. And the only remedy offered for it all is antisemitism.

"And in the country? Isn't it commonplace to see two families with a brood of children lodging in one room, or rather in one farmyard pigsty where there is a larder, walled off with boards, that holds a heap of rotting potatoes and a hoard of food such as cabbage and beets? Unmarried male workers, wagoners, so-called 'boarders,' get meat only at Christmas and Easter. They get fat, or so-called leaf lard, in food laced with rancid salt pork—only in small amounts, since in larger quantities, with its strong odor and the taste of lard, the food would be inedible. These people have no living space of their own. They sleep in stables and cowsheds under mangers. Girls sleep in one room, but often with groups of men in the same room. The married farmhands live in one room amid mud that surges from the walls in spring, and raise children together with piglets."

His audience received all these particulars with a silence that was impossible to interpret. In the meantime, the speaker entered the phase he had dreamed of. He felt as if he were a climber throwing an iron hook into a waiting ring and abruptly pulling his whole soul onto the cold height of courage. At that point he began to present evidence that, though such symptoms of savagery stemmed from many causes, one cause was indeed the indifference of physicians.

"We know how to be diligent in exterminating microbes in the bedrooms of the wealthy," he said, "but we complacently ignore the fact that children are housed with piglets. Which of the medical men of this era busy themselves with hygiene at the Château Rouge? Who of us in Warsaw makes inquiries about how a Jewish family lives in Parysowski Square?"

"What is this?" a voice deep in the room asked, almost in a whisper.

"It's tripe," said a blond man with a face like Apollo, rubbing his horn-rimmed pince-nez.

Judym heard the sardonic tone and saw malicious smiles, but his excitement was rising and he waded farther in.

"Isn't it our duty to promote hygiene in places where there is none, and where such terrible conditions prevail? Who will do it if we don't? Our whole life is one continuum of dedication. We spend our early youth in morgues and our later life in hospitals. Our work is a struggle with death. What can compare with a doctor's work? Farm work, factory work, the work of a clerk, merchant, craftsman, even a soldier? With us, every thought, every step, every act must be a triumph over blind, frightening forces of nature. From every side, from the eye of every sick patient, contagion and death stare at us. When cholera is about to strike, when everyone loses his reason, hurries to fold his tents and escape, only the doctor comes to grips with the disaster in his country. Only at that time do we see, as if in a mirror, who we are.

"At that time they listen to our advice, our recommendations, our decisions and orders. But when the plague is past, those who benefit from the conditions of society begin their hubbub again and set themselves up on more convenient terms, along with the strongest in the group. Our role ends. We move among the crowd and fall in with the thinking of the herd. Instead of seizing the helm of life, instead of using unerring science to erect a wall between life and death, we prefer to ease the lives and enhance the comfort of the rich in order to share the crumbs of material excess with them. The doctor of today is the doctor of the rich!"

"Let me speak!" said a tall, thin, elderly man with whiskers white as milk.

"Let me speak!" the blond man with the pince-nez said harshly and carelessly, lightly rising in his chair and turning toward the host.

A hum of deep aversion drifted through the hall.

"The fact is that medical practice today takes sickness as its reason for being," Judym went on, "and treats the sickness itself without in any way attempting to eliminate the causes. I still speak of treating the poor…"

Someone in the room laughed in a low voice. The hum grew clearer and less polite.

"I am not speaking here of commonplace abuses, of the practices of various railroad doctors and doctors in factories and other workplaces, but always of the state of hygiene. I speak of this: that when a man working in a factory where he rinses iron bars in sulphuric acid and slaked lime all day gets abscesses on his lungs, he goes to the hospital, where they cure him as well as they can, and returns to his occupation. A worker in a sugar mill may be busy producing superphosphate by washing bone char with sulphuric acid. If the interior of the workshop is filled with fumes from the acid, and he inhales gases from the burnoff of potassium picrate, they will cause abscesses on his lungs. He will be ill and, after being discharged from the hospital, he will return to his workshop. In the ice cellars of breweries, pus is discharged from inflamed lungs."

"These are matters related to care for patients discharged from hospitals. They are by no means the responsibility of physicians," said their host.

"The duty of the physician is precisely this: to cure. If he begins to look for appropriate placement for his patients, he is perhaps a brave philanthropist, but assuredly a poor doctor," someone else called out.

"Always 'caretakers,' always 'philanthropists,' Judym retorted. "I don't demand that a doctor find places for the patients he has healed. But the status of physician confers the obligation and even the right, in the name of the physician's own competence, to forbid a sick person to return to the source of the malady that is destroying his health."

"Good try!" "Quite a utopia!" "What a colleague!" could be heard from all sides.

"Precisely what you, respected colleagues, affirm with these protests, I call neglect and disregard for the causes of sickness when it is a question of the poor. We doctors have every authority to destroy cellars unfit for habitation, to make factories and filthy homes healthy, to comb through all the places like Kazimierz in Krakow and the Jewish quarters in Lublin. It's in our power. If only we wanted to exercise the natural rights of our profession, the ignorant would be compelled to obey us as well as the moneyed powers."

With that, Judym closed his notebook and sat down. That was not really the end of his lecture. There was a third part that dealt with various projects suggested by his enthusiastic imagination. But Dr. Tomasz did not feel strong enough to deliver this passage, which was set off by three asterisks in the manuscript; he was quite out of breath. The expressions of the assembled doctors, the discomfiture of the host, and the very atmosphere of the meeting made it clear that the lecturer had been completely written off by his hearers. The message had not been powerful enough to agitate or shock them, or sufficiently novel to dazzle them. They looked at him calmly, without anger, and their looks said: "You appeared to be a fierce lion, but you are only someone's bellows, and—who knows?—perhaps an ass."

When the room had gone completely quiet, the elderly man with side whiskers, Dr. Kalecki, rose from his chair and began to expound his opinions, which were fully formulated and fervent.

"Colleague Judym," he said, "has given us a beautiful lecture that attests favorably and eloquently to his altruistic feelings, his vivid imagination and his studies in Paris. It is gratifying in these times, which are unfortunately so steeped in utilitarianism, to meet a doctor with such lively feelings and a heart so warm and full of sentiment. In the name of those gathered here I take the liberty of expressing appreciation to our colleague for his work."

After this turn of rhetoric, which seemed to Judym to mock his misery, Dr. Kalecki shifted to a critical line of argument.

"The case made by Dr. Judym involves several issues, and touches on heaven and hell. From all we have heard, or so I think, three leading issues can be isolated. *Primo:* a matter purely scientific, the matter of hygiene in the lives of the poor classes; *secundo:* a social issue; *tertio:* remedies. Each of these points is a mountain overgrown with wild forests, heaped with fragments of rock, slashed with ravines, still haunted by witches at night.

"To the first point, then. I do not mention what our friend and reader presented here. Those are facts conscientiously noted and colorfully related. Very sad facts, I might add. As they relate to conditions in France, that issue I must simply leave aside, since I have never given it special examination. I know for certain, however, that in Paris charitable causes draw in ten million—no less than ten million—francs each year. That is no small sum. It is known as well that entire societies of villainous beggars exist there, whole syndicates that support women who pretend to be in childbirth, that send out epileptics, lunatics, all manner of cripples and others with handicaps. When all is said and done, in these discussions we must never forget the perennially wise statement of Herbert Spencer: 'The feeling which vents itself in "poor fellow!" on seeing one in agony excludes the thought of "bad fellow."' By saying this, I do not intend to speak belittlingly of such a phenomenon as Cité de la Femme en Culotte.

"Let us move on to the subject of our conditions here. Our colleague has grieved over the plights of laborers, Jewish communities, and so on. In fact, that is an issue in our country, and here and there things are not well. I must emphasize, however, though colleague Judym may be displeased with me, that those are not matters for doctors. 'Plato is a friend, but truth is a greater': that is given. It would be as if an ambulance doctor called to treat two cobblers who had stabbed each other, instead of dressing their wounds, began lecturing them about the harmful effects of fighting! What can doctors accomplish in such situations? They can educate, educate the unenlightened rural underclass and influence those who employ them. That is all. And that is done, it is certainly done, as colleagues practicing in the provinces attest. It is done more than one would think from a distance, from the exalted position of the devil's advocate. Here, as everywhere, someone chooses what Scripture calls 'the better part,' and philanthropy, at least, ought to choose that part—philanthropy, that sister of human compassion.

"Let us look at the state of the case. We see before our eyes the growth of the spirit of compassion, sacrifice, the true zeal of the upper class to rush to help in those bottomlands of hardship that Dr. Judym pictures so vividly.

How many offerings flowed into the alms pouch this year! How many tears were wiped without words, unseen even by the self-styled advocates of the people! I will not name, I will not point out those among our colleagues gathered here who hurry to answer every call of the suffering, who sacrifice their time, their health and their lives without thinking that they are fulfilling a special mission. They simply do what is necessary, what their hearts and consciences see as their duty, or, I say less flatteringly, what it is their habit to do, or simply their addiction."

"Bravo! Bravo!" Animated shouts could be heard from every corner of the room.

"And let us take one more look. Is it really so bad with us? Hygiene exhibits are appearing, antibegging societies are forming, shelters for the night are being established, baths and recreations for people are coming into being, and finally a hygiene society, to say nothing of compassionate works carried out in silence. Gentlemen, we do not need to blush at the reproaches of colleague Judym that the doctor of today is a doctor for rich people. In all these matters that we are examining, the medical profession has not only provided initiatives, but can say proudly of itself: 'I have played a great part in them.'

"Colleague Judym is a young man. His heart prompted him to words of bitterness, for evidently it has borne much suffering. He cannot admit now to feeling rancor, to harboring bias against the physicians of Warsaw. But when his hair is frosted with white, he will confirm what I have said: that today he expressed angry, injurious judgments. Tonight, sincerely and with all our hearts, we forgive him everything."

All at once and for no reason, Judym felt something like contrition. He had never guessed that anyone would forgive him from the heart for what he had said about hygiene. But before he could find his way around this new thicket of unprecedented feelings, someone else arose. It was Dr. Płowicz, who had asked to speak at the same time as Dr. Kalecki.

"Respected Dr. Kalecki has put into his statement everything it is possible to say about the material presented by the lecturer," he said in a harsh, resonant tone. "In my opinion, there was only one place in which Dr. Kalecki understated his rebuttal to Dr. Judym's accusations. I'm referring to the way the reader imposes on today's doctors the obligation to improve social conditions. It's a preposterous claim, bordering on an attack, when the stern critic asserts that a doctor's work consists in enhancing the life of the rich in order to share the crumbs of luxury with them.

"I'm passing over many things here in total silence. I won't labor the point that the core of life, the essence of human affairs, is the drive of every person for culture, superiority, life in a beautiful residence, even, to our horror be it said, the drive for wealth. I have no idea why physicians should be denied their share of the paltry riches of this sad world. Surely it's because, as our stern and spiteful critic admits, we work harder than those in any profession, and under the most miserable conditions. But as I've already said, I won't labor that point, because, to put it mildly, there is nothing to labor. When Dr. Judym hangs a sign with his hours of business on his door, when he has not only his own student self but a beloved wife and child to shelter and clothe—when we live to see that time, perhaps we will not hear such harsh words about the ethical defects of the medical profession.

"I want to raise another point—to call colleague Judym's attention to the fact that his ideas and his altruistic flights are not well founded. Doctors do not have all the powers that he attributes to them. If they wanted most sincerely and strenuously to force the tavernkeeper at the Château Rouge to apply so-called hygiene requirements, they would in no way succeed. The world is a sharp businessman who does not think at all of giving away the money he gathers so the poor worker can spend his life in a better and more comfortable style. To corroborate that, one must descend from the intellectual heights to this sad world. Preachments, even the most beautiful, do no good here."

Dr. Płowicz sat down. There was silence for a while, a troubled and painful silence.

"I wanted to put in a few words," Tomasz said in a hollow voice, rising unsteadily from his chair.

"Please!" someone whispered from far back in the room.

"Just this…this…I had no idea that my argument—that is, my presentation—would evoke such unexpected points of view. I had no thought of affronting the medical profession. Indeed, I intended to enhance its dignity through the role that I envision for it in society. It seems strange to me that my respected colleagues found a stumbling block in this. After all, I never demanded that doctors should be philanthropists, God forbid!, nor that they should not be wealthy. Haven't I said—I said, and I repeat—that today's doctor is a servant, a physician-servant of rich people? Whether he himself is rich is a secondary question. Because my idea was not properly understood, I will develop it in a different way. Today's doctor does not even want to understand, and in fact tries not to understand this truth: that reducing his mission to zero, he makes common cause with the sharp world-businessman. We are not supposed to serve 'mammon.' One may have money; that's neither here nor there.

"And now for flats, shelters and those well-intentioned baths. I believe that our respected colleague Dr. Kalecki is misguided as to the importance of those things. The establishment of baths by outsiders, by philanthropists, I consider a futile endeavor—"

"Well said!" someone called.

"—since it turns our attention away from the question of who bears the primary responsibility for arranging bath facilities for his workers. When the director of a coal mine comes up from underground, he has at his disposal a bathtub provided by the owner of the mine. What would we think if Dr. Płowicz funded a bathtub for that director with his own hard-earned but still meager assets? Yet if it is a matter of some fellow standing below the foreman on the social ladder, we have nothing against Dr. Płowicz's funding a way for him to clean the soiled abode of the soul. The question lies just here. We lament, we wring our hands over the dirt in the city, the slovenliness of the people, we, physicians, but when the possibility arises of eliminating uncleanness at one stroke—"

"An interesting question: where does that possibility arise?"

"—by demanding the opening of baths by those for whose profit people become covered with sweat and dirt, we go to the city, to the philanthropist. The same…"

"But who is going to press this demand? Who? What authority, and in what way?"

"We, doctors! We, the salt of the earth! We, the voice of reason! We, the hand assuaging all pain."

"How? By what miracle?"

"Let's talk among ourselves. Let's advise each other. Let's issue a resolution and fight the stupidity of society, which doesn't see what Krochmalna Street and the Kazimierz district of Krakow are like."

"Have you lost your judgment altogether?"

"By no means! If they come to me for advice, let them listen! Otherwise I won't be healing, I won't be curing people at all, if I don't destroy the conditions that cause death."

Having said that, Judym almost instantly felt the fragile props of his self-confidence fall away one by one. The bold, unsparing, categorical opposition he had met with tore his strongest arguments from his mind. He wanted to say more about a multitude of issues, but as before, he lost his nerve.

At that very moment a deep silence fell in the room. In the opposite corner several people gathered at a table began to talk loudly of something else. The host rose and signaled to his wife with a look that it was time to invite the guests to dinner. The majority of them stood up.

Judym sat in his place perspiring, feeling as if his head were full of dry sand. He saw the visitors proceeding in groups to the dining room. He was not certain whether he should go or stay. While he was hesitating, he heard Dr. Czernisz's voice beside him.

"If you will be so kind, colleague… Please…"

He rose and passed into the dining room with the others. At the dinner, which for him was a genuine torment, he was seated next to Madam Czernisz. She plied him with pleasant questions, forcing him to express inane opinions about literature, painting, even some law passed by the English parliament. At moments he felt wild rage; he had an impulse to stand up and hit the beautiful lady between the eyes. As if in derision, the reasons for his fury, deep fictions framed in loneliness, forced themselves to the front of his mind from every direction. No one paid any attention to him, so in the intervals between his hostess's questions he could freely exercise his belated sense of what he should have said. Only once in a while someone's fleeting glance fell on him and he saw mockery in it, mockery with a ruthlessness cloaked in social decency.

The dinner ended late at night. Some of the guests returned to the salon. Others, smoking cigars, wandered toward the study, while some, in English style, stepped quickly to the door. Judym was among them. In the gateway outside the building, which had been closed for a long time, several guests knocked to rouse the watchman, who grumbled at having to leave his cubicle. The men were silent and, when the gate opened, only tipped their hats to Judym and said a hasty "Good night." Only Dr. Chmielnicki, a short, heavy-set, aging physician whom Dr. Tomasz had noticed at the meeting, stayed behind and walked in the same direction as he. Chmielnicki was a bloated-looking man with features and ways of moving that Judym associated with Jewish men.

"Which way are you going?" Judym asked.

"Toward Krochmalna. And you, colleague?"

"Toward Długa."

"Well! We're going the same way."

"Not quite."

"Indeed. But why not? I can go a little out of my way. For the rest, I admit, colleague, that it would be nice for me if we walked together. At this hour it's simply frightening to walk on foot. In our part of the city— God help you!"

"Ah, if that's the case…"

Judym walked with long strides. The stocky man ran beside him, wheezing and puffing smoke from his cigar, the end of which glowed perilously close to his mustache. When they had gone some distance from the Czernisz house, Dr. Chmielnicki said, "I sincerely sympathized with you this evening."

Judym had a very different notion about that sympathy, for by chance, as he lectured, he had noticed the fat man. He had seen how he outdid the others in thrusting out a contemptuous lip and making sarcastic faces.

"Why did you feel sympathy for me?"

"What do you mean, why? Aren't you a bit fed up with the excess of friendly criticism? Unfortunately, that's the way it always is with us. If someone rises above the level of the crowd, right away—"

"Respected colleague, I didn't dream of rising above anyone."

"I know, I understand! I'm not speaking of your intention, but of the fact."

"I'm sorry now that I delivered my harangue."

"But why?"

"Because that stunt provoked, among other things, such mockery as this from you."

"You're wrong! On my honor…I'm impressed by courageous people. And I know very well what it means to be ridiculed, to be badgered by that everlasting laugh, like a sick turkey by the flock."

"How?"

"From first grade through secondary school and university and all my life, colleague, I've been seen as funny. Why? I don't know. First of all, of course, because I have the pleasure of being Jewish. Second, because my name is Chmielnicki. My forebears, who, I add parenthetically, were not usurers or swindlers, came from the town of Chmielnik, so they were called Chmielnicki. If they had known how their descendant, a doctor by no means stupid, would suffer with a name that means "field of hops," they would not have chosen such a Cossack name for themselves and for me. They could have called themselves Staszowski, Stopnicki, Oleśnicki, Kurozwęcki, Pińczowski, Buski, and it wouldn't have mattered to them or to me.

"Even my professors jeered at me. I remember that once in Dorpat our late laboratory director asked me in front of the full auditorium: 'Mr. Chmielnicki, do you believe in the immortality of the soul?'

"The question was jocular but unequivocal. I answered, 'Yes, professor. I believe.'

"'And where is this soul of yours?'

"'What do you mean, where? It's in the body of a man.'

"'In the whole body or in a part of the body, Mr. Chmielnicki?'

"'In the whole body, professor.'

"'And if a man's leg is cut off, what happens to the soul? Is a part of the soul cut off as well?'

"I thought for a moment. Then I said, 'No. Surely then the soul rises somewhat higher.'

"This dialogue made me famous far and wide. If today I were to give the world an unfailing way to cure tuberculosis, I would always be remembered as that 'Circassian' Chmielnicki who has an immortal soul that rises higher depending on the circumstances."

"Excuse me, colleague, is there anyone who doesn't carry such a basket of ridicule on his back? We ourselves throw some burden on each person who passes by. Our friends and family do the same to us. Everything comes at a price."

"No! No! What you're talking about is different from my particular burden. Mine is not a basket that can be thrown off, but a hump on my back. I always carry a weight like the one you felt this evening."

"But that was not the same."

"True, not the same, because it was, if you'll pardon me, deserved, somewhat deserved. The ridicule I've suffered isn't brought on by my own fault."

"So this evening I deserved—"

"Well, no! I don't know much about these issues, but, pardon me, it's possible... Such a stern presentation against acknowledged truths, and even, I say in all conscience, against obvious realities! Medicine is medicine. It's an occupation. I studied, I laid out money, I put in a vast amount of work. I am skilled, I have a license, so I treat people. Why should medicine be connected to philanthropy and not engineering, not law, not philology?"

"I don't want to hear about philanthropy!"

"Well, with social obligations. Why has a butcher no social obligations, or a carpenter or poet, only a doctor?"

"You know—let's not speak of this."

"We don't have to speak of it if you don't wish to speak of it with me. But I'm sorry for you."

"Oh, I'm still standing on my feet."

"You referred to those poor Gentiles in Paris. Oh, God! It was a brief mention, but a striking one. Today hardly anyone among us speaks of Jews as people. If someone does speak of them, it's only to compare them to 'vermin' that invade society and devour people. When I read contemporary writings, writings that clearly incite to hatred, to starving out, weeding out and expelling Jews, today, and in the name of the precepts of Jesus…"

"Please!"

"I tell you, colleague, every Sunday's edition of these writings, these antisemitic writings, makes me ill."

"Why do you upset yourself about just anything?"

"Just anything?"

"Yes. Such writings are circulated by evil, miserable people who make a fortune by spreading hate and destroying solidarity among people. They build tenements by sowing this poison. But have you yourselves done much to improve the lives of the masses of Jews?"

"Do we do much? We pour our lives into it. We work day and night."

"Then why, colleague, do you say I'm wrong to challenge doctors to fill their rightful role?"

"Because what we Jews do for each other, we do out of love."

"Exactly! Exactly! Love! It's little you've done, puffed up with your 'love.' I wanted to show those doctors what they ought to do under the imperative, not of love, but of cool reason."

They were on Długa Street, before the gate of the house where Dr. Tomasz lived. Only at the sound of the bell did Dr. Chmielnicki realize that his impulse to talk had carried him far out of his way. Just then a cab passed, so he stopped it and clambered onto the step.

"Colleague—you are mistaken!" he declared. "Medicine is an occupation."

He climbed down again hastily, stumbled in the gutter, seized Judym by the lapel of his coat and said as if it were a secret, "Medicine is a business like any other. Don't forget that."

"All right. All right. I couldn't possibly forget it. I don't even have the means. But if it's given me to live in this world another fifty years, I would see everything I spoke of tonight realized. Medicine will chart the course of life for the masses of people. It will lift them up and regenerate the world."

"Pipe dreams."

"That's certainly what the medical men of the last century said when they traveled around the manor houses with the tools of their profession, asking diffidently if anyone felt unwell, and someone told them that the medical profession would occupy the prominent position that it occupies today. You resent the sarcasm you meet with. Think what would have awaited you, a Jewish doctor, a hundred years ago."

Dr. Chmielnicki fell heavily into the cab and, wishing to drown out the mention of Jewishness, shouted to the driver, "Krochmalna!"

· CHAPTER IV ·

Sadness

ON THE FIFTH of October Dr. Judym went out for a walk on Ujazdowskie Avenue. It was a beautiful day. The sun flooded the sky with a gentle warmth and a light that was still bright, but already disappearing to the unknown country "beyond the ninth mountain, beyond the tenth river." The row of trees along the avenue, the view of which brought back so many memories, was already covered with rusty red.

In the distance, from among the still-spherical treetops, leafless branches popped out like a melancholy road sign. Cadaverous colors, red colors of decay, trickled from the tops, and the pale yellow of decomposition soaked lower and lower into the dark green. Here the flame of death surrounded a still-living leaf like a corona of preternatural mourning; there it devoured the leaf and turned it to rust, leaving only veins of green. The narrow stretch of blue sky was already faint, filmed over with airy clouds drifting in wisps beyond the reach of the eye.

The doctor passed the gate and slowly walked far into the park. Huge maple leaves floated from the trees and flashed above the ground here and there like golden birds. Walnut and sumac leaves stained the grass like spilled, clotted blood. In the deepest part of the empty park, in the shadow of regal black poplars where the sun could not reach, a cool dimness seemed to spread itself and rest. At a distance, where the lanes intersected, illuminated crests of yellow chestnuts exploded in tongues of living fire. Everywhere the sharp, pleasant smell of faded leaves spilled into the cool air.

Avoiding places where people clustered, Judym went along the old allée to the end of the park. Towering poplars that seemed to brush the sky, with spindly trunks and crisp, rustling leaves, grew there. Silvery, longhaired willows hummed quietly as they gazed at the moribund waters of canals.

Spruces like somber monks in black habits, closing off the distant vistas, dreamed in solitude. The breath of mortality had already circled the trees and left a tremulous silence to guard them. From time to time the distant depths gave off a swiftly fading murmur that forced a soft sigh from its hearer. When at a certain time childish noise and laughter resounded, it seemed strange and jarring amid the stern whisper that spoke of death.

Streams of almost white light were falling onto smooth clearings that looked like lakes dreaming between clumps of overgrown vegetation, and cutting in sharp outlines through the cool expanses of grass. Beside paths strewn with leaves lurked pools of blind, dull, still water that received torn patches of firmament and gave them distorted reflections: fragments of elusive silvering dawn with images of black trunks and branches of sloping alders. Every bird resting on a tree sent a shower of leaves from it. Cool exhalations of autumn carried these shriveled remains and deposited them forever on the quiet ground.

The green water of the flat, more open areas caressed chestnut branches below its surface, branches with leaves so yellow that a bright dye seemed to be seeping from them and dissolving at another depth. The leaves were suspended, transparent, delicate. They cast dancing reflections into the centers of the pools that blended with the color of the water to form images of exquisitely gleaming bronze. In one place the sun found a wide path among thinning leaves and dove deep into the water like a spray of molten gold too brilliant for the eye. Every minute the shiny boxes of carriages speeding along on rubber tires flashed between the trees. Their dull rumble, breaking the silence, seemed to harmonize with the chill in the weather. It was an expression of wealth, a force as indifferent as nature itself. In Judym's mind, associations awakened that were silent, but existed like the twang of strings stretched tight.

Dr. Tomasz was not given to brooding over the everyday cares of life, nor did his imagination multiply them. But from day to day, like a myriad of invisible microbes, they were assimilated into his mental processes. Now they were welding themselves into strong assumptions that deepened as he passed from one experience to another. They were the thoughts of a person not born to privilege who happened to be standing at the door of the palace of culture. Prominent among them, camouflaged as love for the poor, was a personal rapacious envy of other people's wealth. For ages it had burned like a fire from hell in the hearts of his forebears; it was their strongest, though most deeply hidden, feeling. In the soul of their recent descendant, the doctor, it did not manifest as blind, mortal vengefulness, only an immense, profound sense of grievance.

During the doctor's childhood and youth, it was from that very feeling that the drive to be a man of the people had welled up. Such a man must run at a gallop where others, the "well born," could go at an even pace, systematically, without difficulty. Later, this envy gave way to personal fantasies, hypotheses, plans and vivid dreams which were often transmuted into passion and prevailed even against the force of money.

Now, on the day of this walk, everything seemed wrapped in the autumn chill.

Judym felt in himself the inarticulable death throes of those old dreams. His feeling underwent a process like the flight of an arrow shot from a powerful bowstring and speeding into space, when at a great height its momentum slows and it suddenly feels its weight. Soon, though it is impossible to say when, that weight turns the arrowhead back down and sends it rushing toward the ground. Whichever way the soul of the young doctor flailed, it struck against some treacherous force, like a swimmer who moves his shoulders with all his might amid the vast sweep of water. He is absorbed only in the struggle with its mild resistance when suddenly his chest collides with an unknown piling.

For the first time in his life, Judym felt that the piling was stronger than the human chest. For the first time he wondered if it were possible to swim only in familiar, proven seas. As he heard the quiet rustle of leaves, a sense flowed into his heart that nothing in the world happens unto itself, that each occurrence is one in a great series of things. He was engaging in an involuntary accounting with himself, a stacking up of things already acquired so as to create a diligent inventory of them. That reckoning showed that what had been acquired was a great destiny. But the old void did not fade from his vision all at once. In fact, it flung itself open, distant and immeasurable.

Dr. Judym saw in the depths of his heart what he wanted to do, what he could do, what a modern man would be ready to lay down his life for. And he felt that he must withdraw from that work.

Nothing that nourished his soul as bread nourishes the body could be translated into action, but must remain what it was—a dream. Now sadness was oozing from all this sense of grievance and desire for sacrificial activism in a wide field. From his vision of the greater good, which had evolved from voracious egotism but was now slowly falling dormant from enforced powerlessness, melancholy was seeping like burning drops of poison. The heart that was imbibing it embraced people, the world, and everything in it, as if in a moment of farewell.

Sadness, sadness…

It freed his dreams from the shackles of thought and penetrated his soul to its depths, as night penetrates water. It stayed with a man one on one, like his fleeting but undeniable shadow. In whatever direction or toward whatever object he might turn his sight, it was there, writhing over the ground, inscrutable and omnipresent.

Dr. Judym walked along the empty lane with his head hanging down and his hands in the pockets of his overcoat. Sometimes he kicked a freshly husked chestnut lightly as it flickered among the dry leaves, or whistled an aria through his teeth—a song heard somewhere, sometime, that had lodged in his memory without his knowing why. He stood by the water at the end of the path, intending to cross the road and walk toward the palace and then to the exit from the park. Coaches dashing by one after another kept him where he was. One hurried past, and a second, and a third. Judym gritted his teeth and followed those vehicles with narrowed eyes. One word attached itself to the melody of his aria:

"Carriages, carriages, carriages…"

He had to stand in place a moment longer because a fourth vehicle, an open carriage gleaming in the distance, was rushing toward him at a brisk trot.

The doctor leaned on a low barrier and looked wearily at the passengers. Suddenly he felt as if he were surrounded on every hand by rays of light and the fragrance of roses. In the carriage sat the three young women he had met by chance in Paris and with whom he had traveled to Versailles.

Natalia, the older of the two sisters, turned her head and recognized the doctor. When he shyly put his hand to his hat, she nodded to him and said something to her sister Wanda and their companion Joanna, who turned toward him from their seats on the front bench. The doctor saw only Joanna's face and her smile before the horses pulled the carriage rapidly forward and it disappeared among the trees. That smile flitted before his eyes like a flash of light, then slowly receded into nothingness.

The sunbeams on the water dimmed and died away deep in the leaves, retreating before the sharp chill that was rising from the water and the ground. Drowsily, as if obedient to the command of those invisible waves of dying light, yellow leaves floated and fluttered in the air. They seemed to be descending dark stairs and choosing tombs for themselves. Judym went on his way with lowered eyelids, absorbed in dreams.

CHAPTER V

Practice

D R. PŁOWICZ'S prediction as to Judym's long-term prospects was fulfilled to this degree, that small plates specifying his hours of business
were put up not only on the door of Dr. Tomasz's residence but in the
entrance hall of the building in which he lived. These signs stated that he
received patients in the late afternoon between five and seven. He spent the
entire morning in a hospital, in the surgical department, where he served
as an assistant. He ate in the city, as he had in his student years, and beginning at five, as the bronze letters etched on the plate indicated, he sat in his
office until seven. He did not allow himself the slightest deviation from the
starting time, and even less from the hour of departure. From the moment
he had rented his quarters he had decided that he would adhere precisely
to this schedule, and he did so with a scrupulousness that permitted no
exceptions, renouncing all impulses and enticements for the sake of building character and especially perseverance.

It was true that all through September, October, November, December,
January, and February no patient, no "lame dog with a ruble in its teeth,"
appeared. But in no way did that entitle him to remove the plate, or to
interrupt or deviate from his program for the formation of will power. It
was well known that the early days of practice...and so on. So Dr. Tomasz
waited unwaveringly.

His quarters comprised what passed for three rooms. The largest—the
office—was separated by an entrance hall from a much narrower one,
which served as waiting room. Both the entrance hall and the waiting
room were bisected by partitions, which divided the first into a hall and
an improvised kitchen and the second into the waiting room proper and
what one might call a bedroom. The entire apartment was situated below
street level in the front of the building, so it was liberally supplied with

moisture and racket from Długa Street, but deprived of daylight. In the matter of furniture, Dr. Judym harbored and put into practice a radical view: "Why am I going to furnish this apartment? For whose good? Will my patient benefit from it? Will sofas and pictures bring me patients? Not in the least."

What he decided to do, he did—or rather, he did almost nothing by way of decorating the apartment. In his office stood a little table covered with tissue paper, and on it an inkwell, a pen, and paper for writing prescriptions. Four wooden stools waited beside the table. An old sofa covered with printed fabric sat by the wall, looking bored.

At least five patients could sit comfortably in the waiting room, where there were two armchairs, a couch, a few stools, a copy of *The Illustrated Weekly*, individual numbers of the rose-colored magazine *The Voice,* and, on the wall, a framed drawing in Impressionist style. All this furniture, except the magazines and the drawing, had been purchased for cash on Bagno Street in a very well-known storehouse with "aristocratic" furniture. The floors were freshly covered with oil-based paint and a mirror was placed in the anteroom (all for the comfort and essential needs of the patients). True, the mirror had some peculiar properties. A patient with an altogether clear mind could experience some confusion of the senses on seeing his face in that plate of glass. A nose always appeared distended like the butt of a shotgun. One eye seemed to be in the forehead and the other next to the right nostril. The mouth, spreading from ear to ear, looked amazingly similar to the mouth of a rhinoceros.

The duties of housekeeper, maid, and doorkeeper tasked with opening the door to patients at the first sound of the bell fell to a Madam Walent, the wife of an itinerant cooper. She lived in the basement of the same building, just under Dr. Judym's office, which greatly facilitated communication by means of heels tapping on the floor. Madam Walent was an old woman, stout, with joints twisted from various aches and pains caused by the dampness of life beneath the ground level. She undoubtedly guzzled, secretly, large quantities of vodka, or Warsaw thunder. Her daughter, a rather pretty girl of about fifteen, filled the role of helper to her mother while waiting to reach the proper age to stroll on the street and be away from their dark subterranean room.

These women ran Dr. Tomasz's apartment with such proprietorial zeal that there could be no question of limiting their authority and even less of altering their ways of doing things. It was impossible to dispense with their services because they both would have bleated at the tops of their voices about cold, hunger, poverty, aches, and pains. To make an issue of every passing matter would not have worked, because they defended themselves on the spot by swearing on so many and such holy sacraments that only a person altogether lacking in sensitivity could suspect them of perjuring themselves. What went on with candles, kerosene, coal, sugar, bread, butter, tea, and the articles that make up a man's wardrobe—that is a secret for eternity.

Almost every item Judym had purchased with money existed in the real world only as an entry in a bill. Apart from that it existed only in his imagination, which was piqued by the evidence of his senses. The candles he had bought were never, literally never to be found. When he crossed his threshold in the evening, Dr. Tomasz always groped his way in blindly and searched in vain for matches, a candlestick, a lamp. Somehow candles did exist and were burned in the apartment; that was attested by an abundance of drops of cooled wax not only on the candlestick, the floor, the sofa's upholstery, the stools, and the bedclothes, but, by a strange coincidence, on underclothes and jackets hanging in the locked wardrobe. The lamp was always empty inside, with a burned-down wick, but undoubtedly splashed with kerosene from outside, and smelled of that precious fuel from a distance of five paces—which in any case showed that what had been bought had been poured out lavishly. Dr. Tomasz never found sugar or rolls in the cabinet, though he writhed with hunger by its doors, yet crumbs not swept up were strewn everywhere, particularly in his bed.

One arm of the upholstered ottoman, which Judym had bought for no small sum, was soon covered with a peculiar grease, and the other blackened with shoe wax and smeared with mud, as they say, to a fare-thee-well. In his imagination the doctor could see, as if in broad daylight, Miss Zośka's pomaded head on one of the bolsters on the expensive piece of furniture, while her hooves rested on the other (his imagination envisioned hooves, not feet). A small table freshly and conscientiously polished when it had been purchased at the shop was soon a hodgepodge of circular marks offering eloquent witness that the doctor's samovar produced first-rate boiling water.

From the beginning Dr. Tomasz had striven for a friendly, fraternal relationship. Before a month had passed he was struggling, and in November he was defeated and taken prisoner. After that, even if he found Zośka lying on the sofa with her hooves heavy with mud, even if he spied Madam

Walent slurping tea at a table loaded with his own eatables, he applied the only feasible, though hardly effective, method, the Italian approach: notice and pass on. There was no other way. He closed himself into his office and left the rest of the apartment to be plundered.

During his office hours Dr. Tomasz did not dare read books. He sat erect at his table and waited. That was in September and October. With time he allowed himself to read newspapers, now sitting, now lying. By the end of December he was putting off reading the newspaper until office hours, and after the new year he began to carry to the office, for just those hours, long works of Zola, Jókai, Dumas, Lam.

Madam Walent always sat on an upholstered chair in the hall at that time of day with her legs drawn up and crossed on a thick piece of felt. At the beginning of a consultation, the old lady coughed, groaned, and exhaled to show that she was watchful. In the middle she gradually quieted down, and soon she could be heard snoring heavily. There were days when noise and rumbling broke out during the second part of an interview. During a nap, Walent had fallen out of the shuddering chair. After each such incident the doctor had to give her some kopeks for arak, since she swore by all that was holy that weakness caused by hunger and an empty stomach had thrown her onto the floor.

Several times the young Aesculapius was called to attend other residents of the house in cases of sudden weakness, usually on Monday. Once in the autumn an old bookbinder from the neighboring building arrived, rang the bell, roused Walent, and caused a commotion. Judym examined him, poked and prodded him, bent him, put him on a sofa, kneaded him, looked him over from every side and sent him away, without charging a fee, of course. After that a silence ensued that lasted for a good two months.

One evening in March, during his office hours, Dr. Tomasz heard his bell ring quietly. Madam Walent opened the door and admitted a small, slender lady in black with a faded, shriveled face. She asked for Dr. Judym and on being told that he was in, entered the office.

"A patient, thank God!" the doctor thought. A warm feeling began to steal over him at the thought of the first ruble he would earn on his own premises. Amid bows on both sides, the lady took a seat and looked around at the furnishings.

"You are ailing, madam?" he asked.

"Oh, yes, doctor. For years, for years together."

"And what is the matter?"

"If it were only one thing! A series of ailments that would have sent a person with less endurance to the grave long ago."

"But the main, the fundamental ailment?"

"I don't know, doctor. Surely the liver…"

"The liver. Well, now."

"Because I have some shortness of breath, sleeplessness, coughing, pain."

"Pain? Where?"

"Oh, such pain! The human tongue cannot express it."

"Pain…rending pain, a feeling of being torn apart, no?"

"Yes, that as well. Often I wake in the morning—that is, I rise in the morning after a sleepless night—and I am ready to collapse."

"And your appetite, if you please, madam?"

"But who would pay attention to all that, doctor? Who would set one's own suffering up beside the suffering borne by unhappy humanity?"

"Watch out," Judym thought. "What now?"

"Surely, doctor, you have heard of our society," she began, adjusting herself in her chair and pressing her bag to her chest, "the purpose of which is the conversion of young women of—you understand—faulty conduct." She lowered her eyes and glanced into a corner of the office.

"I've heard nothing at all about it."

"Well, then. The goal of our society is, first…"

Off and running! Half an hour passed, three quarters, an hour. The lady spoke without pausing about the goals of her society. At the beginning of the second hour she began to speak of means, or rather the lack of means. When more or less an hour and a half had passed, finally there followed a request for financial support for the efforts of the society, which—and so on.

Without hesitation the doctor took out a ruble note, laid it on the table, and straightened it with his fingers. The lady took the donation quickly, wrote something in a notebook, and again, amid bows, smiles, thanks, and Biblical phrases, slipped out the door. After the collector for charity was gone, Walent got a raging cough. To Judym, who was standing in the middle of his office whistling through his teeth, it seemed as though a thunderbolt had been peeking through the keyhole and burst out laughing, choking and snorting.

Such, in brief, was the history of Dr. Judym's early career. The rest of the money his aunt had left him ran out, his credit with the shopkeepers was cut off, and his future was murky. From the moment he had given his unfortunate lecture about poverty at Dr. Czernisz's salon, he had had no standing in medical circles. He could not complain—he had no right to—that people distanced themselves or consciously shunned him, but he felt a vacuum and a chill around him. Older and younger colleagues greeted him politely, as before; there were some whose hats inclined even lower when they greeted him. But a piece of advice fluttered in the air: pack your bags, take your philosophizing and go away, for there is nothing here for you.

Dr. Tomasz understood very well that he had attached himself within a living organism, like a foreign body that blocks the circulation of the pulsing blood. If he would avail himself of the society of prominent people, seek their direction, visit them and become a familiar presence in their households, he would soon become one of the cogs in that machine and would gain a clientele. He understood all that perfectly. He knew how things could be and what he would need to do. But his heretical thoughts and the stubborn adherence to his own views that they engendered kept him from changing his course of action.

He had decided to go the way he had chosen, so he walked, simply put, in half-cobbled shoes.

Early one morning near the end of March, Wiktor's wife hurried over with news about her husband. She talked to the doctor about what had happened for nearly an hour in a voice blurred with weeping, and afterward, having scrupulously recounted all the details, gathered herself up and went away to her factory.

The doctor sat in his apartment for a long time, full of thoughts that were like the dreary end of winter. Everything was going strangely wrong, foundering, piling up like an ice jam on a river, damming up the flow of life. He reflected about how for the present he must help his sister-in-law, he must support her and her family in Wiktor's place, for leaving that responsibility solely on the poor woman's shoulders was not to be thought of. But his finances were in a deplorable state.

He made his way to the hospital, full of bitter thoughts. He left there earlier than usual because some internal incapacity was interfering with his work.

He dragged himself to Wiktor's apartment with a feeling of dread. There he found only his aunt, who was stitching something by the window, and the children, who were running riot in the next room. His aunt's eyes were bloodshot from weeping, her lips were tightly set, and her nose looked even sharper than he remembered. She greeted him with a look of aversion, even disgust. She always saw him as the protégé and heir of the sister she had banished from her life with dreadful invective in years gone by. Now, it was clear, her rancor had deepened and reached its ultimate limit.

Judym paid no attention to her. He sat in a corner and looked with a drowsy eye at the rooms, which had not been tidied. The sight of the rowdy children gave him the idea that now, when he had nothing better to do, he might occupy himself with their education. He tested the boy and was convinced that he read passably, with heavy groaning but no other problems. That feat of reading was the work of the aunt, who was now looking out of the corner of her eye at the exercise Judym and his nephew were engaged in. Karola hardly knew her letters.

It was almost twilight when the doctor left his brother's home. He trudged along with his collar up and his eyes down, feeling numb and lethargic. Reflexively, without noticing either the streets or the people in them, he made his way toward a sweet shop where he sometimes sat and read newspapers. He turned quickly into a more crowded area and met Dr. Chmielnicki on a corner.

"Oh, why are you marching along like a fire, my friend?" the stout man called. "You almost injured me!"

"I? Not at all. I'm going—"

"I see, I see. To someone who is sick."

"Oh, indeed!" Judym said with a deep snort.

"Not to an ailing patient?" asked the favorite son of the town of Chmielnik with a hint of irony.

"I have no patients at all!" Judym said and extended a hand in farewell.

"Wait. Wait a moment! If you aren't rushing to a deathbed, why not have a confab?"

"It's cold. Come for coffee. You'll talk, I'll listen."

"Good! I've come for the latest *Courier*. I have just a few minutes."

They went down the street and were soon seated at a little marble table in the pretty pastry shop. Dr. Chmielnicki, speaking in an undertone, delivered himself of a variety of new jokes, launching into that line of humor with great objectivity, for in it his fellow Jews were presented none too flatteringly. Judym laughed at the anecdotes with his lips, but there was no laughter in his eyes. The narrator's surreptitious but acute sensitivity might have read that expression as insolent. As he was telling one of his particularly catchy stories, he asked unexpectedly:

"But…but perhaps you would go out of the city?"

"What?" Dr. Tomasz exclaimed.

"Nothing! Nothing! I'm on a mission to look for an assistant for my friend Dr. Węglichowski, who is the director of an institute in Cisy. If you don't want the position, I'll have to look for someone else. I had forgotten all about it."

"Well, I won't go out of the city."

"This is no ordinary provincial place. No Kurozwęki, though it's not far from there, or Łagów, which is like Kurozwęki, God forbid!"

"I won't go to Kurozwęki or even to Łagów."

"Ah! Would I take you by the collar and drag you to Łagów? I only repeat what I was told about Cisy. It's an offense on the face of it! Of course you can't go there. How could you? To be in Paris with a surgeon like Lucas-Championniére and then go to Cisy! After all, that's nonsense."

"Not just nonsense. Worse than nonsense."

"Undoubtedly. Well, but it doesn't follow that we shouldn't consider how to fill the position of assistant to dear 'Węglich.'"

"'Węglich?'"

"Węglichowski is my friend from Dorpat. We lived together. He could have been a very able doctor if he hadn't always taken everything lightly. He doesn't like to read; that's all there is to it. And from the moment of the famous revolution in medicine in Warsaw, whoever doesn't read, whoever doesn't want to be taken for a scholar, has to look for places like Cisy. Do you know Cisy, my friend?"

"I don't know it. I've heard something about it. It seems to me that it's in the same region as Kielce."

"Oh, 'seems…' How can such things be? 'To know about what does not directly concern us is good, and to know about what does is necessary.'"

"My friend, are you using that statement as an admonition for me, or only as the model of a national proverb?"

"Excellent! Grand! But to return to Węglich—"

"Oh, that Węglich—"

"But, listen! You younger people know each other. You can point out the appropriate person more easily. The place isn't bad at all. They'll pay six hundred rubles—"

"Folderol!"

"—and provide fine living quarters and complete maintenance."

"And what would one have to do?"

"The usual things. Silliness. In summer plenty of sick people come, so the assistant, together with other physicians, would have to treat them. Baths, you see, soaks, showers—things like that. Frivolities, when you come down to it, and a very busy local practice. This isn't just any post. Perhaps one of your friends could be tempted."

Judym brooded, ordered one more cup of coffee, drank it in one motion, put down his cup and said, "Well, all right. I can go to this place."

"There, didn't I say so? Splendid thought!"

"Where is this Dr. Węglichowski?"

"He's just here, in Warsaw, and tomorrow he will come to you."

"Well, perhaps I should go to him."

"But why? He will come to you. What time?"

"Between five and seven."

"At your place on Długa?"

"On Długa."

"Good!"

Dr. Chmielnicki wrote something in a notebook, looking into it with his left eye as if through a magnifying glass. He put his newspaper on a neighboring table where a provocative woman was grinning broadly at a philanderer in wet clothing, and gave Judym his right hand.

"And so until tomorrow! Splendid idea!"

"We'll see," murmured Dr. Tomasz, hanging his head.

When Dr. Chmielnicki had vanished, he plunged into reflection. "Yes," he thought. "Yes. I must leave here, that's clear. Wiktor's wife can't make ends meet, and I couldn't either if I went for long with the number of patients I have now. I'll go. Perhaps not forever, perhaps for a year or two. What the devil—perhaps when I come back there will be something else."

He went home. That night and the next day the prospect of going away was never out of his thoughts. He regretted leaving Warsaw with all his heart. Abandoning it was even more painful because from birth he himself had been a parochial fellow who knew the country only from summer outings, romances, people's stories, drawings. He had never thought about how one lives in the winter among wide fields with a blizzard whirling over them. Now all that played out before his eyes and threw him into a fit of despondency.

At five o'clock he was sitting in his chair, calmly awaiting the coming cataclysm. Hardly half an hour had passed before someone pulled hard on the bell, which trembled as if from fear, and began to shriek to the old woman to open the door as quickly as possible. A short man wearing a worn beaver hat entered and asked for Dr. Judym. When Dr. Tomasz hurried out to meet him, he heard the expected name:

"Węglichowski."

He was a man of fifty-something, short, perhaps too small, thin, bony. He was one of those compact, healthy, agile elderly men who hardly seem to change for fifteen or twenty years after they first begin to grow gray. He had a pleasant face with regular features and skin the ruddy color of bread just baked. His naturally short, curly beard and mustache, white as milk, set off his face and contrasted felicitously with its color, lending it an expression of particular grace. To see that head was to think: "What a handsome, fine-looking old gentleman!" The hair on his temples, as white as his beard, gleamed silver around a bald spot.

Most noticeable of all were his eyes. They were arresting. Dark as sloes, flashing, they changed with his changing perceptions, expressing understanding, or rather shrewdness of the highest order. He was dressed in plain black broadcloth that fitted him surprisingly well. His plain standing collar and unfashionable black tie were in harmony with his entire figure. They simultaneously signaled a care for his person that had nothing to do with elegance, and cleanliness to a fault—a meticulousness that had become an addiction, a compulsion.

As he entered the office, Dr. Węglichowski scrutinized with a searching look (which was, however, neither stealthy nor fleeting) all the furnishings. He sat down at a distance from the table on the chair he was offered, brushed some dust from the lapel of his coat, blinked, and gazed at Judym with knowing eyes. For his part, Dr. Tomasz felt an unpleasant sense of constraint, or rather a lack of power, in the presence of this person whom he was seeing for the first time in his life and from whom he could have dissociated himself at once. He was also conscious that no force, neither the power of money nor the power of science, would give him the upper hand with this elderly man. As if to dispel this idea, Dr. Węglichowski's face lit with a polite smile.

"My friend from Dorpat days, Dr. Chmielnicki, told me that you would be willing to go out of Warsaw and take the post as assistant." The words dropped softly and quietly.

"Yes, so I told our colleague Chmielnicki," Judym answered, unconsciously echoing the other man's tone, "though that would depend on several circumstances."

"On several circumstances… My dear sir, do you know Cisy?"

"No. Not at all. So little that yesterday I was unable to say in what province, in what part of the country Cisy is located."

Director Węglichowski was silent just long enough to have said, "I'm amazed that you boast about it."

"Why do you want to leave Warsaw, dear sir?" he said aloud.

"The reason is very simple. I have nothing to live on here."

"A living," Dr. Węglichowski repeated like an echo, in a voice that seemed to say that that seemed to him a perfectly sufficient reason, and that moreover the situation of a young doctor without a practice was altogether acceptable and legitimate.

"In addition," Dr. Tomasz continued reluctantly, "there are other reasons. I don't want to conceal them from you. Last fall I gave a reading that expressed my permanent, unchanging convictions, and that displeased the community of physicians. I have no hope of ever being able to widen my sphere of activity here."

The director did not look away from Tomasz as he was speaking. His eyes were not only fixed on the speaker's face, but drew the truth out of it, as a magnet moves inert iron filings and pulls them from their place. After training that inquiring stare on Judym for a long moment he said, "I know that. The story was told me in great detail. I knew about it when I came here. You have been in Paris, dear sir?"

"I have."

"For more than a year?"

"Yes."

"And do you speak French?"

"I do."

"Fluently, elegantly, in Parisian style?"

"I can't assert that I speak like a Parisian. I have an easy command of the language."

"An easy command…When you were abroad, did you ever happen to see bathing facilities? For example, hydropathic baths?"

"Yes, indeed. I saw them in Paris, and especially in Switzerland, in the Albis Montains, in Baden, on Righi, and in other places. I traveled there with an acquaintance, an engineer from a mine who was visiting those facilities. I pulled him out of the Kneipp spa garden in Zurich and took him from place to place. I got tired of that soon enough, so I left him to the mercies of the bath attendants at the excellent Righi Kaltbad."

"Kaltbad…excellent…Please, dear sir, can you give me some information about your temperament? Do you like company, do you dance, do you like a good time?"

Judym had to repeat this question internally to assess first for himself what kind of temperament he had.

"I think I like company well enough," he smiled. "I'm just not well able to be a bon vivant, since my origins—"

"I know about your origins, dear sir, and that's why I've come," the director broke in harshly, looking him as squarely in the eye as if an essential truth were locked into that stare and that tone. "A doctor, dear sir, has a lancet in his coat of arms. Anyway, what are we talking about? Do you know what the terms of your employment in Cisy would be?"

"I don't."

"They are these: living quarters, light, heat, complete maintenance, services, horses, and so on. Salary: six hundred rubles annually. Apart from that you may make use of an office and instruments for a private practice in the winter, while in the summer you will organize a dispensary for outpatients in a special building outside the park. In addition, there is a small hospital outside the park, on Madam Niewadzka's property. I don't know if you are aware that the institute in Cisy and the estate of that name belong to Madam Niewadzka."

"Madam Niewadzka?" Judym asked, overwhelmed by this deluge of information.

"Yes. An old lady, very benevolent, dear sir, very…A matron."

"Wasn't that lady traveling two years ago? Wasn't she in France?"

"She was indeed, with her granddaughters."

"With two granddaughters and a teacher?"

"Yes, with Miss Podborska. How did you know, dear sir?"

"I met them. I traveled with them to Versailles."

The old director's eyes brightened.

"You see, dear sir, what a fine coincidence. Our proprietress will be pleased to see that the new assistant is her traveling companion. As to the medical side of Cisy, that is as follows."

Dr. Węglichowski unscrolled the history of that institution: its first years of existence, its flourishing, then its almost complete collapse, the impend-

STEFAN ŻEROMSKI   83

ing ruin of the whole undertaking, the changes in management, and finally his role in the whole affair. As he prepared to leave, he took from the side pocket of his coat an annual report on ornate vellum, with views, a map, and an insignia, and handed it to Judym.

"This is all I can say for the time being. Look it over. Think it over. When will you be able to give me your final decision?"

"I will give it…I will give it to you…tomorrow."

"Tomorrow at this time?"

"Yes, but I will call in on our respected colleague."

"Certainly. Certainly. At Chmielnicki's home. What time, then?"

"At this time."

"Goodbye, dear sir, and I hope you will bring me your agreement tomorrow."

Dr. Węglichowski extended a hand with a friendly smile, held it in Judym's for a moment, and hurried away.

It was dark. Judym did not ask the housekeeper for a light, but after the director's departure wandered from one corner of his office to another, lost in thought. He had already decided to leave the city. He had begun to turn over a new page in his life. Now and then a biting phrase found its way into his thoughts: "The mercenary man sets about building a career… mercenary… mercenary." But that bitter note, like the longing that made his chest tighten, quickly died away into quiet delight. As dusk flowed into the room, girlish smiles and lovely faces seemed very near, faces almost forgotten, stubbornly flitting away when he tried to seize them with his imagination, as if between dark trees in space. They appeared and withdrew into a dark cloud. He saw one of them in a frame of luxuriant dark hair, a white face, so white that it seemed to spill light around it.

And there was the other one—slender, delicate. He carried in himself a silent, mad passion that transported him, filling his soul with fragrance, ecstasy and sighs.

CHAPTER VI

Naughty Dyzio

ONE DAY near the end of April, Dr. Judym settled all his accounts with the city of Warsaw; packed his possessions into his valise, which he could carry effortlessly from place to place; handed wages and tips to Walent, Zośka, and the watchman; got into a carriage, and had himself driven to the railroad station. He put his accounts in order by drawing on his future salary in Cisy. Dr. Węglichowski had sent over a letter of credit in the amount of a hundred rubles and kindly urged it on him so that his debts could be paid and the cost of his journey defrayed.

Dr. Judym stormed inwardly at the thought of spending money he had not yet earned, but when all was said and done he not only spent it, but spent it so thoroughly that after paying for a second-class ticket in a car going from Warsaw to the last station before Cisy, he only had a few coins in his pocket and two marks worth seven kopeks each. When the train started up, he went to the compartment where the attendant had placed his valise and found a place in the corner of the upholstered seat. Three other people were already sitting in the compartment: an old military officer and two women. They had a great many trunks, and had arranged their personal effects systematically for the ride. The officer had placed his sword and cap in a corner; the ladies had divided between them an abundant collection of baskets, small boxes, large boxes, overnight cases, and other items.

They passed the bridge, then Praga and the last buildings. As he saw the first forest, with birches like a sleepy dream emerging from dark pine woods and fields with their early growth of bright grain, Dr. Tomasz could not take his eyes from the window. In the skies, where the miraculous, benign blue seemed to open the last veils, wisps of cloud sailed along. On the earth, everything breathed with life, growth, and beauty. Sometimes the vacant space of a distant plain opened; then again it was obscured by villages, manor houses, and the beautiful, venerable silhouettes of churches.

He was luxuriating in this view of the landscape when the door opened and a tall, thin woman entered, or rather invaded, the compartment, leading by the hand a boy of about ten. She was plain and so thin as to make the onlooker grateful in spite of himself that women's clothes are made to cover such figures as hers. She had a big nose, pursed lips, and squinting eyes. The conductor and another train attendant threw her luggage after her into the compartment: a heap of bundles, small chests, little wagons, wooden horses as large as real foals, and a few valises and cardboard boxes. The woman left all these things just as they had landed. She only pushed some objects that impeded her movements onto her neighbors' feet. Then she fell onto a seat and proceeded to examine her traveling companions.

The boy stood amid the articles that cluttered the aisle between the seats, whistling. He also looked around at the others in the compartment. In his hand he held a dirty stick with a string fastened to it, like a whip. His hair was grayish, and seemed to grow forward toward anyone who looked at him. His whole figure, especially his eyes, hair, and hands, resembled a lynx or wildcat. His clothes were extraordinarily torn and bore witness to a terrible struggle with the ground, water, and grease. Bruised, bloody legs could be seen through his stockings, which were stretched around his knees and full of holes.

"Dyzio, sit!" his mother said in a fainting voice. As she spoke, she was not looking at her offspring but at Judym, as if she were directing this warm, caring advice specifically at him.

Dyzio acted as if his mother's words had really been spoken to someone else. He leaned with lively curiosity toward the officer sitting in the corner of the compartment and began to scrutinize the buttons on his uniform, taking each of them in his fingers, which were smudged with various substances. The military man assented without protest to the activities of the inquiring youthful imagination and waited with a vague smile for the end of the inspection. Meanwhile Dyzio spied the saber hanging on a hook in the corner and reached between the two ladies' heads with a determined hand for the weapon. At that point the officer moved the boy away from the three of them gently, politely, silently.

"Dyzio, behave," said his mother, "or the officer will take his saber and cut off your head."

Once again the lively boy did not pay his mother's directive the appropriate attention. He started for the window and moved in that direction over the feet of the seated passengers. A cry arose from the ladies and the man in uniform, who accused Dyzio of stepping on their corns. With the expression of a victor oblivious to everything, Dyzio waded on to his goal. He stood straddling two seats and leaned out the window with a movement so heedless of danger that the people in the compartment suddenly saw the back side of his clothes, which were perhaps even more ragged than his stockings. One of the ladies turned to his careworn mother and said:

"Excuse me, madam. Your son may fly out of the window!"

"Dyzio, for the love of Heaven, don't lean out so far. That lady says you could fly out of the window!"

Again, to no effect! For a few minutes everyone was disconcerted by the way the little fellow was leaning out. Then a shout of alarm burst from them all when he pushed himself still farther out, evidently wanting to reach the sign under the window on the outside of the car. He was trying to keep his balance by standing on one leg while the other flailed in the air around the heads of the seated ladies as his body shifted.

The officer jumped out of his seat, took the young man by his belt, and pulled him back into the car. Then Dyzio showed what he could do. First he tore himself from the man's grasp and lunged toward the window again. When he was thwarted a second time, he began to struggle and kick in every direction without caring whether his heels were pounding trunks or feet with corns.

"Please, madam!" the officer exclaimed. "What a beautifully behaved boy! If you would be so kind—"

"Dyzio, I order you by all that's holy!" called the tired mother.

The boy refused to acknowledge defeat. He shoved the officer with his elbows and stuck out his tongue at his mother for so long that people would have paid to see him. There was no help for it. Dyzio was left to his own devices, but somehow he restrained himself. He only looked with particular aversion at the officer and spat in his direction. After a while he sat down between his mother and Judym. He extended his legs and put his feet on the opposite bench, crammed his hands into the pockets of his jacket, and looked at each person in turn with his owlish eyes. There was a fragile silence, and soon he began to attack Judym. He looked him in the eye and jostled him with his arm, his elbow, and his knee. Finally, he dragged his whip from under the bench, planted the end of it like a drill on Dr. Tomasz's foot, and began twisting it down with both hands.

The doctor took it away and moved the boy's hand. That hardly helped, since the youngster repeated his action. His mother watched the sequence of events with a sour expression and finally lisped out, "Please stop. Why are you doing that? Is that nice? Does a good boy play that way? I've told you so many times not to annoy gentlemen in the car. You're making mama very unhappy. You must want the conductor to throw us out of this car as he did out of the other one! What? Tell the truth!"

Dyzio darted a glance at his mother and plunged into new escapades. Judym's hat was lying on the bench. The boy seized it as if he were in a circus and began to twirl it, throw it up, and catch it on the whip handle.

"Ah, Dyzio, Dyzio," the woman moaned. "Don't do that. The gentleman will be angry and scold mama as the colonel did. You must want this gentleman to scold mama. Tell the truth. You must want—"

"I want him to scold you," her son muttered ruthlessly.

Nothing did any good. Only exhaustion finally prevailed over rambunctiousness. The boy sat in an empty seat and, to everyone's relief, yawned once and then again. Finally he went to sleep. Judym very carefully placed the child's feet on the bench and left the compartment. He did not return until the train reached Ivangrod, where he had to transfer his valise to another car. He felt genuine satisfaction at having parted ways with Dyzio. What exasperation he felt when he saw the mother with the mischievous son entering the car where he was sitting! It was a large second-class coach that many passengers shared, and Dyzio took up all the available space.

Around three in the afternoon they approached the station at which Judym was supposed to get off. Then he would travel the remaining five miles by horse-drawn carriage. Alighting from the train and walking by the passenger terminal of this branch line stop, he came upon a large two-horse carriage with a driver in gleaming livery. An elderly Jewish man carried his valise and put it on the box. The doctor hurried over to the buffet in the station to buy cigarettes; as he rushed back, he caught sight of Dyzio and his mother settling into that very carriage. His hands dropped and he fouled his mouth with a long-unused cobbler's curse. Dyzio's weary mother had heard from the driver that she would be riding with a gentleman, and she had already recognized his valise. With an ingratiating expression she made room for him next to herself.

At first Judym had decided not to ride in this carriage for all the treasure in the world. But a series of rapid financial tallies and calculations led to a different decision and put a pleasant, happy expression on his face. With that amiable look he approached the woman and began a conversation full of elegant generalities. Soon the bundles were tucked away, and after fervent pleas from his mother, who feared that, God forbid, he would fall under the wheels, Dyzio sat on the little bench at their feet as the old carriage wobbled into a swampy lane in a little Jewish town.

The woman talked without letup, even when the carriage rattled convulsively over pits, potholes, mud puddles, and dry village dikes. Judym grew queasy at the thought that he might be in this amusing company for the entire five miles, since it appeared from words Dyzio's mother let drop that she and the boy were also going to Cisy. But he was quickly consoled when, as they left the town behind, moist air blew straight into his face from the unsearchable vastness of space, from fields, from forests. Delicate gray vapors rose above the fields, which after long rains were soft and slashed with dark brown streaks of wet soil. They glimmered grayish-yellow here and there, while their higher patches had begun to dry.

Plots of winter crops stretched along and across the land with their wonderful color that changed in the distance from green to bluish, like the feathers on a peacock's neck. White clouds stood high, like banked snow-drifts painted with lovely shadows. From the wings of those clouds the calls of a choir of larks rang out. Over the pale young grain in the fields lapwings turned and turned again, bursting into cheerful cries every minute.

The horses broke into a brisk trot. Thick mud began to spray from under the wheels. The noise of the wind made it difficult to speak, so the conversation became a little less bothersome. Judym immersed his eyes in a landscape that was truly new to him. The doctor had never seen the country—the land, soil, open space—at that time of year. A sacred primitive instinct awakened in him, a dreamlike passion to farm, to sow and tend grain. His feeling diffused and wandered in those wide perspectives. Near a forest where green leaves had just begun to show was a place for a house on a hill surrounded by trees. Alders and poplars were still black. Only a slender, soaring birch was covered so tightly with a thin film of leaves that the bare twigs were hidden. Pale blue hepatica smiled around the trunks. Beside the forest was a glen with a stream flowing through it. A man was moving on a hillside, leaning over, doing something, working at something, planting or sowing.

"God bless you, fellow. May your grain spring up a hundredfold," Judym thought. His eyes were riveted on the place as if it were his family home. But he saw another home: a basement, a damp grave full of reeking vapors. A father forever drunk, a mother forever sick. Blight, poverty, death. What were they doing there? Why did they live in a cave underground, built deliberately to foster sickness in the body and, in the heart, hatred of the world?

Again he looked lovingly at that hill that smiled in the sun.

The carriage passed villages, taverns, forests, and crossroads, and hurried along a muddy highway. Mileposts often came into view. They had sped over some two miles of road when Dyzio gave a sign of life. Until that time he had been plunged into a kind of stupor and had sat inert as a lump of salt, looking goggle-eyed around the ditches.

Judym had just explained something interesting to the boy's mother when he felt the little one tickling his legs. For a moment he thought it was his imagination, but soon he glanced down and saw a look of cunning on the rascal's face, and the thrust-out tongue that had helped with the tickling. Dyzio inserted a hand between Judym's pants leg and the top of his gaiter, pulled down his sock, and ran a long, sharp straw over his bare skin. Judym paid no attention and only hoped that his small traveling companion's mania for mischief would pass, but the opposite happened. Dyzio found another stray straw under the seat—a long, sharp one—and reached to Judym's knee with it. Not content with that, he picked threads from the doctor's socks, tried to pull off his gaiters, and rolled up his underwear as far as he could.

At last, this began to exasperate the doctor. He pushed the scamp's hand away once, twice, three times, all for nothing. The tongue, pushed out to the side, showed more and more clearly that its owner was devising new experiments. These schemes were soon put into action. Dyzio began gathering big, sticky spatters from the mudguard, made a great ball of them, and shoved it onto the doctor's bare skin under the top of his gaiter. Judym threw it out. When the little boy formed another one and put it under the gaiter, he pushed him away harder. When the youngster was starting to do it for the third time, he said:

"Listen! If you don't cut that out right now, I'll give you a thrashing!"

The boy smiled maliciously, took another fistful of mud, and smeared it onto the doctor's bare leg. At that point Judym ordered the driver to stop. As soon as the carriage stopped moving, he opened the doors and with one motion jumped out and pulled Dyzio out with him. Then he took the boy by the back of the neck with his left hand, turned him over his knee, and with his right hand landed about thirty hard whacks on the villain. During the course of this operation he heard a rending shriek from the lady and felt a sharp tug at his sleeve, even the scratching of fingernails, but he paid no attention. The mother of the unhappy culprit snatched Judym's hat from his head, threw it into a field, and screamed as if she had lost her wits.

When the doctor's hand began to hurt, he threw the boy onto the seat in the carriage, pulled out his valise, and ordered the driver to start on.

"Excuse, me, doctor, sir—how can I? How can I? Please, sir, get in."

"I'm not getting in! Drive on to Cisy with that lady. I'm going on foot."

The driver looked downcast and worried. He glanced first at Judym, then at the woman.

"Drive on, you fool, when I tell you to!" the doctor shouted in a passion.

The driver still hesitated, muttering, "The administrator ordered me to come for the new doctor. How did this happen? It would be well if… He … with God the Father…" He shrugged his shoulders and sat still.

"Drive on, damn it!"

"Please, sir, at least sit on the box."

"I won't get on! Do you hear?"

"I heard. But it won't be my fault."

He spat to the side, lightly cracked the whip at the horses, and started the carriage up at a plodding gait. Once more he looked around and saw Judym walking at the edge of the road, carrying his valise. Then he urged the horses on and the carriage began to put distance between itself and the doctor.

The doctor marched along with his load, panting hard and cursing a blue streak. He was in the most ridiculous of all plights, but he did not want to retrace the steps that had gotten him into it; he was in no state to call the driver back and change his tone. To make matters worse, he could see no village and no people. Thin columns of brownish smoke rose from somewhere beyond the sloping hump of a hill, evidently from some ravine. The doctor walked in that direction, over a dry ridge between plowed fields. From that elevation, he truly did see a large village on a plain. It was still far away, but his hope of hiring a wagon shortened the road.

He finally stopped on the threshold of the first cottage. He was tired; he had literally pressed on by the sweat of his brow. The wet, moldering ground he had waded through, the keen air, and his own fatigue worked him into a rage. He went from cottage to cottage asking for horses. There were none at all; no one there wanted to rent any; here and there people looked at him with a smile.

At last a young farmer came along and agreed at once to drive him. He harnessed two small dun horses to a light cart lined with basketwork and darted like a shot over side roads, through holes and past stretches that seemed impassable. The doctor's good humor returned, and he even felt a touch of the high spirits of his student days. A liquor store appeared at a place where the muddy roads crossed. The driver halted the wagon there, bound the horses' tails, and tinkered with one wheel. He went into the shop and came out lethargically. Judym saw that his companion had a hankering for a shot of Leopold and called, "Farmer, have yourself a bottle of spirits."

"With respect, sir, large or small?" said the other man without a second's hesitation.

Judym hesitated. How could he say "small?"

"The larger of those, of course."

The moment he said that he thought of his cash flow and was afraid he did not have enough money. Fortunately he had an adequate supply of kopeks, but very few were left in his pocket afterward. In a flash the farmer pulled out the cork and forced Judym to down a sample. When this ritual had been carried out, the man took the flask, drank half, tucked the rest into his pocket, and climbed onto his seat.

Then the drive began in earnest. The nimble little horses flew like deer. The carriage fell into gullies with prodigious layers of mud, crashed through puddles between fences, flew with violent splashes. The ground in that vicinity was heavy with clay, so the roads were slippery. On downgrades the carriage rolled as if on ice, and only its momentum kept it from turning over. From every hill the farmer drove at breakneck speed straight to the deep, fetid pit that usually forms in such low places. The swingletrees beat the poor nags in the legs and forced them into a mad gallop. The driver turned from one byway to another and raced along some no wider than border strips between fields. More than once he drove through fields to wider roads.

Judym became convinced that they were not going toward Cisy, but it did not matter to him one bit. He was enjoying this wild escapade: the wind whistling around his ears, the mud spurting into his eyes and nose, even finding its way into his mouth and lying in patches on his clothes.

When they had bowled along that way for half a mile, the farmer began to sing. After every song, usually not suitable for print, he took a heavy pull on the bottle and lashed at the horses. They passed villages, skirted forests, and dashed through pastures.

"Is it far to Cisy?" the doctor asked.

The driver turned his pale eyes on him and mumbled something. At the same time he shouted in a hoarse voice and turned the wagon like a shot from a somewhat wider roadway onto a side road. The ground sloped there; the wagon tilted and tore at full speed into a ditch.

Judym felt himself flying into space. He landed with his head in a soft ridge and lay there motionless, unable to move a hand or a foot. He saw clouds, the vault of the sky, and, somewhere far away, a streak of forest. Finally he pulled himself up, sat on the ground, and began to shake with laughter. He was covered all over with clay, since he had smashed three ridges when he was thrown from the carriage.

The farmer lay nearby in the mud, sprinkled with straw from his seat, and looked with vacant eyes at the carriage, which had been turned upside down. The horses walked down into the ditch and eagerly nibbled the young grass. From time to time they looked indifferently at the farmer as if to say, "You see what you've done, you ass!"

After lying prostrate for some time, the driver finally moved and set about lifting the basketwork lining of the wagon. Then it became apparent that the reach, which connected the axles, was broken. When it was set on its wheels, the vehicle looked like a man with a fractured spine. The farmer puttered around, trying to repair the damage, but he moved more and more feebly. In the end he clambered onto the wagon and tumbled in, muttering in a singsong tone.

Judym was in a desperate situation. He was up to his knees in watery clay and his coat, hat, face, and hands were covered in soil rich with manure. His bashed valise was sharing the fate of its owner. There was no help.

He left the reckless driver with his horses and his broken reach on the road, took his valise, and started walking. Evening was coming on. At a distance of about three miles he could see church towers and the glowing roofs of a village. He moved on in that direction, whistling. Every little while he burst out laughing. He had put about a mile and a half behind him in that fashion when suddenly he heard the hoofbeats of several horses at his back. From a wide avenue that intersected with the road two female riders emerged with two men beside them, moving at a fast gallop that brought them even with Judym.

The horses were frothing, steaming, and spattered with mud. The woman in front rode next to a young man who was sitting on a beautiful bay. He was leaning toward the lady and speaking animatedly. The two barely turned their faces toward the traveler, but at that moment it was enough for Judym to recognize Natalia. She turned her face toward him once more, but only for a second. A second. She undoubtedly saw him— she smiled—but then she shifted her eyes in another direction as if she did not have a moment to lose, as if she had no attention to spare even for something so comical as Judym at that moment.

He felt as if he had taken a beating. He heard a mischievous snicker from Wanda, who was riding at a gallop behind Natalia with some older man, but he paid no attention to that. He was utterly absorbed in watching Natalia, who was leaning to the left in her saddle, strong and graceful as if she were sitting in a chair, in harmony with the motions of her mount, splendid in every movement.

He stood where he was, stunned, ludicrous in his own eyes and unhappy beyond words. In the ditch, dirty water sputtered as if it were roaring with laughter.

While it was still daylight the doctor found himself in the village. Then he was surrounded by a swarm of Jews, old men, and vagrants, who greeted him with cackles.

"What town is this?" he asked the first one who presented himself.

"Town? Why you say town?"

"Well?"

"This town named Cisy."

"Good!" Judym exclaimed joyfully. "Here, you rascal, take this suitcase and carry it to the clinic with me. Do you know where the clinic is?"

"How'd I not know where the clinic is? You not from around here, sir? You a little muddy, sir."

"That's no business of yours, you misfit. Carry this to the clinic."

A long avenue lined with old trees, running down to a large park, opened before the doctor's eyes. The man who was carrying his suitcase explained where the clinic was, and the spa, and the castle, and the "countess's" manor, and someone's villa. The lanes and the park were empty, so no one saw the doctor arriving in his suit smeared with clay.

In the large front hall of the clinic the man found a person identifying himself as the doorkeeper. This individual, with a gaping mouth and incredulous air, conducted the new arrival to the "young doctor's" rooms. Judym quickly threw off his wet shoes and clothes, washed up, and changed into a dry black suit. Soon he was ready; he intended to go out shortly and introduce himself to his superiors. He only had to wait for his overcoat, which the doorkeeper had taken to be cleaned. He took advantage of the moment to look around his quarters. They consisted of two rooms, or rather two parlors.

He stood by the windows, which were set about nine inches above the floor. Outside them a narrow avenue lined with young trees, mostly hornbeams, ran straight ahead. Some of the trees already had thick trunks, while others were still saplings. The branches of the thinner trees were trimmed and looked like little schoolboys with heads cropped almost to the skin. Parallel to the avenue stood a thick old wall some six feet high, covered with a sturdy brick coping and coated with mold. Green moisture had eaten away at it from the ground up; now, with spring, it was sporting young, velvety growth.

Between the rows of trees, the narrow, well-weeded allée ran far into the distance through the park. The center was dry, but in the deep furrows on the edges of that spine, dark gray streaks of moisture caught the eye. Young hornbeam leaves, just sprouted, were wrinkled as if they were shrinking from the kisses of the sunbeams and the sighs of the fragrant wind. With their delicate shadows they seemed to be examining the yellow sand, the dark, friable earth, and the frail grasses that were just coming up. They were as cheerful and marvelous as children's eyes.

The stout wall, behind which the sun was already hiding, threw a black shadow like a prison door on the avenue and its lovely secrets. Only at the very end of the park, where it turned at a right angle and intersected with the distant exit from the park, did its rough surface still wear a covering of brightness. There the heavy wall seemed to display a face full of reverie, as if its invisible eyes looked out from the depths of the greening park with a universal, joyous smile. Closer to Judym's windows, two huge poplars stood behind the wall. Their gnarled trunks tore up through the flimsier fabric of younger trees, like bodies in chainmail, their bark-armor covering muscles as strong as the smaller growth and less penetrable. From somewhere higher—no one could tell from which tree—small pinkish-gold hulls flew onto the path.

Judym stood by the open window. He felt a oneness with what he saw.

The force of nature that made trees grow and leaves open seemed to flow through his own body. He felt its strength, and he felt the power to employ it in great work. The hope of the labors that he foresaw in this place filled him with delight. He looked out with a challenging stare.

At last! At last! This was the place in which he would be able to harness himself and plough deeply into the old ground of his aspirations. He would sow. He would work for the masses of people. He would give back to the world what he had taken from it. He would not spare his arm, he would not spare his sweat! Let them know how this man of low origins whom they had accepted into their culture, with whom they had shared a small measure of their right to be active in it, would repay them!

At that moment the powers of his soul had come to rest on something inapprehensible, as if on a sound flowing in space, as if on the rustle of hornbeam leaves that died away among the trees. It was the brief, joyful blessing of the mysterious powers of the world on the sacred right of man to work, and on the strengths, the strong shoulders, that are needed for those labors.

· CHAPTER VII ·

Cisy

THE HEALTH INSTITUTE in Cisy lay in a valley between two chains of hills covered with beautiful forest. Through the center of the valley flowed a stream that created two ponds, the second of which was the engine of the machine that was the institute. Around the ponds an enormous park reached to the wooded hills. The spas, which included baths, hydropathic facilities, showers, and other amenities, were located in a building called, Heaven knew why, Vincent, which stood next to the second pond. In that same part of the property, a hall for entertainments stood resplendent on a hill, surrounded by a grove of greenery, flower beds, lawns, secluded lanes, and hedgerows.

There were villas within the park and outside it, beside roads running in various directions. Some of them stood close to each other in a line, like cottages in a village. Others seemed to seek solitude, cloistering themselves away from the world with shrubbery or simply hiding in the woods. On the other side of the pond, in the middle of the high ground that domi-nated that area, rose the manor and the numerous brick buildings of the Cisy estate. Above the manor, on the summit of the hill, a church with two soaring towers could be seen from every point in the neighborhood.

On the day after his arrival, Dr. Judym paid visits, toured the area, learned the secrets of the institute—and was stupefied. He would not only have to know everything in great detail before the beginning of the upcoming season; he was also expected to take part in the management of it all. Today he would acquaint himself with the chemical composition of the springs. Tomorrow he would study the machines that filled the bath-tubs with water, examine the recordkeeping system, and orient himself to the economic protocols and the running of the hotel. Here and there entire perspectives opened to him, perspectives on things with which he was not at all familiar. Then they vanished, plowed under by new heaps of information.

What interested him most was the corporate framework of the enterprise. Cisy Health Institute was a joint stock venture with a fixed capital of nearly three hundred thousand rubles. There were more than twenty partners. Those partners elected from among themselves a governing board comprising a president and two vice-presidents, and a control commission, also with three members: a director, an administrator, and a financial manager.

The duties of president were carried out by a prestigious attorney residing permanently in Moscow. One of the vice-presidents was the honorary partner Leszczykowski, living in Constantinople; the other was a wealthy industrialist from Warsaw, Mr. Stark. The director was Dr. Węglichowski, the administrator was Jan Bogusław Krzywosąd Chobrzański, and the financial manager was a Mr. Listwa, the fortunate husband of the lady with whom Dr. Tomasz had traveled from Warsaw and stepfather of the naughty Dyzio.

It took a great deal of time for Dr. Tomasz to learn the history of this institute. It is said that history is the teacher of life, and the institute's history, or rather the various past histories that went into it, had a profound influence on daily life in Cisy. As far as Dr. Tomasz could learn from many informants, the history of the institute was as follows:

Cisy had been famous for its waters since the beginning of the previous century. Here and there in memoirs it was mentioned that such-and-such a dignitary had regained his health there. It had not been a health resort in the wider sense of the term, however. Various people had availed themselves of the waters, but only by courtesy of the owner of the Cisy estates, for the springs were located in the park surrounding the old family castle.

From time immemorial this estate had belonged to the Niewadzki family. Not long ago their owner had been the husband of the elderly lady Judym had met in Paris. During the seventh decade of this century, Niewadzki had gone abroad. When he returned to Cisy, he was a broken old man and incurably ill. The overwhelming suffering he had undergone had brought about a fundamental transformation in his outlook.

The old man's overriding thought was to promote the good of his fellow man, and because he himself was ill, his charitable actions were aimed above all at relieving suffering. Since baths in the water from the spring in the park were acknowledged to be beneficial, Niewadzki exerted all his powers to establish a health institute in Cisy. So the business would progress more quickly, he gave the facility he was planning a tract of land amounting to several dozen acres, together with the park, the springs, a portion of the abutting forest, and the buildings on that terrain. He created a partnership and drew in friends of his, most of them scattered throughout the world. His old friend and comrade Leszczykowski, the merchant from the shore of the Bosporus, took the largest number of shares. Lawyers, doctors, and industrialists bought up the rest.

In the early years the institute was headed by an unsuitable director who tried to turn the new spa into a health resort for all Europe right away. Splendid buildings and villas were erected and furnished with such pomp as to satisfy the most extreme demands—a risky experiment that pushed the entire undertaking toward ruin. Aristocratic families came from all over the country and even farther for recreation. The institute tried to gain the reputation of a European summer watering spot and added more elegant amenities. At that time the founder, Niewadzki, died. At the annual meeting it came to light not only that Cisy was not yielding any income, but that it was showing a deficit. In the face of that, and, as often happens, with the loss of its mainstay—the man who had built the institute in the service of an idea—the entire enterprise began to falter.

At that time Leszczykowski, the rug dealer from Constantinople, spoke up. He supported the spirit of his associates; he patched up the deficit from his own pocket; he was outspoken in his demand that the director be ousted from his position, and found a new one who was a friend of his and of the deceased founder. It was Dr. Węglichowski, who had traveled the world as much as those two if not more. As soon as Dr. Węglichowski seized the helm, things took a different track. Above all, the new director refused to manage the economic part. An administrator was named: again a mutual friend, J. B. Krzywosąd Chobrzański.

The next year there was no series of dances, theatricals, races, chases, pigeon shoots, hunts, and such things. There was only a season of genuine curative treatments. A reorganization of the hotel, baths, and other facilities was undertaken—in a word, the building of a real health institute. Dr. Węglichowski made a number of new plans and presented them to the governing board. If its members did not agree to them, he wrote to Lesczykowski, who facilitated everything without hesitation and at his own expense, according to an unwritten agreement.

Old Leszczykowski was a widower. He had Greek stepchildren who sucked him like a sponge. He was a rich man. A storm had thrown him out on the shore of the Bosporus in a torn coat and beaten-up shoes without soles. He had been a ship's porter, a street sweeper, a hawker of European newspapers, a sales agent in a certain French shop, a clerk in a store, a traveling salesman, and finally the owner of some enormous warehouses, a dealer in rugs, and an industrialist, among other things. Through the years he spent in these occupations, all but the first three letters of his beautiful name were lost, because it was possible to pronounce only those three letters in his Persian-Turkish-English-French business ventures. He, the poor beggar, called himself "Old Les" and varied the grammatical form of that fragment as circumstances dictated.

Leszczykowski was the son of a poor aristocrat from a place near Cisy. As a pupil in a famous school in the district of Kielce, he had been friends with the young Niewadzki and with Węglichowski and Krzywosąd. A hard life and his strange career took him away from where his family had lived. This son of a farmer descended from the Piast kings became a merchant. He worked more than twelve hours a day and never took a holiday or a vacation. He was not prone to weakness or error; he was a combination of temerity and invincibility with the strength of a steel machine.

Yet this "Les," amid complex and varied daily and nightly labors, had something else on his mind. A shrewd, clear-headed businessman, more rigidly methodical than any Englishman and not to be outdone in cunning by an Armenian or a Greek, he was in the depths of his soul a dreamer and an ascetic. He slept on a hard bed, he lived in a cramped room, he hardly cared about how he dressed. He designated a certain amount of money for the "leeches," his stepsons, and sent the rest here and there. Almost every day a letter in what he called "human" language lay on his desk, often written from a faraway country. Not one of these was thrown away.

Les was clever. No charlatan ever approached him and cheated him out of a penny, but the latest honest visionary to get his ear got thousands of francs from him. Indeed, his most loving thoughts were of the health institute in Cisy. The sly old peddler perpetually dreamed of transforming the corner of the world where he had been born, of developing it to the highest degree. He accumulated money; he set aside substantial sums. Like a miser, he scraped together a "silent cashbox" for unheard-of undertakings that he would carry out near Cisy, in his Zagorze and its vicinity, some day when he returned.

The silent cashbox was drained by an engineer attending university, a painter who needed to spend time in Paris, a doctor, a technician who was always about to be an inventor, and others. Once again special operations were begun to fill the void. Years went by. When Niewadzki founded the health institute in Cisy, which quite simply could not continue to exist without exerting an influence on the future of that area, old Leszczykowski murmured, "It must be supported." And he supported it in his own way, with his steely perseverance and childlike trust.

Within a few days of his arrival, Judym received a very long letter from Constantinople in which the old emigrant introduced himself and cemented an acquaintance with the young doctor. The letter was written in poor Polish, incorporating English, French, Greek, and Bulgarian expressions, and often what were probably enigmatic echoes of Turkish or Persian languages. Inside was a small photograph of old Les. In a strange way the letter and the photograph complemented each other. The look in his eyes seemed to tell everything that words could not, that the broken language that had helped him amass money lacked the power to convey. It was hard for the doctor to tear his eyes away from the thin face and the dark eyes that stared back at him. The strongly vaulted forehead, projecting nose, and narrow mouth bore the stamp of resignation, firmness, and persistence.

Judym read this rather odd letter several times and became strangely accustomed to its style, as if he found it normal, even necessary. In sentences that were repeated here and there, the writer appeared as a man living far away but with such a strong presence that he seemed to be walking around the places he wrote of. He knew everything in Cisy from the ground up. He called the young doctor's attention to details he had not even noticed yet. He concluded the letter with a request for a photograph and a plea for his new friend to write very, very often.

"I love the young," Mr. Les wrote, "for they set to work without hesitation. You know, doctor, that people are usually lazy, as an Englishman will say. I can't abide that! Our man, a Pole, will do something and then grow old. He works so as not to have to do anything. Then he does nothing and takes advantage of the young. He drinks their blood and leans on their shoulders and pretends that their labor is his. The Englishman doesn't do that. He keeps going forever! 'Forward,' he says. To the end of life. And it's not enough for him to lie in someone else's way; he goes to walk on fresh grass, and the young one comes to where he is and starts from there, where the older one stopped. And we still believe in kismet, like Turks, when, after all, everything lies here with us! Everything can be done! If I were still young, I would do everything. It seems to me that we will support each other, my Dr. Judym."

It had been more than a dozen years since Dr. Węglichowski had become the director and Krzywosąd Chobrzański had been made the administrator of the institute, which during that time had become busy, widely known, and highly reputable. Krzywosąd was a very influential person. He was an old bachelor, tall, handsome, with a fine figure. He wore long mustaches that flowed downward; he blackened them, as he did the remaining hair on his temples, with cheap dye that made them look greenish-gray. He almost always dressed in long boots, wide trousers and a traditional fur-lined frock coat with ornate frog fasteners.

He had traveled the length and breadth of Europe. He spoke probably all Indoeuropean languages, or at least readily pronounced words from a great variety of dialects—and was skilled at almost everything. If the conversation were about chemistry, he would chime in often and accurately. If someone began to speak of painting, sculpture, literature, cooking, gold-smithing, saddlery, the counterfeiting of pictures, the trade in antiquities, tailoring, the shoemaker's craft or the armorer's, and above all of anything mechanical, Krzywosąd's comments revealed a reserve of expertise. As if that were not enough, he could demonstrate in deed as well as word his acquaintance with all these arts. On Christmas Eve he himself cooked soup and prepared fish. To be sure, the soup was a creation all his own, for if he salted it like a soldier, he added a pound of sugar to the bowl to moderate the harsh taste. All the saddles at the institute were his work, or rather the products of his refurbishing. If some people became engaged or married during the season, Krzywosąd asked for the favor of being allowed to make their rings. All Cisy was filled with his work. He himself repaired all the machinery, laid brick with the masons, chopped and sawed with the carpenters, planed and painted with the joiners, dug with the gardener.

Dr. Węglichowski had an enameled watch that Krzywosąd had made and given him, at least according to the signature engraved on its envelope with a burin: J.B. Krzywosąd of the Chobrzański family, Polish nobleman, Paris, AD 1868. In the hall of the recreation building stood a grandfather clock that played an amusing aria on demand, at the pull of a cord. This clock had been damaged and then rebuilt by Krzywosąd as a conversation piece.

In the reading room of the institute stood his *magnum opus,* the so-called

Allegorical Group. It was a small table with stones, crystals, fragments of porcelain and glass, beads, and other objects glued to it so as to create miniature peaks, lakes, and caves. A monk should have come out from deep inside these caves in good weather, but, to tell the truth, one never did. A variety of allegorical figures adorned the highest level of this installation: roosters, soldiers, banners, crowns of thorns. In the center sat a white glass bird rather like a goose, with black eyes that made him look as though he were wearing spectacles.

In the card room stood another showpiece by Krzywosąd; an antique cabinet with ivory inlays and metal fittings so intricate that they had weakened. The date 1527 could be seen inlaid on the upper cornice. It was clear that the administrator was only the restorer of that relic of past ages, but malicious people asserted that he was the fabricator not only of the cabinet, the hardware and the inlays, but of the date on the top.

J.B. Krzywosąd Chobrzański had been in Europe at the same time as Les. But when Les had made his way east, Krzywosąd had gone west, paying his own way, through Silesia, Czechoslovakia, and Bavaria to France. He had roamed around Paris, London, and Brussels, earning his living as he could. In Paris he had been a retoucher for a second-rate photographer on Picpus Street. He was lured to London by a friend who had found himself a niche in a weapon factory. He worked for some time as a common laborer and acquired, it was said, considerable skill as a gunsmith. It was easier, certainly, to accustom his hand to that work than to set a noble spirit on the proper course.

Having scraped together a little money, Krzywosąd returned to the Continent and wandered to Brussels. Not that he was an idler; not at all! He could get up at dawn and work hard all day without catching a breath, then lay his head late at night on a miserable excuse for a bed. He went around in worn out clothes and was ready to give them to someone poorer than himself, provided people knew about it. When anyone asked him for a handout or a loan, he gave it, but he wanted one thing or another in return.

A force that defied explanation pushed him out of the workshop in London: a demand for something better. He never thought of a peaceful life or of great wealth, though he liked abundance. Amid the harshest turns of fate he always aspired to fame, significance, enhanced prestige, influence, notoriety among his own. He would willingly undertake heroic labors as long as they did not become a daily yoke, shackling him to constant, coarsening work that carried obligations like those that bound everyone. Yet for a fairly long time he was a cashier in a tobacco shop in Brussels.

He had even become accustomed to that occupation when a group of his friends who were whiling away some time in Munich got in touch with him. He had seen Munich on his way to Paris, and he liked it immensely. So he went to the city called "Home of the Monks" and found a whole colony there. There were painters, students, artists of every level of talent, craftsmen and homeless waifs, called in German "unhappy Poles." It all teemed like a beehive. Quarrels went on, cliques and factions formed. Assemblies took place, and court processes, even fights.

Krzywosąd joined one of the factions and soon took over the leadership of it. He was an energetic manager. He imposed such order on his group that often the enforcement of rules ended at the police station. His adversaries, whom he aptly called "birds fouling their own nest," he fought with such an iron fist that he was threatened with having his windowpanes broken or being beaten himself. When he had no place of his own to live, the threat was reduced to an attempted assault on him, which he fought off with a crisscross maneuver involving a gnarled club.

Soon after his arrival, before his later work opened before him, he posed for painters. His fine face, with its melancholy expression, its hard, proud air, attracted artists. He gained a reputation for having an interesting head and became widely known as the "unhappy Pole." In time that narrow ethnic designation was transformed into something less defined: "the grimacing melancholic spewing consonants," a reference to the harsh sound of the Polish language to the German ear. But at that time Krzywosąd only posed for his friends, and only on horseback.

Krzywosąd's relations with painters led him into an altogether new field. The community of artists, careless in their behavior, often changing their living quarters, today rolling in gold and tomorrow close to starvation, became a source of earnings for him. Suppose some painter began to move up in his field and left Munich for the wider world. Krzywosąd, or "the chief," bought his artist's tools, old clothes, often some broken armor, drapery, unfinished studies, sketches, drawings, perhaps even cracked frames, for almost nothing, or simply had them left to him. Someone else needed a stylish saddle repaired, a costume sewn, furniture refurbished, an antique glued together. Krzywosąd took every such job and did it—one time well, another time poorly, but he did it. He watched the curious processes of creation; he listened in on discussions; he studied that enormous country, the realm of the painter. He acquired an encyclopedic education in the areas of antiquarianism, dilapidated furniture, art, and crafts. If he was unable to do something, at least he knew how it should be done. If in such cases someone accused him of lack of determination, at least that person could in no way deny that Krzywosąd could expound on a great host of things that were unknown to the average human being.

In time he established an odd warehouse in a large room on Schwanthalerstrasse. There were carpenters' tools in it and a locksmith's workshop, crucibles, retorts, piles of frames, flasks with liquids of many colors, leather, iron. Sketches and paintings, often works of art, faux Persian rugs, and assorted pieces of weapons and armor hung on the walls. After spending more than a dozen years in Munich, he became a fabricator of antiques. Sometimes he managed to glue fragments together according to some existing pattern and make a replica of an antique piece of paraphernalia or household object, then turn it over to a dealer. Or he would wash off a blackened painting purchased for almost nothing and put it on the market as "Italian school" or "Dutch school."

"The chief" was particularly enamored of the "Gothic style." He saw that style everywhere, even in works created in other styles. For him the term of highest praise was the word "Gothic." That was why his collections contained so many things with sharp tips. No object with pointed arches was unworthy of his attention, so he stored away ornaments from iron railings, door hardware, keys, candlesticks in the folk style of the region near Lake Constance, belt buckles, frames, and other such items, not to mention genuine Gothic fragments.

Diverse groups of students and artists often gathered at Krzywosąd's quarters. Their bewhiskered patron treated these light-minded youngsters to outlandish vodka of his own distilling, cheese that he had made, and dry bread which, if he had not baked it himself, he had at least aged in his bottomless cupboards until it turned white with mold. By way of a special favor, at that time he allowed almost anyone to come close to the "weapon" hanging on the wall. He dragged out old, smeared drawings from somewhere underneath it and, with a look as careless as if he were announcing something of no significance whatsoever, pointed to this or that piece of schlock and said, "Peter Paul Rubens" or "Bolognese school, third period of Guido Reni."

After that a presentation of other collected items would begin. For example, there was the little book entitled *Priapeia* in a white calfskin binding. This book was pierced through in several places. When anyone asked what those perforations meant, Krzywosąd explained that it had been a favorite work of King Charles XII that had occasionally served as a target when the king was shooting his pistol. Then there was a cane that had belonged to the poet Seweryn Goszczyński, while at other times Krzywosąd claimed it had been the property of another poet, Wincenty Pol. There was the dagger, studded with seashells, of the Slovak adventurer Beniowski. There was the uniform of an officer from the time of the Warsaw Duchy, which Krzywosąd refurbished by replacing the faded tabs with others of a more or less similar color, and buttons and epaulets corresponding to those of the uniform of the French infantry in the time of Napoleon III. A satin caftan like those worn by aristocrats since the sixteenth century, haphazardly stitched with patches that did not match it, hung behind glass. A peculiar battered cabinet was said to have been the medicine chest of King Poniatowski; a terracotta pipe with a bent stem was passed off as the property of King Stefan Batory.

But "the chief" did not show his collections all the time or to everyone. There were a few people in the colony of youngsters who irritated him and drove him into an evil humor. One such fellow, having met with him somewhere, asked just after a pro forma question about his health, "And something of Van Dyck's? How's that going? In the works, eh? How's it doing?"

The other whippersnapper pretended to be stupid and when Krzywosąd showed his collection, listlessly threw out a query: "I read somewhere—I don't remember where, in some piece of writing—that Szczerbiec, King Bolesław Chrobry's sword, is said to be in your possession, but you don't advertise it for fear the pro-Austrian partisans will send thugs to steal it from you. You can show it to us. Mum's the word, we swear it!"

Yet Krzywosąd had his admirers. He showed them pieces of embroidered fabric that he took from the bottom of the inlaid cabinet, explaining that they were fragments of a liturgical robe and that the rest of it was at Cluny Abbey. A miniature in a blackened frame, he said with a wink and a whisper, had been stolen by a certain dealer from the renowned Brera gallery in Milan.

When the directorship of Cisy passed into Dr. Węglichowski's hands, Krzywosąd began to write to Les with complaints of homesickness. He wrote those letters so often that they made an impression on the crafty merchant, who murmured to himself, "That green monkey is plotting something."

Les had a strange liking for Krzywosąd. Very often he bought his priceless antiques, his Rubenses and Ruysdaels, his hetman's maces and authentic royal memorabilia. He put them all into a green trunk and called it the "green monkey cabinet."

The time came when Krzywosąd admitted in a letter that he intended to return to Poland. Les did not object, and the poor wanderer went back to Warsaw. Soon afterward he took over the administration of the institute at Cisy.

His quarters were located in the lower part of the old "castle." A gate, or rather its remains—Gothic, of course—led to his residence, and because what was left of it was close to collapse, Krzywosąd went to great lengths to shore it up. Farther on and to the right, steep, narrow stairs ran up to his door. In front of the threshold was a balcony surrounded by an iron railing. The balcony, like the stairs, was newly built on by the administrator. To accelerate the aging of the Gothic elements, the rubbish was not swept away, and no one cleared off the traces of the sparrows that had nested in whole flocks under the door. Krzywosąd loved birds. He talked with them and scattered so many bread crumbs that the sparrows had a sinecure and never flew away.

When Dr. Tomasz approached the administrator's door with slow, respectful steps to pay his first visit, this was the scene he witnessed: at the entrance to the stairs more than a dozen farm children, some Jews from the village, and a smattering of nondescript people swarmed, screaming at the tops of their voices. Krzywosąd stood above them in slippers and a blackened jacket of reindeer skin. On the railing of the balcony sat a domesticated falcon whose history Dr. Tomasz had already heard. The falcon had been sick all winter, and been treated. Krzywosąd had poured olive oil down its throat and set it next to a radiator so hot that the poor bird evidently became confused, for the stokers often found it lying beside the door of the large stove, among the coals and ashes. At those times only a glitter in its eye showed that life was still pulsating in the unhappy patient.

Now that the spring sun was shining brightly, the falcon had been taken out of the house for the first time. It sat on the railing, gripping the iron rod hard, looking around, moving, and giving every sign of health. Krzywosąd wanted not only to make a show of the bird, but also of its tricks.

He leaned over and touched it under its beak with his head, appealing to it at the same time to "…bite your master. Bite."

That meant that the falcon should caressingly tweak the remains of Krzywosąd's dyed hair. But either the fresh air or its improved state of health had such an extreme effect on the bird that when the administrator knelt and thrust his bald crown closer and closer, it rose on its feet, bristled, and pecked its "master" on his cranium with all its might until its beak made a tapping sound. The people gathered around, shouted joyfully, and began clapping and jumping up and down. Krzywosąd brought over a long switch and reprimanded the bird.

"I've coddled you like a nephew, you rascal, and you hammer me on the head," he exclaimed. "Go away!"

Having said that, he threw the falcon on the ground and thrashed it with the switch until its feathers flew. The bird spread its wings and with a cry fled into Krzywosąd's apartment on foot. The door slammed shut after it.

Judym opened that heavy door and made his way carefully to the interior, which consisted of a large vaulted hall with a stone floor and two rooms for the occupant. Next to the entrance hall was a room for a heater; in it the falcon was undergoing the punishment it had brought on itself, and Judym could hear its insolent screeches.

The doctor stepped into the room on the left and at once, on the threshold, whispered, "Twardowski the sorcerer! As I live, Twardowski!"

The apartment really did look exactly like the wizard's domicile. The ceiling was vaulted, the walls were extremely thick, and there were gratings on the windows. Near one window stood housekeeping work areas and a high-backed chair upholstered in leather. Deep inside was a wide wooden bed, very old, with a canopy above its intricately carved posts. Piles of iron, leather straps, and boards lay in the corners. On the walls hung the famous pictures of which Judym had already heard.

When Krzywosąd finally came into the room after the execution, he gave his guest an enthusiastic welcome. He seated him in an armchair that cast such a spell on the doctor that he seemed to have been immersed in one of the institute's bathtubs, and launched into polite discourse. When the conversation turned to Cisy, Krzywosąd expressed himself about the institute in general as casually as he did when he was showing drawings by Rubens. Judym noticed as well that he only used turns of style that emphasized his power there.

"I ordered that the entire castle be rebuilt," said the administrator. "I must still occupy myself with improvements to the park. I am thinking of a thorough restoration of the baths, but, as luck would have it, I have no time."

Then he added, "It will be done. It must be done."

He repeated this sentence particularly often: "This suited me, you know, doctor. This did me good. The look of it pleased me, so I ordered it to be built."

The self-assurance of these remarks left Judym unconvinced. He had been informed by other sources that the restoration of a building, for example, depended not only on what the administrator did well or badly, but also on other factors, chiefly the decision of the governing board. But later he came to believe that what Krzywosąd said about his tastes and the influence of those tastes on the running of things in Cisy described the real state of the case.

The treasurer of the institute was Hipolit Listwa, whom Krzywosąd described to his face and behind his back as an old blunderer, or, more maliciously, an overstuffed dud. The treasurer of Cisy was not a blunderer in the strict sense of the word, and even less a dud, but he could not qualify as a man of high aspirations. Fundamentally, he was mired in difficult conditions—in particular, the shackles of marriage. His wife and the naughty Dyzio added such diversion to his life that work in the cold, damp accounting room of the institute, where he sat among ledgers, receipts, and bills, was his only real enjoyment. He only felt alive when he was out of the house. Inside the family threshold he was rather like a broken umbrella: he hid in dark corners, he yielded the field, he was silent. In spite of the modest posture he assumed, he became the scapegoat in all spats with Dyzio, who exercised his wit against his aged stepfather. There were moments when he attempted to oppose the boy, but those experiments ended quickly and occurred less and less often. One word from his wife's lips reduced everything to zero level:

"Hipolit!"

CHAPTER VIII

A Tuberose

LEARNING ABOUT CISY occupied so much of Judym's time, and so absorbed his attention, that he could not think of touring the infirmary, though almost every day something about the "little hospital" reached his ear. Dr. Węglichowski several times mentioned to him, among other communications, "Remember, dear sir, that you have the hospital under your purview."

"Perhaps you and I could look at it," Judym would say impatiently.

"It is not urgent! Acquaint yourself with the institute. The other is a side issue. I say so because…" And the words trailed off.

And so it went. Finally one day the doctor had had enough. He asked in detail where the hospital was located and went there alone so as to at least get a view of the dimensions of the building and its quality. The hope of doing independent work in a hospital that he could almost think of as his own fired his enthusiasm.

Behind the park gate two very large avenues lined with lindens diverged at right angles. One came into Cisy from outside the town, from the direction of the railroad. The other led to the manor, the church, and the hospital. That road was more than two-thirds of a mile long, wide but swampy. At the time Judym was passing along it, it had begun to dry, but here and there slick, miry, washed-out clay from the surface spread out underfoot and clung to his shoes in lumps. Large trees standing over the road were already covered with leaves. In the ditches, streams of liquid loam hummed as they flowed briskly from higher ground.

Deep in his soul, Judym was more cheerful than he had probably been in his whole life. As he approached the farm buildings, which were scattered over a wide area, his heartbeat quickened. The spring wind blew over him, bringing dreams like a schoolboy's—dreams of things to come, of heroism, frantic surgeries, and fragrant lips that promised ineffable kisses. But his expression was unmoved, as befit a sober doctor, when he passed the homes of the administrator, the treasurer, and the estate steward, and went to the left toward the church, passing, on the right, the wide entrance road to the manor.

Beside the church, which was newly constructed of red brick—a fine piece of architecture with two towers soaring upward in Gothic style—sat the rectory. Beyond them, a much older, more spacious building hid among the trees: the hospital.

Judym had no intention of going inside. He wanted to do that in the company of his superior. He went farther on to look over the church, which had just been opened. It was still missing floors, altars off the side aisles, confessionals, paintings, and pews. The brick pillars stood in sand. Here and there were pews hastily knocked together from sawn lumber. Only in the presbytery were there carved stalls. A light of many colors, diffused and muted by stained glass, illuminated the interior. A priest was saying a quiet mass as a group of people stood before the main altar. Judym walked around the left side of the nave, stepped slowly over the sand, which completely muffled the sound of his steps, and drew near the presbytery. While he was standing there, he saw in the founder's pew the three young women he had met in Paris: Natalia, Joanna, and Wanda.

Natalia sat by the aisle. The doctor recognized her rather through the sweet swooning of his senses, through an internal chill that came over his face and his chest, than with his vision. She had on a light hat and her face was covered with a veil of a rust-red color. Her head was surrounded by carved tiles of brown wood that made it look like an exquisite drawing done with a reddish-brown crayon. The sharp lines of her nose and chin, seen through the fabric of the veil, looked as if they were etched in metal, while her eyes could only be seen as dark hollows.

For a moment, Judym's eyes were immovably fixed on her head. He was not sure whether he should bow because he did not know if he had been noticed. Only after a moment did he do so. Natalia nodded almost imperceptibly. Then Judym's eyes also met Joanna's, and there was a fleeting gleam in the look they exchanged. It was the greeting of two young, unspoiled spirits wandering through the world with kindred longings. Joanna's face was radiant, though she struggled with her eyes and lips to restrain her smiles.

The service ended and a small bevy of women from the town left the church, chatting. The doctor walked among the crowd so there would be no indication that he was waiting for the young ladies he knew to come out. But outside the door he paused here and there as if to study the architecture of the beautiful house of worship. When he was standing with his face turned upward, observing the stone arches, the little side doors leading to the sacristy opened. Out walked the priest, still young, who had just conducted the mass, and with him were Natalia, Wanda and Joanna.

And so they met. The doctor greeted the young women and introduced himself to the priest. The priest took him by the arm and began a pleasant, friendly, urbane conversation. He was a likeable priest, stout, with a cheerful glint in his eye and a ready smile. Only a few silver strands wove themselves into his luxuriant hair, and the glowing color of his face was at odds even with those threads.

"Whoever sets foot on priestly ground comes to the priest's house for breakfast!" the young rector decreed.

"Except for women!" Miss Podborska protested.

"With no exceptions. Priests, maidens, and angels are kin, the proverb says. Anyway, I give the orders here, not these young women. And I like that! Isn't that right, doctor?"

"Ah, since there is such a rule—the ladies must give way!"

"Well? And what now? Priest and doctor—I misspoke: doctor and priest have decided, so we are at the rectory," said the clergyman, opening the gate into the new wall that surrounded the church's graveyard.

The priest's spacious, comfortably furnished rooms were full of flowers, printed reproductions of oil paintings, writings, and illustrations. In the dining room there was a cabinet with publications for lay people. In a secluded study stood an ample bookcase, while weekly and monthly periodicals lay on a table. The priest amused his guests with his jovial humor, to which he tried to lend a refined tone, and asked his graceful housekeeper about breakfast, which was soon served.

The rector knew that the doctor and the young women had spent time together in Paris. Above all he was interested in the road to Lourdes, where he had been going for several years. The women tested him to see if he had acquired much proficiency in French.

When breakfast was over, the rector invited Judym out to the study for a cigarette, and the women riffled through the new publications in the living room. The windows in the study looked out on the avenue lined with linden trees. The rector spoke in such a lively, understanding way that every few minutes Judym thought, "What a pleasant, wise little father."

While the priest, with eager curiosity, was asking the doctor a great many questions about the city, he glanced at the road outside. A look of vexation came over his face. Dr. Tomasz saw a young man in an elegant spring coat and a pale hat walking briskly there. It was the spa guest whom he had seen riding horseback on the day he had arrived in Cisy, and noticed later at the common table in the institute. He had forgotten the man's name, so he asked the priest what it was.

"That's Karbowski, one of your patients. Though if he's sick, then I'm a pharmacist!"

"What do you mean?"

"You see… he's a rascal. He comes of a very good family, they say, and inherited a fortune from his father. Well, in two years he ran through it, every penny. He's been in Monte Carlo, Monaco, Paris, wherever people like to be. He gambles, but not like the rest of us: with a strategy. That's the trouble!"

"I didn't notice."

"Well, you will. In the season, as soon as he arrives, he fleeces someone richer, or emptyheaded, or a wealthy youngster, or even ladies, so that they go away in tears. He lives by doing that."

"People like that come here?"

"Nothing easier! That Karbowski—ho, ho! In the winter, when richer company runs out, he sits quiet as a dormouse. Sometimes he goes away and then returns. When things are really tight for him, he borrows from attendants, from people working in the baths, Jewish people, barber surgeons, anyone on the place. I say this because he won't overlook you."

"Oh, it's hard to borrow from me, especially just now," Judym laughed.

"Well, well. He's not in my good graces because he really knows how to swindle a poor man. He comes, let's say, to the barber surgeon, who tucks away a certain amount of money for himself during the season, and asks him to change a twenty-five-ruble note. Delighted to be intimate with 'such a gentleman,' the silly Figaro pulls the rubles from a drawer and spreads them out on a table. Karbowski rakes them into his purse, then pretends that he forgot to bring the twenty-five-ruble bill with him and tells the barber surgeon to come to the hotel. 'You'll come around to the hotel and take it,' he says, 'because I don't want to go running around after the money. I'm going straight to the castle.' But the attendants are

instructed not to let him in to see 'the count,' and in the meantime Karbowski throws himself into playing cards, counting on winning those
twenty-five rubles and paying them back."

"And will he at least pay it back?"

"Today he will if he is pressed to. But who knows what he will do tomorrow? He probably hasn't paid for his room in the hotel for a year. Anyway,
he has something else in mind now."

When the good rector had said that, there was a light knock at the door
to the entrance hall adjoining the living room. The priest murmured something and went out, bringing the doctor with him. In the doorway opposite them stood Karbowski himself.

He was a slender man with a pale complexion and dark hair. A small,
straight moustache shadowed his red lips. He had dark, misty eyes that
seemed to see no one in the room. His hair, smoothly combed back from
the left corner of his forehead, seemed in keeping with his whole person,
which had a peculiar charm. He wore a smoking jacket that fitted him
in a way that set off the grace of his leisurely movements. He greeted the
young ladies with a general bow, kissed the priest on the wrist, offered his
hand to Judym with an amiable nod, and sat down beside Wanda, opposite Natalia.

From the minute the young man had entered the room, that young lady
had been as pale as paper. Her mouth was closed in a peculiar way, as if she
were about to burst into tears, and her whole face had become so beautiful
that it was impossible to take one's eyes off it.

Karbowski spoke to Joanna about a book she was holding in her hand.
While they were talking he opened his eyelids in a particular, almost languid, way and fixed his eyes—eyes that were mad, wanton, and wild with
love—on Natalia's face. She, too, lacked the strength to conceal her expression. Joanna, full of alarm and agitation, spoke spiritedly to Karbowski,
but her words became tangled and stuck in her throat. He asked questions,
smiled, reasoned; he was to all appearances rational, sober, and cool; but
only at fleeting, painful moments did he tear his eyes away from Natalia.
He spoke slowly and in tones so clearly unsuited to what he was saying that
they seemed distant and false not only to him but to any conscious listener.

"You will stay in Cisy for a long time yet?" Natalia asked him.

"Yes, for quite some time. I don't know…perhaps I will die," he said
with quite a deadly smile.

"Die—you?" she whispered.

"So long, so long ago… I'm being treated here to no effect. I've lost hope."

"Perhaps some other resort might help you," said the priest, looking at his nails.

Karbowski stroked his mustache and shot the rector a look that, it seemed, could have killed him. Then he said as if to himself, "Ah, so much time. Yes, Yes. The father is right, another resort. Perhaps I'll go—"

"When?" Natalia asked again.

At that innocent word Joanna quivered and rose from her seat.

"We are leaving," she said to her companions. "Your grandmother will be worried."

Natalia pretended that she had not heard that, but her eyes took on a white glare of vicious spite like quicksilver. Wanda, who was combing through a year's issues of an illustrated magazine, looked up and asked, "Are we going, then?"

No one answered. The priest sat at a separate table and drummed on it with his fingers, looking into space with his lips thrust out. His face did not express unmitigated satisfaction with Karbowski's visit or the turn the conversation had taken. But Natalia and Karbowski were oblivious to that. It was clear that all that mattered to them was to seize these seconds by fair means or foul, to look into each other's eyes, to revive, through smiles and the sounds of indifferent words, the awareness of unfathomable seas of longing. Natalia welcomed the words from the young man's lips with wonderfully graceful movements of her nose and lips, as if each phrase had its own fragrance, like a rose sent from him, and she were kissing it.

Joanna said goodbye to the rector and both her companions followed her example. When it was time to take leave of Judym, and Natalia stood face to face with him, he saw that her fierce eyes were stony with resentment, yet seemed to emit a cry of despair. For a moment he thought he would give his life to have those eyes look at him for one hour with such longing. But devilish laughter roared in his soul and in the midst of his dull pain, something gave way. He and Karbowski walked out at the same time, together with the rector.

A light two-wheeled carriage with its hood folded down stood in front of the porch. The three women got in and the horses quickly moved forward. Natalia did not look around even once. Karbowski looked after the departing vehicle until it disappeared at a turning of the avenue. His eyes looked strangely drowsy and his face was contorted with suffering that neither a mask of pride nor a sociable smile could hide.

Judym envied him everything, even that suffering. He had walked that very road an hour earlier with fire in his heart. He had been eager to work at the hospital; he had had a powerful wish at least to see the walls of the building where he would throw his soul into difficult work as a doctor; and now that hospital had as little existence for him as if it had fallen to the ground. What was more, the aspiration he had felt an hour before seemed at this minute so silly as to be absurd, like something from cloudcuckooland. The reality was that Natalia was in love with Karbowski.

Judym looked skeptically at the devious young man—at his movements and gestures, which were naturally and by training graceful and infinitely sad, and at his clothing, which was tasteful and elegant in the highest degree. He would certainly not have admitted it to anyone, even himself, but he felt that his whole life, all his aims and plans and efforts, amounted to one great folly by comparison with Karbowski's life.

What had it all been for, the treatments he had been trained to administer, the ideas that had inspired him, the labor he had invested? Did Karbowski not understand life as it should be understood? Karbowski was a handsome, exquisite fellow, and for those attributes he was loved by the most miraculous phenomenon on earth, Natalia Orszeńska. Everything about Karbowski seemed reasonable and perfect, even his gambling and swindling. Judym attached no weight to all that, just as we attach no weight to anything but beauty when we look at a mysterious tuberose.

"Indeed," he thought, "a flower like that is the fruit of God knows how much trouble, pain, and expense. It's useless and harmful, by comparison with a blade of hay, an ear of rye, or a clover blossom, but after all, who would think of trampling on it?"

From the depths of the young doctor's soul a bitter sense of grievance reared its head again, and unassuaged envy. Why Karbowski? And why Natalia?

· CHAPTER IX ·

Come!

T HE STORM had passed. When it seemed that everything had gone quiet, new streams of large, heavy drops began beating the ground like whips. Glistening water flowed ceaselessly along the swollen paths, which were reddened from old brick. Little lakes full of glassy bubbles that bulged as if blown through the lips of playful children stood in places where the water was a bit deeper. Streaks of green with fallen tree trunks among them hid in the shadows of chestnut trees. Above, between huge clusters of treetops, was a dazzling fragment of sky with a golden background that glowed like the images of heaven on the altars of village churches. Clumps of feathery violet clouds streamed over it as fast as smoke. Every minute there was another distant rumble: spring thunder.

Very nearby stood an acacia with a thick black trunk and branches that seemed to be made of twisted iron. The monstrous limbs jostled a cover of pale, delicate leaves. Thousands of branches, growing from young acacias that were still bushes, protruded from the shadow of an old wall. Young shoots wrapped in new leaves, with tiny traces of leaves on their very tips, reached toward the clouds, like pampered maiden hands not yet stained by the sun. Once in a while the wind flew up, rocking a bush lightly, evenly, quietly—and then wonderful cadences from leaves swayed in the warm, moist air in drowsy harmonies like music that had lost its voice and, having assumed such a strange form, died away.

Judym sat at an open window in his apartment. A deep joy flamed in him. At moments, a sigh of emotion like the breeze that rocked the treetops sprang up in his heart. Then tender sounds, burning as if from a fire, ran over his lips as he spoke to the enormous trees, the young bushes, the swallows skimming along high above the towers that rose over gleaming space. A mysterious joy drew his eyes toward the end of the avenue, and his heart flew like a fragrance from the depths of his chest. He was waiting for something astonishingly new to him—for the arrival of something.

· CHAPTER X ·

Confidential

OCTOBER 17TH

Today is the anniversary of my arrival in Warsaw. So six years have passed! Six years! The great week of my life. I was seventeen then; now I've lived for twenty-three "springs." If I compare that Joanna to the Joanna of today—what a difference, and not for the better! Joanna, Joanna…

I decided to write a journal again, or rather to revive the old one. Staszka Bozowska, after all, taught us all about that art. She was the first in Kielce to write a proper journal, that is, a journal of her sincere feelings and true thoughts.

Poor, poor Staszka. In one of her last letters she wrote to me: "I really was in this life a gifted author of my journal…and nothing more. Now I've burned thirteen books bound in heavy cardboard and rusty black cloth in my school stove. Goodbye, journal."

She shouldn't have done it! Why condemn confessions that can't embarrass anyone, and for us who live solitary lives take the place (great God!) of lovers, husbands, brothers, sisters, and women friends? No! I will go on writing. I feel such an addiction to it as, for example, men to smoking tobacco. Because of the sneering of the phrasemonger S. I stopped, and I regret it more than I can express. I deprived myself of the pleasure for six years, and why? Because S. made it the target of his wit? Anyway, enough of that.

So many changes! Henryk in Zurich, Wacław gone, Staszka long in her grave. And with me? So many changes!

When I think now of that final night when the telegram came from Madam W.! Within four hours I decided to leave Kielce, to go to

Warsaw—and I went. The telegram said (I know the words by heart): "There is a position with the Predygiers. Come immediately. W."

Ah, that day, that frantic hurry! Getting things together, lingerie, trifles, quickly, quickly. With trembling hands! Amid tears and bursts of courage! Good Madam Falikowska "loaned" me money for the road, and–off I went! A deep, dark night in autumn. How the cab rumbled in the empty streets of Kielce, what strange echoes it made, and what a racket between the walls of the old buildings!

Even taking the railway journey was what one might call an action. Speaking under the seal of secrecy, I was riding on the "iron road" for the first time. The first time—and straight into the world! I didn't get a wink of sleep; I only rested my head against the wooden frame of the car and dreamed anxiously about life. I knew just as much about it as a person going to a doctor because he is tormented by mysterious suffering. As he knows nothing about the fundamental nature of the sickness, does not understand what it is or what its effects may be, what it will do to his body, his lot in life, or his thoughts or feelings, but only imagines things, bringing harsh, shrewd knowledge to bear, trying to understand everything—so it was with me. I fell into life with capital consisting of a railway ticket, a bundle with my belongings in it, five zlotys in cash—well, and Madam W.'s telegram. I left behind two brothers and Aunt Ludwika—who for lack of anyone more suitable took my mother's place when I was attending high school and shared a little of her bread with me, though probably nothing more. Ah, no, not nothing more! I loved Kielce and people there, my brothers Wacław and Henryk, the Dąbrowskis, the Multanowiczes, the hills with the names Karczówka and Kadzielnia, and everything in general! In those years it's so easy for a person to love everything! Especially Kielce.

That night in the train was so sad for me! The wheels beating on the tracks called to me in cruel words. Their grinding crushed my will and strength into a fog of apprehension. I remember those moments of fear before, as if enveloped in a flame, I decided to get off at the first station and return. Return, return! But my car rushed through gloomy places into the autumn night and with its wild iron strength carried me away from everything I dearly loved. Anyway, what could I do? Return to a poor aunt maintaining lodgings for schoolgirls? Live again in a miserable, dark, cramped little room? Sleep on an old sofa amid the stuffy odors of sauces and aunt's eternal shortages, amid worry about butter and resentment that potatoes cost so much—oh, and then the overheated feelings of eighth-graders, so spoiled, silly, and idle? I couldn't. I couldn't at all.

In any event, true to a vow solemnly taken at Holy Trinity, I had to prepare a way for Wacław, who was in seventh grade then, and help Henryk. Old, old history…

It was a morning near the end of autumn, a morning that appeared sick and tearful, when, shivering with cold and, I may as well say it, anxiety, I rattled in a one-horse cab to Madam W.'s. I found Bednarska Street, which wound around like the curving figure of a person or a beast in my feelings, and soon I was walking with Madam Celina to the Predygiers'. I passed streets which, viewed for the first time on such a day (through eyes hardly able to see from fright), were cold, wet, inhospitable, like Mickiewicz's "shell" in which "some strange reptile floats." We went in. We were measured, as if with a yardstick, by the eye of a footman as we waited in a beautifully appointed study. After a long wait full of uneasiness, at last I heard the rustle of silk gowns. Ah, that rustle of silk gowns!

Madam Predygier appeared. She had a Jewish nose but an aristocratic look, in the imperious Sarmatian style, in her eyes. We spoke of me, of my credentials, of what I would teach Wanda, my future pupil, and finally we switched involuntarily from Polish to French. It all ended with a question: how much do I require as a monthly salary? A moment of hesitation. Then I, a woman from Kielce, heroically and without believing my own ears named the highest figure I ever imagined: fifteen rubles.

My own room, complete maintenance, and fifteen rubles a month! Do you hear, you who educate silly children between the toll gates of the capital of the diocese?

Madam Predygier not only agreed, but "very willingly." That very night I slept in a quiet room off Długa Street. I bless the year I had there! Not knowing Warsaw well enough to be able to wander around staring like an artistic version of the proverbial "calf at a painted gate," I sat home like a model governess, working with Wanda and reading. Mr. Predygier's library stood open to me. Never before or since have I immersed myself in so many books.

What resources did I not have at that time! But never mind. I was as good as sugar candy then. "That's the point!" as worthy Mr. Multano-wicz said. I loved my pupil, Wanda, as if she were my own younger sister. I even loved Madam Predygier, though she was hard and haughty with me, dazzling in her grandeur, like a gas lamp. Perhaps my heart would have been large enough to love Mr. Predygier as well if he had not been a rich, repugnant, fat, inscrutable man. During the entire year I only saw two expressions in his eyes: shrewdness and triumph.

Gradually all emotions died away. In that house, between those people and me, no friendship blossomed, no warm feeling. Today I know that there is nothing strange in that. Can the poorest, the most paltry flower bloom in an icehouse?

I remember my first visit to the theater, at a concert of the singing society Lutnia, at the readings. Today I recall only faintly my enchanting, almost mystical excitement when I saw *Mazeppa* on the stage…when I heard the excellent actors delivering Słowacki's wonderful poetry, which I knew by heart, "my" poetry…. Then fate gave me the chance to catch sight of several literary people, whom, in my simpleminded way as a woman from Kielce, I took for descendants of Apollo. Later, only later, I became convinced that far more often they might have traced their ancestry to Bacchus or Mercury. Now I know that talent in most cases is a bag, sometimes full of precious jewels, that any fellow, even any robber, can carry on his back by chance. But then! What overwhelming awe when I came into the drawing room where talent, talent itself sat, invited by Mr. Predygier for a joint of meat!

By the way, today I would still so long to see Tolstoy, Ibsen, Zola, Hauptmann from some little corner, and to hear those who spoke: Przybyszewski, Sieroszewski, Tetmajer, and the one and only "Icz" (Witkiewicz, of course).

But to those great ones I prefer the world I am connected with here: a world that is not so disenchanting, a world of feeling without affectation. Our motherly single ladies, people with humility, with lopsided shoes and shawls faded to rusty red: it seemed to me at one time that the world was made up of such people. The rest, I thought, were temporarily neglected and, when they received the truth, would turn toward it and begin a new life.

I was confirmed in those imaginings by the letters Staszka Bozowska wrote from the godforsaken place to which she had gone. Those letters were nothing more than lofty fictions, the communication of gullible souls. Today Staszka is dead. My eyes and my heart are full of tears.

OCTOBER 18TH

When I began to write, I wanted to enrich my reflections on one thing and another. So much detail comes to me, so many people, events, and feelings. Not everything can be embraced and connected; it disperses like quicksilver and flies away in all directions. Such is our life: full of motion, quick, rudderless.

Tonight I thought of Wacław, and again I felt a tightening at my heart. It really is a terrible mockery: Henryk, who was expelled from school in his late teens, is settled in Zurich, plays at "philosophy," and is fine; and for Wacław, who left high school with a silver medal, did excellent work in natural science here, and was respected by everyone—everything ended so uselessly. It's monstrously illogical. Aunt Ludwika would certainly have said, "It's all because you aren't religious enough.'"

It often seems to me that people have a clandestine similarity to animals: they band together with no understanding among themselves, only with a herd impulse, to persecute distinguished individuals.

OCTOBER 24TH

I was in the theatre. They were playing *The Teacher,* a work highly approved by the entire cadre of critics. I wonder why the author presents his heroine as having been seduced when that was probably not the case. The truth of life is certainly brutal. I know, for example, what temptations Hela R. experienced, or Franciszka W. Virtuous men tied to their wives' apron strings are a hundred times more cunning when they enter these lists than bachelors. Governesses may be smart or stupid, bad or good, pretty or homely, but in this regard they all must be beyond reproach. Perhaps foreign women—that I don't know. It's said that the effort pays off more easily there. But the local element…

A governess, as a stranger in her environment and usually socially inferior, is constantly under something like censorship. Let her only give someone reason to bandy her name about and—she is gone! The scrutiny may be gracious, even friendly, even flattering, but it never stops. It is the same whether she occupies a low, difficult position or, often, a much higher one. It creates a feeling of pride, and makes that feeling more sensitive—a noble pride, which like a walking stick supports one in a moment of weariness and serves as a defense against an enemy. It is a brake, a heavy one, and—who knows?—perhaps altogether sufficient.

OCTOBER 26TH

I'm reading the philosophical poetry of Ludwika Ackermann. In a certain place she says that a woman writing poetry is funny. It seems to me that she's right. Why?

Poetry is the sincere voice of the human soul, an eruption of a certain form of passion. That outburst of the spirit must be a struggle for new things, a giving voice to mysteries previously unheard of.

Until now, a woman has not had the right to see herself as a creator. She is funny when she overlooks the entire enormous gap that separates her from a sincere human being. What new truths about the feminine soul does her poetry contain? Only truths about love (note: masculine). Sometimes a rebellious shout; that is a passing thing that rather impoverishes than enriches.

And often enough it is rebellion for the right to utter something that has already been expressed by men. Most often, moreover, to utter some hypocritical cant or to express, beautifully, interestingly, enigmatically (to men), feelings about the dysfunctional nature of love. All true female poets leave their real personalities in the shadows; Ada Negri, for example, whose theme is the plight of the poor. If a modern Sappho wants to speak and be understood as human being, she must speak as a man.

In reality she possesses all the same feelings, perhaps even more and far more subtle ones, but she cannot and dares not express them outright. Her thoughts run along a different channel; they are purer, or rather not so brutally sensual, passions simply unlike the way they are presented by the authors of today, not only male authors but female. All men are sensual in a way that seems ugly, for example, to a young woman. They are painted that way in art that they themselves created. And men are so naïve in their animal instincts that one must pity them as one pities small children. Anything pretty in the vicinity and—a kiss right away! They feel no obligation to express their gross impulses with greater caution, even for the sake of politeness, out of regard for the fact that the "weaker sex" may feel the same thing in a different way.

On the other hand, at least until now, everything in the way of great art that could come from women (everything equally strong, of course) must first be formed on the masculine model. So it is possible sometimes to read works written by women portraying something like feminine feelings, works that are deliberately lying from beginning to end. This is a kind of coquetry by women of the masculine sort through the mediation of literature. Meanwhile men masterfully defend their regime and condemn all attempts to release into being a different soul and a new, a yet unknown type of art, together with its boundless sphere of mysterious means. The lords of the world would have to undergo a new, fundamentally different critique, which might not be pleasant. Those who sit in judgment in this field today, however—not only men but the mass of women educated in their school—are much closer in their way of thinking to Hindus, who consider a woman unclean since it sometimes happens that she is. In no way does it depend on her will, but it is treated with true Indian simplicity as a fact considered in itself.

Do men of the most elevated feeling, poets, respect the human spirit in women? I think not. They adore a beautiful creature insofar as she is a treasury of attributes they find delightful, though the possession of them cannot be attributed to her as merits. The most celebrated type of woman has been the sort who exercises demonic influence. The ones who are praised perhaps less, but sincerely and beautifully, are the saintly souls who suffer without complaint— sweet beings who do not think of defending themselves, like Ophelia. Women exercising the right to personal happiness, using natural strength of spirit and intellectual ability—there are almost none of those. It's far easier to find in literature the noble aspiration of men to rehabilitate a fallen woman than the return of rights and respect to a woman who is wronged. The latter is neither idyl nor tragedy and so has no "esthetic" impact. Only Ibsen, that immortal truthteller, who through the figure of Justine in *The Wild Duck* laughs at human culture like a devil, like a being not human, saw into the essence of this thing. But he, too, couldn't restrain himself from honoring the proprietary rights of masculine sentiment. The essential feminine poetry perhaps trembled in the song of the slave, when on the Roman magnate's terrace, before the crowd of lounging patricians, she had to sing the song of her country for their entertainment.

We don't know her. When I think of that song and I want to solve the riddle of it, now and then it seems to me that I heard it somewhere behind the fourth wall. Now and then it reaches my soul, and then all day I hear in myself the sound of those strings plucked painfully by bloody fingers. At those times what the poetess says is true: "That is what I feel! It is in my heart! What you say about my song is nothing to me. I sing for myself, only for myself."

But today…today there are still the tears of the woman misled and sold into marital slavery by her family when she loves another—the woman fallen and despised when she is judged by the hypocritical virtue of the crowd. There are still the dreams of a woman innocently and passionately in love, who conceived a child and carries it under her heart. What, now! Is it impossible to draw those sounds from the lyre? That would be immoral, that would promote vice!

OCTOBER 27TH

I've read what has been standing here since yesterday and will still stand, to the enlightenment of the ages. I would like to write truthfully and sincerely, and that's incredibly difficult. I have many thoughts that are half-conscious, as if wandering in a strange neighborhood, which, even if I wanted to formulate them, change under the pen and are not the same. How to write? As it comes, or as it changes when it is put into words? The latter reminds me of a moment in the *Undivine Comedy* when the husband, despairing in beautiful sentences about the plight of his mad wife, hears an unfamiliar voice say: "You are composing a drama."

OCTOBER 30TH

I wrote two days ago about the greater purity of women. Often it has happened that when I am truly and deeply occupied with some thought, I find in the world around me, if not the further development of it, in any case details and fragments that pertain to it. Very

likely that focused thought, like light in darkness, fishes out of my surroundings everything that I would not perceive under other conditions, if I did not know why it came into my field of vision.

I was with Marynia. I rarely see her, but I like her—how can I
express it—instinctively, against my will, perhaps almost perversely.
She is fundamentally innocent, clean, pure, and very simple of heart,
and yet she very much likes more than one, two, or three men. The
erotic element is only a minor ingredient in all this. I don't mean that
it plays no part at all, but what plays a far greater part is a kind of meg-
alomania. When I delicately drew her out, she rejoined with perfectly
genuine naivete that she didn't know why it wasn't possible to be
"occupied" with several people. ("Not in love: nothing of the kind!")

These relationships are altogether distinct, but they are connected
to each other like, for example, layers in a cake. Each is different and
very good; but is the result that all of them, taken together, should
have a bad taste? And indeed, after all this roguish philosophy,
Marynia would not be capable of a whit of that faithlessness that
Ophelia complains of in her song.

NOVEMBER 4TH

One of those difficult days that seem like stern, wicked creatures.
The day is long and doesn't want to go away, like a moneylender who
must squeeze out all that's owed him by a certain time. And when
it finally expires, it leaves a dark shadow behind it—a sleepless night
full of tears, frightening visions, and fears. One of my "well-wishers,"
Madam Laura, in whose house I have given lectures to girls for three
years, conveyed sad news to me with a great show of sympathy. She
heard it in an exchange of gossip with a woman who was newly
returned from traveling. It is this: Henryk reportedly has not been
studying for his doctorate, as he assured me a thousand times that he
was doing, but has incurred debt and been involved in scandals and
brawls. He has been in a duel and in bar fights, been in the local jail,
and been slashed with swords by police. There are too many such mis-
adventures to count, and most serious of all is that he has lied. It's said
that he has not attended lectures for two years. He does not have the
minimum number of semesters required for the examination—in a
word, a sordid mire of facts. I listened to all this patiently, smiling and

saying: "Yes, yes, madam, what a scamp." But there was something quite different in my heart.

There must be a great deal of truth in this if his museum scholarship has been withdrawn. All of it would be nothing if it weren't for the lying, putting one over on me, his stupid sister. If he had told me how things are, I would not have reproached him. I would not even have thought badly of it. He behaves scandalously because he's a vigorous young blood. But to find out about it indirectly, from strangers who unintentionally took out on me the *schadenfreude* that festers in every human soul!

NOVEMBER 5TH

Not much sleep; I only fell into a doze early in the morning, and today I traipse around about as gracefully as a wet hen. Giving lessons was hard work. This despondency chokes a person. It causes her to withdraw, to shrivel, to crumble. I made up my mind to extricate myself from the stifling closeness in which I'm barricaded by this bitter news. No, I won't abandon Henryk! I'll work twice as much, I'll take on more lessons, perhaps even in the morning. If he finishes any course, he would be able to work here more easily. I'll never regret that he didn't manage to enter the polytech, but that's difficult. He really has gone a bit too long without a definite occupation.

NOVEMBER 6TH

To save on expenses I am taking in Miss Guepe. I will lose more than half my living space, but—too bad. My room will only be a partial retreat; even this journal will only be written in snatches. But this will bring in almost eight rubles a month. I must give Wacław some money for a sheepskin jacket and heavy boots....warm underwear. There must be two pairs. Remember, remember, that Madam F. comes on the eighteenth, eighteenth, eighteenth!

NOVEMBER 13TH

I took on a new teaching assignment. I squeezed it in between the Lipeckis and Zosia K. The new work is preparing a girl, Henia L., for the entry class at a boarding school. As yet she knows nothing—not spelling, not the multiplication table, nothing. A large room, dark as a cellar, with one window looking out on a narrow yard. At this season, before the sun has set it is already evening there. Henia and I sit opposite each other at a table and speak, both of us, in strange voices.

"Ces enfants ont trouve leurs mouchoirs, mais ils ont perdu leurs bonnes montres."

First I say that in a loud voice, and then she forces out equally strong sounds. She must think that one has to speak French in that sepulchral tone. In a large, dark apartment everything reverberates as if a secret ritual of the Freemasons were in progress. Sometimes strange sets of ideas come into the little girl's head and she asks me questions to which there are no conceivable answers.

After staying there for an hour, I hurry as fast as I can in rubber galoshes deep into the Powiśla district to the Blums' with the urgent information that "In the declarative we announce concrete actions in relation to the referenced subject. In the imperative, actions ordered or forbidden. In the conditional, actions only possible, assumed, or intended." An ingratiating cousin is always waiting there.

Today is packed, absolutely packed like a Jewish bag, with lessons. I am so accustomed to systematic walking at specified times that on Sundays, as I while away the hours after lunch in idle chat or reading, I feel anxious twitches every minute and I jump up like a lunatic. My very legs jump and do logarithms of the routes to Smocza Street or Dobra Street.

Who would have believed that I, a lowly creature from Kielce, would someday come to be paid sixty-two rubles a month in the very center of Warsaw for the dissemination of mysterious knowledge in various streets!

Guepe has moved in. She has the cardinal flaw of Frenchwomen: she is a chatterbox. To be honest, I benefit from this, because I must talk with her in the evenings and, in parrot-like, truly feminine style, I take on a Parisian accent when we speak French. But I sleep poorly. At midnight I'm still laughing at her adventures, and often I can't sleep afterward. Bells toll the hours.

I'm weak when I rise and something in me trembles like our old wall clock when it was started up. The strange part is that in such cases I don't want to sleep at all unless I am tired, exhausted to the point of collapse. When that happens, I'm unconscious, I don't know what people are saying to me, and I answer the prattling little sweetheart with nonsense.

NOVEMBER 15TH

On Sunday I read many beautiful things. Until now I have had subjects on my mind that are not my own, not closely fused with the spiritual part of me.

Few feelings can fill the heart with such a demand for positive action as the cold, hard awareness of how much was suffered, how much was borne, for the happiness of the generation living today, of which we here are a minuscule part. There is a strange brotherhood going back to those who fulfilled all their obligation in their time. It is impossible to think of anyone living with such reverence, such sacred veneration, as those who remain behind us in the twilight of oblivion.

I've come to the conclusion that if it is not possible to cure heavy moral suffering and subtle, persistent, deep worry, it is in any case possible to deaden them with pressures of a certain sort. When one is so sad that tears come for any reason, one should read, for example, the "Report on the Activities of the Trade Bank From the Seventh Term," or "The Eleventh Regular General Assembly of the Stockholders of the Warsaw-Terespol Railroad." When one studies such things consciously and resolutely at the appropriate moments, they produce an effect of enormous otherness, of their own ruthless, steely character, that affects delicate, tender feelings as strongly as Schleich's anesthetic. That salt so numbs the nerve stems for some time that it is possible to cut painlessly with a lancet through the places affected by it.

It is a different matter when the suffering is severe. Then the "Eleventh Report" flies from the hands like a terrible weight.

NOVEMBER 17TH

It seems that I'm unable to write such a memoir as I intended. I have too little persistence. It would be hard for me to assert this morning, when I'm calm, almost cheerful, that I won't be drowning in despair at twilight, unfortunately—even without great cause. Lack of money, Wacław's silence, thoughts of Henryk, some small, trivial, empty occurrences of the autumn day, things Krasiński so rightly termed "paltry," and most often some distant, remote disaster, not mine, not a friend's, but in this city: it throws me into sadness, or rather into a painful coldness. It's by no means peace! Oh, no! Peace is a precious state. Worry and poverty teach us to feel peace as happiness. It's impossible to record these passing states here, just as it is impossible to look in the mirror when one is moved to the depths by something. And there is no way to recreate them using beautiful words and parallel phrases, since that would produce something altogether different. A multitude of things have passed and continually pass, and I am not only unable to present them and assess them, I can't even mention them in passing. Sometimes I am so lacking in strength that I could easily sit on the edge of the sidewalk on which I rush from one lesson to another, and rest amid the laughter of the passersby.

The ladies I pass are so happy, going for walks or to wherever they go at a leisurely pace. They carry on pleasant, charming, cheerful conversations with fashionably dressed men. Who are these people? What do they do, where do they live? I don't know them at all. The world is so small, so cramped, and at the same time so vast! A person in it is a poor captive running continually over the same path, back and forth, like the Wilanow railway.

In my mind I turn back to the places I was before, and I think of myself a few years ago. I was better then. Today I could not tire myself so with work, no matter what good I might do.

What will happen? Will I go on becoming worse and worse? In Kielce then, in our Głogi, in Mękarzyce, and here in Warsaw sometime ago, I made efforts to be different. Now I am impulsive, full of negative thoughts. What an ascetic I was with regard to comforts! Now little things vex me.

I have thought long about this: what exactly has changed in me? I used to have a great deal of faith in the goodness of people; that is why I was ready in my heart to rush outward to them. I had the grace of utter, wholehearted devotion to nonmaterial things, to things of a different order.

I am so cold now! I hardly remember those springs of delight. I have become insensitive to the suffering of others. I can say that I am more inured to my own poverty (or perhaps not so inured).

I really do have warm feelings for many people these days, but I often imagine that I do not love Henryk and Wacław as I used to. I will still do what I can for them and for others, but I do not feel the old happiness for the simple reason that I must work, I must be of service. I still have a great deal of enthusiasm for good and fervent natures, for those who go to great trouble and despise hidden evil, but that is another matter. I do not know, I cannot say sincerely, whether I love such people or whether I only want to march in their ranks out of a calculation that to do so is safest because victory lies that way. This is "that road on which the soul descends in the dark, into the bottomless night of darkness…"

Before now I was surrounded by people with dignity, with deep, quiet, modest, tender natures, often as enduring as iron in their goodheartedness, prone to utter neglect of themselves for the sake of others. They were even-tempered and united in their aspirations. To be in their presence was so good; it so inspired trust; it was so quiet for the heart. They were my parents, our neighbors, certain people in Kielce. Was my soul different, or only capable of blind credulity?

In my old world there was not even one person who seemed repugnant to me. How many there are today! For example, that cousin at the Blums' who opens the door for me and helps me take off my wraps: I am waiting patiently for him to accost me in that corridor sometime and eat me with his eyes. The teacher who comes to his cousins seems attractive to him. I cannot demand, after all, that he not open the door and help me off with my cape, but I find him as repulsive as a centipede or a dirty comb. It amazes me that he does not feel the disgust that it seems to me I exude. But perhaps in the sort of love that he has in mind, feelings of revulsion on the weaker side do not come into the calculation at all. That ought not to concern me in the least. I am perfectly free to treat such a person as objectively as, let us say, a ram or other representative of the animal kingdom, but I cannot. In the wider view I am a bit too interested in this matter; I write about it so much that it arouses suspicion. Could this "disgust" conceal a touch of satisfaction?

November 18th

To Waliców Street by tramway. Only when I had gotten into the car and paid the conductor did I see, sitting in a corner, a fine-looking man in a top hat. I have seen him three times. He wiped away the steam with his hand every little while and looked out through the clean space on the window.

What was he looking for? If it were a woman, what a happy one! Who is he? What does he do? How does he speak? What thoughts are concealed in that masterpiece of a head? I see his thoughtful face before me constantly, and, in my imagination, his whole figure. Today during lessons at the F.s', involuntarily, with no effort, only half knowing what I was drawing, I sketched that profile with its very subtle combination of features, full of harmony and a valiant strength. It was a good thing that he got out on the corner of Ciepła Street or—who knows?—I might have fallen in love with him.

All day for no reason I had a pleasant feeling, a joy somehow, as if in a moment I were going to meet with something supremely delightful. When I tried to understand what had happened to me that was so nice, I seemed to see his face, and those eyes looking for something out of the window.

May he meet with everything good in life.

NOVEMBER 19TH

The most notable Song of Solomon says: "Who is this that cometh out of the wilderness like pillars of smoke, perfumed with myrrh and frankincense, with all the fragrant powders…"

The most notable words! It is a real description of feeling. "He that cometh out of the wilderness…" Words without sense translate the essence of the feeling as precisely as algebra.

NOVEMBER 20TH

"By night on my bed I sought him whom my soul loveth: I sought him, but I found him not. I will rise now, and go about the city in the streets, and in the broad ways I will seek him whom my soul loveth: I sought him, but I found him not." Immodest, humiliating! These words: a blush. Every letter burns with shame. Well—and when it's true? When it's true.

November 22nd

That cousin again, with his smile stuck to his lips with gum Arabic! When he stands in the doorway after I ring the bell, I am simply weak. I feel at once that I am red as a beet. Try as I may to regain my proper color, it is all for nothing. I turn red in spite of myself; my hands tremble. This fool imagines that he makes a thunderous impression on me, and he only offends me. Why isn't this the one from Song of Solomon?

To blush in the company of good, refined people is not at all so painful. It isn't as if I wanted to use vulgar language, smack my lips, or look at indecent things. But here! I read somewhere that in Egypt talismans were sold that had the power to guard the buyer from spells. "From the glances of girls sharper than the prick of a pin," it was said, "from women's eyes, sharper than knives, from the glances of boys, more painful than the lash of a whip, from the glances of men, heavier than the blow of an ax." How I would like to be safe from those last, from their glances!

Today Madam B. detained me in her cluttered drawing room, and that "man of letters" slipped in right away with silken steps. I felt his presence, though I did not raise my eyes. He began saying trite things which he had surely heard from someone more intelligent. On Nietzsche! There were strong indications that he considered himself a "superman" and a student of the philosopher, of whom he has formed his estimation from articles written in Warsaw. He is especially brilliant when the openings of his sentences promise something of consequence:

"For madam ought to know…"

"No doubt madam thinks that…well, now…"
and he only spouts a thought that is familiar to me and as unnecessary as some hackneyed commonplace. His conversation is only intended to emphasize certain phrases. I wonder if this superblowhard is brave enough to accentuate these phrases when he speaks to one of those rich ladies who could answer him with boldness equal to his? God help him then! What does it matter that such a person offers me proof of his low regard, taking advantage of the fact that I am a teacher? Is that going to hurt me? It is not at all deserved. I cannot bear it without annoyance, but, after all, I can make light of it. I must, at any

rate, because no other form of resistance could protect me from such fraying of the nerves. Incidents of that kind keep me from seeking out company, as does a lack of courage in social situations. I know that I would not reject a good person because others are contemptuous of her, but I am not bold enough to defend myself very forcefully.

NOVEMBER 23RD

I will have to give up lessons at the Blums'. It's too bad! I can't make a scene in the hall or complain to that lady. I had to defend myself. What I did today I will not spell out here, but he will remember that moment! Anyway, how miserable it all is!

Long ago I thought that hate was evil. To be angry, to nurse resentment—that is another thing. Hate is a desire to injure someone. I would not do anything bad even to that womanizer, but I would not be very sorry to know that something bad had happened to him. Over time I may develop a desire for revenge. Why not? If one walks on stairs, one must descend to where they lead. I know that, but I do not feel angry at myself when I feel hostile toward someone. Who knows if, when you come down to it, hate is evil and immoral? This kind of hate——who knows? But why must I be asking these questions, why must I be debating about this?

NOVEMBER 26TH

Quietly, very quietly, Miss L. has died. Certainly she left no deep regret in anyone's heart. She was loved, so to speak, out of duty. Good Heavens—the worst of people, when they die, often awaken lively, sincere regret. Who can be seen as a model person, even a model disciple of Christ, if not she, that motherly single woman? She was a creature not only pure in spirit but amazingly pure in body, one of the divine messengers on the model of Christ's "bruised reed that He will not break" and "the smoking wick that He will not quench," as St. Matthew says. She spent her whole life in teaching as if she were in a religious order.

Perhaps she had hidden flaws; perhaps in secret, with some shrewd eye looking on, she committed a sin that no one else knew about. But in her life, weighed as if on a merchant's scale—the life of an old teacher whom people made fun of—I find no offense. Work, dull work—instinct for work, passion for work, vision for work— arranged systematically as a theorem in geometry. A life spread over school years and quarters, delighting in the harvest of nothing more than the fruits of the nation's culture. I never saw anyone who so rejoiced with "exceeding great joy" when beautiful works of literature appeared, such as *The Flood* or *Pharaoh.* She was truly happy to be living at the same time Sienkiewicz was writing, and she had a picture of him in a garland of ivy in her little room.

I could not agree with many of her opinions, or rather I did not concur with her in my heart when she spoke. For she spoke from another time. There were new forces in the world that she could not understand. She lived in the old order that had been trodden underfoot by Bismarck's "power over law." How did she apply the old laws to the new life? Very simply; it could not have been simpler. She exorcised her zeal into work; she poured it into her duties. It was hard, certainly it was hard, to compress that passion into such a small space. It must have been slowly, over a long series of years, that she created a system, a compartmentalized system. To teach grammar and style, to teach writing as Miss L. did, is something no one else can do. Her way of teaching, pedantic, fierce, almost nagging, was driven by enthusiasm.

Beside Miss L.'s coffin I made a decision to imitate her. Not to mimic her, but truly to follow her example. Her life was cultural to such a high degree that it would have been asinine folly on our part to neglect the excellent examples she set. Men, after all, imitate Englishmen, people of another country and type, people from abroad, and we, seeing someone like her here, where we live… And so: 1, to stifle in oneself lapses, weakness, exaggerated sensitivity, and chiefly, chiefly, sighing sadness; 2, constantly to urge oneself to perseverance and form one's will; 3, to arrange premeditatedly and critically a plan of activity; 4, to execute with precision what one decides after consideration, no matter if the river rises; that in particular. And in general, to preserve purity of soul and not to harbor anything ignoble. Simply do not give it room. If it takes on the tempting form of novelty, freshness, strike the vileness down with all the force of one's spirit.

Beside Miss L.'s coffin it occurred to me that the just person lives here on earth far longer than the fool. The small, shrunken, smiling remains of Miss L. affected me more today than many a learned debate. Her teaching did not end with the moment of her death. Indeed, what she had done became altogether comprehensible then, as if it were a perfect book and we had finished reading the last page of it, together with its conclusion. Dr. Muller as well not only lived that way, but also healed others after his death. At the moment he was dying of plague, he prescribed a way of disinfecting his body so that contagion would not be carried to any of those close to him for four days after his decease. There are people who achieved supreme strength on earth; they did not fear descent into the grave. So their deaths are mysteries of great consequence, full of veneration and sadness. The deaths of people who fear death cast a dreadful, terrifying spell over them; it makes them think, or rather smother and drown in thinking, of that decay of the body in all its indescribable hideousness. That spell is like a monster, loathsome, mindless, and above all omnipotent.

But one thing more. Would Miss L.'s life have been equally useful if she had been married and had children? Would it have been more useful to the world if instead of so many pupils she had only brought up her own children well? And would she have brought them up so well? It seems to me that this, too, is motherhood, and motherhood in a higher degree: to educate human souls as she did. Our mothers make light of mother-educators. Giving birth to children is a great and miraculous business of nature, but not a credential for an educator. Meanwhile any woman can bear children. Perhaps I am guilty of heresy for writing this opinion here, but I believe it is true. My thought is this: the world is full of women who are neither wise nor good, but beautiful and healthy. They are Sabines, who will surely be abducted by men who want them for wives. But the result of those abductions is not that every Sabine woman becomes a treasury of knowledge. The duty (but also the right) to raise better and better generations, if the point is for generations to be better and better, must be taken away from Sabines who are neither wise nor good and given to homely women like Miss L.

November 28th

Today, in the light of the principles I have adopted, I calculated my income and expenses. Material consideration of the events of the last three months of my life, and yet more material efforts to predict the future, showed that I'm spending almost twice as much as I've earned. It's true that I sent underclothes to Wacław and money for two months to Henryk, and, most important, I paid Siapsia Bożęcki forty rubles from an old debt of Aunt Ludwika's, but then I contracted debts to Marynka herself worth a hundred rubles and more. I was terrified by my extravagance—actually, by my poverty—and I've decided to limit my expenses to the minimum.

I began by buying a ticket to the theater together with Marynia. Molière's *The Imaginary Invalid* was playing. Marynia and I reached the same conclusion: often one reads, and in particular hears, that in the world "everything has already happened." On this premise that "everything has already happened," various ladies and gentlemen indulge in things that really were possible only in the past. Watching such a play by Molière, one sees just how humanity has advanced, not only in the field of medicine but above all in the area of ethics. Yet anyone who wants to can still see, in the vicinities of Radomsko, Kielce, even Sandomierz, such barbarians as we see on that stage, and no doubt all this belongs to the epoch Molière described.

A small observation: I am despondent because of Miss L.'s death and other circumstances, but after all, I can burst out laughing at any funny remark. I have always flattered myself that I am lighthearted; now this attribute seems stronger. Nothing about me is fixed and unaltering. I can enjoy myself very freely, not only at the theater but with any little wag at all during lessons, even though I have my sadnesses.

How is it possible to trust oneself, then, when there is inside a person a hidden demon that cannot be caught by the ears? Obviously it must be the strength of this earthly casing of flesh, some animal force, that needs laughter as plants need to be whipped by the wind. It would be fitting to chasten this dwelling place of the spirit.

November 30th

His name is Dr. Judym.

December 1st

I am not superstitious at all. I do not believe in signs. When something of that nature occurs, it is very painful to me—now in particular, after last night. It seems to me that I am standing before powerful, brutal people who will do me harm.

I fell asleep late, tired and sad. In a dream I saw before me a dark hall, rather like a court in Zurich, where in fact I have never been. People in drab, dark uniforms led me in. In particular, one—where did that face come from?—whom I still see. Those people told me that Henryk had committed murder. Fear such as I had never known before overwhelmed me. At the same time, I felt in myself a resolve as formidable as that message: I won't let this happen! I stood by a window, set into the thick wall, that let bright golden sunlight into the ominous-looking room. In the distance were white mountains and a dark blue lake with waves. Then a voice sounded: "Bring him in!"

Henryk came into the hall. There was a smile on his pale, gaunt face, but what a terrible smile! I felt as if this smile were cutting through me. When I wanted to come near him, a very ordinary-looking man came in, carrying steel scissors. Henryk sat on a chair and his smile became more, still more malign. The barber cut his hair, my dear little brother's beautiful, light hair. Its curls rolled over his black clothing and fell on the dirty floor. Someone took me by the hand, but who was it? Oh, God!

I tried to speak, to scream, but there was no sound in my throat. I could not even pull a sob from my chest. Guepe called to me.

I awoke and then sat down, overcome by a terrible feeling. I can't express it. That pain in the midst of sleep, a hundred times worse than any pain during the day, and that mysterious, clairvoyant premonition—perhaps, ah, most certainly an omen of future suffering unknown to me, suffering so deep that to comprehend it is anguish. I couldn't move a hand or foot. The horrid dream flew slowly away and a quiet joy that it had been a dream, a joy like a blessed sunbeam, trickled to the depths of my heart.

Who could love anything in the world as I loved my brother that night? It seems that people love their families more than anything. I don't like those family feelings of mine or value them, but nothing has such cruel, unfathomable power over me as they have. And why is that?

Is it right to feel such devoted love for people who perhaps do not deserve it?

Indeed, there are so many things—so many people and issues—in the world.

What have I written here?

DECEMBER 2ND

Henia has the measles, and I have a free hour. I dropped in at home and I am sitting alone. Ah, how unpleasant! Brownish fog is drifting into the sunken yards. It's just four o'clock, still daylight, but I can't see the turrets of the roofs that are always outlined on my horizon. Only the nearby chimneys, the square brick ones and the round, narrow, metal ones alike, are reflected in the wet, slippery, flat surfaces of their roofs, like poles and pilings in standing water. Every day now, walls that are gray and yellowish are blue with cold. The windows have almost disappeared, or they loom like sunken eye sockets in the face of someone near death. Thin mud dribbles like saliva over the asphalt walk at the bottom of the yard. Just outside the window I hear a monotonous rustle. I lean out, I strain my eyes, and through the moist pane, as if through a spider web, I see something in the fog. A pile of yellow clay—and in it something moves, something rummages, as they say here.

A cap with a visor pressed onto a colorless head tightly as a skullcap; a soiled doublet; an apron covering the figure from the waist down; shoes, hands, a spade. The stove fitter's boy works the clay to be used for tiles. Every minute he pours water onto the thin mass and shifts the sticky mud around. His movements are frog-like, quick, fluttering. He wades in the yellowish, miry loam, each leg quickly jerking itself out and submerging again, jerking itself out and submerging again. His boots are soaked, covered with sticky lumps.

In my lodging, the housekeeper ordered that the fire be lit. It is warm and snug here, but the breath of autumn squeezes in through the crevices in the windows. Fog, more and more dense, does not fall away but crowds in from all directions, clings to the walls, creeps, spreads out, shrinks, and slides through space like drifting mud.

Is this fog? The heart groans with suffocating fear. It seems to me that something deceptive has taken the form of fog—that something is scrutinizing the earth, the human habitation, peering into the window, trying to see the terrified hearts.

It's death.

A figure is moving in the gateway, a mass with a human shape. The first streetlight has been lit and a yellow glow spreads through the reddish twilight. It reaches a pile of clay and bursts onto the silhouette of the little stove fitter's boy.

And I'm lighting a candle quickly, as quickly as I can, and I'm trying to read. In vain. The swishing of the spade and the rattling of the bucket reverberate in me like an echo in a stony hollow. I hear the child's every step, I feel every movement he makes in his wet rags. It seems to me that long ago, long ago, I saw a day like this, that I even experienced these very feelings. That is what I think as I look into the bruised, soggy world, absorbed and digested by darkness. I don't know when my thoughts flow into harmonious words, in reverent sounds that embody all this:

> Don't waken them until the darkness changes
> Accursed dusk where eyes of saints are blind
> Don't waken them in the autumn night of sorrow
> In the moldering chill where cold locks spirits' wings.
> Today the fruits of toil, crops full of blood
> From sodden fields have now engulfed the chanters
> Don't waken them with prayers and with singing…

Where do I know those words from? Whose words are they?

And just there, in those damp waves of mist, the small, stooped, ragged figure of my beloved old teacher, Marian Bohusz, moves and vanishes. The wind tugs at it and the cunning cold closes in on it; cold, the last messenger of earth, which is the habitation of cutthroats. In my thoughts I run after him over trackless wastes, lonely, unpeopled places, where patient death waits for the unfortunate. I search for him, I pursue him over river banks, in currents and depths of wet loam, in dried reeds among the rushes and carp—wherever that pit of death is in which the tenderest heart, such a heart as was never seen or heard of, was extinguished, burned out by perpetual feelings.

In the shadow of pain.

And there, from the twilight that envelops the world, in the tears that spill into my eyes, his face appears. Half-blind eyes look at me, the bold, frenzied eyes of the sage. They stream with tears, tears that roll down the faded face and etch long, bloody furrows on the cheeks.

Eternal rest.

DECEMBER 4TH

After a very long absence, I visited Miss Helena yesterday. These are not meetings at teatime, but late in the evening. My deep gratitude to dear Miss Helena dates from the times when no one, no one here knew me. She helped me find teaching work and did it with no thought of gain, which is worth remembering. At her receptions, to be sure, I do not feel in my element. Perhaps it is because I go out for enjoyment only after a day's teaching and I forget many of the fine points of drawing room behavior. And perhaps it is because the literary people or artists who gather there are too great.

The main contingent comprises the "immortal youth" of the current season. I must confess that I am not enamored either of fashionable books of the season or of "immortal youth."

Yesterday, as I went up the stairs to Miss Helena's flat, I was overcome by genuine cowardice. At the moment when I had to enter the drawing room, where a certain number of people (note: men) were gathered, I felt quite unprepared. I had forgotten a thousand things that would have helped me appear to advantage. It was a true case of stage fright. It is clear from this that the company of men has its charms for me. I admit that I like it very much, but the men must be sensitive, understanding, and not pedants who will treat my thoughts and words disrespectfully. All men are interested in young women, and I would not be truthful if I denied that it is pleasant, oh, very pleasant, to be the object of attention. If I go in with the goal (unconscious) of drawing such attention, I always find so many flaws and deficiencies in my appearance that I have an urge to turn and run for shame.

Miss Helena's drawing room is as it was some time ago: lovely big palms, sofa and chairs in the style of a Japanese house. Dimmed light as formerly. Various distinguished personalities in their places on the sofas. Everything centered on our celebrities. My entrance was not noticed and there was no pause in the conversation, which was very lively. The deplorable "woman question" again. Poet Br. was discussing it with the aid of triumphant aphorisms. For him, that question "does not exist." Who prohibits a woman from doing whatever she likes? She wants to learn, she learns. She wants to be active like a man, she is free to do that as well. For his part, Poet Br. makes bold to assert that women ought to exercise their rights, but predominantly in the sphere of ethics. To perfect the soul, to place the soul beyond the brute strength of a man to apprehend or surpass. What good is it if a woman becomes a lawyer, a medical doctor, or a professor of mathematics, if a strange longing for something beyond her grasp wrenches her from one of these professions, even when it is the authentic profession for her (as in the case of the Russian mathematician Sofja Kovalevskaja, whose interests in political philosophy and writing sometimes interfered with her career)? According to him, women striving for what is called emancipation deprive themselves of one of their real strengths—charm—when they do away with their graceful lack of awareness about things in the world.

For Poet Br. there is something brutal about a woman who has no question to ask a man. At the close of his disquisition he posed a truly difficult question to the female world: Is it possible to say confidently that women who gain absolute freedom will not use it as badly as men do today? After all, there is a mass of bad women, and as psychiatry tells us, the deranged behavior of women exhibits far more radical evil than that of men. The poet agreed, when he was pressed to the wall, that that is precisely the aggregated result of the actions of the world, but he "did not believe" that it was possible to change that ratio by the means that women attempt to use.

From my corner under a palm I dared to speak up, weakly, of course, and not in my usual voice, but tremulously (let that be attributed to my alarm in the presence of so many lyricists, playwrights, novelists, and "esthetes"). With that humble organ I stammered out a few sentences. Seizing on the speaker's last expression of doubt, I said that it was not at all possible to share that doubt if one believed in the beneficial action of culture on the human soul. A young woman who has finished university can be as evil as an uneducated woman, but the moral actions of the first must of necessity be better than those of the latter, and the surrounding world will be altogether better off. As higher culture spreads, differences created by the inferiority of the female mind and the lack of effort to develop it are erased. If there is a void in a woman's soul that striving toward some light could fill, it is natural that in that void the fruits of anger, stupidity, and faulty education will grow. That is why the statistics in hospitals are so catastrophic for women.

As for the statement that an emancipationist who has nothing to ask a man about is "brutal," I admitted that today there is still no such woman. Simply because of her lesser physical strength she can't win in competition with a man, even if she has before her a road free of obstacles and traps. If ignorance not only "does not commit sin," but apart from that confers "charm," then in spite of every effort, a woman will be "quite charmingly" more ignorant than a man for a long time yet. Today in any case it is not at all a matter of becoming the equal of men, but of being not so far behind them in everything, even in hospitals for the mad. Finally I dared to throw in a little dart, as if as witness that governesses are in fact inferior to poets of the masculine gender. I said that it may be quite charming to need care, but at just the time when there is no care, no care at all in the whole world, a woman feels that there is not one whit of charm in needing it.

I made these statements in this gathering.

As I was returning to my room, I thought of all this again and felt a certain uneasiness—not just slight but considerable uneasiness. Will liberated women not abuse freedom as men do today? The contemporary lot of women is certainly a consequence of their moral state. If it were a matter of struggle and victory, one would have to say that when men have the right to do as they see fit, that same right should extend to women. But indeed the point is not to win a battle, but to bring about a good. Incidentally, my conscience so easily shudders when there is talk of these issues that it's obviously affected by the strength of superstition inherited from a line of female ancestors.

I don't know life. A few times I've read things that make the hair stand on end and the body tremble as if one had malaria (Guy de Maupassant, Ovid). Walking along the streets, I often come upon some sight that not only terrifies but dumbfounds me, while hundreds of people move past it as they move past streetlights or signs. There exist some evils unknown to me, things full of cruelty and shame, in which women take part. Who taught them such monstrosities? Or did they themselves find all this in their own souls? That's why I'm frightened by Poet Br.'s opinion that women could abuse freedom.

Does that mean that one must throw up one's hands? No, never! Whoever is guilty of the terrible sins humanity commits, one must lift oneself from the dirt. Both men and women must do that.

December 5th

Yesterday I mentioned Ovid. I don't know myself why it came into my head to read him again.

Among her mountain of sentimental romances, Guepe has two lovely old books from the last century, published in London and entitled *The Love Books of Ovid*. In the second volume are the witty, charming, and decadent "Elegies of Love," and the prettiest of them, which begins with the words "the most charming bird in the world, my glorious parrot."

I translate it for myself this way, in my inept language:

"Parrot, the voluble visitor from India—is dead! Gather for his last rites, pious birds. Follow his remains as a throng of mourners. Beat your breasts with your wings. Tear your cheeks with your claws; snatch, for lack of hair, the tousled feathers from your heads. Instead of funeral trumpets, let your enchanting songs ring out. Philomel-Nightingale, forget the crime of Tereus, who cut out your tongue. Long years should have eased your sorrow. The fate of Itys-Pheasant was tragic, that is certain, but, after all, it was so long ago! Weep, all winged creatures who steer your flight into the crystalline air, but above all, despair, Turtledove, companion of the dead. Yes, O Parrot! What Pylades was to Orestes, Turtledove was to you. But what did your faithfulness and the beautiful color of your wings profit you? And what of this—that at once you pleased a most beautiful woman when I brought you to her as a gift of love?"

There is a strange freedom in this—life itself is portrayed as contemplative, not purposeful, but even and bright. Ovid himself accuses himself of being "a poet with his own lightmindedness." It is clear from other works that he has terrible dark recesses of pain, but escapes

from them to his beautiful, spoiled, wicked women with amazing eyes
and hair the color of "cedar from the dewy valleys of sloping Ida."
He loves one string on his lyre that rings through so many ages and
for so many generations. It is lovely and so strange. Just next to this
exquisite sadness, which we can feel as vividly as if it were our own, are
incomprehensible pages, terrible in their inhuman cynicism, such as,
for example, the monstrous elegy number thirty-eight. One gasps on
reading it, as if death itself had snatched one's breath. Unfortunately,
there is marvelous poetry in hideousness—poetry that flies from those
ancient pages like the fragrance of strong perfume, or roses picked a
thousand years ago that garlanded the poet's temples.

December 7th

Tired. Tired. It's late at night. Snow mixed with rain weeps outside the
window, rumbles in the gutters like a pauper's lament, and glazes the
stones in the yard, which are lit by the wavering glow of the lantern.
In spite of themselves, the eyes are fixed on faintly flashing puddles
that tremble with the falling drops.

I must confess secretly that I am far different than before. There is
certainly some nervous fatigue. My nerves…I trusted their stability so
much, like the strength of the leather traces drawing the large carriage
when it drove down toward Głogi.

And now, after each surge of emotion—pounding of the heart after
strenuous work—headache, heaviness alternating with distraction,
mechanical responses. How poorly I sleep! And after a sleepless night
I have a continually irregular heartbeat, a sensation like sand in my
eyes, a ringing in my ears, pain in my throat—and some sort of detest-
able anxiety. Though in a given day I have a clean conscience, though
I have tried with all my might not to stain it, I am not happy or free
in my mind. I run to my lessons like a driven thing. I conduct them
like an idiot. When, for example, I solve a problem in arithmetic with
Anusia, I only understand the first words of each thought clearly. The
rest I chatter out like a barrel organ playing its melody. Immediately
after pronouncing a sentence, I hear the meaning in my head as if
it were someone else's phrase that a discussion with another person
was keeping me from understanding properly. There is no strength in
my nerves. Poor, tired, and numbed, they have no rest. Every obstacle

becomes onerous for them, and I really want to cry when a chance for recreation comes and there is no desire for it.

But the hardest thing of all is returning home from lessons. My legs move as if they were swollen. Shoes that are wet, as they were today, are troublesome and heavy; my mud-spattered dress does not look like real clothing or part of an ensemble, only a horrid rag. Ah, clothing that reaches the ground! Certainly it is pleasing, beautiful, and perfect, but only for ladies who never walk on the muddy streets, only ride in carriages. For us who must roam around the swamps of poor neighborhoods, it is genuine torture. It is unsightly to tuck the skirt up higher (impossible in any event, for ten men will begin to peep), and the hands go numb holding it, minding it—as one must or be spattered and wear a pile of dirt. In one hand I carry an umbrella, books, and notebooks, and in the other I must eternally be nursing the train of my skirt, and in this way I hurry along the sidewalks. Modesty allows decolletage—uncovering the bare arms and bosom— but forbids showing the world the legs above the ankle even in thick stockings and high shoes. I wonder if in the moment when fashion dictates that we fasten the tail of a kangaroo behind us, we will do it as piously as we do now, wearing skirts with trains.

Today as I ran to the Lipeckis' on the fourth floor, wet, muddy, and steaming like a tired post horse, I heard music halfway up the winding stone stairs. Someone was playing very proficiently behind the third door. I stopped for a moment, first to hear what was being played, and then for some other reason; to this moment I do not know what. Harmonious tones instead of painful questions began to flow all around me, began to look at me like great blue eyes full of tears. They had compassion on me like good, beloved brothers, and saw in me something worthy of sympathy—some unwished-for changes, evidently, for they sobbed with grief.

But then they began to smile in my heart—to call me as if with affectionate names, and so strangely, in such an unearthly way as I will never hear in this world. It was as if I were enveloped from head to foot by spring, a spring I spent long ago, years ago in Głogi when my mother and father were still alive. With my closed eyes I saw a path to a slope under a large pear tree, with buttercups among spring water all around, and long streaks of viburnum, blackberry, and wild hop. I saw water glistening beyond the sluice, and rushes like green wands.

Silver fences near the very top wound toward the sun, and perch with
dark stripes thrust their sharp backs out of the cold current. A wooden
figure of St. John stood among the dikes by the pond and the black
alders with twisted trunks.

I cannot write…

December 9th

When a person moves about in the world for years, continually coming in contact with new people, she takes on an uncanny discernment
about human beings—not only at the level of thought, but even with
the swifter perception of the eye. I manage to sense what a person is
like far better and with more certainty than I would if I took to long,
systematic study, to conscious observation (though I never abandon
that). Sometimes I'm still deluded by the worldly game of friendly
smiles, often so well played, but the error only persists for a moment
before an unpleasant internal sensation quickly warns me. At such
times I wait patiently, and life, that trustworthy friend, brings a confirmation of my instinct. It's happened that way so many times!

Apart from that intuition, I have a few other means of getting at
the truth. Note: I do not provide information to satisfy curiosity and I
do not answer spiteful remarks. I simply do not condescend to notice
certain smiles, words, allusions.

Well-bred people quickly reach the conclusion that I'm numb as a
post, an exceptionally dull creature. Then the truth emerges

Have I ever had an inclination for such inquiries before? I don't
think so. Life, like flint striking sparks, brings out all things in us.
There is none of my former naive humility in this—not a bit! Rather
there is some untoward pride. I often think that I'm more distant from
people in my heart. Where am I going—to some phantoms seen in my
sleep, to some pure, heroic shadows? They are my real companions.

The world we live in, the world that surrounds us, is half intelligent, half barbaric, and chiefly cunning. In it, cleverness serves malice, and malice is practiced for its own sake. The point is always to
assert someone's inferiority, and the more so the harder that inferiority
is to discover. Women, our angels stoking the home fires, practice this
trick masterfully!

We are all so advanced in the art of prattle at the expense of those close to us that when a man first approaches a strange woman he must be asking himself: what sort of animal is this? In this empty life, dissimulation reigns supreme. Lying not only is not condemned, it does not even arouse instinctive disgust. Everything evil is tolerated with moral neutrality. In the most egregious cases, sophistry helps to give things an unreal appearance, or people simply pretend not to know facts that have actually been discussed in great detail. It is in this atmosphere that the upbringing of innocent children in the home breathes like a flower.

Even if we had an inborn love of lies, we would have to destroy it for the harm it does. But in our moral striving, we are stung as if with a lash by the continual awareness that there are people living beside us who simply have no longing for a moral world, who are not at all disheartened by seeing abuses. The suffering of single individuals who feel this longing seems a stray sentiment, irrelevant, unconnected to anything, like a peculiar quality either obsolete or premature. Can these feelings really be so lonely? They will perish like grain among thorns in the divine parable.

How many times have I tried to fan the flame of a love of truth in the soul of one pupil or another! To blow on the dying coal of the wonderful power that brings a person so much happiness! How many times have I met with resistance entrenched in a wall of derision! My mission arouses mockery. Then I always feel lonely and abandoned. It was the same today.

Maniusia Lipecka is what is called a brain. She really does have some fine capabilities, but they certainly run in one direction. Here is what she devised: when Grandpa Hieronim came over, Maniusia asked him on the quiet for forty pennies for "sealing stamps." When Uncle Zygmunt dropped in—the same. With Aunt Tekla—the same. Meanwhile the little trickster had no intention of buying stamps. She stashed the money she collected in her piggy bank. When I suggested reining in this knack for amassing money at the age of eight, her mother resisted with wide eyes. According to her, this behavior was a sign that the girl will be clever and thrifty.

Our feelings cannot sleep. They must find expression in actions. I am developing a deep aversion to what passes for morality in the upper stories of middle-class homes. The stamp of hypocrisy pressed out by society's poohbahs suffices for everything there. Every single woman would tremble at the very idea that she could be negatively branded. Could I myself boast that I do not care a whit about what Mrs. Lipecka, Mrs. Blum, or any other mother busy with the systematic spoiling of her children under the pretext of education is whispering? By no means! I can't ignore them all. I should say not! But I know you, God's little beasts! I know that if the resistance of your children to the ethics I try to teach them hurts and worries me, it's not because the lot of you were wise and good.

December 10th

A letter from Wacław. Here is what he writes:

"The road was tiring and oppressive, and to make it worse, my tooth hurt. It didn't give me a moment's peace for nine days. Actually it was not the road itself that wearied me so, but staying overnight in wooden cabins. It's impossible to know what to do with yourself. You can't go out for very long, since a minus fifty-degree frost is no joke. It's difficult to read, and there's the state of continual waiting, the fear that the reindeer will run away and we will have to stay in this hole for several days. All this spurs us to hurry. The reindeer have run away several times, but Jaś and I managed to herd them together fast enough. During the entire journey I haven't lost one day. '*Nulle dies sine linea*'; you see how fine it is to know Latin. '*Linea*' in these parts means about thirty miles, thirty miles a day. The reindeer are good everywhere, the road with slight exceptions passable, so we dash along at seven or eight miles an hour.

"Sometimes the overnight cabins are awful! I had read and heard so much about them, but the reality greatly exceeds the ideas one forms. They are huge, low buildings without floors, without reinforcements, with smoking chimneys, with chinks in the walls; in a word, like me: all flaws and no merits. At first glance they have a poetic look, especially when fire lights up the walls covered with white frost and icicles, and something like a thousand vanishing diamonds begin to sparkle. But aesthetic satisfaction gives way to disenchantment when that dream of beauty begins to drip onto the traveler's nose and clothes. At night in the cabins I never undress; rather I dress warmly, which is not especially pleasant. And as long as the fire burns, it is so "hawt," as the Lithuanian women say, that you can't find a place to hide, while at the same time your legs and back are freezing. Sometimes, instead of the cabins, we manage to spend the night in a yurt, but these 'furnished rooms' are not without their drawbacks. A dozen or more people of male, female, and indeterminate gender nest in a small yurt with dogs and calves, in direct proximity to the animals. Add to that the smell of rotting fish and one has to hop out nimbly to catch a breath.

"In the morning we're off again. The endurance of the reindeer—amazing! You have to see them (though I don't advise it) pulling the weight of the loaded sleds when they are tearing toward a steep mountain crag or dashing over muddy patches of grass barely, just barely, covered with snow. We hurtle through the mud! The skis jump and tremble over the tufts of grass like a boat on water in a blowing wind. The night is dark; we can only see a low white plain. The drivers shout to urge the animals into a faster run. Behind me I hear something like the wheezing of a locomotive, and every little while the benign face of a deer with antlers appears from the left or the right, shaggy with hoarfrost, steaming, tongue hanging out like a dog's. When the frost is strongest, the deer stop panting and close their mouths.

"When we're moving, we have to lean continually first to one side and then to the other to keep our balance. If we lose it, we have to hit the ground with our feet. We drive into forests, we dart over hills, then we slide into valleys again at a mad pace. Deer run like the wind and the skis fly until it takes your breath away. At the bottom of a downgrade the front skis slow down while all the next ones slam into each other and bounce in all directions. In the valley there are clumps of grass again, and again that hopping of the skis as if on choppy waves. Because we're forced to this constant gymnastic exercise, we're warm, but our legs are cold, and in the insane rush over tufts of grass in the dark there is no way of getting heat to them.

"At last a column of sparks appears in the distance. A yurt! We greet it as joyfully as sailors greeting a lighthouse. After some minutes we settle into warmth, we eat and drink like Homer's heroes, and soon afterward to sleep, to sleep! Well, and so it has been every day for three months and two days. My camera, glass, tools—I have carried them all with me safely, which surprises me extremely. They are going to send me film, paper, and everything in general from Yakutsk. How is it there with you, my sweet girl, my dear sister…"

DECEMBER 15

For some time I've been looking and longing for the sight of joy. I try to find cheerful books. It would give me great pleasure to see someone's life full of happiness. I have around me either impoverished, unhealthy existences or struggles against overwhelming adversity. At every step it's possible to meet people who are pleased with themselves, but nowhere does one see cheerful people. There is contentment where needs are small, but nowhere, it seems, is there the happiness from which cheerfulness springs. A human being is created for joy! Suffering must be fought and eliminated, like typhoid and smallpox.

DECEMBER 24

I came back from Christmas midnight mass. We were all there: Miss Helena, Iza, and my tots. Frost. Snowflakes glittered and crunched under our feet. From my window I see only silver roofs. Rows of enchanted palaces stood in a poor neighborhood.

The moon is shining.

The telephone wires are covered with frost. They are white, like cords of thick cotton that a very, very old grandmother rolls into balls. There is something strange about this clear night and its purity. An inexpressible grace lies on the walls washed with moonlight.

In this quiet, surely all struggles with weariness have stopped, and the iron fist of violence has grown feeble with remorse. If at this moment a bandit wanted to bury his stiletto in his victim's chest, his hand would weaken. For now angels descend from heaven to earth and take the sighs of wronged people to their immaculate hearts.

Someone will pray now.

In a manger, lowlier than a poor worker's baby, lies the One of whom Isaiah said, "He will strike the earth with the rod of His mouth." Perhaps His kingdom has already begun, perhaps "the year of the Lord's grace" is already coming. May souls suffering for the good of many be strong, Lord, may they find respite!

December 26

Holidays! I sleep, relax, and pay visits. I have collected a stack of books and, beginning tomorrow, will throw myself into heavy reading. Guepe has gone away for a week.

For lack of space, the S. family's Christmas tree has been brought to our apartment. At night I have the pleasant smell of spruce. Ah, to ride sledges through the snowy forest that shines with icicles on a winter evening, when shingles crackle on roofs! What is it like there now?

Empty fields. Not a murmur, not a rustle. The moon moves above vast space. Here and there a wild pear stands lonely and ragged amid the snow, casting its bluish shadow.

January 7th

Wacław is dead.

I had a message from that lady a week ago.

March 23rd

As I browsed through the bits and pieces in the drawer of my little table, I found this tiny note. I opened it and my eyes fell on words written two months ago as if the note were something new! Such coldness and indifference together. Is this about my misfortune? Where is the sense of it? I don't feel it. The words are hollow and only have a form, a shell that uses the language of grief that everyone knows.

Long ago, when I was still at home, my late father showed me wheat in Głogi that was infected with smut. We were walking at dawn along a little stream called Kamienny, beside a field under a mountain. Father tore off an ear and pulled out a grain. It looked exactly like a grain; the outside was the same color. But if you touched it with a finger, powdery specks of black fungus flew out of the golden hull. My feelings are like that. There is none of the good bread of sisterly affection in them, only powdery smut.

MARCH 25TH

There is something I would like to describe here. I begin to feel a need to disclose it in order to exorcise it from the depths of my soul. I am so numb. I have no feelings, not even agitation.

I am like the pool of Siloam when the angel has flown away. I feel that something in my soul, some power that was in it long ago, has died, and what remains is worthless to me. It's cold and cowardly. I can do nothing new in the world. There are still good creatures who value what remains of me, but can I myself endorse the idea of giving any value to something that's like a miserable rag left from what had been a garment?

There was a time when I thought that I was altogether shattered. Now I see that it is not so. Only my personal happiness is broken.

I want to rebuild in myself the strength of life. I challenge myself with the memory of Miss L. I set about working with all my might. But that's all. That's all.

I constantly feel that someone has prompted me about what I need to do, taught me what I need to do, tried with all her soul to help me, and I, like a boor, do not trust her. Often this or that friend comes to me and talks about her hardships. At such times I am happy enough to listen, but happy in a way akin to contempt. I look at another person's tears and think to myself how fortunate she is to be able to cry like that.

I say nothing.

I know one wise word of which Wacław knew nothing. The word: Be hard.

He would have killed me with a look if I had said that one must love life itself above everything.

MARCH 26TH

Often these days I don't know what's good and what's bad. It seems that I don't do anything "bad," but I'm not certain that such conduct has any value. At times I feel that a "good" deed would be something quite different. Of course, my understanding of things hasn't changed, but no commonplace sayings can have any effect on me.

MARCH 27TH

Of what use is suffering? Is it possible to believe that such anguish is a normal, ordinary necessity? For whom? When long days are full of it, it becomes an incomprehensible enigma for the mind, a mysterious torment, the meaning of which, inexpressibly grave, hidden but imperious, hovers over one's head like a mystical bird.

Black, sinister raven of misery!

MARCH 29TH

I had a long moment of introspection out on some open land. Muddy clumps of grass, barely covered with snow. It's very unpleasant for me.

APRIL 2ND

I don't know what's happening to me. There is some feeling, the strongest and most acute sadness yet. Longing... sadness without any subject, goal, or thought. Ah, no—there is a wretched, fleeting, helpless scrap of thought. This bit of thought holds in itself the certitude that what caused my sadness is the most important, the most precious thing, the only thing of value. It's strange: with the help of that tiny atom of thought one divines the true content of life, sees great spaces, vast, distant worlds of which our healthy everyday common sense knows nothing.

Longing. Longing. The feeling one is least able to articulate, a state void of all consolation, a constant, monotonous pressure at the heart.

Yet it is itself longed for, because it gives rise to an anxious desire to feel that misery again. The wintry coldness I experienced was not a good state. Now I begin to recall all those cold feelings as if they were iron tools that are coming apart.

Long ago, perhaps eight years ago, Henryk and I walked one time through our birch grove. He had a revolver in his pocket. Wanting to show off for me, he took out the gun, aimed and shot. The bullet hit a young birch at an angle. A stream of sap gushed from the wound for so long, so long that I couldn't bear it and fled from the forest, When I reached the edge and turned my head, the stream could still be seen oozing over the white bark. The sun looked at itself in that sap and sparkled as it does in a squalid puddle on a road over which calves wade.

April 3rd

I don't know myself what I want. I long, or rather I wither from long-ing. I would like to go, to run away. I am like a very sick person who does not know herself what hurts her most. She feels unwell and she does not have the strength to move. Anyway, if she were able, the change of position might be bad for her.

April 5th

I think that if I could listen to a little good music, I might still be unhappy, but not at my wits' end. Tears are stronger than the will. That's why I suffer and can't manage to change anything in myself. Everything remains as it was, the same purposes, the same duties. I understand that, but still I have no strength. I can't accuse myself of a lack of resolutions; I have so many of them on my lips! There is only some small thing, some very small thing missing.

April 6th

I get up in the morning, I go to my lessons, I carry on with everything as I should—and I laugh at all of it. It has no more value than feeding the wind. I have no desire for anything. I ask myself what I might want, and always, without saying so, I find that I wish only for one thing: not to be.

That thought thrusts itself forward with no transition from a past frame of mind. Tears flow and that wish is in them.

April 7th

With Antosia L. I'm working my way through literature...Greek. I'm conversant with as much of it as I heard of from Wacław. I read everything he had read from that time, and even absorbed a great

deal of Greek language and history. At present I am reading the trag-
edies of Aeschylus, Sophocles, and Euripides in the translations by Z.
Węclewski and K. Kaszewski.

Who would have thought that on the pages of these works one
could meet one's own pain—that in those times there were sisters who
were forbidden to bury their brothers?

My pupil read in a steady voice Aeschylus's *Seven Against Thebes*.
Here is what Antigone says there:

> *Strong are the bonds of blood that unite me*
> *With my unhappy mother and my dear father.*
> *So bear patiently, my heart, the injury under which*
> *he writhed, and sacrifice your life for the dead*
> *from sisterly love. No ravening wolves*
> *will rend his body. That will never happen!*
> *For with my own hand I will dig a grave*
> *and do him that last service, though a woman.*
> *In my full linen robe I will carry him out*
> *and bury him myself. No one shall stop me!*
> *A person of courage will devise a way to do this.*

Mad girl! No, no! Away with such models! I am of sound mind, my
ideal—that obedient Ismene, who respected the edict of Creon. I will
not go to dig a grave for Polynieces.

April 11th

A holiday. I won't go out today. I am so broken and in so bad a state
that I might have been sitting in a dark, airless dungeon. Fits of weeping come over me lately. When I cannot snivel during lessons, I choke
back the tears and carry them from place to place. During the holiday,
when Guepe goes out and no one sees me, I indulge in this inexpen-
sive diversion for hours at a time.

April 20th

Today, coming back from the lessons, I took an unaccustomed road:
Jerozolimskie Avenue. It was warm and somehow the air was clear and
full of light. Far beyond the Vistula, blue forests spread before the eye.

And look! My heart began to pound and take fright for no reason, like a poor, stupid child. I avoid weeping because if I sob during the day, I will surely not sleep at night, and then the next horrible nightmares come right away, one after another. Oh, those phantoms in the night! I should have torn my eyes away, but I could not. There was no way on earth.

I will go away from this city! I don't want to. I will tear myself away from myself, from my thoughts, my resolutions, my work, obligations, everything.

Earth never seeded by man! Open land, empty, untilled ground! Tall trees humming blithely in the forest!

The Vistula railroad goes that way, toward our old home. Nothing can cause such a transport of joy as this mindless fact. If only I can drag my soul along until June, I will wash her in the snowy waters of my own countryside.

MAY 13TH

A warm, clear evening. The moonlight spreads illusory silvery-gray figures on the stones of my courtyard in a magical design. The old, dirty, polluted alley is changed, unlike itself, as if it were dreaming. Tonight even poor, unfortunate people rouse themselves and turn their eyes to the bright stars that remind them of long-extinguished feelings.

What strength these sights ought to pour into our hearts—into the hearts of young creatures who do not pull the heavy carts of an unkind fate, into the hearts of those who value their souls above everything, who are capable of loving very deeply and have not yet sold out the strengths flowing from pure hearts or the valor that throws down the gauntlet to all wickedness!

JUNE 4TH

I'm writing these words with a rusty pen in a hotel in Kielce. (Here in Kielce, as far back as human memory can reach, there have always been rusty pens for the convenience of travelers.)

What an upheaval! I'm here in my own friendly town. Yesterday I discontinued all lessons, I rejected two invitations for holidays, to the

Lipeckis and to that Madam Niewadzka from Cisy. My packed-up odds and ends I entrusted to Guepe who is staying in Warsaw through the summer, and I, burdened only with thirty rubles and a little sack, left *toute suite*. I don't care what happens to my physical being. I only know that I will be at Krawczyska, at Mama's and Papa's grave, and in Głogi… and the rest makes no difference to me! I will certainly go to Mękarzyce, to my uncle's family, the Krzewińskis. Perhaps I will stay there all summer, or perhaps only a few hours. It makes no difference to me (as I wrote above!).

Just now it is not I who control things, but gusts of emotion— Lelum-Polelum, the ancient wind gods. They carry me where they want, like horses given their head. For a long time I had confined them in an iron stable, and every day I slammed the gate, beating my fingers against a slab of granite. Now let them run as they will. I would have traveled immediately, but it was raining buckets.

Bad, ugly Kielce! What I see outside the window, instead of the blue I yearned for, is a new cluster of clouds and streams of rain. But never mind! I must explain how it was.

I arrived at night, or about four in the morning, and found the street number with difficulty. So it is; in the city of Kielce, Miss Joanna has no one.

Home fires die away quickly and the fragrant smoke of the family shelter blows away in the sharp wind. The human nest endures as long as a spider's. In my mind I sift through persons here who certainly still live between Karczówka and Pocieszka, but I find no one who would look me in the eye with brotherly understanding if I were to relate the history of my grief, of the dirge-like sadness that was like the shadow of death. I cannot think of anyone—how can I say it?—with eyes that see deeply. They are all goodnatured people whose dull hearts do not penetrate beyond their family walls. God love them! I have already learned to move among people with no warmth for me as among monuments in a cemetery. But never mind!

My avenue toward Karczówka! The distant view of the mountains that I dreamed of for years in Warsaw!

Six o'clock strikes in the bell tower of the cathedral. Greetings, sweet, booming sound of the clock! How you frightened me at one time, with what profound alarm I listened to you when I first came from Głogi to school! And see... but away with memories! I must not think of things long past or crying fits will start.

It's quiet. Only rain chatters in the drainpipes, and from time to time a city vehicle rattles by.

This day in Mękarzyce.

I'm here at my uncle's. It's very late; what blessed silence! I'm spending the night alone on the "other side," in the old room, the "little room." I'm happy. Oh, how happy I am! I walk quietly on my toes in this empty room with old household bric-a-brac that remembers the dead, and I revel in the consciousness that it is not an illusion. Here, in Mękarzyce! I stayed with my deceased mother in these low rooms when I was three and four years old. A ceiling with two beams, a little crooked; walls whitewashed with lime that had fallen away here and there, revealing dry, hard larch wood. A window sheltered by clumps of dahlia, mallow and lilac, the varnish washed from its frame by rain. The latches, old latches in strange shapes, decoratively forged by some disciple of the Biblical craftsman Tubalcain, covered with a layer of rust so thick that it made truly beautiful things from the iron. When I think very hard, I seem to I see in my sleep the man who nailed in those bolts. He was a young blacksmith.

I was about four years old then. Everything here, the scorched windowpanes, the door, the walls, the furniture, the old lithographs, has something moving about it. All these things exist, unchanging, through decades, in the same places. They endure the effects of the changing seasons and become like indispensable elements of nature in this place. Each of these objects has its own history and simply belongs to the family. The old house is warped, it leans, it is a bit out of plumb, but fundamentally it remains the same as years ago. It is a family home, with a field, an orchard, trees and flowers. Someday, perhaps, it will crumble into dust and perish from the face of the earth, just as a human being does.

The dogs are barking. Lured by the light in the windows of the room, which are usually dark in the evening, they settle just outside the panes and yelp ferociously.

But to the point. Every written work must be composed point by point. First the introduction. And so: Today I went out of Kielce before noon. The rain subsided a little, though it didn't stop. It sowed its wet chaff, sometimes only sending down a coarser grain. I hired a cab for four rubles (four rubles!) and off I went! My driver tied up the tails of his skinny jades, wrapped his legs comfortably in a saddle cloth, and drove the carriage, which moved with an extraordinary clatter, out of the city.

When we got onto the highway, our dear old highway, scarred with potholes, watery mud began to fly up from under the wheels and could not be stopped by the vents of the cab, which were clanging like janissary music. A torn apron helpfully covered me as it could. Soon a lake of water formed on that friendly object and ran from place to place like quicksilver.

I was tired, drowsy, and even happier than I am now. My attention, or rather my smile wandering in space, was focused now and then on two lanterns that served, I believe, as decorations for the vehicle. When all is said and done, their broken glass and missing tops left them nothing except that honor. One of those vestigial components of the four-wheeled vehicle was attached to the main iron bar with twine that was soaking wet. The hulking figure of the driver, in a blue hooded coat tinged by rain, came between me and the world, and a lone yellow button on the back of the coat, which bore the image of a coat of arms, drew my eye. All visible space was sprinkled with fine raindrops. Far off, the outlines of hills could be seen in the misty dark gray air. Their shapes, as I saw them vanish one after another in the fog, to me were true expressions of grief. As soon as they came within my line of sight, I felt that they were hurting me.

So the heart of that little girl of long ago tightened as she was being driven away to school and said goodbye with her eyes to these beloved hills.

The cab jumped from pothole to pothole, staggering every moment like a person with a syphilitic spine who conceals his defect so as not to lose his employment. It slid around turnings as if in moments of despair it wanted to throw itself suicidally into the ditch. A village appeared, with cottages as gray as its fields, though their walls had been whitewashed at one time.

Willows with thick trunks sporting pale, abundant young branches; wild pear trees in fields, as wild as in those times. Where the ground tilted downward, a river ran through a valley. The river flows from my village, from Głogi. We drove down from the hill onto a long bridge.

The drenched horses walked one foot after the other, steaming. I leaned out and my eye lighted on clean water trickling over stones and coarse sand, water that flows around my parents' house. A barrier. The carriage stopped. We had to pay a few pennies. I searched for them in my pocket—no, I searched with all my senses for the sound of that river, which down there below was speaking to me with its splashing.

We moved slowly uphill again. Beside us walked stooped people, splashed with mud, covered with hair that can only be called shaggy. They were chatting about something to each other, yelling in an ugly way and quarreling. I recognized one face, that of our man, Wicek Michcik. He was the same as in the time of my childhood except that he had aged a little. The horses moved on, and in the clank of iron, the rattle of the wheels, I heard words read not long ago in the Bible. Clearly a secret thought lived in me as if written with a steel burin on lead: "There will be no remembrance of the wise or of the fool forever, for the days will come when everything will be forgotten, and as the wise man dies, so also does the fool."

That cynical bit of wisdom from an arrogant king who understood "all matters under the sun" brought me no pain. Rather it was like a perfect truth that harmonized with everything, as a liquid quickly fills every point eager for satiation. Everything in me was soothed, quieted down, seemed to lie down to sleep. I snuggled into a corner of the carriage and relegated to memory the somber words that had come to me without my knowing why.

From the hill the view opened out to level ground. Far, far away I saw the trees of Mękarzyce. Then again a quiet joy began to burn in me, a joy which has not left me yet. I knew that I would not find what I was looking for, but the view of the sleepy woods, the long, wide, empty spaces overgrown with small juniper, poured warmth through my veins. There was the forest, alien and unwelcoming, in which I had never been, but in the other direction there were the avenues of Mękarzyce, enveloped in mist and seeming to be interwoven with it.

Then it occurred to me that I hadn't notified anyone—that I actually didn't know if my uncle's family were living here. Perhaps they had moved away. Perhaps they had died. I hadn't written them for so many years! I began to count. It was more than ten years since I had been here.

Toward evening my cab went off the main road and into a lane between a double row of poplars. I saw old, broken buildings, the house settling into the ground, fences broken.

I went into the familiar hall: no one. I opened the first door a little and jumped like a three-year-old: the faithful old piano, the picture of Prince Józef above it. But of course!

And now as I write these sentences I feel that I'm a stranger here, alien, alone. What of it? The rustle of the old poplars, which terrified me so many times when Mama and I were leaving here late at night—after struggling to reach this place, I was hearing it again. Was there a tenderer voice on earth?

JUNE 5TH

A day and a short evening have gone by. I've been in the stable, in the cowshed, in the workers' quarters, in the field, in the meadow. I don't know what this really is—if it's an illusory calm—but I feel very good. I have no urge to cry. I even have an (unpleasant) aversion to rushes of emotion.

Wacław's story quite wearies me. On the day of his death he passed it on to me like a legacy. Under the hard law of inheritance he imposed futile winter months on me, tearful days and sleepless nights crammed with spiritual labor as sterile as speculating on the causes of things, and as stern, compulsory, and necessary to life as breathing. Now I scarcely understand that that happened to me. It's passed like a flood in the mountains. Only scattered hunks of stone and slime hanging on bushes indicate how far the destruction reached.

Yes, no doubt: God created the village, the devil created the city—the bourgeois devil. People living in the country are so healthy and so openhearted in their health that they appear to me as living stories that defy belief. And I come of just such people!

Today at five or six in the morning my dear uncle began shouting at someone from the porch. I jumped up in my nightclothes and ran out like a madwoman, thinking that there was a fire or that we had been attacked by bandits. It became apparent that uncle was haranguing someone in front of the stable. Nothing more.

Perhaps it is improper and ignoble to characterize impartially people with whom one is staying (and family to boot), but I can't control my astonishment. Are those really Aunt Valeria, Uncle Hipolit and their daughter, my cousin Tecia? I knew these people, but they are completely different. No! I was different. I saw them with the eyes of long ago, eyes formed by this place. Now there's not a trace of the girl I was, but they are certainly the same. Not much changes here. Years accumulate, backs stoop, hair grows gray, the house settles, and apart from that, everything is as it was in the old days. If Grandpa Józef were to rise from his coffin, he would find few things that were strange to him.

And me—what has happened to me? From just the creature I was, rooted in my home ground, came a runner dashing everywhere after lessons—something in the nature of a butterfly having emerged from a cocoon (if I may use such an elevated metaphor). In conversations that went on all day today with Aunt Valeria and Tecia, I seemed to be undergoing an examination on the subject of my life. I recalled vividly not only both these kinswomen but, in rich detail, myself.

I must be presenting much more material for astonishment to them than they are to me. That, at least, is how I like to explain their indifference to me. Not that they are cold on the surface. We kiss each other and weep often enough, but there is no heart or even pity in it. When my aunt kisses me, her tears flow because she thinks of her other, younger daughter who married an engineer and lives at the foot of the Ural Mountains. Tecia broods about herself, compares my free life with her heavy, confining family responsibilities, and cries for herself. Uncle does not think of crying, since that is not his idea of a useful capability ("sobbing is women's business"). On the other hand, he speculates about what I'm doing in these parts and constantly familiarizes me with his business difficulties, moaning about the poor winter crop, interest rates, dry spells, flatworms, hoof and mouth disease. He expects, poor man, that any minute I will burst out with an oration about my need for a loan of money. He would sigh his heart out with relief if he knew that I want only air, earth, and water.

Yes, this world is altogether strange to me. These people are conscious of nothing in the world apart from Mękarzyce and have no views except on what affects them financially. My old aunt and uncle are occupied with nothing beyond the bounds of their folwark. The light of their lives is Felcia, now Madam Balwińska; the dark side is Tecia, who has not married and who—I hope I err in my prediction!—will be an old maid. This family's horizon is so tightly closed that I cannot find myself on it at all, even this moment as I sit here. My whole life would be strongly suspect if they were not so indifferent to it. I read that in their eyes when I tell them everything frankly and they listen with smiles that pass for sympathy.

Wacław's story!

In essence we are strangers to each other.

I hear long, detailed paeans about how attractive Felcia was to that engineer at a ball in Kielce, how he courted her, the proposal, the wedding, the departure, the birth of a child. In these family sagas Felcia is a heroine. Everything happened to her. She fulfilled all expectations.

Tecia is the disappointment. She has still not been "pleasing" to anyone and if she was ever courted, there is no point in talking about it, for nothing came of it.

In her parents' thoughts and feelings, her very name evokes worries: "those several thousands" in dowry, and "trousseau." My good aunt interrogates me: What do I think? Is it better to give more in cash or invest more in the trousseau? What do I think? "For in the wider world you have more opportunity to observe these things than we do in the village. With us here, some think one thing and some another. In this place the prevailing custom dictates that for the trousseau one does not give this or that." Aunt thinks that it is better to invest such and such an amount in silver, because "silver lasts for life." She voiced this maxim with such feeling! I was adamantly in favor of silver.

Poor Tecia sits in Mękarzyce and waits. All her being calls to mind the foot of a Chinese girl, molded in a wooden form from childhood. She smiles, speaks, recounts things, jokes and cries after the pattern set by my aunt and uncle. Uncle has a habit of describing certain things that are foreign to him as "foolishness!" or, more mildly, "surely some foolishness!" or, in the best case, "there never was the like!" or, without pointing a finger, perhaps out of politeness, the same expression: "there never used to be such foolishness."

Tecia uses the same turns of phrase. Sometimes, when I say something that sounds odd for Mękarzyce, she quickly scrutinizes her parents' faces and smiles as they do. I'm not speaking of thoughts and opinions. All these opinions are the same as they were decades ago, when Aunt Valeria was a girl and studied in Ibramowice. Tecia, though she is alive today, is, properly speaking, a young woman from the times of Klementyna Tańska Hoffman. The world has moved forward a hundred miles since then, and its progress has brought both good and evil. In Tecia's room, which adjoins aunt's and uncle's room and is farsightedly protected, there are some books. They are bibliographic landmarks, so-called "good books." Moralistic books for young people by Klementyna Tańska Hoffman, of course, and piles of translations from English. Among all this goodness lies, oh, horrors! the erotic *Poems* by none other than Kazimierz Przerwa-Tetmajer himself.

Where did this come from? It came by accident, borrowed from some neighbors as "something to read." It was also read, I suspect, in the face of family disapproval.

But isn't Tecia's situation better than mine? Oh, it is certainly better here.

A family home, quiet surroundings, people to take care of one, the peaceful atmosphere that I sighed for in Warsaw! Excitement doesn't penetrate the wall of boredom here, but neither does pain. Here Ovid doesn't fall into one's hand nor evil speech into one's ear, and the sharp hook of deceitful thought and the rawness of images of life don't wound. There is such silence here. If a voice from the world drifts in, it's like the echo of lively conversation carried on behind three walls.

But, dear Tecia, if it were up to me to choose your lot, even at my parents' side, I would not. Never! I am a human being.

A hunk of dry bread, but my own! A future without wealth, but formed by my own hand! On both sides of my stony, solitary path the modern world unfolds like ripening grain in fields the eye has never surveyed. My heart and mind feed on the culture of the living world, a culture in which the element of good increases from day to day.

And I am nourished by that growth and rejoice in it, where it flows in the veins of humanity "like blood," in Mickiewicz's phrase, "through its deep, invisible passages."

June 6th

Today I traveled to the grave of my father and mother at Krawczyska. I walked from the highway over a wide ridge between fields. There were no ruts there, only heavily trodden paths. Beside it, on the right and the left, dark, steel-colored rye with new brown ears was swaying. Far off on the plain I could see huge trees and a white wall. That was the place.

The cemetery was filled with graves, so its boundaries had been widened without removing the old walls. A part of a wide mound at the entrance was surrounded with very roughly hewn timbers, and yellowed graves were arranged peasant-style in a row next to the fence, by the spruce tree.

The gate to the old cemetery was closed. No one came in there, neither the living nor the dead. It was a place dedicated to those who had been sleeping in the Lord for many years. The shingles in the little roof that had covered the old walls in days gone by had decayed and fallen off. Only exposed, rotted beams that had supported the roof shone like bones in the sun. Here and there a solitary shingle nail with an iron head gleamed, protruding with no purpose.

I moved the gates, which were joined together by the bolt, now yellowed from rust, of the big lock. They glided apart quietly, with no resistance, no grating; so might the gates of paradise open before souls. I went into that sacred ground. Luxuriant, dark grass was covered with dew. There were poppies and clover blossoms of lovely red; I stepped on them with every move. None of the graves could be identified. Not one! Here and there the ground had sunk. I felt in my heart that unfortunate people must be lying in such low places. In one spot a great wooden cross had fallen to the ground and crumbled into powder. The blood-red print in the shape of a cross lay there in the thick, succulent grass as if burned with a firebrand.

My parents' graves were not marked at all. I didn't know where they were. I looked around for them, then I walked all around the cemetery. Not a trace! I looked for the bush that I remembered from the time that Mama was laid beside it. In vain.

Spreading clumps of pale birch, which my father loved so, appeared as whole thickets and streaks of white. Perhaps they gleamed, handsome and fragrant, at the head of his resting place.

They all sleep here together, farmer by farmer, the people who plowed this land, sown themselves today with flowers, like a meadow. Humble—they inherited their places in this burying ground.

Birds were singing high and low. Now and then wings of warm wind carried the rustling sound of young grain, bent the branches of bushes, and quietly passed over grass untouched by anyone's foot, like an angelic caretaker painstakingly preserving the hallowed silence. Green plants bowed under its transparent feet. A slender acacia, with a tall, straight trunk and slender black branches that seemed to fly toward the sky, rustled with alarm more eloquently than the other trees; its translucent leaves swayed in the bright sunlight. The consecrated tree seemed to be saying something. I thought I would hear its melodious phrases. Listening deeply, one becomes aware that it only sighs perpetually.

In the depths of my soul, I begged that someday I might meet...

JUNE 7

Tomorrow I leave. So at least I've decided. I can't deal with this! The comforting experience that marked the beginning of my stay has given way to internal irritation and quarrels that I wouldn't have had for all the treasure in the world. The attitude toward the villagers, the servants, the workers on this farm! Perhaps it's because of the laughable idealizations of a city woman—that may well be the case—but I can't bear this backwardness. I can't breathe in this atmosphere.

"You should try living among these rascals!" says my uncle. "There, at your place, it's easy to manage everything, sitting at a table with a book in your hand."

I will not be living among rascals, and I will escape. This is my only success, that I can go away when I like and to where I like.

My grandfather Józef's farm workers experienced just such a state of emancipation in the time of the Warsaw Duchy, when shackles were removed from their feet, but together with their boots. I, too, removed shackles from my feet together with my shoes, that is a fact of history, but I can also go freely from place to place, like the peasants of that time. Where will I go tomorrow? Weep with happiness, my heart: to Głogi.

JUNE 10

Kielce again, in a hotel. My expedition is over because my money has run out. "I return to Lebanon, to my home," wrote the poet Słowacki. Głogi, Krawczyska, and Mękarzyce are behind me. I am altogether well and calm.

It only remains to relate in order how everything happened. I escaped from Mękarzyce on the ninth in a farm cart, very early in the morning. The previous day I had ordered, in the village, a pair of mares and a wagon loaded with straw. It may have been an affront to my aunt and uncle, but it was not my intention to hurt them, only to avoid being obligated by their hospitality and to be free to do as I liked. Once I hinted during a conversation that I wanted to be in Głogi, and they stared at me as if I had announced to all the world something that offended human feeling.

"What for?" cried three voices at once. "Why, a Jew lives in your house now, Lejbuś Korybut."

The cemetery at Krawczyska—that was understandable, but the thought of a trip to Głogi, where Korybut lived, was treated as something simply silly, and from the farm-stable-Mękarzyce viewpoint even impossible, since it would take the team of grays. Tecia asked me with that smile that was so like her parents' what I was thinking of doing there.

"You will go to that Głogi," she said. "Well, and what will you do there? Where will you stay, with Jews living in the manor?"

In short, if I had left Mękarzyce with horses and a carriage, I would have drawn everyone's attention to myself. So I decided to use a ruse. When the cart drove up in front of the porch, I only said I was going to Kielce, and without delay. Under this pretense I apologized as sweetly as I could for my departure. I gave and received family kisses, which are used in designated (very great) proportions and unnecessarily, in the same way, for example, as honorifics in letters. I left.

Outside the village, when we had almost reached the highway to Kielce, I interrogated my driver about what he was willing to do.

"Take me to Głogi first," I said, "and only after that to the city."

The farmer stopped the horses on the road and began to consider. He muttered something about hay, fodder for the horses, a wasted day, and having to go four miles out of his way. Finally he declared that I must pay him an extra five rubles. Of course, I agreed. If the unthinking man had demanded ten and my wraps and my suitcase to boot, I would have assented.

Very soon we turned, and moving along through pastures, bypassing Stróżów, we went upward. It was perhaps six in the morning. The day was made to order: warm, only hazy with bright, delicate strands of the night clouds that still lay drowsily on the lowlands at the edge of the woods, like spider web. I sank into an illusory lethargy. My heart was more watchful than ever, but its elation was overlain by the silence of our mountains and forests.

My wagon slowly reached the pass and we found ourselves in ruts left from an old road, now overgrown with grass, that was marked "Up." Hazel and birch grew there, almost into the forest. The farmer cracked the whip, we passed a ravine with loamy soil near the summit, and—look! Far away below us, I could see Głogi. From the meadows, from the river, from the pond, mists rose and vanished in the highlands. The white walls of our house gleamed amid the greenery of the garden and seemed to see themselves in the depths of the water.

The young horses, unaccustomed to the roads in these parts, could not keep the wagon steady. The swingletree bumped against their legs, so we dashed full tilt from the steep side of the mountain through the juniper and stopped short at a stream. Only then did the horses pull their little heads out of their collars, which the taut traces were pressing against their ears.

The driver stopped and I got out. I showed him the road he should take to the other side of Głogi, to the tavern by the highway to Kielce.

"I'll be there at noon," I said.

The farmer looked at me out of the corner of his eye, but was reassured when he noticed that my suitcase remained in the cart. When he finally drove away, I walked along the path. The grass had not yet been cut. I was surrounded by my flowers, which were overgrown. I walked in happiness that was like a cloud. Those flowers, which I knew by their fragrance before I saw them, could be seen from the meadow: pale lavender wood anemones, my born sisters, the dearest to me. I did not pick any. I only stood over them, kissing them with my eyes. They asked me why I had left that country, why I did not live in my family's village. But in a pasture by my path, I saw something unfamiliar: a large creeping willow bush. It stood alone.

"I don't know you," I said to it. But at that very moment the curtains of my memory parted. It was he!

A poor stray dog had wandered to our kitchen on the day I was born. No one knew where he was from or what his name was. The day he came, he was given something to eat, like a guest. From that moment he stayed around the yard. We nicknamed him Bandit. He was a well-behaved, good-natured, faithful dog. Mama liked him; my brothers and I were very fond of him. When we returned home after holidays, the first thing we heard from a distance was always his bark-ing. When we went away, he looked at us regretfully.

By the time I was fourteen, he was so old that he never moved from his place. He was gray all over, and deaf, and had stopped barking. He lay in the sun and looked around with sad, senile, sleepy eyes. When anyone came near him, he still wagged his tail, raised his head, and smiled like a human being.

One day at dawn we heard him whining. I ran to the window and saw the marksman Gązwa in the pasture. Bandit was tied to a stone about a dozen steps from him, pulling and tugging. A flash from the gun, blue smoke—then a boom.

Bandit barked once. Twice.

When Wacław, Henryk, and I ran over moaning, Gązwa was gone. Bandit lay dead. One of his front paws was still twitching. He went cold in my hands.

We dug a hole there. On the old dog's grave we planted a branch of willow.

This tree is Bandit. His warm blood is in those shoots. I drew near and touched him. He was covered with a layer of white dewdrops like an air plant, or a white vestment. Perhaps the trunk of the black bush would give a joyful bark or the moribund leaves would move. No. Only cold, heavy, silent drops fell onto my hands.

I walked through the meadows to the spring. The old pear tree under the crag and the slope in the distance were exactly as I remem-bered them, and even the rocks over which one walks.

It was the same with the spurts and bubbles of water that hopped from the spring, blossoming on the surface like perpetual roses that live in summer and winter. I sat by the spring and the world faded from my sight. Birds sang in the thickets, where streams glistened as they flowed over little beds running from the slope. A sandy path crossed them not far away.

Above the spring glowed a red mass of centaury, which mama and I used to pick in this very place. She used a preparation made from the plant as a remedy for headache. Hardly thinking what I was doing, I put my hand down and plucked a few of those resistant flowers, but immediately, as if they were punishing me for their deaths, I was seized with a terrible feeling. It seemed that I was tasting the bitterness of centaury and that drops of it were trickling to my heart.

I walked away. A low ridge leading to the manor stretched before me. New groves of trees had sprung up. Everything was different, changed. Only the sparks flaming on the ripples of the pond and the slick stalks of the rushes were the same, and the fragrance of sweet flag and the moist smell of willow. The yellow and white water lilies smiled at me from their broad leaves and infused my heart with the wine of joy.

I noticed that the great alders by the water had been cut down and that there was no St. John's wort. A deluge, I saw, had brought down the floodgate, for it had been replaced by a sluice to let out excess water. Now nothing was trickling out at all, and I was also struck by the absence of the melodious hum that had lasted as long as my childhood happiness. All of that was gone, like the water that used to flow there—was irrecoverable, like a drop that leaks into the sea and is dissolved.

The old black mill beyond the ridge had also dissolved, into greenery. The larch over the road had grown out still more. Two pussy willows beside the workers' quarters were utterly decayed and only a pair of green stems grew out of their dying trunks.

I stopped in front of our home.

What devastation! Fences, flower beds, paths—all obliterated without a trace. Even the wild grapevine by the porch torn out, the porch itself demolished, the paint peeled off the walls, the windows broken. I went into the hall and pushed ajar the door of the large room in which both my parents had died. It was full of Jewish odds and ends. In one corner stood a bed heaped with eiderdown comforters.

I ran out as fast as I could.

None of the adults saw me right away. Only a little Jewish boy probably six years old crawled out from somewhere and blocked my way. When I stopped in the yard, about ten people suddenly crowded around me. They walked along with me, asking me who I was and what I wanted. I said something to them. One elderly man stepped along beside me, looking me over and asking questions. I passed the courtyard and the linden trees and made my way toward Bukowa. The old man, who wore a satin coat, kept walking and speaking without a pause. I plodded along, unable to say anything. At last he stopped. He scrutinized my every step from a distance, and his children peeked out from behind the bushes.

My soul was wrapped in gloom, my heart was chilled, and I could feel nothing. Only a fierce, painful, vengeful thought illuminated the spot like lightning. The place was the same, but everything had passed with time, flowed away with the water. Only the impassive ground had been left alone and was persistently green, as in ages past. Nothing that had been my father's, my mother's, mine, or my brothers' had survived. The place that had been permeated with the work, thoughts and feelings of all of us had been taken over by someone else.

In the home where my parents had made their last moans, which for me was the holy of holies, strange people were chattering. Trees that had lived as sacred, mysterious symbols of matters hidden from mortal eyes through years when I was longing for home; roads with ruts of yellow sand, which like golden cords drew me to this country amid the tears and twilight of winter nights; my meadows, and the sheen of water in the bends of rivers among the alder trees: a newcomer falls heir to all of it! All those treasures of my soul only represent paltry profits.

And that newcomer, like us, will pass away and go down with his huckster's brain into the land, which devours everything. At that moment I saw the true face of that land! I saw it smile toward the eternal sun, and in that smile there seemed to be a jeering parody of my love for it, like a cynical confession that it had never seen me, that it did not know who I was at all.

It is not the land I loved. It does not respond to the love of the human heart. And when the soul struggles toward it with all its might, it reveals in a dreamy glow some transcendent goal which it is not in the power of a human being to achieve.

Suddenly I stopped beside a ravine, in a quiet corner between fields. Strength I had not known I had came to me.

I was so close to my parents that I could almost hear them, almost touch them with my hands. It seemed that they were behind me— that if I were to turn around and go in through the gate, I would see them under the linden trees. I had not felt the grace of such closeness even in Krawczyska.

It was quiet. The feeling persisted for a little while.

Only after that did I feel with all my heart the terrible execution that death carries out. Where are they? What have they become? Where have they gone from this place?

All my body trembled to the depths of my heart. I crumbled into dust before death, begging to be worthy to possess the secret.

Where is my father? Where is my mother? Where is Wacław?

Then again I heard in myself the words I had heard on the way to Mękarzyce: "For that which befalleth the sons of men befalleth beasts; even one thing befalleth them: as the one dieth, so dieth the other; yea, they have all one breath; so that a man hath no preeminence above a beast: for all is vanity."

And again, like an inexpressible pain, I whispered with lips stiff from terror the verse of the wise man of God: "Who knoweth if the spirit of man goeth upward, and the spirit of the beast goeth downward to the earth? All go unto one place; all are of the dust."

I had no strength. In dull despair I dragged myself into the undergrowth on the hill. I went in among the birches and wandered around, seeing and hearing nothing. I don't recall when and I don't know where I fell to the ground. A deep wish for death came over me. I felt only that wish, and it was the last beat of my heart.

It lasted for a long time.

But then my mother came to me from the deep earth in the cemetery in Krawczyska. She forced her way through the earth, through the loam, the sand, the bedrock. In that moment I was not lying on dead, fallow ground. I felt that I was in my mother's embrace, on her beating heart. Deep, earthy, quiet emotions infused me. My words can't express what happened. Death took fright and went away. Grief and tears stopped.

Oh, the bright flowers of my valley!

VOLUME TWO

· CHAPTER I ·

Large-hearted Provincial Ideas

D R. JUDYM had a great deal of work during the season. He got up early, the more eagerly because before six o'clock his room under a metal roof—the room for which he had left the splendid salons of the city in June, bringing his *lares* and *penates*—was simply sweltering in the heat. He made notes at the weather station, looked over the rooms where the bath attendants administered hydropathic treatments, checked to be sure things were in order at the bathhouses and the springs, and before eight o'clock was in his hospital.

At ten he was sitting in his office, receiving a certain category of the sick (predominantly the young chronically ill) until one. After the midday dinner he occupied himself with entertainments for the ladies, with organizing amateur theatricals, walks, foot races, and so on, as well as the keeping of all sorts of records. He was obliged to treat such diversions as part of his work whether they suited his inclinations or not. All this engulfed him like a new element.

He was surrounded by swarms of young women who were edgy, idle, insistent in their desires for new sensations. Without quite knowing when, Judym became a young fop, stylishly turned out and spouting cheerful cliches. The interesting, amusing, pleasant and subtly demeaning life of a little health resort, where a temporary population from every end of the country and every sphere of society came together and was concentrated into something like one family, made him absolutely giddy. Suddenly he found himself spending time in the company of wealthy women and being initiated, not merely as witness but as arbiter, into their most closely kept secrets. He was sought out and even competed for by the inner circle—and sometimes, with an inward chuckle, he was called on to make decisions about something he called tone and taste.

Once in a while, when he returned to his room late at night from some sparkling entertainment, he reflected on the glamor of life, on the new forms of it that he was coming to know. When he thought of the microcosm that was Cisy, it seemed that he was reading a romantic novel from the end of the last century, full of sensuous indulgence, portraying a life worth nothing but nonetheless possessing a certain charm. The power of the senses, artfully concealed in pleasing forms, becomes something unfamiliar to the everyday, commonplace nature. There were moments when he was captivated by the eloquence of discreet silence, flowers with symbolic meanings, colors, music, words that continually shied away from something.

The people from the manor now and then attended balls and other gatherings, and at those times the queen's scepter passed to Natalia. When she appeared in a bright dress, she was so dazzlingly beautiful that everyone alive would have died for her. No doubt she sensed that collective madness, which spread widely among the men because of her regal eyes, but she did not condescend to see it. She was always cold, indifferent, as if detached from life. Sometimes she took greater pleasure than usual in the entertainments and smiled alluringly, but as soon as she noticed that one or another man interpreted her passing humor in a manner favorable to himself, she dashed his hopes with one glance or a smile of another sort.

So it was with Judym.

Emboldened by his success with the other ladies, Dr. Tomasz confidently approached Natalia. During one gathering she singled him out several times, chatted gaily with him, and of her own accord mentioned Paris and the outing to Versailles. Judym's head was in a whirl. His feelings reached such a pitch that in a moment of recklessness he decided to mount an all-out offensive. During the next contradance he began to speak of Karbowski, who had not been in Cisy for a few weeks. Natalia concurred when he said that Karbowski did not seem a very agreeable person, and greeted his words with quick nods and discreet exclamations.

A lighthearted flirtation lasted for quite a while. Then the doctor drew closer and, encouraged by his apparent success, wanted to take things further and change the subject from Karbowski to himself. But he was stopped dead with fear, for he saw such a flash of haughtiness in her eyes as he had never seen before. It seemed to him that that imperious look from her narrowed eyes, that expression that insulted him in cold blood, stabbed him, plucked him to pieces—tore him to shreds, as the claws of an eagle quarter its living prey. The words he wanted to say rolled up and stuck in his throat like a fistful of flax.

Pale, with clenched teeth, he sat as if he were shackled, unable to leave or stay.

All these circumstances got in the way of the doctor's concentration on matters concerning the hospital. It was as if two currents were racing each other in his life that summer. The more one of them dashed forward and headed off the other, the more the latter exerted its force. The doctor felt something inside himself continually hindering his efforts with the sick. He strove against it by working very hard, but the more passionate his efforts at the hospital, the more helplessly he succumbed to the world of amusement when he was once more in contact with it. Yet with all this, things were well with him. He lived without stint and had no idea what it was to have second thoughts, to be bored, to feel depression.

The hospital had been built very near where he was living. It had been there for several years, erected by the idealist Niewadzki, but after his death it had been used in unintended ways. When he felt the need, the administrator of the estate deposited beets, randomly discarded barrel staves from the distillery, broken parts from the threshing machine, and other items in the hospital rooms. At other times attendants, the administrator, the bursar, the estate steward, and other functionaries borrowed beds for their guests, and dishes and utensils were stolen in impeccably careful Slavic style. Often a homeless mother-to-be on whom someone had taken pity lay there during her confinement, or a farm hand ill with colic, or a child with smallpox.

Dr. Węglichowski was in charge of the hospital. It would be false to assert that the director approved of the storing of heaps of scrap metal there. Indeed, it must be admitted that once in a while he burst his sides laughing at it. But neither could it be said that he was deeply engaged with the sick. When someone was feeling very poorly and was put in the hospital to "locate the infection," Węglichowski sometimes arrived and scribbled a prescription. In most cases the medicine even helped.

Often the rector, the young ladies or Madam Niewadzka found some sickly individual and the happy patient was packed off to the hospital. If he was a favorite of the priest's, a plate of broth with noodles would be brought from the rectory, or a dish with a boiled chicken leg. If the young ladies from the manor were his caretakers, he ate the most delicious remnants from the serving dish, often to the detriment of his health.

In the wider picture, that hospital building, standing off to itself but amid farm buildings that served to generate profits in known ways, represented on a modest scale the fate of a noble idea in a material world. It stood abandoned, powerless, timid, sad, as if with folded arms. Dr. Tomasz felt a passion too deep to stifle every time he was near it. When he looked at the hospital in its present state, then thought of the man who had established it for a certain purpose—the man who had thought long and hard of how it should be built—he felt such a rage as if that unknown dead person were lashing him with words of contempt. And that was not all.

As soon as he had arranged a receiving area for his patients in the first well-lit room, an avalanche of Jewish folk, old men, world travelers, indigent people, consumptives, and cancer victims came crashing down on his shoulders—in a word, all the weeping, woebegone dregs of a smelly Polish town and no less smelly Polish villages. The doctor sorted through this material and took it under his care. Some patients had to be taken into the hospital for a while, so he had to put it in order, and he did it by force.

He paid agents to search out all the beds that had been dragged away, and no pleas prevented his taking them back. The story of his acquisition of new mattresses, quilts, sheets, and pillows could fill an oversized book. The most beautiful and distinguished female guests at the spa mounted an amateur theatrical to pay for two bathtubs and water heaters. All the furnishings for the office, the pharmacy, the kitchen, and other departments he captured from various people. From one he wheedled six plates, from another he coaxed knives, forks, spoons. He forced one person to buy glasses; he won a bet with another for a length of percale for the hospital linen.

Madam Niewadzka took an interest in the young doctor's efforts and even wept and thanked him "in the name of the departed." But she herself was so powerfully influenced by the general manager Worszewicz, who had no patience with the vagaries of the peevish farm people, that she could do nothing much on her own account.

All the same, at her request the ground on which the hospital stood was encircled with a sturdy new fence, and the gardener was ordered to maintain the orchard around the building with the utmost care. That was Judym's first important gain, since from that time he was king of the consecrated terrain surrounded by the fence. No one, neither worker nor passerby, was allowed to carry anything out or even set foot inside. The wrought iron doors were tightly shut and equipped with a bell.

The second important gain was Madam Wajsman. She was a widow whose departed husband had had a little money, but at this time she had none. Madam Wajsman accepted the position of supervisor of the hospital at a salary of four hundred rubles (which was paid, quite simply, from the "silent cashbox" with pedantic regularity and in the deepest secrecy by Les, through the mediation of Judym) together with housing, light, and fuel, all provided by the manor.

The third fundamental issue was the provision of food for the patients. In this matter Judym proceeded as if he were Machiavelli. He worked on the general manager with the help of female guests primed for the effort. He resorted to abject flattery; he tempted the man with promises. He put him into the hands of the three young ladies from the manor, and he gained his point. The general manager agreed to supply the hospital the year round with specified quantities of potatoes, flour, buckwheat groats, milk, butter, vegetables, fruit, and other foods, and signed with his own hand a contract cunningly drafted by Judym. The resort was unable, at least in a certain measure, to refuse its help. Finally the rector, the vendor who supplied meat to the manor and the resort, and certain wealthy townsmen, coerced by the doctor and the rector, made commitments to supply the necessary provisions in kind to the hospital.

In this way, by the middle of the summer, the hospital was revived and full of ailing people, coughing, groaning, and wheezing to the doctor's delight. In the garden, old, wizened women, children with greenish skin shivering in the sweats of malaria, various "silly" Jewish ladies, and all sorts of doubtful characters "who neither plow nor sow" warmed themselves in the sun. There was not a week in which the doctor did not perform an operation. He removed cysts and sores, he drilled, he pierced, he cut things out, he cut things off, he stuck things together. His worst problem was the lack of assistants and the extreme scarcity of instruments and dressings.

Madam Wajsman could not bear the sight of blood (especially peasant blood and, dreadful to relate! Jewish blood). She loathed vagrants and in general despised people of low class. At every step the doctor had to watch her and force her to hide her contempt for farm workers.

The management of the resort watched the young physician's activities out of the corner of its eye, so to speak. It could not be said that anyone opposed him or thought badly of what he was doing, but neither could it be said that anyone shared his desire to set the hospital on a better footing than ever before. Dr. Węglichowski treated all his measures with the same irony as the pilfering of its beds by the attendants. If Dr. Judym demanded active help of a material kind, Dr. Węglichowski agreed, groaning, and doled out, of course, as little as possible. When the hospital was full to overflowing, the director was not happy, though he did not allow anyone to see—or Judym to feel—his displeasure. Yet he joked about the "chief of the wards" in an indulgent but exaggerated style.

From time to time he went to the hospital and supervised its operations as he had in the past. He stepped into the rooms with his hat on and a cigar in his mouth, spoke loudly, asked questions, snorted irritably, reprimanded Madam Wajsman, shouted at the sick, and briefly examined this patient or that one, writing prescriptions in a wide hand or ordering Judym to give one medication to one patient and another to another.

The "chief of the wards" listened most obediently to these directives and followed each one in a way that allowed for no contradiction. His aim was to win Dr. Węglichowski over to the cause of the hospital, to draw him into its work, so he let pass the jokes and the prescriptions he disagreed with. Even if a "rascal" the director abruptly ordered off the hospital grounds was someone Judym knew, the young doctor forced himself to defer. Things went on that way until the end of August.

In the last days of that month, the number of guests began to decline. Carriages, carts, and the resort's omnibuses began carrying away a large group, or at least a family, every day. Dr Judym bankrupted himself buying farewell bouquets in which forgetmenots upstaged the other flowers. For the first time, a morning chill rose deep in the park, cold white dew spread over the lawns in the evenings, and here and there a yellow leaf wove itself into the treetops like the first gray hair on the head of a mature man.

A quiet sadness came over high-spirited circles of friends. Feelings of affection strenuously hidden came into the open. People who only then had a great deal to say to each other found the evil day of departure hanging over them.

Judym's heart was not touched. To him, passing "impressions" were like rain that soaks the earth, making it seem incapable of anything, and then endowing it with powers of creation. This passing shower quickly dried and Judym's soul became focused again, pushing him to redoubled work.

Early in September, when the rains came, a very large number of children in the farm hands' quarters fell ill with what was called the "fever."

Those quarters were located in the large, damp park that spread like a great cape over the slope of a hill from the top, where the manor stood, to the river that flowed through the meadows. There were sheepfolds, cowsheds, and housing for the farm workers. The general manager of the estate, a man of great energy and skill in the management of land, had turned the idly flowing water to use by creating several pools near the edge of the park, in a bog fed from underneath by a hidden spring. The water fell through neatly arranged pipes from one pool to the next.

The pools were set in ground with a high peat content. Loam thrown onto the banks and dikes softened in the sun and, when the time was right, served as fertilizer for the farm. The water flowed away from there into a long basin with ponds that spilled over into the park at the resort, greatly enhancing the look of the perennially acidic banks. A place so wet, with the dead water held back in these containment ponds, let off a heavy vapor that the sun could not dissolve.

It was just there, in the workers' quarters and in the village on the opposite side of the meadow, that the fever flourished. The children from there who were brought to Judym were shriveled and green, with lips as black as if they had been rubbed with coal, and eyes that did not see anything. Their periodic attacks of fever, their constant headaches, and their appearance as of dead souls in living bodies forced Judym to examine these cases at length. He concluded, sadly, that he was seeing victims of malaria. He took a tour of the low-lying areas on the quiet. He was convinced that many families had been touched by the devastating disease.

He saw that people who had lived in the village all their lives tolerated the infection better than the itinerant workers on the farm, who came from other places and fell victim in far greater numbers. Judym only took children who were very sick to the hospital, treated them with quinine, and kept them in the garden in the sun, dispatching them to various jobs and sending them little by little for schooling. But he could not take even a quarter of them. On the higher ground, and in the warmth, their conditions improved. Then, however, they had to return to their homes by the water.

Those homes, built many years before, were relatively sound. They had brick walls like the sheepfolds, barns, granaries, and other buildings on the grange. Housing those families in another place was out of the question, since the expense would have been very great. Their houses stood at the center of life on the farm.

The first time Judym casually asked the general manager if it might be possible to move the workers' quarters to a drier place, the man looked at him closely, as if the doctor had suddenly danced the cancan or turned a somersault in the presence of older, respectable people. Judym did not lose his presence of mind or lower his eyes. He waited a moment for the powerful agronomist to answer him, and when no answer was forthcoming, he said very courteously, "In those buildings there are large outbreaks of malaria. The pools that have been put there are a very important contributing factor."

His hearer's cheeks flushed and his eyes went bloodshot. The pools had been his pet project. He himself had designed them and stocked them with fish, and he derived considerable income from them for the estate. Throughout the year the fish were used in the clinic kitchen and sold for profit. They were an important item in the estate's books and with skillful management might become even more so. Apart from that, the pools produced other commodities: sludge and ice.

The general manager still said nothing, but his eyes flashed. He changed the subject with murderous politeness.

After having broached the subject that one time, Judym hardly saw the likelihood of an agreement or compromise. It would be necessary to bring pressure. In all matters relating to the management of the farm, Madam Niewadzka could only be approached via the general manager. The young women wrung their white hands but could do nothing to help.

The autumn came on. After rainy nights, something that was like mud in space hovered over the meadows and the lower park. Anyone who breathed it for very long felt headaches and a pulsing in the veins. Then, too, Judym noticed that in a building near the ponds the air was, if not exactly like that, very similar. Leaves flying down from enormous hornbeams and willows dropped into the basins of standing water and rotted there. Masses of algae frothed on the surface of the ponds, and when the algae was torn away and thrown on the bank, it spread a foul odor. Visitors who came to Cisy to recover from malaria were not cured, and two cases of the fever were even contracted there.

When Judym communicated his observations to Dr. Węglichowski, the older man scrutinized him as the general manager had done, though perhaps with a bit more humor. But the director declared with a certain tartness in his tone that there was no fever at all, and certainly not malaria.

"The main thing," he added, "is not to say anything at all about it."

He kissed Judym lightly on the forehead and clapped him on the shoulder with a friendly, brotherly hand. Judym was astonished, but said nothing to anyone.

In September, the receiving rooms at the hospital were full of children large and small. Languid, sleepy beings, hardly speaking, sat or lay wherever there was space. The rooms were stuffy and full of an indescribable lethargy. It seemed that there was a drunken school there where nothing was ever taught at all. The children glared at things blindly, with no expression in their eyes, with no impulse even to eat. If one of them was sent out, he crept mindlessly forward, cradling his head on his arm.

When a place came free, someone took it and closed his eyes, not to sleep, only to avoid looking at the world—to pull himself into himself like a snail into a shell and feel a warm relief. Girls with withered bodies and faces ravaged by the pain of headache sat motionless on the floor, wrapped in shawls and aprons, ready to endure whole days in the same position so as not to crawl through mud and rain. When the doctor came in, all eyes looked at him as if he were the autumn daylight. Once in a while, somewhere in the room, lips stretched into a smile.

This sentimental hospitality toward youngsters not bedridden was flagrantly contrary to the traditions of the hospital, and began to irritate people. The general manager said bluntly that it was leading to demoralization of the worst kind, and that he would not be responsible for it, was "washing his hands" of it. The truth was that Judym himself did not know what more to do. He was giving out quinine like flour, and getting results, but what it might ultimately accomplish he hardly knew. When sick children came to the hospital like sheep to the fold, he allowed them to sit and lie around, but when so-called "fathers" sent by the stewards and overseers pulled them out to work with their fists drumming on the backs of the young necks, he did not protest, because he lacked the authority.

So things stood when, one day, Dr. Judym received a note from Madam Niewadzka requesting him to come to the manor without delay. As soon as he arrived, he was led to a little room where the elderly lady usually passed her time. Both her granddaughters were there, and several other members of the family who as a matter of habit stayed at Cisy during the season. Judym had been in this room several times before, but the presence of such a large group sapped his self-confidence.

Madam Niewadzka extended her hand to him and directed him to sit beside her. "I have asked you here, doctor, to confer with me," she said.

"I'm happy to be of service."

"In the matter of those youngsters from the farm, there is no way, is that right?"

"None."

"Worszewicz doesn't want to hear your plans to move Cisy to another place—to the Świętokrzyskie Mountains, for instance?" she teased him gently.

"He doesn't even want to move a couple of barracks higher on the Cisowska mountain here, let alone the Świętokrzyskie Mountains," the doctor said in a tone that echoed hers.

"Hmm. That's not good! But Joanna has proposed a different scheme."

"Miss Podborska?"

"Yes, yes. She wanted to give up her room in the wing to house those with malaria, to relieve the hospital of them. Anyway, she has some ideas that I don't fully understand, but they are bright as a flame and tender as a morning glory and I have to give in. The place would have been in the passage, you see, doctor, beside the housekeeper's lodgings. Now we've arranged a surprise for her birthday in November. In the south end of the left outbuilding there is an old bakery, absolutely empty today. It's a very large room, it's dry, and it lets in a lot of light. I've asked Worszewicz to order that the rubbish be taken out of it, the walls whitewashed, the stove renovated, the windows caulked. Perhaps you would agree, doctor, to relocate the children there. Let it be heated in the winter, and reclaimed. This is for her, for Miss Podborska, for the tie that binds—"

"Would I agree! But—"

"Ah, well, thank God."

"These children don't need cures, only dry quarters here on the mountain. Where is Miss Joanna?"

"No, no, there is no need to tell her! This malaria ward will not open until November and then ceremonially, in her name. You see? She will deal with the motley crowd there. It's her project—under your medical supervision."

"Ah, yes," he whispered.

A feeling of distaste, even rebellion, rose in the gloomy recesses of his soul and then receded.

CHAPTER II

Old Men

D<small>R. WĘGLICHOWSKI</small>'s house stood on the hill overlooking the entire park and its environs. It belonged to Mr. Les. When Dr. Węglichowski decided to accept the duties of director, Mr. Les began immediately, under the supervision of a competent person whose services he requested, to build a "shack" for himself in Cisy, where, as he wrote, he desired to live out his life. It was a wooden villa, unpretentious and compact from outside but with a variety of amenities inside: alcoves, pantries and cellars, secret storage places, garrets, and more, so constructed that they made it a home of great value.

When the house was ready, Mr. Les in a madly multilingual letter requested that Dr. Węglichowski live in it so as to keep it safe from burglars, fire, and war. Węglichowski rejected the proposal. He had no intention of availing himself of a donated house (since that was Mr. Les's strategy, too crudely formulated for anyone not to see it). Then Les wrote a letter with yet more chaotic spelling in which he inveighed in Turkish against old comrades who considered a friend's home a strange house.

"There is no friendship of the old kind anymore!" he wrote. "You have converted everything to money, and since it is so, then pay, pay rent, as you would to a Jew or a Greek. For I am not a Jew or a Greek, and I don't intend to be a grifter in my old age, so I demand that you turn that rent over for the training of some ass from Cisy or near Cisy in a useful craft, in basketwork, weaving—something that he would go on developing in the area, I don't know what and I don't know how. After all, I am stupid in these matters, as, for the rest, I am in everything not directly related to haggling with Asians."

So Dr. Węglichowski willingly accepted. The rent was determined in collegial fashion and paid according to Dr Węglichowski's wish, first to the gardener, who was studying in Warsaw, and then to another farm worker.

Dr. Węglichowski's wife, Laura, was particularly pleased with the house. She was an exceptionally interesting person. She was well over fifty, but she carried herself elegantly. She darkened the gray strands of hair that slipped from under her black head coverings so strenuously and systematically that they took on a peculiar hue—the color of silted hay, which has dried out in the sun but cannot lose a deep greenish-black tint. The color in her cheeks was always as high, her eyes as lively, and her movements as nimble and forceful as long ago, when she was a girl of eighteen.

Madam Laura was slender and not tall. From the time of her residence in Cisy she had changed by degrees to a "lady of the house;" she devoted a great deal of time to pitting fruit, frying, baking, and boiling. Yet it cannot be said that she could not see the cosmos for the cooking pot. Indeed, Madam Laura liked to look at the wider life, and with a penetrating eye, which often led to excessively categorical solutions (between the roast and dessert) to complicated questions.

Her life abounded in details that could have filled a novel, or rather a travelog. Her youth and early years of married life had passed somewhat apart from the world, on rough roads, in commonplace work, in hard, heavy suffering. That way of life curbed Madam Laura's innate temperament and shaped it in a peculiar way. At first glance, the doctor's wife seemed a chatty woman, cool and decisive. She had no patience with excitement, sniveling, sensitivity, or mawkishness. More than once she fired off an opinion that was rather acerbic.

At bottom, however, she felt things more vividly than anyone around her. There were issues that instantly aroused strong emotion in her, and at such times she looked like a pussycat with its hair on end. She spoke briefly, tersely, like a leader giving orders to his squad of infantry, at the head of which, of course, stood Dr. Węglichowski. Whether he was henpecked will remain a secret until the end of time. In broad, general questions of principle he seemed to be second in command, while in matters of all sorts that required clever strategizing, he was the master who issued the orders.

The little world of Cisy gathered nearly every day at the home of Dr. and Mrs. Węglichowski: Listwa, Krzywosąd, the general manager Worszewicz, the priest, Judym, and several guests who were staying at the resort for long periods. In the summer, and particularly as the fall came on, there were games of Russian whist on the little veranda, which was shaded with wild grapevine. From the time Judym arrived in Cisy, he found that the regulars at these whist sessions shared not only friendship but accretions of thoughts and imaginings, enjoyments, and antipathies.

Some of these people liked each other mutually and without selfish motives. Madam Węglichowska liked Listwa, and he her. The young rector mocked these "amours" in an elegant way, while Krzywosąd jeered at them like a saddler. Madam Laura laughed often at the old bursar, but she was fond of him and defended him from harassment by his wife, by Dyzio, and by the whole world. Listwa returned this care with nothing short of adoration; his unwavering admiration refused to admit a word of criticism. Krzywosąd inserted himself between the Węglichowskis, kept close company with them, and, being aware of all their merits, errors, and eccentricities, did what was necessary to remain master of the field. He succeeded brilliantly; in him Dr. Węglichowski had a true right hand. Krzywosąd executed everything the director's way and foresaw his wishes four weeks in advance, but in exchange widened, step by step, the extent of his own power.

In spite of his keen mind, strength of will and firmness of character, Dr. Węglichowski often acquiesced to Krzywosąd, let him have his way, and even cloaked his actions in the aura of his own authority. The two of them complemented each other and created a strong, utterly indissoluble unit of power. Worszewicz enjoyed the society of these people, and they liked him. Day after day he sparred with Krzywosąd, who annoyed him with everything he said and did, but in spite of that he was quite fond of the versatile administrator. That circle formed a world of its own.

These were people of proven, unimpeachable integrity who had seen a great many things in their lives, so in that small locality it was seen as an honor to be among the whist players at gatherings of the directorate. Judym and the rector came into this group ex officio, so to speak, from the nature of their social positions. They were well received, of course, but they could not be part of the inner circle.

Judym could never get a real hearing, could never convince anyone of anything. They listened to him attentively, they agreed with his opinion or refuted it, but he knew very well that it was all just conversation. Between him and the group there was a barrier that could not be breached. He was always struck by the way these people looked at things in the present time, or rather the pattern into which they placed all current phenomena. It was as if contemporary life in Cisy, for the directors and their friends, was only a frame for events that had already happened. Everything that was or could be important lay in the past.

The people, events, conflicts, changes, joys, and sufferings of those long-ago times had a force of reality that overpowered new things. Everything contemporary was almost imperceptible to them, trivial, without value or influence, most often laughable. Judym, on the other hand, lived so intensely, throwing himself into the present moment and seizing it in his hands, that those bygone things only bored him. So he could find no path to these people.

At every step he felt that he must either take the management of the resort's affairs into his own hands or work together with them in such a way that they would think they were doing it. After several months had passed, he was convinced that only the latter was possible. The connection between the administrator and the director was so strong, and they so deliberately kept a tight grip on everything, that there could be no thought of doing anything in spite of them.

After the season ended, Krzywosąd repaired the pipes that took hot water to the bathtubs with his own hand, and when Judym called his attention to the fact that he should not have done that—that repairing the pipes was work for a professional or during the season a disaster in the form of burst pipes might result—Krzywosąd answered him with a few anecdotes and went on doing things his own way. When Judym turned to Dr. Węglichowski with the same advice, the director smiled and responded politely that that was Krzywosąd's territory—that in his devotion to Cisy, Krzywosąd went too far; that he worked with his own hands to save pennies for the institute; that he was, in short, a phenomenon. Moreover, he cited six examples of Krzywosąd's impeccable integrity. When Judym tried to make it clear that he did not doubt the nobility of Krzywosąd's character and had not said anything against it, but that, on the other hand, the pipes… the director repeated his statement and ended the conversation.

That process repeated itself perhaps ten times, and in the most varied circumstances. Each instance made it clear that there was no active way to influence the course of affairs in Cisy without being hand in glove with the administrator. At such times the young doctor thought of working with Krzywosąd and so gaining some mastery over him. In the autumn, when all the recreational activities had stopped, he set about doing all sorts of work. As Krzywosąd's deputy he organized the record books, which in Krzywosąd's scrawl were impossible to decipher. He cast an expert eye on matters involving the kitchen, the garden, the farm. He planted trees, rode to the court in town, built, remodeled, saw to all kinds of furniture resto- ration, and drafted contracts, among other things.

His zeal won not only Krzywosąd's approval but everyone's. People will- ingly delegated work to the doctor, who turned his hand to every job. For him, all this was a means of reaching a long-term goal: to dry the wetlands of Cisy, to do away with the pools, ponds, and retention basins and, against that background, to institute a series of cleverly considered reforms. From time to time, with very little ado, as if nothing were in the wind, he put out a feeler and assessed the situation to see if movement in a known direction were possible. But every time he had to pull back and return to the usual performance of tasks for Krzywosąd and Węglichowski.

As soon as it was noticed that the work of the "youngster" was driven by philosophical values, he was tactfully removed from activities that had been permitted him as if he were a promising little boy who had been polite. But nothing disheartened him. He continued to act on the idea that with time he would know Cisy by heart from A to Z, gain mastery over it with his work, and in that way take possession of it.

Deep in his soul, the elemental willingness to work gradually changed to a destructive obsession. The entire resort, the park, and their surround- ings became a hidden passion for him, an internal world with a life of its own, like an embryo. When he thought hard and seized on a bold move, it always turned out that he was up to something: new devices, different bathtubs, walkways, gardens for children, gymnasiums, shelters for the workers, and other things, other things—until the resort would have been a "Cisy museum," too elaborate and expensive to maintain. Often at night he would wake up and rack his brain over a trifle, over something that would have interested no one else. Then he would wait impatiently for morning, get up at dawn, and do something, carry something, dig some- thing, measure something.

Certain undertakings that were absolutely essential to his system, to his sanitation plan, he carried out himself with a furious energy. No one could understand why he busied himself with a side issue unconnected with the year-in-year-out life of the resort, with its established procedures. Those around him smiled indulgently and composed anecdotes about him on the sly, not to interfere with him or injure his feelings, but because it was the natural bent of those calm, respectable, entrenched, complacent people.

By winter the young doctor had become so indispensable at Cisy that he was a part of the place, like the bath houses and the springs. The staff, the laborers, the local farming people, the businesspeople, the manor, the guests—in a word, everyone had come to understand that if something hard needed doing, a little cash must be unloaded to the "young one." Meanwhile at all times of day and even on winter nights, through frosts, snowstorms, slush, on a small sledge or on foot, he made his way in thick boots over the roads between the villages to patients with smallpox, typhus, scarlet fever, diphtheria.

As is usually the case with strong people in this world, he was spared no punishing exertions. Everyone who could used his services. But Judym thought nothing of those hardships. He felt himself to be as good as anyone else when he was building a fortune and a reputation. The harder he worked, the more strength he felt in himself—felt a momentum and a passion that grew powerful and formed itself through difficulty, like a muscle.

In that life, however, he felt with his whole heart the lack of an ally. Now and then he made mistakes, he rushed needlessly in some direction, and in the end he noticed that those who sat on the side were laughing at him— that they had watched and known beforehand that what he was doing was ridiculous.

There was one partner, but he was far away. It was Les. The correspondence that had begun when Judym arrived in Cisy had grown into constant communion. No lovers ever expended such stacks of paper as these two pragmatic dreamers. Judym laid out his projects and explained the principles behind them; Les pointed out ways in which they might be realized.

From the beginning Les had also written the governing board, striving to convince them that such and such improvements should be made in Cisy. Everyone, of course, objected to his solutions to issues related to an institution he had never seen. Les had to back down and be silent, for he was discredited. People began to wonder who had put wind in the old philanthropist's sails, and it was not difficult to guess. Krzywosąd was among the first to divine the truth, and he secured his own interests by writing long letters to Les himself and presenting matters in a different light. Fortunately, the old merchant knew the "green monkey" very well and loved the resort too much to let his sense of what was going on be easily muddled. In Judym's letters he saw the outlines of his own plans, which were born of nostalgia—as if the young doctor's ideas were the advanced corollaries of his own thoughts.

So he did not quit. When his varied and crafty ways of working on the director and Krzywosąd brought no result, he directed Judym to fall back on the "silent cashbox." So it was with the hospital and a host of other things. If those in charge would not agree to some innovation, Les funded it through Judym's mediation. The board of governors grimaced, smiled sardonically, and displayed their wit in whispers, but in the end were forced to accept it with thanks.

Through the entire autumn Judym observed, examined, and measured the ponds inside the park, especially the basin that let water into the first of them. The basin was arranged so that, just at the point where the rivulet entered the pond, a dike was built that raised the level of the neck of the rivulet by a foot and a half. The excess water fell with a babbling sound to the pond. Krzywosąd had constructed this reservoir so as to adorn the park in a way he had seen at various aristocratic residences.

Judym reached the conclusion that to eliminate the dampness of Cisy, it would be necessary above all to do away with this invention and, later, the first pond, and then to turn the next into a reservoir that would power machines in the resort. Then the bottom of the little river should be raised to the level of the water in it and the stream allowed to run over a bed of hard-packed stones. To this end, a type of dam would have to be built in front of the park and the height of the river raised as it flowed through the open valley, over a large space. The stream of raised water would race down to a hard bottom in the park, trickle briskly through it, and flow down to the first pond. In this way, leaves from the trees would not decay in the reservoir, the spring thaws would not raise them to the pond together with the slime, and the water in the ponds would not be so unhealthy.

Judym was terrified at the very thought of broaching this project with the people who managed the affairs of the resort: the director and the "green monkey." But it was not possible to carry out all the work at Les's expense. Just then, in February, the time came for the reviewing commission to visit Cisy. The commission, consisting of three people chosen from the group of partners, came to the resort once a year, toured it, skimmed through the books, ate dinner, and went back to their occupations, since it was known that in the hands of Węglichowski and Krzywosąd the institution was running admirably. As he went into the dining room one day, Judym saw three gentlemen unknown to him who were speaking animatedly about Cisy. They were obviously versed in matters concerning the resort.

"The commission," he thought. A tremor ran along his nerves and, at the end of that covert path, seemed to ground itself in a firm decision. "Now," he resolved, "I'll tell them everything!"

At the midday dinner, a lively conversation started up. Judym joined in, but with the goal of learning about the newcomers, sounding out what sorts of men they were. He could not find out much. At one moment they spoke very intelligently, unwittingly supporting reforms, and then again they showed such commonplace lack of information that it was disheartening. Dr. Węglichowski invited the commissioners for a meeting in the treasurer's office, where, after a rest, they would come together and review the books, accounts, and, among other things, the new plans for receipt books proposed by Judym. Taking advantage of the politeness the director and Krzywosąd lavished on him in front of the commissioners, Judym asked Dr. Węglichowski in an aside to allow him to be present at the meeting. Dr. Węglichowski, rolling a cigarette as was his habit, fixed his penetrating eyes on him and asked straight from the shoulder:

"Why, colleague, do you want to be at this session?"

"I want to present you gentlemen with my plan to make Cisy a healthier place."

"To make Cisy a healthier place…beautiful. That is what all of us here think of, as we are able. Your thoughts are valuable, I don't doubt, but are you about to express something far more advanced than what we all know—Krzywosąd, for example, the gentlemen of the commission, whom you heard talking so knowledgeably, or—well, myself?"

"What I really wanted to say was something different. Perhaps it is not well judged; the gentlemen will judge. I would like to expound it clearly and offer it for consideration."

"Have you found, my friend," Węglichowski said slowly, with an airy smile, "that we have slipped a little in the matter of salubriousness?"

"By no means…that is, in my view, Cisy is too damp."

"So you don't want to find any more of your much-touted malaria? The malaria you found in the summer?"

He spoke with what appeared to be a benign laugh, but Judym could not restrain himself and said, "It seems, unfortunately, that no one manages to avoid it."

Dr. Węglichowski made a clucking sound, pulled hard on his cigarette, and said, looking at his assistant through the smoke, "You see, dear Tomasz, we must proceed according to the rules, and they do not give you the right to participate in this council. You are not a member. We must abide by the rules. That lack of respect for rules—it is our national failing. That saying, what is it? Law is law, and friendship friendship. Our motto—"

"Director, sir—"

"Pardon me for interrupting you. Our motto ought to be something else: 'The law is hard, but it is the law.'"

"Ah…if the rules forbid it," Judym whispered. "In that case—"

That refusal did not so much vex him as lower him in his own eyes. In general, Judym easily succumbed to the illusion that he had no right to many privileges that were accorded other people. Memories of things gone by were part of this idea—the sense of his origins and what he felt as undeserved access to higher levels of life.

Accordingly, after the conversation with Dr. Węglichowski he felt in the depths of his heart that deterioration of his self-respect, the cowardice of the rational will. He went off to be alone; he threw himself on a sofa and tried to suppress a miserable feeling of humiliation. At the moment when he was exerting himself to the utmost in this futile effort, an old bath attendant who acted as a butler in Dr. Węglichowski's house in the winter knocked at his door to convey by word of mouth an invitation from the director's wife. Judym knew that the commissioners would be there, so he purposely drew out old Hipolit, who had brought the invitation.

"The director has not been on the hill from morning on," the old man said.

"Well, and whom are you having over there today?"

"Those three gentlemen from Warsaw, the administrator, and the land steward from the manor."

"Good. I'll come."

He knew then that the invitation had been issued in the morning, and Madam Laura was putting it into effect without knowing about the disagreement after dinner.

That evening he found himself in the Węglichowskis' salon, being greeted by the director with the utmost politeness, and surrounded by an atmosphere of kind, polite, almost doting solicitude. He felt that it would be very difficult for him to shatter this spider web, but he knew he must. He must. Yet the memory of the reading of his paper in Warsaw so nearly strangled him that at moments he hardly knew what he was going to say.

Before supper was served, when the usual circle of guests mingled with the visiting trio, Judym joined in the conversation and began to explain in a very determined style his theory about the management of the ponds. Dr. Węglichowki listened patiently for some time and all at once, at the appropriate moment, dismissed the matter with an adroit aphorism. He brought up another matter: the cost estimate for a new and profitable villa for the sick of modest means.

The discussion moved onto other tracks. Judym knew he would hardly escape being a laughingstock if he harped like a maniac on his theme of raising the riverbed, but he ventured, "Gentlemen, allow me to return once more to the matter of the river."

"Oh, please do. Please," said Dr. Węglichowski. Judym glanced at him and saw a gleam in his look that could poison a man.

He began to present, from the ground up, detailed proofs of the movement of a drop of water and the strength of its fall from the river to the pond, and of the type of fog that covered the meadow near the water.

"We cannot destroy the basin," Krzywosąd put in hastily, "since it holds the excess water in the spring. When the thaws come, you will see, doctor, what happens. If the riverbed is raised, the water will overflow the banks and flood the park."

"The meadow," Judym said. "Not the park."

"Yes, the meadow, but we have planted the most beautiful trees on it."

"What of that? What does anyone care about your trees?"

"What?" said Dr. Węglichowski. "I will show you, friend, what those trees cost! We planted thuja, ash, the loveliest Weimut pines, even plane trees, not to mention those exquisite hornbeam copses."

"Director, sir, what does a sick man who comes here for his health care about a copse—or even thuja? There's mud there! The meadow is soaked with putrid water that stands in a stagnant channel. It's imperative to destroy that channel right away, and cut the meadow with several ditches. To dry it! To dry it!"

"To dry it!" Krzywosąd said with a laugh.

"I think that Dr. Judym may be right," said a member of the commission. "Someone complained in my presence about dampness in Cisy, about a strange chill that comes over the place after sunset. On the fields round about it is still warm, this person said, heat still comes from the ground, but over the ponds there is such a chill that one feels a cough scratching the throat. I'm not familiar with the situation, but since Dr. Judym confirms it…Even my wife…"

"Oh, these young doctors!" Dr. Węglichowski cried half-jokingly. "It seems to them that wherever they set foot, there lies America, which, of course, they must discover right away! After all, gentlemen, I live here winter and summer, I know this institution, and I wish it well. Don't you believe I wish it well? So then—what do I care that there exists a canal that creates moisture…if it creates moisture. But I say that these are idle notions, caviling. The canal is necessary, just like the bridge, the pond, the road, so we keep it. If it is shown to be harmful, we will get rid of it. But to begin such work for a baseless idea and throw in hundreds of rubles, money that is not ours, after all, that will bring in no income, that will be wasted—"

"In that case we should make a slight amendment to our advertisements, to the descriptions of Cisy. We should not say that certain ailments will be healed here—stubborn fevers, let us assume, or diseases of the respiratory system—for no one can expect it."

Dr. Węglichowski wanted to reply, but he restrained himself. His jaw trembled a few times. Only after a moment did he say in an icy voice, "I am also a doctor, and I know, more or less, what it is possible to cure and what it is not. Surely…I don't know that as precisely as our respected colleague Dr. Judym, but inasmuch as…I have had cases of malaria here that were treated with great success, serious cases, so I see no need to delete statements in the descriptions."

"In my opinion"—one of the commissioners turned to Judym—"your view of the matter may be a bit extreme. After all, the number of guests is continually growing."

"The number of guests, if you'll excuse me, sir, proves nothing. One article by a learned physician offering evidence that Cisy is not healthy for those who pay for the air that is supposed to cure them could bring everything down. The institution could collapse in one year. I, too, wish this beloved place no harm, and that's why I speak."

"'One article by a learned physician'; do you hear?" Dr. Węglichowski muttered quietly to Krzywosąd as he rolled a thick cigarette.

"Anyway, is cost the concern?"

"Oh, yes, we know!" Krzywosąd laughed. "You will find the sum necessary to cover expenses, doctor, in the pocket of the worthy Les. But is that proper? The old man will give, that's certain, but he doesn't even know what he's giving for."

"And is it good, is it good to urge that solitary man to incur such great expenses?" Madam Laura interposed. "Yes, he is wealthy, but he is not a millionaire, not even very rich. What he will earn he will give away. It is still possible that in his old age he will have nowhere to lay his head."

"That's right, doctor," said the commissioner who had taken Judym's side. "Leszczykowski spends too much on these things. We simply cannot permit this. I could understand if it were a trifle, but such fundamental matters—it's not appropriate."

Judym was ashamed. The thought crossed his mind that at that moment Krzywosąd suspected him of intending to use to his own advantage money that Les would send to raise the riverbed. That thought was so unexpected and so overwhelming that it choked out everything else. He went silent and distanced himself from the conversation.

So it was that his bid for the right to transform the reservoir in the park came to nothing. After the commissioners departed, everything went on as it had before, and to all appearances relations were not altered. The director behaved cordially to Judym, and Krzywosąd treated him with exaggerated politeness. But cold hate lurked under the surface.

In his humiliation, Judym saw his initiative in an even brighter light. Its rejection seemed to him destructive to the health of the patients and an antisocial act. What was in essence a minor issue grew in his mind to unprecedented dimensions and blotted out much weightier matters, as the moulding on the roof of a pigsty in front of a window from which we look out covers a vast mountain range in the distance.

His antagonists, director Węglichowski, Krzywosąd, Listwa, and Worszewicz, were not really arguing about raising the riverbed. Each of them was using the issue to settle some score with Judym: the director for the hospital, Krzywosąd for his humiliation, Listwa for marring the silence that was the delight of his life, Worszewicz for Judym's recommendation that the workers' housing be moved.

Above all, however, all four of them resented Judym because of his youth. If one of them had murmured over a card game about the same thing Judym had proposed, he would have won their agreement, though not without bursts of the stubbornness typical of old men and a stipulation that the one who had such an excellent idea should be the one to execute it. But since a young person had stepped forward with the suggestion, the old men felt as painful a blow to their sense of worth as if he had showered them with abuse. So they cut off discussion and, without reaching an agreement that included all sides, decided not to let "such a whipper-snapper" take charge of the matter. The director was particularly adamant.

Apart from his youth, Judym as a fellow practitioner of medicine irritated the director. Without being aware of it, the old physician did not consider Judym his equal as a doctor, and when the younger man spoke or even smiled in the name of medicine, it took will power for the director to clench his teeth and keep from using a short, insulting name. What was there to say when the younger man wrenched himself from under his elder's influence and acted on his own?

Every measure imaginable flashed through Dr. Węglichowski's imagination, deluding him with the hope of swift and absolute satisfaction. None, however, appeared sufficiently and flawlessly effective. To oust the enthusiast for some reason that the lips of rumor could help to inflate to the scale of an offense… But in that case he would have to run the hospital himself, and do it in the way that Judym had done it. Otherwise Judym's reputation with the crowd would grow to an unprecedented and detrimental height. To use harassment, ridicule, a series of trivial stings, humiliations, and annoyances to force him to leave of his own accord…But in that case, would the son of a cobbler not avenge himself in his "scientific" way, not take such a dig at Cisy in some fifth-rate publication that the devil himself could not pick it apart afterward? Dr. Węglichowski cursed the day he had turned to Judym with a proposal that he take the post. In a passion he tore at the net of his own making, a net with some remarkable loops.

Until this time, Dr. Węglichowski had traveled a straight road in life, always, as he liked to say of himself, "speaking the truth and not asking what the rest would think." He had never cheated, never resorted to a trick. He had never fought any human being with a hidden dagger. People everywhere knew him as a "man of integrity." He himself had not only been used to this appellation, but to this image of himself, as he was used to his fur coat and cane—until, because of his struggle with the "youngster," he was groping in darkness for the first time in his life and looking in himself for something unknown, some different weapon.

Judym felt this internally and wanted to fight all the more zealously because, without the sanitary reforms that would begin with the raising of the riverbed as the art of reading begins with the alphabet, it would not be worth it to work at Cisy. Accordingly, in total silence, amid polite bows and the drinking of tea as newspapers were read, a covert battle raged.

Early in March, after hard frosts that had held the world in iron claws almost throughout February, a thaw came. The snows melted away rapidly and the ground was no longer frozen. The river in the park rose, overflowed the artificial dike by the first pond and flooded its banks. Judym stood beside that miry water as it rushed along in a deep current and saw the confirmation of his argument. The weather was warm, bright, springlike. Lost in thought, he did not notice when Krzywosąd and Węglichowski came up to him.

"And what would happen now, doctor," said Krzywosąd, "if the canal were not here? Where would all this water go?"

"You should ask instead where these heaps of rotting leaves from the canal will end up. They're going to the pond at this moment, to give off that 'fresh air' you make people coming from far away pay for."

"'You know this tale, so listen,' as the playwright Fredro says," Węglichowski laughed, clapping Judym on the shoulder.

"We fulminate in the newspapers at the public that runs like stampeding sheep to the foreign spas. Which of those spas would put up with things like this?"

"Dear sir…"

"No! No! I am not forgetting myself. Not at all! I talk about how people rush abroad when you gentlemen want me to. Let a German in here and watch what he will do. Which will he get on with first: building a splendid ballroom or cleaning out the pond?"

"Well, come, Krzywosąd, come on," the director said. "We still have much to attend to."

CHAPTER III

"The tear that flows from your eyes"

WITH A FEW hundred rubles put up by Dr. Tomasz, his brother was able to go abroad. Wiktor remained at home for a couple of days, amid the tears and pleas of his family. When the moment came, however, he left.

It was early on a February morning. The lone horse that pulled the cab trudged along the streets as its tired driver burrowed into a sheepskin. Wiktor and his wife sat in the shadow of the raised cover. The children, nestled at their parents' feet, felt a pleasure in the ostentatious ride that they could not articulate. The lean, haggard horse, that four-legged laborer, slipped on the frosty stones, stumbled when his buck-kneed legs hit pits blown out of snowdrifts, and hauled the curse of his life—the cubicle on wheels—up Żelazna Street toward the Wola tollgates.

A gale was blowing from the cross streets, from the Vistula, wreaking its fury against everything. It hit weary draft horses in their nostrils and their muzzles, which metal bits forced open, as they dragged great freight wagons over the savage pavement with every muscle and with all their strength. It stung the eyes of poor people who, beginning at dawn, had been rushing hither and yon looking for a hunk of miserable bread. It snatched from all sides at a little stray mongrel that huddled up to a cold staircase. It tried to pull out the latch hooks and rattle the doors on shops. There were seconds when it seemed to be enraged at the sight of signs—when it lunged and seized the big letters with its teeth, jerking them in all directions, as if it intended to shake the absurd inscriptions from them onto the ground. Farther along its way it met tall buildings, burst onto their roofs, and from there it puffed snowdrifts onto the dirty streets.

Delicate fibrils cut the view like living, moving spiderwebs. Snowflakes were flying so swiftly and so continuously in one direction that they appeared to the eye as long threads. They seemed to have been spun off a distaff from a visibly growing drift under a reddish-brown fence, and their opposite ends curled up on telephone wires, circled mechanically around poles with transverse arms, and flew with machine-like speed somewhere above the gutters.

Entangled in this net, the street messenger fidgeted on a corner. He hopped and stamped, bumped one leg against the other, rubbed his hands, and ran for short distances back and forth, back and forth. When he turned his face to the north, the wind, lurking around the corner, leaped at him like a tiger, sank its claws into him, and pushed his breath into his throat. Then this little fellow with his hunched back turned around and shuffled in place as the gale beat him in the back and pushed him forward, blowing up his long gray coat. At moments he hid from the blustering wind, huddling in a recess in a wall and standing there without moving as if he were dead.

A powerfully built Jewish wagon driver with a whip in his hand and a large red rag wound around his head walked along with wide strides. He wore three cloaks and big felt boots. His face, unshaven, florid, and flogged by the wind, towered above the crowd, and the look of his bloodshot eyes from under knit brows was like a gale. This field soldier of the street, a man who belonged to the road like a milemarker or the barrier at a bridge, a man ready for communion with storms, snow, and frost, fascinated Karola and Franek. They forgot everything else; as the cab moved slowly away, they went on looking at him and pointing him out to each other.

On Srebrna and Towarowa streets the crush of wagons forced the horse to go one step at a time, so that the cab crawled along, swaying like a boat in the potholes. The children's eyes bulged with curiosity. Here were freight wagons creaking under the weight of crates of goods: black wagons loaded with coal, others with ice, bricks, wood. Beside them walked drivers covered with blowing snow, with frost-streaked beards on red faces, shouting and urging their animals on.

Among dirty buildings, the wild shapes of factory walls popped out, not losing their black color even in such a blizzard, as if they were oxidized to that hue. Behind roofs like peaked stairs glittered dark steel panels, set in so that no human eye saw God's world between them. Among the stifling walls the panes struck the eye with a glare not their own, alien to their nature, like a cat's eye seen against the light. Now and then, a great brick smokestack or a black iron chimney fitted with wires soared into the sky, throwing gigantic clouds of brownish-gray smoke onto the walls of neighboring houses and into their windows.

The convulsive motions of the carriage pushed the passengers' hats down onto their foreheads so that they covered their eyes. Wiktor sat without moving, looking from under his drooping hat brim at the images that moved past. Now and then a tear rolled from his eye and, unnoticed by anyone, ran over his hollow cheek.

When they passed the tollgates, the hubbub stopped. They were surrounded by fences, vacant lots, orchards, extensive yards with heaps of coal, lime, and timbers. Here and there gaunt, solitary houses came into view, looking as if they had been formed of windblown red sand. Their second-story doors looked out onto nothing at all, and since they did not open onto balconies, only onto two reddish braces that protruded from their walls but supported nothing, they seemed to harbor the intention of throwing themselves from their hinges and leaping into space. Soon the last of these dwellings disappeared, and behind a fence, fields tilted away— the domain of the wind. In the distance the city was dimly outlined like a vague symbol of something, a symbol full of pain and grief, such grief...

Now the freezing, violent gale blew into the carriage. It roared menacingly in the trees by the road. Sometimes among the traces, as if through the horse's back hooves, it gave a terrifying whistle. The whole family huddled together. Apparently from instinct, Wiktor's wife, feeling the cold, pressed her knees to her husband's legs. He sat stiffly, thrusting his hands into his sleeves and looking straight ahead. In his thoughts he was already far away, imagining the journey, envisioning his unknown future with fallible premonitions. From somewhere—from distant impressions received God knew where, from allusions dropped in his hearing—he formed a strange tool to acquaint himself with an unknown destiny.

His eyes wandered over the snows by the road, which were as strange as events, as thoughts, as everything. There were the shapes of virgin snowdrifts, formless, not compatible with anything, lavish with peculiar effects, like baroque ornaments. Some resembled distorted, crooked leaves, full of kinks, reminiscent of nature but deviating greatly from her true forms: leaves that do not exist, large but malformed, or again like titanic arrows that could pierce the walls of Holy Cross Church. Hills came into view and wooed the eye with their gentle shapes before dissolving. Hideous snow caverns stirred memories of the worst pain of life—dark, unknown anguish—bringing it to mind vividly, like a frightening cry. From right and left the world was veiled by a dark storm cloud. From this eyewall of the blizzard, the frantic wind blew out flying snow and propelled it over the land.

Around noon the cab finally arrived at its destination and stopped in front of a building, standing alone in an open space, that connected the railroad track with the world. At its base was a small shop with a gaudy sign. A Jewish family lived on the premises; several representatives of it appeared at the door when the cab stopped. The Judym children, almost numb with cold, stared wide-eyed at this structure built from partly decayed beams, no doubt taken from a defunct inn or barn. It was painted a flesh color with red ornamentation around the door and windows. Wiktor got out and asked one of the onlookers if he could get a glass of vodka to warm himself. A bottle was brought out right away and the rest of the family also had a glass apiece. The driver was forced to swallow two, since after the first he could not clearly taste the essential flavor.

Gray outlines could be seen in the mist. The Jews explained that that was the railroad station. The train for Sosnowiec would appear in about forty-five minutes. Wiktor had to hurry. The family was going to accompany him a little farther, but before he reached the town where the station stood they would turn back, get into the waiting cab, and return to Warsaw.

Then they all walked quickly, quickly along the edge of the track, over the frozen path. Wiktor ran in front. It seemed to him that it was late, that the train was coming, and so he ran quickly. They hurried after him, mimicking his movements. Sometimes he slowed down and spoke in broken sentences, directing his wife to do this or that. She still wanted to bring up a thousand things; she hoped that something might stop him, even for a day, for a few hours. Her thoughts became tangled and, like those snowflakes, spun around her brain. In her mouth, in her throat, inside herself she felt the burning taste of the vodka and a blurring of the senses. That was nothing to her; it was all such a grief!

There was a tightness in her heart as if a slender thread were wound around it, cutting. But above all there was the unreasoning certainty that whatever someone did in the world, any time, for any purpose, she alone had to carry the burden of it all. She must feed the children. He, Wiktor, was going away. There was nothing to be said; she must... Oh, how that vodka burned! Such smoke in the mind, such foolish smoke! She had to understand, after all, what and why. Since the children had been born, she had had to carry them along with her. Like an animal. An animal. All the world knew: the father could go away and she could not. She was a mother. That was what she was called: mother. Of course he must go; that was still generally understood. The knowledge lay under the heart like a child conceived, like a wound lying open with sand perpetually sprinkled into it. Inside the bosom lay the assent to his going.

Several hundred steps before the first houses in that out-of-the-way place, Wiktor stopped and said the goodbye that had to be said. His voice trembled.

On both sides of the wide, hard highway over which they were walking, dark creeping willow grew. Deep brown, round, slippery wands from its branches bumped against the sturdy wooden barrier with its coat of black paint; the sound was like a cruel, penetrating voice. The wind cut along the ground under the barrier and swept thin folds of snow from the road, uncovering dark ice and ridges of clods churned up by cart wheels.

"Wiktor," moaned his wife, "don't desert me. Fear God, Wiktor."

"Oh, good grief… now…"

"It's as if you were throwing me aside!"

"Well, it's time. The train is coming. We must be sensible."

"Don't forget that these children are yours, after all—Wiktor! Wiktor!" she sobbed in a low, fearful, dying voice.

"I'll write as soon as I get work. I'll send the first money I earn. What are you thinking—" he seized her quickly and hugged her, then the children.

Before they looked around, he had gone down the road. They trudged after him, but he waved once and then again to signal them to go back. Once he shouted to them to return, for the cab driver might lose patience and leave. Then they stood still and looked at him. They saw his overcoat, which had served its time, his wide, shabby cord trousers, baggy in the knees, which did not cover the tops of his gaiters, and his rusty hat, a flat-top bowler. Only his face had disappeared from their view.

The woman turned to the children and said between sobs, "See, that's your father there, going away. Your father…there…"

This information did not impress Franek. He stood quite calmly, picking his nose with a finger. Wiktor's figure grew dim amid the flying snow, then suddenly moved downhill and out of sight. The woman grabbed Karola's hand and ran back, as if to lose as little as possible of the time for which the driver had been paid. She began calling to Franek, who with unfeigned satisfaction was dropping little lumps of frozen dirt onto the highway.

CHAPTER IV

At Dawn

Very early in the morning Dr. Judym went out to visit his chronically ill patients in the neighboring villages. It was early April. The meadows were still wet, the farmlands dark. Deep mud puddles had stagnated on the roads and were swelling now from a fine, steady rain, a rain that fed a moving fog, flying from within the smooth, slowly sighing breeze. It was possible, jumping here and there through the ditches and clinging to the fences, to cover at least a few miles of road without being drenched.

The doctor was wearing a warm jacket and thick boots. He walked along, lost in gloomy thoughts and whistling a certain famous aria with the main motif so out of tune that a European could only get away with it in Cisy, and then only in an open field. The road stretched along the edge of a forest, over hilly, precipitous ground. Here it fell into a ravine, there it climbed up a hill, then again, like a straight seam, it cut through a field in a cleared space in a forest. On very wet ground in the low areas, bright expanses of grass brought to mind the miraculous flush of life on the face of a man who is seriously ill and close to death. Moribund wetness still lay on the small farmers' plots. The doctor scrambled to reach a higher point that would enable him to view a wide area and see the face of the sun, which had not emerged from the hills opposite, though it was already floating above the level ground.

Spring moisture trembled in the forest as he advanced along its edge. Wet mosses hung on spruce gnarls like gray, dead, winter furs; every minute dark drops trickled from them. That dripping was the only movement among the sleeping trees, and the drops seemed to exude a damp, sour forest smell. Here and there on the trunks hung ragged patches of bark. The spring had saturated them with water, as if they were ugly rags, and was slowly pulling them toward the ground. The interior of the partially cleared woodland was still covered with a humid darkness in which the forest vapor curled. The aspen trunks had a yellowish hue. Hornbeams were dark and glistening like steel from the rain. On the pale bark beneath the tops of pines, damp streaks were outlining odd shapes, sketching contours of things, drawing silhouettes of peculiar faces. Wet trunks and thickly clustered branches sagged under the burden of rain; between them a leaning birch or a young aspen with a multitude of fresh buds scattered over it like red hot coals lured the eye, as if the tree were a sleepy ghost that could not be chased away.

The sight of such trees is pleasing to something in a man and arouses deep emotion. Dr. Judym thought that feeling was a bit sentimental, or maybe even worse, but he could not overcome it.

"It's certain that this sentiment can't be cut with a microtome or examined under a microscope," he thought, "but what of that? Sentiment exists and is an accomplished fact, just like the most thoroughly documented bacillus!"

Preoccupied with such elemental thoughts, he walked in among the trees, sat down on an old stump, and waited. Dark clouds formed a wide dragnet that stretched from one end of the horizon to the other, hanging like long bags. Every hole in that net shook out warm rain that flew like fine sifted grain. In the background there was pure space, a delightful sea-green ocean of it, with which the purple of the morning light mingled. White and reddish clouds appeared at the very edge of the far horizon; they aroused strange stirrings of the heart, like the lovely open eyes of a woman when she is dreaming. It was silent, so silent that he seemed to hear the sprinkling of the quiet rain in puddles pecked by the falling drops. Little streams ran everywhere, like children full of glee, who do not know why or to where they are bounding so joyfully.

In this silence, the rumble of a carriage struck the doctor's ear roughly. Soon horses wrapped in a cloud of steam came into view at the top of a hill, and then a chaise. The bays were tired and so spattered with mud that they were gray. The carriage had been through a swamp. Even the driver and the person on the seat showed the signs of a long journey.

Judym looked hard at the face of the woman sitting on the chaise and recognized a person from the manor: Joanna. She was wearing a pale green French coat with a hood, which was pulled over her head to protect her from the rain. She seemed to be dozing.

The doctor was overwhelmed with curiosity about where Joanna was returning from at this hour over a road that did not lead to populated areas. Only half knowing why he did it, he rose from the stump and walked to the edge of the highway opposite the carriage. When he was only a few steps away from it, Joanna raised her head and saw him. A look of confusion, even fear, came over her face. She pulled her hood over her forehead, then turned her head away. The doctor bowed to her and with an inquiring smile stopped near the chaise.

"What escapade is this, Miss Joanna? Where have you been?"

"As you see, sir. On a journey."

"I see. I even see that it must have been a long one."

The driver stopped the horses. For a moment Joanna plucked at the edge of her coat with a troubled air. What people called her "impossibly" honest face showed that she was trying to hide something. Her cheeks reddened and she said softly, "I went to confession…to Wola Zamecka."

"All the way to Wola? And why at night? You shouldn't do that again. Did anyone see you? It's raining, it was cold in the night, and you're all wet! Pardon me for intervening without being asked, but as a doctor I consider it my duty to point out these things."

Meanwhile he was by no means acting from professional motives. His heart was pounding. That face with lowered eyes inside that green hood, that lovely, untidy hair falling out onto her forehead, and especially the eyes, the eyes and the flaming blush… It was like the charm of this peculiar forest; it blended with the sun that was drifting from behind the mist over the silent, dreaming solitude. Judym stood helplessly by the steps of the chaise, looking with narrowed eyes into her shy face.

"I beg your pardon, miss. Why is something being hidden from the gentleman, from the doctor?" the driver said unexpectedly, turning aside. "The young lady and I didn't go to confession, if you'll excuse me, doctor."

"Felek!" Miss Podborska shrieked.

"If you don't want…" Judym said, tipping his hat. "I wouldn't like to cause the slightest pain—"

"Well, this matter won't be covered up even if we stand on our heads, the way people run their mouths," Felek chattered on.

"What on earth—"

"We went, if you please, doctor, to look for that young lady, Miss Natalia."

"To look for her?" Judym whispered, astonished. "What do you mean, to look for her?"

Instead of answering, Joanna rose quickly and got out of the carriage. The look on her face was agonized and her body shook as if she had a fever. Her eyes signaled to Judym that she wanted to tell him the whole truth, but not in front of the driver. They walked a few steps along the road leading up the hill. Felek understood and shook the reins lightly. The horses moved slowly down the hill, one foot at a time. The rattle of the carriage wheels over the pine and spruce roots that cut across the road muted the conversation.

"Natalia left home without her grandmother's knowledge," Joanna said.

"Alone?"

"No."

"With Karbowski?"

"Yes. With Mr.—Mr. Karbowski." She spoke with her coat pulled around her as if she were pierced by the cold. "Her poor grandmother! How terribly she's suffering about this! She went to Grandfather January's grave right away and lay in the chapel with a cross. We didn't know…we didn't know where she was. There was such a panic!"

"Well, and how did you find out?"

"Yesterday Mr. Worszewicz learned from someone that Natalia had gone to Wola Zamecka. I don't understand how he could have known that. He's such a clever man…He guessed that they would marry in that very church, the church in Wola. There's a priest there, reportedly not a very nice person. And indeed he agreed to perform the wedding. That's why her grandmother sent me last night. I went without delay. We drove as fast as the horses could go, but it was all for nothing. They were married already. When I arrived, it was all over. They had gone. They said to tell anyone who asked that they were going straight out of the country."

"Excuse me, but that was…that was not unforeseeable. Perhaps not exactly that, but something of that kind."

"Oh, doctor! What a role I've played in this affair!"

"You played a role?"

"I was her teacher, her mentor, you might say her confidante. I suspected, I even knew about this love. I couldn't bear that man, and I suppose that was why I believed that all those feelings would pass. Now anyone could say that this happened because of my influence. Anyone could say that, and unfortunately they would be right. I often talked with Natalia about how a loveless marriage involves many things that I find despicable, and how she should not, she should never…Who could predict that she would interpret what I said in this way?"

"Please calm yourself. Discussions of that sort would make little impression on Natalia. She has a bold, independent, ruthless nature."

"Oh, yes, ruthless. In a letter I'm taking to her grandmother she expressly states that she is going to take the money she inherited from her mother, which was deposited in the bank, all her personal fortune, since now that she is an adult she has the right to it. That's what she wrote to her grandmother: 'As an adult…'"

"Is it a large fortune?"

"Reportedly quite a sizable one."

"Karbowski will have something to squander for a while."

Joanna stopped as if she had just remembered something. She threw Judym a bright, knowing look and said, "But I'm saying all this with no thought for the pain it must cause you."

"Me? Pain?"

"Ah, after all…After all, you were in love with Natalia. I'm so sorry—"

"I? I in love?"

"Please don't think I told you all this out of spite!"

"Your sympathy is wasted on me, madam, for I'm not at all aggrieved. I give you my word as an honest man that I am not in love with Miss Natalia. No! No!" he cried with joy in his voice and his eyes. "I don't love her at all!"

That denial, that confession, ended their conversation. It drained it to the dregs. Still side by side, they walked a few dozen steps in silence, for it was impossible to say more. Joanna quickened her pace and said, "I must go."

Judym escorted her to the carriage.

When she gave him her hand, her face wore a look of painful anxiety, like the face of a person who, with the force of premonition, perceives something that her senses cannot yet embrace. He looked at her with wide eyes. When he helped her jump onto the steps of the carriage, which had stopped in the middle of the muddy road, and felt her next to him, almost in his embrace, he had a strange illusion.

Who would have believed that it was Joanna herself, that this was the fragrance of her hair? Until now he had seen her as a fellow human being, a sister, with a mind and a heart, a being from his own sphere, from the circle of those who never take their ease but labor with the joy of kindred spirits for something obscure, high, and incomprehensible to the mass of egotists. And now he was mad with happiness: she was not only that! A dream that seemed sacrilegious slid through his heart. It was as if the color of her hair and its delicate smell had become his property forever.

An aching solicitude and an inexpressible tenderness filled his heart, a misty compassion like the fragrance of flowers. These were alien to him and awoke wonder and musings.

The carriage grew more distant and disappeared around a bend in the road.

Judym felt then as if his heart were tightening and trembling. He stood on the edge of the forest and reproached himself severely for letting the conversation end so soon.

There was so much yet to be said, there were so many things of immeasurable importance! Every word that now emerged from the dimness had its eternal existence, its own form, its sense and place, its content and logic, like an inevitable, indispensable, perfectly placed tone in a symphony. Whole landscapes were locked into each word, spring terrains where wet fields gave off fragrances and tall trees rustled.

He trudged along with a lagging step in the direction he had been taking in the first place, toward the villages on the other side of the valley. When he reached the top of the hill, the sun burst from the clouds over the wide forests. His soul went toward that light like a giant whose shoulders reach the sky.

He stopped where he had been before and looked at the prints of Joanna's small shoes on the muddy road. His eyes lighted on those neat furrows in the sand and in his ecstatic imagination he saw the feet that had made them. He saw the slender figure that had flitted over them and its subtle beauty, which awakened indescribable delight.

He closed his eyes and looked into the depths of his soul. In that moment quiet knowledge descended on him: the cheerful whisper of a vexing riddle and the solution to a difficult question, simple as pure truth. He welcomed it with a joyful laugh:

"Why, yes! Of course! That's my wife."

CHAPTER V

On the Road

AT THE beginning of June, Wiktor's wife received a letter from her husband in Switzerland directing her to come to him. He wrote that he was working in a factory and earning more than he had in Warsaw, that his expenses were high because he had to take his meals in a tavern, and that Swiss food was not good for him at all. He enumerated such dishes as soup with Swiss cheese, potato salads, and drinks like grape cider, astonishing everyone with the outlandishness of such cuisine.

She had no choice. She could not earn enough by herself to maintain the house and support the children and the aunt. She was afraid that her husband would abandon her and perish somewhere at the end of the world. Since he wanted her, since he ordered her to come, she could do nothing else.

She sold their odds and ends, obtained a passport, and started out. Someone she knew told her that the Germans forbade the transport of silk dresses over the border, so she undid the seams of her best clothes, put the pieces on under her outer garments, and, carrying a green wooden trunk, went on her way. A group of Wiktor's friends gathered at the station. The aunt sobbed; the children were elated at first. She herself, unaccustomed to inactivity, dozed constantly in the train car. She had bought a ticket straight to Vienna, where a friend who spoke Polish was going to be waiting for her.

She could not manage even one foreign phrase. She was taught words: *Wasser, brot, zwei, drei,* and more, but they became entangled in her mind.

The train crossed the border and night fell. In the car people were still speaking Polish. She took heart. "So this is what it's like abroad!" she thought. "One can still converse with people perfectly well! They speak like us, just a little differently."

She arranged the children next to her and curled up. Her nerves, accustomed to continual watchfulness, took advantage of the moment. She fell into a sleep, that sleep in a third-class car that is a strange, half-waking state when one feels every rattle and tremor, is aware of everything, and at the same time is a thousand miles away.

The train flew through the dark. Often the lights of a station struck the windows and after an instant died, as if carried away somewhere by the whistle of the locomotive. When the train stopped, electric bells could be heard vibrating. In their whine she heard ominous phrases that burst into thousands of identical shudders.

She felt all this in a dream. Wide-eyed fear wafted onto her from every direction, then was transformed into pleasant sights and conversations with her family, or into the commonplace, familiar, tiresome sight of the inside of the cigar factory. Her senses, conditioned like draft animals to stuffiness, rattling and thumping, loud voices, and annoyances, were drifting now into unknown spaces. A sweet, ignoble but victorious subliminal feeling of superiority to everything that was left behind in Warsaw, everyone who was now working amid squalor, pervaded them.

She was going out into the world. The world. The world. To Vienna. When someday she appeared in Warsaw again, she would not let the aunt impose on her with advice for every situation. What did the aunt know? What could she know? Had the aunt, for example, ever been in Vienna? Had she seen the world, or Europe?

In her half-dreaming state she seemed to see the old woman here beside her. The blubbering aunt was sitting on the trunk, under the window. Where was this—in the old apartment on Ciepła Street or somewhere else? Some lodgings in an attic or a basement? Dusk was washing over a corner of the room, dusk and damp and sadness. A pale light from the window fell only on Aunt Pelagia's cheek and on her lean, clenched hand. The old woman was saying nothing and everyone knew that she would say nothing. She was not to be mollified. True to her habit, she had bleated all night; now she was silent, only looking coldly from under her eyebrows. Sometimes a brief, pale, sickly smile flitted over her tight lips. But to sigh, to speak with anyone… She is aware of everything. Ho! Ho! Nothing is hidden from her. Three months from such-and-such a day she will mention what happened at one time and another, at what hour certain words or looks fell.

Teosia felt absurd, unbearable regret. She wanted to turn to the aunt and shout a question at her: "Why the devil do you sit there like Copernicus on his pillar? What is that about? Have we stolen something or burned down someone's house?"

But not that, not that! She did not want to say that to her at all! Aunt would have not just one but a hundred answers. This was about something else. After all, she had had to go away. She had had to follow her husband to where he ordered. Let aunt say that she had done badly. Yes, all right! She would free herself from the old woman once and for all. But there was one thing, one thing. What a grief! She could not look at the aunt, she had grown so repugnant, but at the same time she could not tear her eyes away from her!

Suddenly something jostled her and pressed her against the wall. Still dozing, she leaned sideways and her arm rested against the man sitting beside her on the bench. He was a tall, burly fellow with a pipe between his teeth. He sized her up with angry eyes and muttered something. He had a large, dark face and a hooked nose. He had come into the wagon while she was sleeping. By the feeble light she looked stealthily at this new figure and at several others that filled the compartment. These were people who had come sometime before, for they had managed to fall asleep. One was snoring noisily, while opposite him a man in a hard round hat was nodding. Only the hat was visible because his head had fallen onto his chest and his face was hidden in the raised collar of his overcoat. The hat slipped farther down and his body moved forward in a way that grew more and more comical. At any moment, it seemed, the man and the hat might come tumbling down on Karolina, who was asleep in the corner of the opposite bench. Teosia wanted to shout, but a strange fear made her shudder.

Someone else was sleeping in a corner. A thin face leaned against the wall, shaking when the wall shook and bumping noisily against it. Spasmodic snores burst from the mouth of the sleeping man, which was open as wide as it is possible to imagine.

Teosia felt a vague fear as she looked at those people. She glanced out the window and began to notice with astonishment the area through which the train was passing. The short spring night was dispersing. A gray, flat landscape loomed in the distance, and at the sight her heart tightened so painfully that it seemed to be choking her.

"This must be a foreign country," she thought. She looked with great fear and humble respect at the faces of the people sleeping in the car.

The train sped on into more populous areas. Reddish factory buildings appeared on a tract of cleared land. Houses and churches were everywhere.

It was broad daylight when a great river appeared, and rows of smoky black walls. Soon the train stopped. Everyone left the car, so Teosia got out of her seat. The children were sleepy, lethargic, and pale, and she herself was unsteady on her feet. When she was standing on a broad platform, a shabbily dressed man approached her and said in Polish, "I recognized you right away."

Teosia looked into his face and remembered it. He took her things and ordered her and the children to come with him. They went out into the town and walked for a long time along various streets. The man, Kincel, was a chatty fellow and a good friend of Wiktor's. They had run across each other again here, in Vienna. Wiktor had written to ask him to assist his wife on the day she arrived. He would help her to her next destination. He had not gone to the factory today because he wanted to do all he could for them. They were tired—well, well, that was life. Straight from Warsaw! And what about this Warsaw? Nice little place, Warsaw, though you couldn't say that it's a hotbed of merriment, and it can't hold a candle to Vienna.

Teosia murmured something. She found the presence of this stranger embarrassing. She wanted to rest as soon as possible.

They entered a very poor neighborhood and climbed to the fifth floor of a large house. Soon they were in a commonplace, cramped apartment, a home of a working family. Wiktor's friend was married to a Viennese woman who understood not a word of Polish. But she chattered to Teosia and the children in funny phrases, asked them a thousand questions, laughed, and rubbed her eyes. After breakfast she spread a wide sofa with quilts and Teosia laid her head on them, but could not blink an eye in spite of her fatigue. Hour after hour passed as she brooded about how she would continue her journey to Wiktor.

Only now did it become clear to her that she was among foreigners. Wiktor's friend who spoke Polish became as near and dear to her as a brother. When he went out of the room, she trembled at the thought that he had gone away and might not come back.

Toward evening they had to leave for the station. Their caretaker helped them find places in a large transport wagon where they were packed in like herring in a barrel, and took them to the Westbahn. There he bought Teosia tickets to Wintertur in Switzerland and, as they were waiting for the second bell, he quickly taught her a number of German words. He ordered her above all to remember two of them: *umsteigen* and Amstetten.

His pale, bulging eyes were fixed on her and his Adam's apple moved as he said, "Amstetten—that is a station where you will transfer to the *zug*, or train, that runs to Salzburg, and *umsteigen*—that means transfer. Keep asking the conductor: Amstetten? Amstetten? When he says Yes, or nods his head, then transfer to the train for Salzburg. *Umsteigen!* Understand?"

"I understand," she whispered, quivering with fear.

He was teaching her a dozen other essential expressions when the second bell sounded. A crowd of people swarmed through the doors and into the cars.

Kincel found comfortable seats and secured them for his protegees, though not without difficulty. He had to wage a contest with a fat man who tried to cram himself onto the same bench. Teosia, of course, did not understand what was going on, but she gathered from the men's tones that a scene was brewing, and she asked their guide to smooth things over because it was all intimidating to her. He relented and found seats for the children, stowed the luggage on an upper shelf and continued to teach her new words. But the third bell rang with a short, angry shriek and their companion disappeared through the narrow doors of the compartment.

The car was full of people and noise. Despair overtook Teosia as she listened as hard as she could to the talk but could not understand a single word. "Amstetten, *umsteigen*, Amstetten, *umsteigen*," she seemed to hear Kincel whispering, long after he was out of sight.

The train moved out slowly. At intervals, fiery white lights from outside leaped onto its windows like the flaming maws of animals chasing the moving nest of human beings. The last one flashed and the train rushed into the dark as if it were lunging forward and flying away from the light. The children were fussy. Karolina sniveled loudly and Franek squabbled about nothing. Teosia was simply torn apart inside. The lack of any supportive certainty was choking her. She was in that terrible cycle of feeling when a person cannot master herself, when something inside snaps, explodes like a powder charge into a blind physical act. She had a stifling feeling in her throat; she was overwhelmed by confusion. She sat quietly on the bench but she was not sure that after a moment she would not leap up, throw the door open, and run away as the train was running, rush forward into the deaf, frightening, boundless dark. She could not have said how long this lasted.

Suddenly the door to the compartment opened and the conductor's lantern shone straight into her eyes. Teosia took out her tickets and gave them to the man. He looked at them hard, cut them, gave them back to her and said in a droning voice, "Amstetten, *umsteigen*…"

To Teosia those words had a tender, comforting ring. Perhaps the Lord would help her understand everything as well. Glory to God in the highest! May His name be blessed.

The glow of the conductor's lantern died away in the doors, and the car was in partial darkness. The din of conversation still filled it; laughter and shouts from some repulsive women broke out from the corner opposite the Judyms every few minutes. But it was no longer all so painful to Teosia.

The train rumbled, rumbled…and when she could listen intently, it was possible to catch the words-not-words that flowed from under its wheels. Oh, no, not words. It was like the change that song makes in a human being: the unknown spearhead of music, like a bee's stinger, that is left in a person's soul by deep, sacred tones. It is the same thing, the same effect of melody, as when the cycles of "Bitter Lamentations" resound under the vault in the vast interior of the cathedral of St. John in Warsaw:

> *The veil was torn in two…*
> *the earth quaked, and the rocks were split…*

The train's song transported Teosia, carried her beyond the past, present, and future vexations of life, tore her away from the pincers of adversity, drew her painlessly from her husband, from memories of her parents, from love and hate, even from Franek and Karolina. Everything was strange, cold, alien. There, somewhere far, far away, the music drew her with it to holy fields covered with bright grass. Pearly dew lay on flowers. One whose bare feet and bloody legs were washed by that clear water became once again a human being—became herself, whole, a lone, free soul. Gentle tears flowed to the heart like miraculous medicine that quenched the fire of every wound. Cool peace, or perhaps a fragrant wind, breathed on the frazzled forehead.

Sometimes despair still descended. Sometimes deadly foreboding so sharpened the eyes that they saw misfortune like a terrible mirage. But all that slowly subsided, subsided.

The murmur of quiet rain started up. The crowd in the car changed. Plain people came in. Villagers in short jackets with pipes between their teeth rode past one or two stations and then alighted, giving their seats to other groups. The air was terrible, so bad that little Karolina grew queasy. When she quieted down a bit and went to sleep, Teosia sat by her in a corner and slept through the loud shouts of "Amstetten!" that came from outside the window.

Most of the people in the car got out, a completely different set came in, and she knew nothing of it. When she woke up, it was day, and the wagon was almost empty. From the windows she could see a hilly, strangely green countryside. Beautiful meadows stretched between the hills. The car stopped before noon and all the passengers exited the train.

"This must be Amstetten," she thought.

She pulled her bundles from overhead, gathered them up, and got off. Trembling, she read a different name on the station. Then again she was overwhelmed by anxiety. Had something gone wrong?

The station was small. The train she had come on switched to another track, detaching from its locomotive. It stood empty, like a carriage without horses. The travelers scattered; even the porters vanished from the platform. Teosia did not know what to do. She stood beside her things, looking around in fright. It seemed to her that hours went by as she waited without knowing what to wait for.

At last a railway agent came out of the station, approached her, and asked her something in German. She understood nothing, of course. After a while she managed to force out a timid, inquiring squeak: "Amstetten?"

The railway employee smiled at her, asked another question and then another, and when he received no answer, went away. He was back a moment later, throwing phrases at her. When he saw that she understood nothing, he took her hand, led her off the platform to the yard, and motioned toward a city in the distance. Then she realized that something was awry. She took her ticket from her pocket and showed it to him. He read it, stared at her, shrugged his shoulders several times, gave her back the ticket, and began waving his hands and speaking again as clearly as he could. Finally he muttered something sternly, hoarsely, and walked away.

She waited at the same place, hoping that he would come back and tell her what to do. He did not appear again. In the meantime freight wagons, cabs, and coaches began rolling into the yard. When she tried to go back onto the platform, a porter blocked her way, loosing a torrent of words, and escorted her back toward the station.

It was very hot. The children were hungry and thirsty and whining. The ailing Karolina was staggering on her feet and complaining of a headache. Teosia had to find a little tea somewhere, since the child was crying and begging for it. She trudged in the direction of the city, carrying their belongings in her hands and on her back. She walked along the bare, sun-drenched highway as huge wagons hurtled past in clouds of dust. She was in distress; she had lost her strength and very nearly her mind. She would not have been at all surprised if someone had thrown her from the road into a ditch and kicked her.

She saw moving wagons, houses at a distance, and the outlines of lofty towers and factory chimneys, but apart from that, every moment she caught sight of things that were unheard of. It seemed that a curving white-washed fence had something different to do here. Something was running from a beet patch, something invisible and so frightening, so loathsome! So appalling! She spied it in a vapor that trembled over the ground; she felt its terrible eyes in her chest, her joints, her heart, in the roots of her hair, in her numb fingers. It was the Evil One coming from behind the fence on flexible feet that grew into the ground. He choked with laughter, then he expanded, shook, elongated, crumpled. He had such long hands and eyes, eyes that bit like a dog's muzzle. Saviour! Merciful Saviour!

She wiped the sweat from her face and rubbed her eyes to make the phantasm go away, but she could not. Fear enmeshed her like a wide web that someone was winding around her, winding, winding. And that soft whisper, a familiar whisper, still remembered from childhood…

Franek was walking ahead of them and began to play. He gathered little stones and threw them into people's gardens: one, two, then a third. After the fourth there was the distant tinkle of a broken window. Teosia heard the noise, realized that Franek was responsible, and felt a sudden bitter aversion to the child.

"I'll take the mutt and strangle him!" she thought. "Before I get far they'll begin to harass me about that window. Just see how they'll come running!"

She walked along the road and stared wild-eyed at Franek, who was looking around with his hands in his pockets and whistling. Every minute she was forced to stop, rest her bundles on a heap of broken stone, or lay them on the ground. Sweat drenched her; every seam cut into her skin. Her heavy legs felt as if they were swelling and bleeding. Little Karolina dragged herself along beside her mother, not like a dearly loved child walking, but like a bucket of water so heavy it numbs the arm. In that way they trudged to a bridge over a wide gap with pale blue water rolling through it.

The bridge was noisy. Every pounding of a wheel and stomping of a horse's hoof resounded for a long time. At the entrance to the bridge Teosia sat down, utterly spent. She looked at the city that glowed in the sun on the other side of the river. For a short time pure, peaceful thoughts filled her mind and seemed to be telling her to walk toward a bright meadow, to urge her on with wise words. But she could not see that meadow in her heart. Despair struck her like a mountain wind.

"Why am I going on?" she asked herself with a stifled sob that seemed to tear out her insides. "After all, this is not Wintertur or Amstetten. What city can it be?" she exclaimed aloud, looking at it with dry eyes.

She sat weak and uncomprehending, like chaff worried by the wind. The children went down from the walkway and amused themselves by throwing stones into the gorge. They could have fallen headlong into it and she would not have noticed.

A voice roused her from her torpor. A tall policeman in a uniform and helmet stood over her and said something, looking pointedly at the bundles and the children. She looked him briefly in the eye and said aloud in Polish, "Bark all day, dog! I don't care."

The soldier repeated what he had said more loudly. Teosia said angrily, "What's the name of that city?"

The German's eyes widened and he began to speak again. When she gave him no answer and paid no attention, he took one of her bundles and motioned to her to put it on her back. She sighed with longing to spit in his eye and even made a physical move to do it, but restrained herself with a great effort. She walked a few dozen steps back, feeling more dead than alive. A cold numbness slowly turned to a confused plan, though she did not have the strength to understand that. Her fragmented thoughts seized on that muddled subliminal inclination, struggling only to know what it was and immediately act on it.

The policeman was already gone, so once again she rested her bundle against the iron barrier and stood still, looking around her without seeing. She only felt the weight of her pack burning her back and that treacherous urge that gave her the hope of peace. She stood there for a long time, as if she were screwed with iron nuts to the gravel in the pavement and to the barrier.

In the middle of the street, omnibuses and carriages were rolling toward the railroad station over the round stones. Suddenly Teosia's eyes lighted on a two-horse cab and the people sitting in it: a young, handsome couple, elegantly dressed. The woman, in a modest straw hat, was shielding the man with a pale parasol. Both were laughing at something and casting happy, amused glances around them.

Teosia reeled as if someone had pushed her forward. She called the children to her and followed the cab, saying audibly to herself, "Such happy people, so happy… Maybe they will help me. Saviour! Merciful Saviour!"

The cab was moving slowly and Teosia, running as hard as she could, managed to stay within sight of it. The passengers' heads tilted toward each other every minute. Twice as quickly as she had traveled in the opposite direction, Teosia covered the distance between the bridge and the station.

She stopped in the station yard just after the cab. The young couple had alighted and were standing by as the porter took two trunks from the driver. Teosia did not know what to do, but she waited for a moment to speak to them. Why to them? She did not know. Now all her being was concentrated in one explosion of will: she would speak!

Suddenly the young woman said to her companion, "Take the number from him and let's go to the hall."

She was speaking Polish.

Teosia staggered on her feet. Her eyes darkened. Like a drunkard she went up to the lady and began to bleat out phrases broken by a smile, a shriek and a sob: "Madam! Madam! Oh, my lovely one! Madam! Angel!"

The strangers turned to her with good-natured smiles. They exchanged perhaps a dozen phrases in French, then listened eagerly and sympathetically to her rather incoherent account of her adventures. The woman in particular inquired curiously about everything. Teosia showed them her ticket and assured them that they were not dealing with a beggar or a swindler. At the woman's request the porter took her belongings and carried them to the hall along with their luggage. The children each got a cup of milk. Only then could Teosia cry, and for a moment even the other woman had tears in her eyes.

The man went to the cashier with her ticket and stayed there for a long time. Then he returned and informed them that everything was in order, and that as a result of his complaint, Teosia would return to Amstetten with them and from there travel the right way when they transferred to the train for Italy. Teosia shuddered at the idea of separating from them, but they both calmed her with assurances that they would not let her get lost— that they would direct the conductors and managers to see that she reached her destination, Wintertur.

The young lady began to question Teosia intently. Among other things she asked, "Have you come from Warsaw, madam?"

"Yes, madam, from Warsaw."

"And what is your name?"

"My name, dear lady, is Judym."

"Did you say Judym?" the beautiful woman asked in astonishment. Her lovely blue eyes widened.

"Yes, madam."

"That is—your husband's name is Judym?"

"Yes. Judym."

"Really?" The other woman whispered. Her curiosity was palpable. "And perhaps a cousin of your husband's is Dr. Judym, Tomasz Judym?"

"He's my husband's brother! His brother!" Teosia cried. "Do you know him, dear lady?"

"Yes, I know him slightly," said Natalia. Turning to her husband, she asked, "Do you hear?"

"It appears that you had admirers in all spheres of society," Karbowski returned.

"I would like to see our ambitious little doctor now!"

"It really would be interesting! And how would he greet his relatives, who are traveling in such an original way?"

The hall began to fill. Bells sounded; the train pulled up to the platform and Teosia was seated in third class. The Karbowskis traveled in first. Evening was coming on.

At the stations where the train stopped for a few minutes, the young couple came out of their car and chatted with Teosia and the children as they strolled around the platform. Natalia took an interest in the health of little Karolina, who was sleeping uneasily in her mother's arms. She brought her wine, something to eat, and some medicine to relieve her lethargy. She gave the family a slightly wilted bouquet of flowers, half a flask of perfume, her fan, and various elegant trifles for Franek.

As the pair appeared on the platform and walked together, speaking ardently and caressing each other with their eyes, lips and words, Teosia never took her eyes off them. She whispered tender names, sweet, rustic, almost peasant-style pet names, and her whole soul breathed blessings on these strange, lovely figures.

"May your husband always want you as he does now!" she whispered. "May you always be his darling. May he love you until death itself. May you have beautiful, large, healthy, wise children. May you give birth to them without great pain. May you never shed tears over them at night."

She pressed the bouquet of roses tightly to her lips and drank in the fragrance of it. That perfume mingled with admiration and love for the elegant young woman. The scent aroused her gratitude and transformed it to wistful delight. Her attention was riveted by Natalia's every movement; she followed her with her eyes and saw her in her mind's eye even when the train left its place and moved swiftly among hills gilded with sunset.

In Amstetten during the night, the Karbowskis parted ways with their protegee. Before that, the conductor of the train for Innsbruck busied himself with her with such extraordinary zeal that his spasm of solicitude had clearly been inspired by a "remembrance" of at least five gulden. The Judyms were placed in a locked compartment of their own.

Teosia was so tired that she could not get a wink of sleep all night. She lay on a hard bench and strained her eyes looking at the window.

It was a bright, moonlit night. Near morning, mountains could barely be seen on a wide horizon. Their ridges, round at first, grew taller and more jagged. Teosia was seeing mountains for the first time in her life. That sight, which inspires such awe in a person from the lowlands, from a city, was like a continuation of the past day. In her mind these sights and events were reflected as if in water, and created an astonishing picture. She looked through the window, not at the mountains, but at that picture inside herself. Her heart fluttered and the internal vision melded into a beautiful collage.

"What kind of land is this?" she wondered. "And is this the earth?"

Who were those exquisite people she had seen there, near that city where she had been in such distress? Or were they people? Who had told her to follow them? And—?

At this question her heart weakened and dissolved in tears. With unspeakable trepidation, she asked the deep night, the chain of mountains and that holy reflection in herself— the reflection in something tender and unresisting, as if in a sea of tears—"Who sent them?"

The highest summits were silvered with moonlight. Their sharp, fang-like peaks now had a gentle, human look. They seemed to be brooding, to be meditating and looking with stony eyes into the cloudless azure that was sown with stars. Yet it seemed that, like a human being, they could see nothing there.

Now and then Teosia looked into a chasm when the train ran along the rocky ledges of the Arlberg route. Somewhere below, in the gorge, in deep, deep crevices, the greenish white foam on the waters of the Inn River flowed over drowsy, slippery black boulders.

Those sights did not arouse wonder in her. She accepted them quietly, cautiously, thoughtfully, and hid them away in her heart with the cherished memories of her life. Sometimes pitch darkness filled with smoke and racket surrounded the car. Teosia did not know what it was, but she felt no fear. That night she was immune to weakness of body and agitation of spirit.

The silver mountaintops grew dim, as if someone had taken them down from the highlands. Steep gray surfaces and ridges of rock appeared more frequently out of the shadows, breaking up the darkness on the lowlands. From high above the land the mountain daylight was descending.

In that way the Judyms traveled all the next day and through the next night. The children's exhaustion became a dull faintness. Bumps appeared on their lips for lack of proper drinks. All three were coughing and thrashing in their sleep.

In Buchs the Austrian conductor handed Teosia over to a Swiss attendant, who eyed the travelers sardonically. Their baggage was examined, they were closed into the car again, and they moved on.

In the glow of a new day something not of this world soon appeared. Teosia looked at it and could not believe her eyes: the cold, blue, mysterious Lake Walensee. The first beam of light falling from the mountaintops to the land below glided over waves that trembled in the cool dimness of early morning. That crystalline depth descending into a dark chasm made Teosia's heart tremble again. It seemed that she was seeing those waters in her sleep, that she was walking ecstatically through them, and that a holy secret lay on their stony bottom.

Meanwhile, the shore of the lake curved rapidly and shut the blue water away from view. The train sped out onto a wide expanse of green grass. The mountains were out of sight; only subalpine spruce forests stretched out into the distance. Meadows white with bastard balm extended as far as Teosia could see; among them thick clusters of fruit trees created an orchard impenetrable to the eye.

Around eleven o'clock the train stopped at Wintertur. When she heard the name, Teosia was overwhelmed with alarm and afraid to leave her seat. The conductor opened the door and gave her a signal to leave the car. When she had gotten down the stairs with her bundles and her children, she saw Wiktor elbowing his way through the crowd and looking for them. The sight of him irritated her. When he saw them and came running up, she hissed: "Where's your common sense, man, dragging us so far from home? Oh, Jesus, Jesus!"

"Did I order you to come? You didn't have to. Look at her! A husband's welcome! For three days I've been dashing over here like a fool, meeting every train."

"A welcome, you say! Look how it is with these children. They have sores on their mouths, I don't even know…You're the smart one! It's something that we didn't die on the way."

"Again, so considerate! I traveled that same road, after all. What was I supposed to do, shorten it or what?"

"Oh, shut your mouth. Really—"

"You were the one who shut my mouth so I couldn't welcome you. If you don't like it here, get on the train and go wherever you think fit."

He took Karolina in one arm, put a bundle under the other, and led them past the platform. They walked in silence along a gravel-strewn road. Houses, mostly with two or more stories, stood beside the road in small yards with iron fences. Each window was covered with a green blind. Those dwellings, like everything around them, seemed to be blossoming— to possess in themselves the verdant health of plants. Branches of grape vine were fastened on the south-facing walls, and grayish-green bunches of fruit hung abundantly among the leaves.

"You have a place to live, Wiktor?" Teosia asked more quietly.

"Indeed I have."

"One room?"

"Two small rooms and a kitchen. Cramped, but not bad."

"Far from here?"

"A little way. Not far."

After passing several crooked, crowded streets, he soon led them into the entrance hall of a narrow tenement and onto narrow stairs, very clean and so heavily trodden that the wooden treads were worn thin. The stairwell was musty, though the furnishings there were clean and gleaming. On the third floor Wiktor opened a door and let his family into a flat. True, it was cramped, with ceilings so low that one's head touched them, but it was pleasant. Both rooms were paneled in wood and colored blue with an oil-based paint. A very large heating stove with brown tiles reached to the center of the first. Windows, two for each room, filled the outer wall. Teosia looked at these quarters with a smile and felt as if she were still in the train, so vividly did the two painted, gleaming, box-like chambers remind her of the compartment in their car. But in the second she noticed a bed lavishly spread with covers. She began to undress right away.

Wiktor went out to his factory. The children did not want to go to sleep and hurried out to the city with their father.

Drowning in down quilts, Teosia let her eyes stray over the clean walls and plain, spotless furniture and tried to fix them in one place. Everything moved as she looked at it, moved endlessly, like the train cars. The wall slid out of its place and went on moving. The chair, the chest of drawers, the wardrobe, the big bundle lying in the middle of the first room—everything continually moved somewhere. When she closed her eyes to push it all away, an unending line of train cars unreeled before her vision and deep in her brain. Their wheels, knocking, rushed through her whole body, through her head and chest, with vibrations, roaring and screeching. There was no pushing it away, no rest.

She was perfectly conscious of how time was passing; she heard voices from the world outside; she understood where she was; but she could not quit feeling the driving motion of those cars even for a second. Among the noises from the street, one in particular captured her attention. It was like singing, like the chanting of lessons or a choral prayer by a group of children. Teosia heard not only the general tone but each individual voice as distinct from the harmony. There was something so inexpressibly cheerful in it, so sweet, that she could not resist it. She rose from the bed, threw on her clothes, and moved furtively through the room, looking out to see where the voices were coming from.

On the other side of the narrow street, at the same height as the Judyms' flat, were the open windows of a large room. Some forty children between four and six years old were sitting there on little wooden stools. They were chatting, laughing, crying, romping, and quarreling, but at regular intervals, at a sign from a stout older woman, each of them took a crochet hook in hand and began to work. Then, following the leader's voice, the whole choir nodded and sang that song, executing every move with the hook. Teosia did not understand the words, but she could not keep from joining in with the melodious sounds:

"Push in, wrap thread,
    pull out, drop…"
She was amused and totally engaged.

"What can this be?" she wondered. "A school? But would anyone send such little tots to school?"

Meanwhile the room full of children again erupted into chatter. The little ones shouted, played, and chased each other, but after a certain time elapsed, the recitative could be heard again: "Push in…"

As she watched these frolics connected with work and heard the sing-song babble, which was not really music but was rhythm that made work painless, she had a strange feeling. Huddled against the wall, not moving her eyes from the picture before her, she thought of something that had never occurred to her before. Scarcely comprehending the deep, wise realization that was breaking over her, she felt an agonizing regret. In her mind, walls, windows, and blinds moved without ceasing, and a storm of tears flowed from her eyes. She sighed for herself, and not only for herself. In her powerless, tormented heart she saw her children growing up in the gutter.

A violent banging on the door roused her from these reflections. Someone was rattling the handle and knocking. She was afraid to open it, so she sat cowering for some time, but when the person beat harder and harder, she unlocked the door. A tall man in a vest came into the flat. His look was so stern and his eyes so full of rage that she sat back on the edge of the bed in fear.

The newcomer began to shout and wave his hands. Every moment he showed her leaves that he was holding in his hands, then threw them onto the floor, then picked them up and put them in his pocket. He approached her and asked her some questions. When she maintained a diffident silence, he shouted more loudly. He went on in that way for a quarter of an hour. Finally he went out, slamming the door.

Teosia had hardly managed to regain her composure when he was back with a whole fistful of leaves. He put them on the table and with flashing eyes spoke again, repeating in a German-Swiss patois after every few words, "Go away!"

Without knowing what gave her the impulse, she began to yawn. She covered her mouth with her hand, but the man saw it and burst into a paroxysm of fury, shaking and stomping. She watched him warily from head to foot and swore to herself that if God would let him leave the flat again, she would never be so stupid as to unlock the door. The quarrelsome fellow did rush out, still shouting on the stairs. Quick as a wink she locked the door, lay on the bed and burrowed under an eiderdown. She lay half asleep for two hours, then was awakened again by a knocking at the door. It was Wiktor, the children, and the angry Swiss.

Wiktor mumbled something, rather to show his wife how to converse in German than to clarify the issue.

"What does this man want with us, Wiktor?" she asked.

"Our children stripped away his vine."

"What vine?"

"You see, here they have grapevines on the walls. This burgher had the whole front wall of his house covered with them. Franek and Karolina came and tore away all the leaves and pulled the stems out of the ground. So the clod is so angry he's shaking like somebody with the plague."

"Why did you do this?"

"It's the end of the world, that we pulled off the leaves!" Franek flared up. "Now you have something to make a hullabaloo about, Mama."

"That boor said he came to you here," Wiktor said to his wife.

"He came. He even came twice. He said something and I listened. He got it off his chest and left."

"Oh, a person can never get along with these Swiss. This country is like a prison! If you stamp your heel on the floor in your own flat at ten in the evening, the whole house is down on you. You can't talk to someone out loud, you can't keep a bundle of wood in your kitchen, you can't light a fire when the wind blows, you can't sprinkle kerosene to start your stove or right away you'll be fined twenty-five francs. Damn it, I don't know what you *are* allowed to do here!"

Meanwhile the Swiss man was talking to him without stopping for breath. Judym explained to his wife that he was asking why the children had done this to him—why they had destroyed the grapevine with its ripening fruit, and who had taught them to be such hooligans even in childhood.

The matter was put off until a later time, since Wiktor himself did not understand perfectly what the other man was saying He only knew that they would certainly evict him from that flat and that he would on no account be able to find another in the city. That sent him into a rage. He cursed the "clods" until the air turned blue and railed at them in Polish and in Swiss. Finally he said to his wife, "I tell you straight out that I don't intend to stay here."

"Where?"

"Here."

"What are you saying?"

"I'm going to strike out for America."

"Wiktor!"

"This is captivity, not a country! Yes, I earn more here than in Warsaw, but do you know what they pay Bessemer workers in America? Wąsik-iewicz wrote me in detail. That's what I call money."

"What are you saying? What are you saying?" she stammered. "We'll never get home again!"

"To Warsaw? Too bad! How am I going back there? Are you daft? Anyway, what the devil for?"

He thought a moment and said, shaking his head, "My dear, Bessemer is everywhere in the world. I follow it. Where they pay the most, that's where I go. Am I going to stay in this hole? Nobody is that stupid!"

Walls, windows and furniture reeled before her eyes. She fell onto the pillows like dead weight and looked with stony eyes at the painted timbers in the ceiling, which moved along with her somewhere into the beyond, into infinity, moved, moved…

CHAPTER VI

At Dusk

IN DR. JUDYM's life a remarkable epoch was beginning. To all appearances his existence did not alter; his duties were the same. So were his aims and the resulting friction.

At a deep level, however, the young doctor almost became a different person. What he did, what kept him busy, was the outer shell of his essential nature, while deep within it the intrinsic spirit blossomed. His treatment of the sick, his execution of matters related to the hospital and the resort, his attendance at the manor and in the neighboring villages underwent no change, and indeed were carried out with greater ease, but that was only the burn-off of excess energy. Something new, as new as spring after a hard winter, was engaging Dr. Tomasz's inmost soul.

Between one sunrise and the next it was as if enchanted groves were closed, hidden behind high walls, remote from this world. A fragrant memory persisted, an impression he had received on the April day when he had arrived at Cisy for the first time, stood in a window, and looked far down the lane through the park.

The branches of tall trees were still bare, gray and slender as hazel sticks. Their color contrasted vividly with the strange blue that rose and stood like sparse wisps of smoke over the ground, between the trunks. The first fragile, wrinkled leaves had barely sprung from the tips of the thin lilac branches. Heavy clusters of flowers like golden knurls seemed to float down from brown chestnut twigs. The beaming fire of the sun fell on the wet ground, flew away to its cerulean kingdoms, and was lost in the varicolored gowns of clouds. Bright plots of grass appeared on gray, steaming ground. The first blades were quivering, turning and tilting toward the sun. The joyous twittering of birds and the distant cheerful cries of children could be heard, and all space was filled with the odor of violets.

Against this background, with every sunrise an acute darkness of the mind arose. It made everything appear with double clarity, like stars in an evening sky. All external things were connected and separated differently than before, and all objects appeared full of wisdom and order. Everyday thoughts fell out of their domains like young birds that are startled out of their nests and look at everything with astonishment.

What was spring for? Why did night pass and day dawn? Where did the diligent clouds come sailing from, clouds that were sometimes as innocent as children's dreams and sometimes as terrible as bowels chopped with an ax and streaming blood? For whom did the spring flowers grow and why did their fragrance spread on the air?

What are trees, and why do they shed, in broad daylight, something on the earth that resembles night: their enchanting shadows?

Evenings—when the moon was set out in the radiant sky, which, as the Bible says, was the work of God's fingers—were transformed into a sacred mystery. They were an unfathomable secret; the heart sighed with longing for them as for the supreme form of its happiness.

At twilight Joanna often came to the park with Wanda, who was now her only pupil. There, without prearrangement, they met Dr. Tomasz. The three of them walked in the dark lanes talking of impersonal things, scientific, artistic, social. There was a particular charm in the fact that they hardly saw each other's faces or eyes, only dark figures, dark persons, dark beings like souls. Only in the sound of a voice could they become aware of the dreams they shared. Sometimes—rarely—they met in social settings and then, when the lips uttered indifferent phrases as they did in the park, the eyes carried on a different conversation, full of questions, answers, pleas, avowals, and promises—a conversation a hundred times more eloquent than words.

Judym was close to madness at the very thought that he would see his "fiancée." That was what he called her to himself, although he had still not declared his love to her or asked for her hand. And when he could see those eyes that glowed with the miraculous grace of love, he felt that blood was beginning to flow from his heart, that sweet death surrounded him like an ocean wave and carried him to the feet of that vision. The joy and sweetness of those moments together was so incomparable that it even put a damper on bodily desire.

Judym was not obsessed with Joanna in a carnal way. He never had dreams of tearing her chaste clothing from her. Something like an aromatic haze surrounded her and veiled her from such thoughts. Above everything, above beauty, goodness, and intelligence, what he loved in her was his own or her love itself, that enchanted garden where the person entering acquires an unearthly knack for comprehending everything. He shuddered to think that if he should willfully touch that heavenly grace which, God alone knew why, had crossed his path, if he stretched out his hand to see that unearthly thing more closely, it would instantly be gone. At the thought that it would disappear, cold death took over his inner being.

And so two streams of feeling continually flowed in his heart: longing and fear. When he looked at dainty, elegant Joanna, the basement on Ciepła Street rose before his eyes like a specter from which he could not disconnect himself. He thought of his family, the family of a craftsman, and his aunt and the companions of her amusements. He imagined that he himself, cowering, ragged, hungry and downtrodden, standing on the very brink of want, was in that dark cellar. And look! A dim figure was descending the stairs. He heard the quiet rustle of her gown, the fragrant ripple of her approach. She walked down slowly, stopping on every stone. She carried in her farseeing eyes the momentous message of her love.

He was free to look at her, but if he rose and spoke even one pleading word, if he touched the hand she extended, something ominous would ensue. For there is something that lies in wait, that bides its time patiently and watches with fixed eyes as one takes each step.

One day during the last half of June, Judym was on his way to one of the most distant villages. He deliberately shortened the walk, taking a short cut over footpaths to pay his visits more quickly and get back before sunset. The path went along a river that meandered through underbrush at one end of a long meadow, in a valley between two flat hills. The little trail, pressed out of soft ground and hiding in the shadows of trees, was only dry on the surface and still gave way underfoot. All around were grasses, basket willow, and creeping willow. Judym was walking quickly with his hands in his pockets and his eyes down, hardly seeing anything around him, when at a turning he met Joanna.

He was so taken aback at first that he did not even greet her. He took a few steps, wondering if she had been waiting for him there or if it was a dream. He would not have been at all surprised if she had vanished like mist from over a meadow. Nor did he feel happiness. He looked at her pale face with its confused expression and observed indifferently that her straight little nose, seen from the side, did not look like itself. At last he guessed that this was some sort of miracle. He would not have to wait for her in the park, or hurry to the sick, or find ways to shorten the remaining hours until twilight, for she was alone here with him. There was even a certain disappointment in this.

"Are you out for a walk, madam?" he asked, feeling as he spoke that he was behaving like an utter commonplace fool, for the moment that was passing was immeasurably important and would be remembered all his life. But in an instant that conviction was lost in forgetfulness and indifference as complete as if someone had poured a bagful of sand over it.

"I walk here every day, if, of course, it doesn't rain."

Judym knew that this was a fib. He knew that she had come to that place for the first time so as to meet him. He heard her words perfectly clearly, but they seemed to come from a distance. He did not understand them in any case, for he was preoccupied with the joy of seeing into her heart.

"And Miss Wanda?"

"Just now Wanda is riding with Mr. Worszewicz."

"You don't ride?"

"Indeed, I like riding very much. And it used to be…it used to be… My goodness… Now I can't. I have to be careful. I have a slight heart defect or some such, for every ride gives me a pain just here where the beastly thing beats. After that I can't sleep."

Hearing this, Judym felt a literal, physical pain and such grief, such deep, measureless grief, that he had to clench his teeth to keep from bursting into tears.

"Why haven't you consulted a good doctor in Warsaw?"

"Ah! A good doctor doesn't give advice about such things. Anyway, who would pay any attention to it there? Not to ride—that's easy."

"It's not a heart defect at all, and there's not a hint of disease about it," he said with a smile. "It's common, the most commonplace fatigue. Your organism is unaccustomed—"

"My organism—"

"…under the influence of forced exertion, suffers for a time from exhaustion. It might be well if—this is a simple thing—you could muster your strength and ride the gray mare two or three times a week, not so long as to tire yourself."

"You think so?"

"Yes, indeed. You must look lovely on a horse." He spoke without a moment's premeditation and really with no sense of all the words conveyed.

"Ah, that's just therapy!" Joanna said without looking at him. A golden smile, the most beautiful of smiles, encased her face like a sunbeam. Her lips and eyebrows twitched happily. For a moment Judym waited in vain for her to pronounce the tenderly eloquent phrase that lay concealed in that ravishing smile. A low blush like dawn washed over her cheeks.

"Excuse me," she said, blushing still more deeply, "have you ridden the tramway to Chłodna Street or Waliców Street sometimes?"

"I have. Yes, of course. Why do you ask?"

"I was only asking. Several times I saw you riding in that direction. You were a bit different at that time, not exactly as you are now. Or perhaps you looked different in a top hat. That was about three years ago or even more."

"Why did you notice me at that time?"

"I don't know."

"But I know very well."

"You do?"

"I surely know."

"Tell me why."

"Because…" Judym went pale. He felt the skin on his head tingle and a cold shudder run through his whole body. "No. Not now. Another time."

Joanna turned her eyes on him, looked at him with a candid, earnest expression, and was silent. They walked a long way.

The cottages in the village to which Judym was heading were scattered along the edge of a meadow at the top of a flat hill. The road, narrow on the lowland, turned into a wide cow path furrowed with many ruts and enclosed with a pole fence. Joanna walked a few dozen steps along that larger road. Suddenly she stopped and asked, "Are you going to the village?"

"Yes. To the sick."

"I won't go there."

"Why?"

"No, I won't go."

"Are you going back home?" he asked with disappointment in his eyes and voice.

"Yes, I must. Anyway… will you be long?"

"Not very. Half an hour."

"Ah, yes. I'll wait here. Or better—"

"Joanna—"

"Or better there, at the edge of that hill."

"Oh, good. Lovely! A lovely idea!"

He walked quickly along the road. He would have run full speed; he would have—the devil take it!—completely neglected his patients. He was only restrained by a superstitious sense that she was waiting there and that he must fulfill his duties. That certainty caused him boundless delight. He felt that something was approaching, something like a tryst, an agreed-on time of shared joy, and right away he was glad, again superstitiously, that happiness had come of itself, that he had not asked or importuned for it.

He wanted to deal with the sick as quickly as possible, but as if out of spite, women with children and men with injured fingers gathered in front of every cottage he approached. He had to examine them and administer dressings. It was nearly dusk when he finally hurried out of the village and looked for Joanna with burning eyes. There were moments when he lost control of himself.

"She's left," he whispered, choking back tears like a child.

Just then, as he approached the hill, he saw her. She was sitting on the ground among enormous junipers.

"Let's not go by way of the meadow, because it's growing foggy and damp," he said as he drew near her.

"Which way, then?"

"We can go over the mountain, straight through the fields, and from there by the edge of the Łaziński forest."

"Well, good. But we must go as fast as we can. It's almost night."

They climbed to the summit and found themselves in a field surrounded on three sides by woods—leafy trees on two sides, a pine grove on the third. The wall of trees grew quiet as the sun went down, painting motionless stands of hornbeam with gold and the birches with tints so vivid that the eye could distinguish the precise shape of very distant leaves. In the boundless distance beyond the ravine from which they had emerged, at the far edge of fields shimmering with grain, the sun was setting. Its level rays lay on bright roads, on glittering sheets of water that were usually hidden, on colorless surfaces of village houses. The figures of Joanna and Judym as they walked cast two shadows, as if two immense reflections of their existence walked in front of them, drew close to each other, blended, and then moved apart. The purple and gold glow of objects was soon gone. The disc of the sun slid into the ground and was submerged there. The distant grove of leafy trees grew dim and far away—far away—disappeared.

Judym looked at the landscape and felt something he could not explain. He had been there many times, it was true, but it seemed to him that he had experienced the same feeling in that place before, sometime, sometime…

This was the place he had been coming to all his long, wandering life.

"Why is this so?" he mused, looking into that mysterious open space. "Why is this so?"

And for a moment, for the wink of an eye, something like an answer found harbor in his mind, something like the ring of a word the wind brings from a distance but immediately snatches from the ear and blows away.

A part of the field, as if shunned by people, was covered with plants that had seeded themselves. Beside it lay another patch of ground that was plowed and dragged to cover the seed, an unusual sight at this time of year. That ground was still warm, spongy and soft. It did not impede the feet like sand on a dune, but warmed them from the depth of its fine, airy soil. Joanna's feet, in slippers, sank into it. Neither of them paid any attention to that detail, but both were aware of it.

The gray hue of the soil began to rise, began to absorb the colors of the forest that had gleamed a moment earlier and to spread near and far in a quiet, warm, fragrant twilight.

"I didn't tell you earlier why you noticed me when I was taking the tramway toward Chłodna Street. I think I know."

"You know?"

"Yes. I know."

"I'm very curious."

"You must simply have had a premonition then."

"A premonition of what?"

"Of everything that was going to happen."

"What on earth—"

"That I was going to be your husband."

Joanna did not show astonishment. She walked on calmly. Her pale face looked as if she were in a trance. Judym leaned toward her.

"Would it be for the best? Do you know what you're doing?" she said in a deep, quiet voice. "Think well about this."

"I have thought it all through."

That hard pronouncement did not reach the core of the matter, but it had such a decisive ring that she did not answer back.

Only now did Judym feel how completely he wanted her. Everything else fell out of his field of vision. The dusk bored into the depths of his soul and everything in him went dark. It seemed that the drag of the soft, deep earth in which their feet floundered had no end, that it stretched through hundreds of hours. The gray dusk, the desire-enhancing abdication of light, caused wild delight. It was an unknown element that seemed to diffuse itself into a flame and precede that sacred, divine, mysterious night like a cheerful cry in the wide emptiness above the earth.

Judym embraced his "wife" with his right hand and felt her left arm on his chest, her head next to his cheek. He leaned over and plunged his lips into her luxuriant, windblown, girlish black hair, on which something fragrant had breathed.

Tears flowed from his eyes, tears of boundless happiness that was locked inside him and that he would never know again.

They were startled to find their feet touching hard ground at the edge of the forest, but they did not slow their steps. Darkness stood like black marble in the pine grove; now and then it was slashed with a vein of gold by a firefly. They saw these golden threads and, though hardly aware of them, stored the beautiful soft glow in their memories forever as a precious treasure of life.

It was so quiet that they could hear the distant trickle of water from a sluice. Joanna thought that that voice was saying something, that it was calling. She raised her head to hear. Then she felt something like hot coals on her lips. Happiness like warm blood flowed to her heart in a slow wave. She heard a question, quiet words, holy words from the heart. She could find no phrases on her lips. She spoke with kisses of her deep happiness, of the sacrifice she welcomed with all her soul.

CHAPTER VII

The Rage of a Cobbler's Son

K RZYWOSĄD WAS ATTENDING to the removal of slime from the pond in the way he had done for years when, in the first half of June, so many guests descended on Cisy that it was not possible to complete the work. The slime was only taken out of the part of the pond on the river side and put in the moving current. The rest formed a swamp that the pond water could barely cover. After the water was drained, the drying mud, coated with a rough green blanket of aquatic weeds, gave off a hideous odor. The men working with wheelbarrows and shovels got fevers; even Krzywosąd himself had a fever and chills.

In such difficult circumstances, when there was no way to cart the rotting ooze past the park in front of the new arrivals, Krzywosąd had an inspired idea. Without telling anyone, he ordered that at a certain place the dike be dug down to ground-level and below; a sloping chute of boards about a foot and a half wide set into the opening, and a stream of water released into it. The water would trickle to the bottom of the drained pond and create a type of cascade that would rush down in volume to the riverbed. Krzywosąd put in place a dozen or more robust people with wheelbarrows and others with shovels and ordered them to take out the slime, cart it over the planking into the gutter, and throw it onto the wooden stream bed. The water rushing from above would wash away the slime and carry it toward the Baltic Sea.

It was such a neat trick that everyone was astonished at its originality. No heavy carts carried leaking slime around the park. No mud-spattered people slouched around the paths. The pond still stank, but it was calculated that if the work were stepped up, the level of the pond would be lowered in two or three weeks and the water could be held back.

Judym, up to his ears in love, knew nothing about this. When he saw this piece of hydrological engineering for the first time on his way across the dike to the institute for lunch, he stopped, speechless. He was so baffled that he asked the first worker he saw, "What are you lads doing here?"

"We're letting the muck out to the water, doctor."

"Letting the muck out to the water?"

"Yes."

"But that water runs by your villages. What will people give their animals to drink, and how will they have water for other uses?"

"It isn't our doing. The administrator ordered us to chuck it out, and the problem is solved."

"And since he ordered you to, you chuck it out, and the problem is solved!"

"Farmers have already come running over here from Siekierki," someone said. "They protested to the administrator that they were in trouble, that the water in the whole river was fouled, but the administrator cursed and chased them away. That's what they got for their trouble."

Judym turned away and walked along the bank of the stream with the intention, not yet clearly formed, of seeing if the river really was fouled. He walked for a long time over the freshly mowed meadow and looked with growing outrage at the grayish-brown, loamy effluent that slid lazily along the riverbed.

At a certain moment, however, his anger subsided. The radiant thought of something sweet replaced it. Judym forgot about the river. He forgot as completely as if reality had receded from his vision and he saw a dream far more actual and impossible to doubt than the pond, the river, the mire, the workers, or Krzywosąd. Only in the park did he regain his sense of his surroundings and look up.

He saw Krzywosąd and Węglichowski standing by the newly built sluice.

At the sight of them the young doctor felt physical revulsion. It seemed to him that the two figures themselves gave off the disgusting fetor of the slime. He decided not to go near them, to pretend that he did not see them, and to go away by a different route.

Why was he, among a hundred thousand, concerning himself with the whole business of the mire? Was this a more serious abuse than a billion others? Why was he devoting so much attention to it? Let these old geezers do just as they pleased! It was their affair. Instead of lolling in bed for years now, let them have their fun, this pair, this walking cemetery! He had done his utmost. He had pointed out everything that in his view was good or bad. They didn't want to listen; they were doing what they wanted. Well, so be it!

He went on his way at a fast walk. Above all other arguments, one remained at the forefront of his mind: "This is the role of a health resort: to supply the least advantaged layer of the population with fouled water for drinking. Instead, that layer…Ha! Ha! What a perfect image of the entire affair! That stinking muck in the river—that's the health resort's doing! Quite an illustration of the high-sounding phrases about the 'social role of the institute in Cisy!'"

He could endure it no longer. He would only aim this witticism at them and—enough! He would say that to Krzywosąd. No, not to Krzywosąd! He would say it to Węglichowski face to face and the discussion would end once and for all. It would be a Pyrrhic victory for them.

It was as if that argument were seizing him by the collar and turning him from his path. Its clarity of fact and its rational logic were so blinding that everything disappeared before them like a shadow before the light. At that moment no one could have beaten Judym into tempering the force of his point about the institute.

Krzywosąd and Węglichowski saw their young assistant coming and pretended to be carrying on a discussion of something more important than anything else in the world. Only when he greeted them did they turn toward him, without for a moment interrupting their spirited treatise on the hair used to stuff mattresses. Judym was silent for a long time, looking casually at barefoot, shirtless workers, partly submerged in mud, who were pushing large wheelbarrows.

Everything inside him was boiling. Everything was turning upside down. In his mind he repeated his wisecrack to himself and crafted it in good literary style. He wanted to express himself in an innocently malicious remark that would land like a light prick but poison the minds of his adversaries forever. Finally, struggling to control himself so that not one quiver of a muscle would betray his emotion, he said, "What brings you here, gentlemen, if I may ask?"

"As you see, colleague," answered the director, who was a bit pale.

"Yes, I see what I see, but I confess that I don't understand it."

"It's not possible to cart the mud here, so Krzywosąd is flushing the pond with water."

"Ah… flushing the pond."

The director went silent. After a moment he asked in a cold tone with a hint of anger, "You are not pleased with what you see, sir?"

"I? Indeed, why should I not be? As a subject for a domestic landscape painting…"

"As a subject for a domestic—"

"It is a principle of sound economy to use every means of enhancing the profitability of the enterprise. Since I have—" Krzywosąd put in.

Judym ostentatiously ignored him and repeated with emphasis, turning only to Węglichowski, "As a subject for a domestic landscape painting. I believe that what we often refer to as the role of the institute in the history of the region, attributing to it some social or hygienic significance, is only parochial claptrap, meant for effect, for self-promotion, calculated to gull hysterical ladies. For me this is merely a view, the same as any other view."

"These lectures of yours are offensive! I am an old man—"

"And I'm a young man who can't at a given moment be an old one."

"My dear sir!"

"I'm a doctor! I consider being your man-of-all-work unworthy of the position of doctor."

"Respected colleague!" Krzywosąd muttered threateningly. "Please choose your words well. What do you mean, man-of-all-work? *Nec sutor ultra crepidam!*"

"Well! Well! Spare us your Latin!" shouted the director. "I'll teach you to speak Latin!" Turning to Judym after a moment, he said quietly but emphatically: "Your admonitions will exert no influence on me or anyone else."

"I'm well aware of that. I—"

"If you're aware of that, I don't understand why you interfere in something that is none of your business. It has nothing to do with you, dear sir."

"Matters of hygiene have nothing to do with your man-of-all-work?"

"This is not a question of hygiene at all, and still less is there a man-of-all-work. What notion are you harboring? What do these things have to do with each other? Hygiene!"

"There is hygiene, but for the rich. Let the farmers and their livestock drink slime from our pond. I'll tell you in a few words, director: I protest unequivocally against what's being done here!"

"Protest, sir, for all you're worth, for all you're worth! Krzywosąd, tomorrow hire me twice as many workers as we have today."

"Mr. Piorkiewicz," Krzywosąd called to the steward, "send someone to the village and get eight or ten more people to come to work." He turned to Judym and said with a hearty, sarcastic laugh, "And what do you say to that, reformer?"

"I say nothing, you old ass!" Judym retorted calmly.

Krzywosąd fixed his eyes on him for a moment. Then he went pale, raised his fist, and took a step forward. Judym noticed that and lost sight of everything else. He took one leap at Krzywosąd and grabbed him by the throat, shook him ten times or so, and pushed him away.

The man had been standing with his back to the pond. When Judym threw him backward, he flew off the dike, fell into the muck, and was immersed so deeply in the watery swamp that they could hardly see him. The workers flung down their shovels and rushed to help him.

Judym did not see what happened next. Rage covered his eyes like a cataract. He went his way spewing loud, vulgar curses.

· CHAPTER VIII ·

Where the Wind Blows

As EVENING came on, Dr. Judym was handed a letter from Węgli-chowski with these words: "In the light of what has passed, I hasten to inform you, respected sir, that I regard our agreement, concluded a year ago in Warsaw, as no longer in force. Your servant, Węglichowski."

Judym read it carelessly, turned over, and looked sleepily at the design on the slipcover of his couch. He had known very well that such a letter would be brought to him any minute, and persuaded himself that he was waiting for it with contempt.

He tried not to think of anything, only to rest, to quiet himself, to cool down and attend to what had to be done before he left. He was even pleased with himself for achieving tranquility consciously, systematically. With a penetrating inner eye he noticed that he had developed a vibrant, morbid passion for Cisy, which now had to be struggled against lest it be transformed into something foolish. He closed his eyes and began earnestly making an effort to enumerate, in a low voice, certain chemical bonds. But he had hardly whispered three names when a question arose that pushed him from his seat as if something had hit him:

"Why hadn't I gone home before that row?"

The regret hidden in these words was so relentlessly painful, so piercing—it burst from inside him with such force—that it was like the end of an iron hook stuck in a living lung, a hook that tore the lung and ripped it out. But when the pain was at its most intense, when the hook seemed to be pulling with all its might, another agonizing image loomed: Joanna's smile when he met her in the meadow.

Throughout the entire incident, Judym had forgotten about her, or rather had been unable to remember her. Her appearance now was a shock that left him helpless, hurt, and speechless.

"What's to be done? To leave, to separate? Now, of all times? Today, tomorrow, the next day?"

The feeling that overwhelmed him at the very thought of leaving was silly, weak-minded, and miserable. It left him shaking with fear and mad with grief. Everything in his soul came apart. Courage and resolution blew away like chaff in the wind.

Evening fell. The smell of blooming roses came in through the open window. Above the wall that enclosed a part of the park, between the tree trunks, a red-gold sunset gleamed. A warm twilight filled the room and spread slowly along the lane between the hornbeams.

Judym still saw the charming distant perspectives of the lane and the gray wall, but at some moments he lost sight of everything, as if the dark had devoured his vision. In spite of all his efforts to fend it off, he fell farther and farther into impenetrable blackness. He felt that all the emotions of love had fallen there with him and would be scattered like dust at the terrifying bottom. He lay helpless as a log, experiencing a tremor as sudden resolves formed in his mind, while in that same moment he had a strange sense that they foreshadowed only the presence of a miserable sickness in his soul.

He heard a rustling that caused him stinging pain. A female figure appeared in the blue glass of the window. Rather from the tears that flowed to his heart than from the strength of his vision, he was conscious of Joanna's presence. When he was standing by the window and pressing her head to his chest, she began to speak to him quietly and rapidly. He could not comprehend what she was saying; he only felt that his power of thought and feeling had returned. A sigh burst from him: "Tomorrow…"

"Tomorrow…"

"I can't be here a moment. Not a moment."

"What was it for? What was it for?"

"I had to do it. It wasn't up to me. My own efforts have taken revenge on me now. If I were a placid man, if I went along with everything… 'He who struggles with the world must perish in time to live in eternity.'"

He quoted that sentence with delight, with a certain peculiar, pleasant boastfulness, a delicate pride. Only then did a fragrant little mouth find his lips and press a wonderful kiss on them.

"Where will you go?" she asked, tearing herself from his arms.

"I don't know. To Warsaw, surely. I haven't thought about it yet."

"What have you thought about?"

"About something completely different."

"What?"

Instead of answering he put out his hands, but at that instant she disappeared. His heart and lips overflowed with words of great tenderness; she could hear none of them. He looked into the twilight that was enveloping the garden, the twilight that seemed to be her element—the element from which she came, the element that she was. It was full of lovely scent and filled him with madness.

For a long time—until late at night—he was by himself, plunged in sleepy anticipation, imagining that she was watching from the dark. The moment came when this spell dispersed as if a damp vapor from the darkened park had frightened it away. Judym remembered that in the morning he had to leave.

He had not thought even for a moment about where he would go, but again paroxysms of grief tugged at him. He lighted a lamp and with lifeless eyes looked around at his winter quarters: two very large rooms on the ground floor of the old castle. They still contained some traces of the old, archaic grandeur. The walls were hung with tapestries in frames; the doors and windows were set in graceful woodwork. Simple gilded mouldings ran around the ceilings, blossoming here and there into filigree in royal style. Old console tables with mirror tiles flashed in the corners of the room and between the windows.

From deep in an old frame over the beautiful hearth, the portrait of a young woman with bare arms and a glowing expression seemed to say to every viewer, "Love life above everything." Thick, luxuriant coils of hair lay on her forehead like clusters of black flowers. Her purple lips, one cheek, and one arm were illuminated by a delightful radiance like the dreaming silver of the moon. A satanic charm was locked into the lines of her face— perhaps love for the creator of the painting. Judym liked to look at "his" portrait. To him the lovely divinity on that canvas was like a force that pulled one into the past, into antiquity. It allowed him to see, through subtle clues, that those who had lived in those rooms and known enjoyment and suffering there were proud gentlemen, and later had gone away somewhere, like clouds passing overhead.

Now, as the lamplight fell on the portrait, on those charming, elegant, pleasant rooms and the comfortable furniture, he trembled. It struck him that he did not have the strength to leave all this. Every piece of furniture seemed to emerge from the dimness and hold a memory. Each of them was like a devoted friend who had absorbed some detail, some particle of the secret of his love for Joanna, and now laid everything bare. Here in this apartment, everything was Joanna. She had never been in it, but joyous dreams and thoughts full of happiness concealed her as if in a mysterious residence that no one had ever seen. The old portrait knew about her and its smile seem to threaten to spread the wonderful rumor to everyone at any minute. What inexpressible charm was hidden in its silence!

A little table in the corner was littered with books. At the sight of it Judym sobbed inside. When he had run into the room with the delightful secret he had discovered in himself after seeing Joanna at the edge of the woods, he had sat over that table, caught up in the music of blossoming rapture, resting his head in his hands.

Now grief took that moment in its wicked fingers—that moment that was like the lovely ornamental flowers whose seven calyxes always bloom at the same time. That grief tore away and crushed their flame-like petals.

At the sight of all the contents of the room, Judym felt a shabby emotion that reared its ugly head like the forehead of a seal poking up from moment to moment out of dark water. He fell to thinking and, closing his eyes, probed for a way of apologizing to the director and making up with Krzywosąd. He thought of the scheming wife of the old bursar. She could be useful...

He threw himself onto the sofa and dreamed deeply, desperately, despicably about how he would manage everything. A hundred times he organized his plan, his intrigue. He would go away in two days, he would go away the day after tomorrow. Tomorrow! No, not tomorrow, not for love or money. For a whole day he would work his hardest to win over the director and that shrew. The women would bring about an understanding between him and the director. The director, for his part, would talk Krzywosąd into a good humor.

When he returned, he would begin a new life. Oh, a new, quiet, domesticated life! This once it was time to be through with foolish things! Time to become a serious man! He and Joanna would be married quietly that very month. Again everything would be pushed aside for the long-term plan. They would walk along the lanes as a couple. Ladies who were guests at the spa, beautiful ladies and plain ones, would pass, dressed in their best. All eyes would be on him and Joanna. Judym would feel like a common man who talks like a close friend with a distinguished, famous person in the midst of an envious crowd. He would boast about his fiancée, he would show off her dazzling, all-conquering beauty, her every movement, lithe as the tremulous young branch of a tree. They would walk among the crowd without seeing anyone, absorbed in themselves as in the fragrance of a tuberose.

Not until daybreak did Judym sleep briefly. He woke chilled. He sat on the bed and looked around in astonishment. He had to leave: the realization was like a millstone falling on his chest. He did not brood about it, nor did he wish to push it aside. He only mustered the strength to lift it.

For about three hours he packed his things—clothes and books—into an old valise. Just before eight, when the mail wagon went out to the railroad, he was ready, with a quarter of an hour to spare for breakfast. He drank a cup of coffee in the restaurant as hastily as if someone were pursuing him and went to take a parting look at the hospital. When he was standing at the gate of that facility, in which he had invested so much passionate effort, a new, unknown spring brimmed over in his soul. A smile of superiority played around his lips and his eyes took on an icy expression. Still wearing that smile, he passed through the rooms, briefly examined a boy who was ill with typhus, and walked out without saying goodbye to anyone. He did not even glance toward the manor and the windows behind which lived the heart of his heart. Only at the corner of the lane, before the hospital was out of sight for good, did he turn around and gaze at it for a few seconds with narrowed eyes. His face tightened and twitched spasmodically. Then he walked away with long strides.

The mail wagon was already standing in front of the castle veranda and the driver was asking him from a distance to hurry. Judym ran quickly to his apartment to pack something into his valise. He quickly unfastened the buckles on the leather straps, opened the lid, put what he needed in the proper compartment, and began to fasten the case as fast as he could. When he had done that, it seemed to him for a moment that he was in another place.

He was in his aunt's entrance hall. He was hurrying to his lessons, right away, right away! He had to hurry because, first, his life depended on it, and second, he might get a bad mark on his report card, and third, his aunt might notice that he was still there, appear in the doorway, fly into a rage, and kick him in the teeth or spit in his eye.

He must go. He must go.

"As fast as you can, you wicked mutt!"

Why was there such unutterable pain in his heart? Why far worse than then? Always and everywhere…

For a fleeting instant, something stood by him like his own shadow, something so familiar, so near, so very, very near, as near as a coffin: loneliness. It seemed to speak in an unintelligible language that made his blood run cold and his hair stand on end. "Nothing," it said. "Nothing. I will wait."

After a moment he was in the wagon. On the way to the station he felt an outer calm that was even pleasant and stimulating, like the onset of fever before a serious illness breaks out. He did not think of the affairs of Cisy. He did not regret anything. He felt only an overwhelming aversion to the new landscapes that passed by and a genuine fear of the station, the train car he would soon enter, and the other passengers. When he found himself in the railroad station, however, he made his way into the crowd and forgot those painful feelings. He squeezed into a second-class compartment and since no one was there, he threw himself onto an upholstered bench, hoping to sleep.

To sleep…to sleep…

He was worn out. He felt tons of weight pressing him down. He smoked one cigarette after another. His eyes were tired. They were turned toward the window, absorbing the color of the sky, sometimes the treetops, the telegraph poles and wires—inanimate as mirrors that hold an image without being conscious of what it is.

Up and down, up and down over the window the thick parallel lines of telegraph wires ran incessantly. Now they moved slowly, slowly, lurking near the bottom of the window frame until suddenly they hid behind it, as if they had fallen into the ground. Then after a moment they flew up like startled birds, hurtling all the way to the top of the pane. Then again they stopped in the middle, motionless, as if lost in thought about where to go next.

"If they go up," Judym mused. "If they go…"

His heart tightened and he sobbed, because the wires he saw in that small, transparent templum, like an oracle in the sacral field of vision, tilted downward and moved slowly, like a soundless mocking laugh.

Then his soul was enveloped by phantasms, nameless half-feelings, superstitions, aberrations, fears. They rushed in from somewhere unexpected, like rough streaks on a shining sheet of water. They sighed and fell away. Then they appeared again like water plants, like algae, like long strands from which white lilies bloom on the surface—like flat ribbons and threads that wrap around the body of a drowning man when he is choked by water, loses his force of movement, and, without strength, falls to the bottom.

They seemed to wait in the depths with clenched claws during long days and nights, constantly on the watch for the person overcome with despair. These creatures are deceptively charming, unlike anything on earth, without intelligence, without sense. They are neither bushes, grass, nor plants. They sway ceremoniously with their slippery green, brown, or yellow bodies touching each other. They hold mysterious assemblies, as if they were humming something, rocking in time to a melody of waves flowing over their heads. How strange they are when they look into the eyes of a drowning man! A sensible man who rips them from the water and throws them dying on the shore, who separates and examines them, sees that they are only paltry water weeds. Not so the drowning man, who looks at their stems with green hair, with hands that flex like a hydra, with lips that titter as they kiss, with eyes hidden by loathsome, shaggy lashes.

Judym wandered around among his premonitions like a drowning man around the bottom of the water. From moment to moment he stretched his arms, shook them off and floated up. Then he saw something like the phantom of Joanna; he remembered the rustle of her dresses and the fragrance of her lips on his. But such moments were shorter than a word, and were dispersed by an awareness like death, after which the memories were infused with unremitting grief, the same yet perpetually new. The grief flowed from his heart and attached itself to every rapidly disappearing view, to every thicket of woods that remained nearer Cisy—and, like an industrious worker, his grief showed him greater, ever greater distances.

Most bothersome of all were particular irritations, blind spasms of the nerves. Images, thoughts, fragments of reasoning, syllogisms, concepts, tore at him like pincers. Then the most vexing pain burned his soul like fire; the flaming claws of powerlessness bit into it, turned it inside out and shook it. He castigated himself senselessly, like a drunken beggar wandering without a goal.

The train made station stops, ran on, stopped again. Judym was oblivious to that. Only at the large terminal where several railroads intersected and there would be an hour's wait did he have to get off and go into the hall. In the crowd he felt weaker, more aggrieved, more hopelessly at a loss, and unhappier than he had ever felt in his life. A piece of furniture reminded him of his winter apartment in Cisy, with its elegant silence and peace, and the memory moved him to tears. He missed those places with a pain in his heart, with weakness in his hands and his legs. He reproached himself no end for his obstinacy, his quarrelsomeness and the scenes he had caused, especially the recent ones. With clearsighted disgust he saw the folly of everything he had done in his last days at Cisy. He tried to purge his memory of it all, to efface those recollections. Now he admitted that Krzywosąd and Węglichowski had been absolutely right about everything. He realized how well-judged and tactful Węglichowski's behavior had been. If he had caught sight of their faces in the crowd, what a welcome sight it would have been!

Someone in the crowd said "Cisy," and he could not control his feelings any longer. He walked among the throng clenching his teeth and his fists, choking back sobs.

Just then he saw, like a curse, a familiar face among the people milling around the hall. He turned away from it involuntarily and at first had an impulse to run away. Not for anything in the world was he ready to talk with anyone, particularly with this person. He sat in a dark corner and scrutinized the fellow from the corner of his eye so he would not be recognized, even if he had to hide his face in his hands. He would have gone to the most eccentric extremes of poor breeding just to avoid contact.

This acquaintance was the engineer Korzecki, a tall, slender, dark-haired man in his thirties. Judym had met him in Paris and later traveled with him in Switzerland, where Korzecki was staying for his health. Partly in the capacity of physician, partly as a fellow countryman and companion, he had followed Korzecki around from one institution to another for three months at his own expense.

At that time, Korzecki had been overworked and sick with nervous exhaustion. They had long conversations, engaged in contentious sparring, and, often irritating each other, wandered around without other company. At last, after one of their sharpest disagreements, they went in opposite directions: Judym returned to Paris and Korzecki to Poland.

Just now the sight of his companion from the Swiss excursion was unbearably painful. Korzecki walked slowly around the hall and out to the platform, then returned.

He was a handsome man; tall, well built, distinguished. His clothes were in the latest style and perfectly tailored. With his pale overcoat and

traveling cap, yellow shoes, and leather valise, he stood out from everything in the hall like a shining product of Western European civilization
among the colorless, insipid inhabitants of Lesser Poland.

The first train moved out, significantly reducing the crowd in the station. Judym did not know where those people were going. Nor did he care
at all in which direction or toward what destination he himself was going.
He was traveling toward Warsaw, the great common home of all wander-
ers. But when he would arrive there—whether he would stop on the way,
or where—he had not thought about at all.

Deep in his own musings, he paid no attention at all when Korzecki
came and stood before him. He only noticed him when he said, "It can't
be—such a respected Aesculapius looking as if he were in a drunken
stupor!"

Judym quivered and looked askance at the man, whose presence just
then was unwelcome. Nevertheless, he extended his hand and touched his
smooth glove. "Where have you come from and where are you going?" he
asked slowly, in a way that was almost insulting.

"I'm going home. And you?"

"I—where the wind blows."

"That's a highly original direction! Does it lead to some residence in the
form of a point moving in space?"

Judym stifled the words he might have uttered in response. Reluctantly
he forced himself to raise his eyes to the other man's face. It was the same
face, but more worn. As before, the eyes glimmered like two flames: dark,
deep, sad eyes, often hollow and sunken, now and then gleaming with hate
and passionate energy, like the white fangs of a tiger. One, the left, seemed
larger and very often motionless. Their most sincere, most truthful expression was irony. When that intimidating vision, unrelenting, heavy, penetrating as an X-ray, was turned on someone who was talking, it sometimes
took the speaker's breath away, as if the barrel of a revolver with its dark
opening had suddenly been put to his head.

Judym always feared those looks more than the most adroit logic. Their
merciless scrutiny never trusted a single sentence that came from anyone's
mouth; it was like fingers thrust to the root of every thought, every emotion, every reflex, to the hidden things a person is not strong enough to
perceive in himself. Korzecki spied even the most deeply hidden untruth in
those he conversed with. He uncovered every pose, every trifling element
of falsehood. And when by luck he found one, he threw himself with joy,

with wild pleasure, into frolicking with it, jerking it about, like a cat with a mouse in its claws. A thousand expressions of feigned wonder and fabricated outpourings of admiration, cunning incitements to further innocent hoaxing, shot from his black eyes as if they were coated with quicksilver—until at last a truly devilish look crept out of them, followed by the dull blow to the chest that deprived the victim of the power of speech and paralyzed his thought.

"I heard a vague rumor that you were living in the country," the engineer said, sitting at a table.

"In a medical institute."

"Ah, yes! In Cisy."

"Yes. In Cisy."

"Well, and is it a good place?"

"Not altogether."

"May I be so optimistic as to assume that you can endure it?"

"I have just left it."

"For long?"

"Forever."

"Voila! Forever…I don't like the word 'forever.' Was it the material conditions?"

"Frankly, Korzecki, I'm quite unstrung. To the point that it's difficult to speak. Be a good fellow and don't be offended."

"I noticed, and I apologize. It's good, at least, for a person to speak candidly. I understand and I'll disappear like a dream. Only one little word: where are you going? Do you need money or any sort of help?"

"No, no! It seems I'm going to Warsaw."

At that moment he heard, not far off but quite near him, Joanna's voice. He felt a tightening in his heart and his eyes glazed over, as if life were flowing out of them.

"I'll say a few words and go away," said Korzecki. "May I?"

"Speak."

"I say this: come with me, good man, to Zagłębie. For a short time or a long time; it's up to you. Rest your body, rest your soul, look around."

"No, no! I can't go anywhere."

"I'll say even more: in one business there, there is a vacancy for a doctor. You could put your name in. The rest—later."

"I'm going to Warsaw," Judym muttered, not knowing himself why he rejected this proposition. Above all, the idea of having to talk with

Korzecki sickened him. As if divining his thoughts, Korzecki said, "I won't talk to you. I won't even ask you anything. Well?"

"No. No."

"Where do you intend to stay in Warsaw? In a hotel? When a man is tired and his nerves are giving him trouble—"

"What do I have to do with nerves? But my nerves will still make me sick, these stupid nerves! I can't bear this excessive nervousness."

Korzecki's eyes widened slightly and a little smirk darted across his face. Then it disappeared, to be replaced by an expression that was seldom seen there: profound respect and attention. Judym looked at him and felt relief. Really, where was he going? To Warsaw, to ramble around the streets, stifling spasms of anger and longing?

"My presence would make your life miserable," he said much less gruffly.

"We'll go in separate compartments, even different cars, if that's the issue. They'll give you a sleeping compartment and you won't even be able to see me."

"What are you saying?"

"Never mind. I know what I'm saying. Anyway, I have an interest of my own in this."

"What interest?"

"A certain interest."

"But I bought a ticket to Warsaw."

"What of it? I'll go right now and buy you a ticket to Sosnowiec. Sit here quietly and worry as much as you can in so short a time, and I'll hop over to the ticket window."

Judym watched him go and enjoyed the sight of his pastel-colored outfit as it moved through the crowd. A sigh of relief escaped him. For a brief moment he thought about Zagłębie and what it would be like. In spite of his aversion to new places, and in particular to a place with a name that suggested damp bottomlands, he preferred going there to being in Warsaw.

Korzecki returned immediately and ostentatiously showed Judym his ticket, then quickly tucked it into his pocket. The train arrived and Judym mechanically followed his guide to the first-class car. He was alone in a compartment and quickly threw himself onto the seat, trying hard to think of nothing at all. When the wagon shuddered and began to move, he felt a deep pleasure because he was not traveling alone and not going to Warsaw.

No one came into the compartment. Only after an hour did Korzecki enter silently, with his deep leather suitcase in his hand. He sat in the opposite corner of the compartment and read a book. When he took off his flat cap, Judym noticed that his bald spot had become much larger. His thin, closely cropped hair was still black around the crown of his head, but the white gleam of bare skin was striking to the eye.

He read attentively. From time to time an expression of cold contempt flitted over his beautiful lips, and something like a smile—the kind of smile he wore when as a self-styled cynic he was carrying on a spirited conversation with someone who was putting on airs. His eyes treated the page on which they were fixed as ruthlessly as it if were a person. Judym watched him from under his eyelashes and out of nowhere a strange idea entered his head: what would have happened to Joanna if she had been the wife of such a man? At that moment he wanted to see her eyes, to remember them, but his vision was drowning in his own tears, which seemed to be dissolving his eyes and face like a flood.

He lay motionless, trying with all his strength to stifle spasms of suffering. At one moment he felt a fevered desire, a passionate longing, to speak of Joanna to Korzecki—to unburden himself of the whole truth, everything. He had almost begun to speak when something, some trifling reminiscence, brought down the idea like a heavy pellet hitting a bird in flight. He forgot where he was and what was happening to him and, racked with longing and feeling more dead than alive, rifled through his memory.

Around five in the afternoon, Korzecki closed the book and pulled his heavy suitcase from the shelf. As he prepared to leave the car, he said quietly:

"It's time to get up, Judym. We're here."

They walked out onto the platform. The station was large and busy; they passed by it quickly and got into a waiting carriage. The well-fed horses carried them briskly through the town, which looked as if it had been built in a week. The houses were new and crude, constructed hastily, with little care. There were ruts and deep mud puddles in the streets, and spatters of dried mud on the second-story windows. Old shacks and dwellings in the style of the Piast era, six hundred years earlier, huddled beside the new buildings.

The area beyond the town looked as if it were constantly being ransacked, not with the aim of improving it, but of plundering whatever it contained. Nothing was left in the place except offscourings, remains. Every second the eye was tormented by pits, ditches, canals, drains. Here and there stood clumps of pines growing sparsely like rye in sand, so that it was possible to see what was happening beyond them. Some spaces were overgrown with stunted pine, that misshapen pariah of trees, and others with juniper.

Highways, roads, paths ran in every direction. Every now and then the wheels of a carriage rumbled over the railroad. Chimneys could be seen everywhere, chimneys with smoke trailing into the distance over the vivid blue sky.

The road ran along beside factory buildings of all sorts, which formed grotesque enclaves scattered among rows of human dwellings. Near the factories one could see large, deep holes, in which foul, contaminated yellowish-red water stood with no way to flow out. The sight of those pits filled Judym with a sadness beyond words. It was a painful, disgraceful picture. The water could never leave them, flow away, escape, move backward or forward, or even soak in without a trace, be lost to memory, and die. It had no use, not for drinking, not for cleaning. It could not even reflect clouds or stars in the skies. Like an eye put out, it looked up with a terrible glint, a mute cry that haunted a person. Cursed by all, it served as a container for infection. And it would be there forever, with no death to end its filthy existence.

Not far from these craters stood slag heaps, piles of coal dust as large as real hills. Here and there they had been torn apart by rains and storms that cut diagonal gaps within them. Coal dust mixed with shale smoldered in these strange heaps, the color of burned brick, that erupted here and there like fiery, bloody tumors on that sick and mistreated land.

When the carriage finally rolled onto a wide, well-maintained highway, they could see their destination at a distance: the Sykstus mine. Its outside buildings were like three conjoined wooden windmills, so covered with black dust that two panes at the foot of one of them caught the eye with a pleasant steely glow. At the tops of the two highest prism-like towers, amid clouds of steam and smoke, the wheels of the underground elevators turned first in one direction, then in the other. Black jetties of coal extended from the buildings in all directions, and the huge wooden ribs of catwalks rose above them.

The mine spoke; its voice could be heard from far away. A man in thick boots and a jacket that reached to his knees stood on one of the catwalks. He was black all over. He must have said something because he was waving his hands, obviously giving an order to people below who were hard at work shoveling up black lumps. Water stood all around in ditches and containment basins—or rather not water but a colorless, dark, dead liquid. It lay heavily in the torn earth, which lacked the strength to cover with grass the parts of it that had been stripped bare. Black powder was falling from the sky, and no sooner did the sun bring anything to life on the ground than the dark particles destroyed it.

Behind the mine's enclosure lay a dumping area for stone mixed with coal. Farther on, a great splotch of black dust sprawled, like a huge patch on a torn garment. A ragged stand of tree trunks bristled behind it, withered by blistering heat, stripped of branches by storms, and thickly sprinkled with coal dust drifting through the air. In Judym's eyes those projecting remains, the stumps of lush trees beheaded long ago, were like the faces of injured beings, of misery stifled and trodden into the ground. They seemed to be weeping with rending, terrible sobs that no one heard. As far as the eye could see, an unexpected field of rubble ran down along the sterile ground whose reason for being had been annihilated.

Judym looked at it as if it were the landscape of his soul. He saw perfectly every logical necessity, the workings of all the intelligent, productive laws of industry, but at the same time he felt an irrational emotion running beside them independently, like a restless, stormy river—but quietly, existing in its own right and subject to its own laws. In his soul he wept for this land. Some shackle of unfathomable sympathy joined him to these places. He saw something in them that reason could not grasp and even imagination could not keep pace with.

Korzecki ordered the driver to stop in front of the check house, and asked about something. The carriage went into the yard. Both men alighted beside the sorting plant and went into the accounting house. It was a small one-story building, grimy as a chimney sweep's clothes. In the first room they entered, Judym found a free chair by a window and sat down. Korzecki asked him to wait there and went to the next room, from which the voices of people with excellent lungs resonated.

The room in which Judym was sitting was empty. Two cabinets painted black and filled with papers stood ominously in the corners. A table and a register lying on it were covered with particles of coal that seeped in through chinks in the windows, which trembled along with the entire building. Behind the windows, cars were being pushed along railways by muscular workmen, with much rumbling and slamming. Lumps of coal flew into those moving wagons from the grates of the sorting plant. He heard constant banging mingling with harsh shouts or crude laughter.

An electric lamp that was fastened to the table began to burn feebly. Judym's head fell onto his entwined hands. The light filled his heart with a terrible pain. He seemed to feel the weight of the moving wagons in his shoulders; he thought black, shiny lumps with angles sharp as axes were falling on his head. The wild yells of the workers, the shouts of the foremen, the indescribable racket of the sieves in the sorting plant, and amid all of it the periodic moan of the bell when a cage went down the shaft into the gallery, all fell on his ears like the voices of ghosts. The sound of the bell was particularly terrifying. It sounded like something being choked, and reached to his heart as if it were sounding an alarm. It was like a human moan, like the *vox humana* in the organ in the Freiburg Cathedral.

Judym slowly raised his head and saw ink, a pen and a scrap of rough paper in front of him. He began to write in poorly formed letters: "Joanna! Joanna! What shall I do without you? My life was beside you, all my heart, all my soul. Always I feel that one of us died and the other wanders through the world in a cemetery that never ends. A tolling bell groans terribly in my soul, stammering out some phrase that I can't quite hear…"

He broke off, feeling that he was not expressing what was essential, that the real, merciless truth that tore at his heart could not be laid out in words. As he was sitting hunched over the paper, he felt that someone was standing over him. It was Korzecki. Judym rose from the chair and saw that the other man knew his secret.

"Pardon me," Korzecki said. "My eye fell on the paper involuntarily, without my realizing that you were writing a letter. I only read the first few words."

"It wasn't a letter!" Judym muttered. He tore the paper to pieces and tucked it into his pocket.

"I apologize!" Korzecki said softly, delicately, in a voice Judym had never heard from his lips before.

"Are we staying here?"

"Heavens, no. We're going on."

"Where to?"

"To my place. I don't live here, after all. You may be spending enough time here, after a while. On the way we'll have a look at the clinic."

"How far is it?"

"Two miles. Are you tired?"

"Yes. I'm ready to drop."

"We'll be home very soon. I'll phone them and tell them to have tea for us."

"No! That's not necessary at all. I, at least, won't eat. I won't put a thing in my mouth."

When he had said that, Judym blushed without knowing why. Korzecki noticed and said quietly, "And if I order you to eat beefsteak in the name of Miss Joanna?"

He took him firmly by the shoulders and kissed him. Judym returned the gesture with a hug but felt humiliated and went quiet, thoroughly confused. He had an oppressive sense, as he had had when he first met Węglichowski, that he was a captive, dependent on a stronger will. He was deeply exasperated at the thought that his secret concerning Joanna, a matter extremely private and sacred, had been revealed to Korzecki, who seemed to know everything. There was even a second when those delightful and painful events lost a little of their charm.

In the carriage Korzecki fell into silence again, into his lethargic, immovable numbness. He came to life only for a moment, when he showed his companion a house in the shape of a box, with evenly spaced windows and a flat tin roof. It was the clinic. A cluster of very commonplace people were standing there, one with a rag fastened over one eye, another with a thick bandage around a hand, another with an expression of acute internal pain on his face.

Judym saw them all as if through a pouring rain. The thought that he might come and treat these people, might occupy himself with their suffering, was as dreadful to him as the suffering itself. His thoughts were arrested by a phrase he had heard from someone: "the rabble." From whom exactly? From whom? It crept into his mind and tormented him, for he was so close to recalling the occurrence, close to all the circumstances that attended it… After a long effort he found himself at Versailles again, in Marie Antoinette's chambers, and he heard the phrase from Joanna's lips. How well, how completely it expressed the essence of the thing!

"If you liked, perhaps you could have the post of doctor at the Sykstus mine," said the engineer.

"Not now, not now! I must rest for a few days."

"I'm speaking of the future. I talked with someone, a fellow with influence. It would be a good thing if you settled here. It's boring and dismal, that's true."

He was silent and sat with his head down for a while. Then he whispered melodically to himself: "Thou wilt sprinkle me, O Lord, with hyssop and I shall be cleansed. Thou wilt wash me and I shall be whiter than snow."

He turned to Judym. With some embarrassment, with a pale blush on his face, he explained, "Sometimes an unexpected image comes to me. From where, I don't know. A feeling that seems to come from under the ground. At just that moment I thought of our church, an old church in the mountains. The portly priest came out in a white vestment with two other people: the organist and the sexton. That odor of herbs, of grain, of trees with young hazel nuts, for it was August fifteenth! The priest intoned, 'Sprinkle me,' and went out to the church by a path that formed between the farmers, like a path over which cattle are driven to pasture. He sprinkled holy water to the right and the left, slowly raising his hand. Meanwhile the organist himself sang. His voice was pure, calm, masculine. His face—it was clean-shaven—had a look of profound concentration, almost sternness. When he sang that sweet phrase, 'whiter than snow,' the tone of his voice was a bit sharp, a little hoarse.

"I can hear him at that moment…oh, God! Usually when he began the verse for the second time, the priest returned and then drops of holy water fell on the foreheads of those who stood in the patron's pew. Drops of holy water…cool, holy drops…And that melody, plaintive, trusting, that song like a child's song, that sigh of the simple soul who is not afraid! Don't you see that from the depths of those phrases, straining eyes, flooded with tears, look into Heaven? 'Thou wilt wash me, and I shall be whiter than snow.'"

Evening fell. In the distance, electric lights spilled their pale blue glow. The hum and clatter of human activity could be heard. The carriage drove rapidly into a small street in something resembling a backwater town and stopped in front of a shabby one-story house. Judym followed his host into the house and then upstairs.

The apartment was spacious but empty as a doghouse. In one room, coatstands stood like eccentric scarecrows. In another an iron bed hugged the wall. The third held a card table and another bed, together with a few small necessities. "Make yourself at home as best you can in these elegant rooms, and I'll get us something to eat and drink," Korzecki quipped as he left the apartment.

A little later a man as black as coal came in, carrying the suitcases. He kissed Judym's hand for no apparent reason and began to bring in glasses, chipped plates, and knives and forks from the neighboring premises. Korecki appeared soon afterward with the news that there would be steak and beer.

"Don't you admire the Spartan austerity of this apartment?" he asked, taking off his stylish coat and cap.

"It will be fine when it has a mistress," Judym said to make conversation.

Korzecki laughed loudly, too loudly, and snickered unpleasantly. But then he stopped speaking and noisily began to wash up, splashing his face with water, snorting and huffing. When he had wiped his face with a rough towel he said, "That's an awful thing you're promoting. Mistress of the house! Ha! Ha! Mistress of the house! What an expression!"

"What's awful about it? You're perhaps a year or two older than I am."

"What does age have to do with it? It's nothing to do with youth or age."

"What, then? Well, what—"

"If you like, I'll find a young woman for you."

"I've already found one myself."

Korzecki's eyes lit with an ominous silver glare and looked steadily at Judym.

After dinner they sat opposite each other in silence. Judym, though he was tired, felt no inclination to sleep. Indeed, he welcomed conversation.

"I'd like you to settle here at Sykstus," Korzecki said quietly, "for a purely selfish reason."

"What would be in it for you?"

"Simple! I dragged you down here for no other reason than that I had something to gain."

"Well?"

"You know me, after all, or rather you knew something of me several years ago. Since that time I've pushed on bravely in my chosen direction."

"Didn't the Swiss cure help you in those days?"

"Bosh! Oh, it helped. I'm as healthy as an ox now. I work here as an engineer. I get up at five, I go to sleep late, and I have to have strength and a sound mind to be equal to the task. It isn't about that, about health— how can I say it? —superficial health—"

"Oh, more mystical terms!"

"If you like! It's—I would just like for you to be nearby, with your honest eyes, your scholarly medical vocabulary, and your sturdy soul, your soul—don't take offense!—from the lower echelons, even with your mysterious Miss Joanna…"

"Now, listen. About that——"

"Nothing. Nothing. I'm not saying anything objectionable. It's so good for me when you sit at my table!"

Judym heard in Korzecki's voice what he saw in his look: a note too high, quivering helplessly toward some dizzy, unreachable zenith.

"What's your trouble? Tell me," he said in a kinder tone. "I'm at your service, wholeheartedly and with all the power I have, though I know you'll annoy me sometimes. And I will heal you."

"Don't worry about my annoying you. It's nothing. I'm only like a steel bayonet on the surface. Inside, I'm as weak as wax. For the rest—I'm going away."

"What does that mean?"

"Nothing. Just talk. I, if you please, have undertaken a spiritual task that ought to be called the education of the will, or, properly, the struggle with fear. I would like to achieve such mastery over the body and its so-called nerves that I will not be dependent on them."

"Not be dependent on your nerves?"

"Well! Have I put it badly?"

"Very badly."

"I want to know life and death so closely that I can look indifferently at one and at the other."

"Those are phrases. That way a man can only know life."

"Take Andrée, the explorer, for example! The people who boarded his balloon knew death more closely than life. They saw fields of white, glassy with ice, in the glow of the northern lights. They saw themselves in their loneliness there, and they saw death coming from a distance. They had seen it all winter in warm, comfortable homes, among commonplace conversations with refined women. And one day they got up and went out for their meeting with that unknown. If only I could develop such calm in myself!"

"We don't know anything about how those people looked into the eyes of death. Perhaps they felt passionate surges of ambition. Perhaps they weren't calm at all. Perhaps they felt only a lust for fame. That—and fear."

"Ambition! I like that! To die of my own volition, to die when I choose, when I myself choose, I—master, spirit, to take it in my own strong hands, to take it on my terms. Yes, there may be some ambition in that! Andrée and his companions formed their wills to such a degree that they could fulfill their intention. The point is to wake from sleep and, when death stands beside our beds, to greet it with a smile as if it were an April morning. Oh, God! Not to be afraid of death!"

"That's impossible. It's against nature."

"It's only immeasurably difficult. For other people, in any case, it's not a serious issue, or even, though this sounds rather simpleminded, a high priority. But for us, unhappy sufferers from nervous illnesses… It's possible to fight the fear of death per se, but it's impossible, impossible for me, to suppress the fear of something, a random fear, the gift of sleepless nights. Lately I haven't been able to sleep alone. A certain miner spends the night in my entrance hall."

"You see, your nerves are unhealthy."

"Just a moment. This miner is not unintelligent at all, but wise. I talked with him until I was ready to collapse in order to follow his suggestions and sleep, but in the middle of the conversation he tumbled onto the bed like a log. I found it so comforting that he was snoring near me. I sat on the couch for whole nights. If I had wakened him after midnight, that fellow with exquisite nerves—nerves like steel cables—and said to him: 'Man, you're going to die just now,' we would see what would have happened to him! He would have quivered. He would have writhed on the floor. He would have prayed and fainted from fear. And I, who was dreaming here myself as if turned to dust, whose nerves seem to wander all over the universe, I, the sick one, touched death with a finger, challenged it on my terms, looked at it in my ironic way as I would look at a man I hated. Now I feel that if you were staying in this place, I could sleep. On such a night I could think: 'Judym is not far away. I'll get up in the morning and I'll see him. I'll go to where he is.'"

When he said that, the doctor felt a cold tingling, as if a slippery green snake were creeping over him. Korzecki seemed to be watching him, but his vision was really turned inward, to his soul. There was a smile on his lips, a cryptic smile that pulled the eye to it, like the glow that can be seen now and then in a chasm in the mountains. His expression was not pleading; it carried no demand for sympathy. He had only explained the situation in a detailed, concrete, articulate way.

"So you aren't afraid of death?" Judym asked.

"I battle with it. One time I win, another time it wins. Then I have night terrors, like a small child. See: I'm sitting here with you, I'm talking, I'm calm and cheerful. I don't even know if sadness can exist. What is sadness? I know nothing of it. I'm like a Philistine who would go into a fit of laughter if someone told him that there was a grown man in the world who is afraid of 'something.' But an hour might pass and that depersonalized apparition would be standing over me. I would begin to be afraid of being alone, to feel such terrible, such terrifying suffering! Human language has no name for it. Terrors… Only the fearsome music of Beethoven some-times creates a gate to that cemetery where ragged corpses lie in pits run-ning with blood, where a human creature who has lost its reason howls and wanders, wanders forever in night that doesn't end, searching for rescue."

"You ought, so far as it's possible, to take walks in a field. To devote every free moment to diversions. To take train rides, and most of all to avoid all excitement."

"Yes: to go for a spade and dig myself out of the mud I'm lying in! But there is no place for me on earth."

"Nonsense!"

"I know what I'm saying. I can't live as millions do. Indeed, I often run away for two months in the Alps, in the Pyrenees, on a little island on the shore of Brittany. I swear off newspapers and books, I don't open letters. And what do I get for it? Always and everywhere I see the world reflected in myself, in my disturbed soul. At times when I don't expect it, rage against some foul thing seen long ago bursts out, wakes me from sleep, brings everything back to mind, shows me everything. Helpless rage, and the more helpless, the greater it is!"

"Perhaps a complete change of your way of life? Throw off all your obli-gations. Go—I don't know—back to the soil."

Korzecki thought for a few minutes, then spoke.

"No. That's impossible. Until he dies, a man must wear a certain sort of clothing, have this kind of linen and not another kind. That's inviolable! I have to earn a great deal. I couldn't wear the cord fabric they make around here, in the Łódź style; a fellow must bring it to me from abroad. That's inviolable! I also need to go to Europe, to see the art in the spring salons in Paris, to know everything, to read new things, to know what's new in the human mind, to go with the world, to ride the waves. That's inviolable! Ah! I understand what you say: go back somewhere, back to my place in the forests, spend my life on the land, like those happy people who are completely independent of everyone! I understand you. But that's not for me. I know too much. I need too much. And I have an excitable nature. In a place like that I would find some nincompoop and get into wrangles with him."

"Ah, yes!" Judym laughed.

"You'll say again: avoid intense emotion. Not only do I avoid it, I have no intense emotion in my life! What emotion should I have? Let the philanthropist have emotion. But in spite of my knowledge, some emotion that I don't understand lies in me like a thief who has stolen into my apartment and only crawls out of his hiding place at night. Meanness, abuse, evildoing, injury, misery…I pass by them calmly, coolly, I kick them, I spit at them. I always repeat to myself the highest, the most powerful, the divine words that He pulled out of the shadows of human language: 'Is this your concern, or Mine?' But without knowing it at all, I draw the pestilence into myself.

"A few weeks ago a little boy died here, the son of one poor miner who carted coal to the lift. I'd brought him a little red cap from Milan, a gift from the road that I got for a franc. Here in this garden he ran and jumped for whole days. That little head with its red cap… When I learned that he had died of diphtheria, I took the possible effect on myself very seriously, devising plans to avoid thinking about him. Well, and somehow it passed…until once, near evening, as I was sitting in this chair, I raised my eyes and saw a red spot moving along the wall. And I heard that gleeful voice.

"How do I know what that spot was? It was a red stain of sadness, a sadness as terrifying as the death of such an innocent. Night came, and with it my troubles. Insomnia: one night, two nights, three, four. I went away for two days. I rode the mail coaches wherever my eyes led me. I stood in the window and looked out at the landscape. Well, thank God, the red spot disappeared. I slept in a hotel. You will laugh at me, but so it was: that red stain was done away with, rubbed away by green, pale green."

"Your nerves are unhealthy."

"Oh, yes. But I have another sickness as well: an overrefined level of awareness. It's a thorn in my side! To be in possession of the truth is a misfortune. It's torture. There is too great a gulf between truth and this vale of tears, Zagłębie."

CHAPTER IX

"Open a New Vein!"

WHEN HE AWOKE the next morning, Judym did not see his host. He was alone in the empty apartment, which was unadorned by any pleasant or elegant furnishings. He felt as if he were in Paris again, on Boulevard Voltaire, with vile, alien air all around him. On the wall of the room where he had slept hung a small oil portrait of a man with a slender face. Its resemblance to Korzecki's face struck him immediately.

"It must be his father," Judym thought. "What an oppressive face! If someone wanted to paint pride in human form, he wouldn't hesitate to take that for a model. Those eyes don't seem relax their hold on the viewer for a minute, and they say, 'You boor! You ragamuffin!'"

He could not stay in the apartment. He drank a cup of milk that he found in the room next door and went out. He wandered around the small streets of the factory settlement with his head down, looking at everything with the keen scrutiny which, except in moments of deepest sadness, is always seen in men of modest origins.

A dense cluster of brick buildings, two-story for the most part, formed a dingy village. Along one street there were two long buildings with some fifty windows at the bottom and along the second story, like a sheepfold. Old, very old plaster had peeled away from their outer walls, revealing bare blackened brick, dirt, and leaked moisture. No trees grew around them. Not even a stalk poked up.

At the fronts and backs, in front of the doors and halls, lay piles of rubbish and puddles of wash-water growing putrid. The residents of the rooms had decorated the window recesses as they could, painting them pale blue or brown; the window frames created a true polychrome in this strange human shelter. Here and there hung a white piece of tulle by way of curtain, and some green plant soaked up water in a clay vase.

Farther away, beyond the settlement, houses that could properly be called brick huts stood on both sides of the highway. Each was as like its neighbor as if they were two drops of water. These primitive buildings, always dark because they had never been plastered, were dilapidated, leaning toward collapse, barren of any decoration. Deep in the black walls, from which fine particles trickled on all sides, the windows glistened eerily with panes that were red, blue, and greenish from being overheated.

These dwellings carried the mark, even the stigma, of the transience of their occupants. No one cared about their condition, neither the owners nor the temporary inhabitants. No one felt an attachment to these quarters that were like hotel rooms, where a wanderer might shelter his weary head from cold or rain but at any time might abandon them and move on. These buildings reminded Judym of villages he had seen on the Italian slope of the Alps, in the vicinities of Bellinzona, Biasca, and Lugano, where here and there lived men with minds blunted from the struggle with nature, which had given them nothing but a piece of bread and a gulp of vodka. Pushed from place to place, such people hung on in vegetative states from day to day.

A listless dog shuffled from one yard to the next, looking at the passerby with the utmost indifference. A wet, dirty, sad child in a gray frock the color of a swamp roamed about aimlessly with the enfeebled air of an old woman.

In a big ditch on one side of the highway a little river flowed briskly, contained by hard banks. Its red water, pumped from the bottom of the mine, deposited sludge the color of brick dust on sand, grass stems, and rubbish tossed into it.

It was a foggy day. Now and then a fine rain fell. As he walked, Judym saw a new red brick wall every few minutes, or a house that had fallen down twenty years before. The whistles of locomotives speeding through the fog in all directions, the signals from the mine like dull sighs, the wheezing of machines working everywhere far and near, carried him into emotional territory that was strange to him. He was not himself. He could not locate and get a grip on his feelings. They were still alive in him, but something had happened to them.

This was a troubled, difficult, despairing time for him, but not only because Joanna was not there. Thousands of painful emotions tore his heart. Some sights and sounds seemed to swallow up the longing for her, to devour it in their cavernous throats. Only the muted, lost echo of it

was audible in their speech. One such sound was the moaning cry of the
mine's bell that rang at a distance when the buildings belched great clouds
of steam and the spools on top of them were set in unwearied motion.
Another was the rattle of coal wagons rushing over the scooped-out
ground.

As he walked slowly along the highway, every now and then he passed
railroad tracks that crossed it. Next to one of these spurs he saw, as if
through sleep, an aged man with blackened skin sitting in a booth half dug
into the ground and, with a clouded, almost blind eye, keeping watch on
the crossing. The tracks went straight to the mine, where large wagons full
of black lumps with a dusting of lime were continually in motion. Farther
along them, another man was bustling about. Wearing a lambskin cap and
resembling a moving pile of coal himself, when he wanted to stop a loaded
wagon hurtling at full tilt, he sat on the thill fastened to the brake, tucked
up his legs, and with all his might and weight held back the wheels.

Greetings and words of respect for these people drifted through Judym's
mind, but he had no strength to utter them. He walked around them in
silence. His chest quivered, and in it his heart. In these dark, dirty figures
his most private, most genuine inner feeling greeted his own mother and
father.

"That's my father. That's my mother," he whispered.

Near a wide wood-frame house a man stopped him with a word: "The
engineer is asking for you."

Judym went into that building and met Korzecki.

The enormous room, lit by electric lamps and cluttered with kegs, was
partly divided by a balustrade, like town offices. The senior foreman and a
superintendent were sitting at a table as a list of workers who were coming
to the mine for their shift was being read. The reading was done by numbers, which were being called out by a strong, shriveled man, a German
who nevertheless cursed and vituperated excellently in Polish. Black figures
standing around the room answered with the names of their fellows who
had not showed up. The superintendent, who had been a worker and then
was promoted, roared every minute, "Quiet! Shut up! What a racket! This
is not a tavern!"

At the other end of the hall, bread was being given out. Every now and
then a new miner walked in, knelt devoutly in the center and said a prayer
with his face turned to the table, as if he were expressing adoration for
the majesty of the foreman. Now and then the whites of his eyes flashed

from under his eyelids, as if from deep within his face. Eyes were the only expressive parts of these faces. Anger, joy, smiles—everything else was hidden by a seamless mask of coal dust.

"Could I see the mine?" Judym asked Korzecki.

"What, today? How are you after that trip?"

"What do you mean, how am I after that trip?"

"Close your eyes and you'll see exactly as you do with them open."

"So it's not possible?"

"Why, certainly it's possible, but I didn't think it would suit you today. But since—you want to go down, then?"

"Yes. I want to."

"Bula." The engineer turned to someone in the group. "Go and get two lanterns ready, and shoes for the gentleman, and a jacket and hat."

A little later they went into the yard. Judym was overtaken by the mood of the day before when he saw the sorting plant and its rollers, which gleamed with spiral grooves that seemed to writhe as if they were screwing into their casings. Carts with coal, which had been brought up in the elevator from the depths of the mine, stood on small tracks and, with strong hands pushing, spilled their cargo onto the grates of spiral rollers. From there thick hunks like cobblestones flew down onto the grates below, and the fine powder and nut coal were sprinkled into sieves that pushed them out onto the edge of a chute.

Iron sieves on curving shafts, making motions like those of a manual shifter, shook out fine coal and created something like sluices for two streams. These streams flowed lazily but endlessly toward an outlet with railroad cars below it.

In the neighboring room, beside the elevator shaft, Judym gazed at the steam engine that rotated the two spools on top of the mine. Two steel cables that supported the elevator turned on those spools. One cable went down to the tunnel, the other went up. As he looked at the glittering cylinders in which the pistons worked, Judym was really searching for a bell that was hidden somewhere.

Wearing thick boots and leather jackets fastened with buckles, holding brass lamps in which wicks soaked in oil burned, the men stood in the elevator. For a second, when the elevator was still even with the floor but its planks shook, Judym felt his throat tighten. Soon his composure returned, but there was a ringing in his ears and a slight fear in his heart. The black timbers lining the shaft flashed past his eyes like an endless series of stairs.

When the elevator cage stopped, they walked out into a dry corridor lit by small electric lamps, where throngs of people moved briskly and lines of horse-drawn carts came and went. From these first lighted passages, Judym and Korzecki made their way by winding paths to machines that pumped water. Here the lamps ended and the only sources of light were lanterns carried by hand. The floor was smooth. Tracks lay along the base of the corridor. The carts with the day's harvest of coal ran over them continually, pulled by trained horses.

Doors, invisible in the darkness—placed here and there to let air into the passageways "where no light shone"—were opened by the mysterious hands of decrepit people who were ending their days here as attendants. When the engineer passed those doors, he called, "Good luck! Open a new vein!"

"Good luck!" the darkness answered.

There was something in that sound that wrung the heart. They stamped themselves on the mind, the figures of those aged men, barely distinguishable in the dark—those black lumps that in life dwell in a grave, that dream in it to the end of their days like spiders, waiting patiently for the moment when they enter the earth forever, when they go into that cold womb for the everlasting "shift." A chain of dark captivity shackles them to this place. In the dozings of old age, surely they see the warm spring sun and bright meadows sown with flowers.

The corridors differed very little from each other. Some were hewn out of coal exclusively. Some had recesses with brick walls, built in as barriers against fire or wet, loose sand, which they called quicksand. An ordinary walk with a semicircular ceiling changed gradually into a corridor with props on which lay timbers, or flitches, supporting a ceiling. These corridors led to a chute from which layers of coal fell. Timber was pushed through a wooden gutter that ran down next to a black pit. A steel or iron cable moved beside it, pulling carts in.

Darkness, darkness thick with acidic fumes, was illuminated now and then by a small lantern in invisible hands. There were stairs in some places, or, properly speaking, rungs nailed to planks. Here and there, one walked over a slippery board. At the bottom of the mine, about two hundred and fifty meters underground, a cold, damp draft drifted through the corridors. There was a whole network of those passages, and it was painfully unnerving to walk through them; a fish must feel such uneasiness when it finds itself near a densely reticulated net.

Judym and Korzecki walked in a direction that seemed to be along the right-hand side to a passage that rose steeply and at a slant, forming a blind tunnel. Soon they had to bend double because the floor above them was so low that a cart full of coal could hardly pass under it. Somewhere far off, as if at the summit of this mountain, small, pale yellow lights moved from place to place, and in a cavelike chamber that suddenly appeared, the sound of several people at work could be heard.

"Good luck! Open a new vein!" Korzecki called. The choir of friendly voices that answered made an acute, strange impression on Judym. From deep in his soul he also called to them, "Good luck! Good luck!"

Just then, it was as if a new spring of longing for Joanna had burst its dam in his heart—longing that was more poignant than at the moment of their parting.

Miners in black caps and leather belts loaded coal powder as coarse as grains of corn into long paper cartridges. Openings in the proper places were drilled by long steel spindles with ends like the points of pikes. When the loading was done, a fuse was set into each casing and held in place with rubble tightly packed from the top with a rammer, like powder in a barrel. One worker lighted two fuses, another lighted two, and a third lighted two. In darkness thick with smoke and dust, bluish streaks of fluid appeared, dripping from above. Small flames flew to the wall and disappeared.

At that time the ladders were hastily pulled away and everyone rushed to the neighboring walkway. They waited there for about ten seconds before the first explosion sounded. A current of air surged into the adjoining passages and cells, carrying a strong smell of powder. Lumps of coal came crashing down behind an adjacent pillar, and on every side something inside the walls spattered with a rapid slamming and rustling, like rats running behind tapestries. Then came a second explosion, then a third and a fourth. Smoke filled the passages and moved lazily to the lighted aisles. In the distance the roar of dynamite charges could be heard; they left a sweet smell on the air.

In one place, Korzecki called a miner by name and left him with Judym while he went to survey the work in a different part of the mine. Judym remained in the dark with a phantom holding a lamp. Nearby, a dozen people or more were busy propping up the next story. For a while Judym and the miner stood without speaking to each other. Finally Judym raised his lamp and saw the blackened face of the old man, whose gray hair was escaping from under his cap.

"What are you doing here, sir?" he asked.

"We're making a deck between the walkways. We choose a slab. We take one whole slab after the next, the length of it and the width, we prop up the ceiling with a pole, and—on! Lagging is set up off to the side. I beg your pardon; it may be that you're not familiar with the mine, sir?"

"No. I'm seeing it for the first time."

"So you—"

"What is lagging?"

"It's blocks set on end to serve as a wall. From the front as well, from the walkway at the end of the section, another such wall is built and an empty place like a door is left. And a whole section is made and the pieces cleaned off it. Just these poles are removed, and others are cut with an ax. When a miner hard at work in deep silence hears the first faint slam of the floor, then it's grab your pickax and away from the pillar! The ground breaks up in that place and everything will cave in with the rubble. Above, at the top, it all falls down as if it were in a funnel."

Judym lifted his lamp and studied the walls. Their faces, smooth or rough, bore outlines made by sharp iron that were like some diligently engraved cuneiform script. Walking slowly along a smooth wall, he imagined that he was reading them—reading a history of the pit in words composed of slanted signs tending now in one direction and now in another.

He seemed to see himself standing in a miraculous forest, a primeval wilderness uncultivated by human hands, through which no human foot had walked. All around grew giant ferns with trunks three people could not reach around, horsetails expanding upward like trees, eerie clubmoss and other unseen flora—mystical beauty and monstrous ugliness—sigillaria, odontopterids, lepidodendron. These behemoths, bound together with chains of liana, multiplied on soft, boggy ground where exquisite mosses and indescribably lovely flowers shed their fragrance in the sultry blackness of ancient shadows. Sweet, torrid years pulled these trunks and branches, which only eyes and wings could reach, from the earth toward the clouds. Throughout ages, moist, rainy winters enriched the soil. Untrammeled gales, spawned on prairies and in the snows of mountain ranges, flew in to pummel the wilderness, howling like young lions.

Then the wilderness cradled deep within her a song that roared like the sea. How often thunder cracked in her, and hurricanes trod her down, plundered her, and tore at her! Wild clouds with red sparks lit her singing depths. Then she grew hot as a vast pyre. But when the rains stopped, perennially young spring came with arms full of lilies, like a girl seeking her lover, and with playful lips blew the dust of plants onto the water-soaked ground that dreamed of the shade of branches. A new ocean of green washed over that ground, and through it dashed flinty hooves of fire, and the spokes of its cart as swift as the gale.

Once more, the random war cry of a jaguar fell on the silent thickets of the young forest, and the death-portending shout of the ruthless eagle tore through them.

Then great seas that had lain idle deep in the land burst their banks. Rampaging currents uprooted vast forests, carried them in their foaming waves like a flotilla of battered boats, and pushed them into the hollows of the lowlands. There they swept the measureless mass down as if into a grave, to be covered by layers of soil from the mountains. Through thousands of years, life was extinguished in those plants, in whose branches birds without number had nested, and a secret decaying action began. The enormous pressure of the collapsed layers, the inflow of water, and the passage of centuries created a process underground: the creation of water from the oxygen and hydrogen of these dead bodies and the extraction from them of carbonic acid and carbon monoxide. Only coal remained—immense quantities of coal, which like a solitary spirit of darkness had nothing to connect with.

Over millennia its terrible outer husk grew lifeless, cooled, and died. Agonizingly, it accreted and huddled into itself like a being under a curse. Nothing remained for very long from the old layers of plants and earth. All that was left—like a lone echo from the fatherland where everything bloomed, grew, and propagated in the skies—was the faint outline of layers of trunk or the imprint of an ethereal leaf in black, funereal stone.

The long works of nature, the results of physical fermentations and reactions unfathomable by human thought, man seizes as his spoils in brief, clever, mechanically facilitated labor. He comes into a sacral abyss with a small, pale flame and a short pickaxe. With the strength of a paltry arm he carries away what an ocean hid there. He takes the entire deposit, from outcrop to dip, rakes together the pieces, and delivers them to the world, leaving only a heap on the surface and a void below.

The earth does not give up its labor and its wealth without a struggle. Simple and indifferent as a child, it learns betrayal from man. It lies in wait for him with the lumps he moves so that it can throw them at his head when he does not look around. It sheds deadly gases in its cells and lurks like the tiger, the lord of the dead wilderness. It spills out invisible subterranean waters; it drains off water from dark lakes, accreted drop by drop through untold ages and gleaming on cold granite. It opens underground basins of quicksand, which were moved by heaps of rubble, and their loamy silt fills passages strenuously hewn out.

"The guardian spirit of the mine has not carried you off?" Korzecki's voice sounded unexpectedly as he emerged from the dark.

They moved down the long walkway. From near and far, lines of horse-drawn carts rolled along. Each of those equine workers had dragged those accursed carts behind him for whole years. When the men passed an advancing horse, he turned his head and eyes aside because his eyes were dazzled by the yellow glare.

At last they came to the shaft through which they would be catapulted a hundred meters up from the bottom of the mine. Water poured in streams there, dripped into the elevator, leaked over the wooden supports. Judym and Korzecki stood in a wet elevator among drenched people with angry faces who were yelling to each other; in only a moment they were carried up onto the upper surface. From there they walked through a damp, dark, cold passage that seemed endless. In some places the ceiling was subsiding; it warped the beams and ground down the linings. Not even mine lights illuminated the deadly blackness. Sometimes nothing could be heard but a distant rattle and the shout of a carter. Again a miner-horse appeared out of the gloom, turned its sad, longing, hopeless eyes away as if it could not bear the sight of a man, and vanished in the perpetual grave.

At a certain moment Judym heard a conversation in the darkness in front of him, or rather a monologue. Someone exclaimed in a forceful voice, "Fuks, I say, there's no pileup!"

After a moment of silence, the same voice rang out with redoubled insistence: "No pileup, Fuks! No pileup means no pileup!"

Korzecki pulled Judym over to the wall and explained in a whisper, "Sometimes a wheel on one of the carts, which are coupled together, jumps off the track. Then the horse, in this case named Fuks, stops, because he doesn't have the strength to pull, and anyway the next carts immediately derail. The driver must put the cart in place and set it back on the track. When he has done that, he calls to the horse to let him know. But sometimes he attaches one cart too many and then the horse stands still, thinking that the extra weight is the result of a derailment. The driver assures him by shouting that there is 'no pileup,' but the horse pulls lightly and then stays in place, since he still feels too much weight. Then the carter must convince him, so he walks along the carts to the very end and then once more solemnly shouts: 'Fuks, no pileup!'

"At that point the poor horse accepts that he is being exploited, musters his strength, and drags the burden of his pitiful lot along in the dark. Perhaps he even becomes conscious of what it is. Perhaps he even quietly sighs or clenches his teeth. But he must stick to that agreement, because when he dreams of something different or tries to protest by, let's say, stopping, the driver might thrash his back with the whip, and that wouldn't improve their relationship."

"Well, but you should forbid that!"

The engineer raised his lamp and said with a bullying, sarcastic smile, "I do forbid it. I sternly forbid it."

After a moment he added, "I forbid it. I forbid it with everything in me. But I don't have the strength anymore…"

· CHAPTER X ·

A Pilgrim

On one of the days that followed, Judym and Korzecki went to see Kalinowicz. It was a clever gambit, an undertaking worthy of an engineer, to cultivate the acquaintance of a person of influence.

"Who is Kalinowicz?" Judym asked as he walked down the street that led to the home of one of the powers of Zagłębie.

"Not to know that! Not to know something so elementary! Well, he is an engineer, but a great one."

"Is that all? Why do we have to see him today?"

"Because it's a smart thing to do."

"It's going to storm. It's hot as hell." After a moment Judym added, "I'd rather get a whipping from Aunt Pelagia than go on this visit just now."

"Come. There will be a storm," Korzecki rejoined, looking around the neighborhood.

They were standing on a rise. A town lay below them. There were rows of houses very like each other, black, veiled with smoke. Within a relatively short distance, fires from large blast furnaces erupted as if from the craters of volcanoes. A strong wind snapped away patches of flame from those fires as if it wanted to throw them at the town. Trees were sprinkled with dust and smoke, like the workers in the mine and mills. The green of grassy spaces was covered with something like a funeral shroud.

On the far side of the forest and a line of hills, a steely cloud with dark underpinnings stretched along the horizon, moving slowly. A chilling gale flew from it, dying down now and then. It seemed to creep around the walls, drift under the fences, peep into the gutters and perch on trees whose uppermost branches quivered restlessly, fearfully. Sometimes it sped full tilt into the middle of empty streets with a roar and a whistle, like the vanguards of invading armies from far away. The men saw chimneys all around, pouring out slanting columns of smoke jerked about by that wind.

From the dried puddles that filled the whole length and breadth of the streets, mountains of brownish-gray dust flew up every minute, darting over the houses and the factories like grotesque retorts, and hurling itself down onto human dwellings. This flying mud covered a town that was sad to the eye, queer, cold, and somehow illicit, like a dodgy business deal.

Beyond the town, the director's mansion stood on high ground, in a shady garden. As they were walking in over narrow, carpeted stairs, Korzecki, stepping far to the side so as not to tread on the carpet, said in a low tone, "Now summon all your powers, for the time of testing is upon us."

A butler led them into a salon with windows that looked out on the town. A soft, fluffy rug muffled their footsteps. The wheels of satin-upholstered chairs were also silenced and moved without a rustle. On the walls hung pictures and engravings in prodigiously wide, magnificently ornate frames.

With a modest air, Korzecki sat down in a chair. He adopted a pious expression as, with his eyes, he directed Judym's attention to the ceiling and wallpaper. Judym looked at them in spite of himself, and saw a painting depicting a landscape with ruins and a shepherd boy. But before he managed to take a good look at the wallpaper, the voice of their host sounded in the doorway.

"Respected engineer!" he greeted Korzecki. "Sir, you are a rare and welcome guest."

Korzecki returned the greeting and in a voice full of gravity pronounced the name of his companion: "Dr. Judym."

The host reached out and pressed Judym's proffered right hand with a bow which, in view of his corpulence, must have been somewhat difficult. They seated themselves in satin chairs, immersed their feet in the softness of the carpet, and carried on a conversation about nothing, that is, about subjects without the slightest importance. They spoke of the look of the neighborhood, the climate and hygienic conditions of Zagłębie, and other droning nonsense.

Their host was a man with an air of superiority, almost obese. His head was bald, shining and strongly domed; such a skull was fit to carry an iron helmet. His bristling mustache with its upward swirl suited it perfectly. His straight nose and his eyes, large and stern under bushy brows, bespoke the noble blood that pulsed in his veins. His gentle movements and the delicacy of his manner seemed to hinder that powerful figure. Yet the wide lengths of excellent cord that swathed his legs and torso produced the effect of clothing thrown on casually and provisionally.

Korzecki, looking respectfully around the drawing room, leaned toward its owner and whispered, "I see something new."

"Well, what?"

"A little piece, but it's dazzling."

"That clock?"

"Yes! Yes!"

"I bought it in Munich," the director said with discreetly concealed satisfaction. "To tell the truth—for a song." After a moment he repeated, "For a song!"

Soon he rose and helped his guests to a closer view of a French Empire clock that stood under a bell jar on a cabinet shelf. There really was something very pretty about its unpretentious lines and the simplicity of its surfaces.

"And is the one by Uhde framed?" Korzecki asked spiritedly.

"Oh, yes, yes! And I tell you, friend—exquisitely. Perhaps you would like to see?"

"Oh, if you would be so gracious—"

"Please. This way, please."

"How is Miss Helena? Is she still absorbed in the art of Rops?"

"Ah, yes, she and her Rops…this way, please, gentlemen…"

All three went into an adjoining study that was sumptuously appointed. The floor was carpeted and the room was filled with furniture over which a splendid desk reigned. Candelabra, figurines, photographs in standing frames, paperweights, and many, many books were piled on it. The walls were hung with paintings and drawings and a bookcase, masterfully carved, glittered with gilded titles.

"Have you seen this little folly, sir?"

Korzecki squinted and with a look of the most profound curiosity examined the indicated picture.

"I bought this piece in Milan, in that—you know, gentlemen, that hole in the wall—where DaVinci's *Last Supper* is. Yes, I dropped in there. It was hot. Outside the window I heard some officer shouting to muster a division of those knights Menelik later swept out of Ethiopia like rubbish. I saw that some young Italian boy was copying the *Supper*. He was as lovely, the rascal, as the most wonderful painting. His hair was windblown and his eyes, nose and mouth were like a hawk's. He was painting away. He jumped to his easel and cut with his brush, cut in all the meaning of that word. I saw that he had only done one figure and the rest were barely, barely sketched. That picture, I tell you, gentlemen, was a thousand times more striking to me than the original. What an expression! What a face! The look of those eyes! An apostle indeed… and not only an apostle, but a man who asks agonizingly: 'Is it I who am going to betray you, Lord and Master?'

"I couldn't restrain myself. I said to the little painter, '*Signore* painter, how much does this picture cost?'

"He looked at me and muttered that it wasn't painted yet. I told him, as I was able, that I didn't care. I pointed to that apostle and shouted that I wanted him just as he was. He glanced at me suspiciously, like a wolf, and painted on. When I asked him again, he growled, 'A thousand lira.'

"'Oh,' I said, '*signore*, isn't that a bit much?'

"Finally, after some haggling, I pawned the little beast off with six hundred francs and took the picture almost unpainted. Here in the house my daughter and I simply cut out our apostle and threw away the rest. But what a face! Isn't that so?"

"Oh, yes. Really. You have something here."

Then Korzecki leaned toward Judym and whispered so that their host heard him, "How tastefully this home is appointed, isn't it?"

The director smiled slyly and said, "Tastefully, eh? You flatter me! Anything so as to… It isn't easy living in our style, the august Sarmatian style."

Emboldened by Korzecki's words, he led his guests to the next drawing room, which he called the "studio."

"But we were going to see the Uhde!" the flatterer reminded him.

"Certainly. In the studio."

When they entered that room, a woman of perhaps nineteen rose from behind a wide table to meet them. She wore a pink gown of fabric so light that it allowed the viewer not so much to see as to feel its lovely shapes. Her hair was pale, almost white—the glistening color of a spruce freshly planed. Her eyes were blue like her father's, but not so stern and cold. From a distance she made a strange impression on Judym, as if she were a rose barely in bloom. She had been writing or drawing something. The unexpected entrance of two men from outside the family circle confused her a little; she squeezed a pencil in her right hand as if she were at a loss; only as she greeted them was she forced to drop it on the table.

Meeting her in the workroom freed Judym and Korzecki from the obligation to tour the more distant rooms in the house. They returned to the first drawing room. The young woman, whose name was Helena, walked with Korzecki, and carried on a friendly, relaxed conversation. Her pretty, round face, blossoming in rosy tints that came and went, was turned toward him, and her bright, restless eyes gazed at him with insistent curiosity.

Korzecki was grave, as if he had suddenly aged. He spoke in a cool voice without sarcasm or malice. He looked at her musingly, but with a certain aversion. Judym, listening with feigned attention to the director's opinions on industrial development in Zagłębie, heard snippets of their dialogue. Several times he caught names: Ruskin, Maeterlinck.

Before he managed to grasp the meaning of their conversation, a man a little over twenty came into the room. He greeted Korzecki with a firm shake of his right hand. In a moment he introduced himself to Judym:

"Kalinowicz."

"A son, no doubt," the doctor thought.

The young man turned to Korzecki with visible pleasure and began a conversation with him. Helena listened in, and soon even the old director turned his chair in their direction. Judym, feeling shy and strangely sad, listened to the buzz of talk, but his feelings wandered far afield. It seemed to him that he was hearing strange, beautiful singing, perhaps one of Grieg's songs growing distant among high mountains—particularly in a certain place on Righi, under the lonely summit of Dosse, where he had been once in his life.

"Who's singing that, and why?" he thought dreamily, arranging his feet on the fluffy carpet as decoratively as he could.

"...nor do I intend to admit defeat!" the young man exclaimed. "Not at all! You will not prove that! There are certainly standards to distinguish good and bad."

"And...since they exist..." Korzecki said quietly.

"We know, after all, that slavery is a way of life to which we must not return. You know that as well as I do. And every man—"

"So—what of that?"

"Our awareness is a standard. The good of society—"

"Just so: the good of society! We always talk as if we know what the happiness and the good of society are, but the happiness of the individual never concerns us."

"Oh, that! That! The happiness of the individual man, the individual," the director put in, waving a hand.

"The happiness of the individual must be subordinated to the general good."

"That's a statement of violence against the human soul," Korzecki said with a conspiratorial glance at the director. A mischievous smile flew like a spark into his eyes and onto his lips. "How many people the Holy Inquisition burned at the stake on that principle, under that standard!"

"The Inquisition!" the young man fumed. "What the devil do you drag in a thing like that for? But what is the happiness of the individual? Answer that, sir! I don't understand it."

"Actually, it's something so far from us that you don't in the least understand it. Something we don't know at all. What was the philosopher Leopardi speaking of, saying that 'the hope of his cherished dream does not vanish, but desire does'? Happiness: a bright meadow full of flowers where the human soul can walk freely. The possibility of action, speech, thought, of at least feeling, at least breathing freely. The search for gratification—"

"I understand: pleasure in the Greek sense."

"What you have is consolation. Pleasure is something else!"

"I understand you. But one note on this: a mentally ill person with persecution mania, or even better, a suicide, seeks gratification by trying, for example, to gouge out his eye. Do we have the right to permit him to find that gratification?"

"A mentally ill person is at the mercy of an atrocious force which, quite simply, turns his thoughts and feelings upside down, which—but, sir, what a poor example!"

"Why?"

"Remember Dr. Pinel, who first removed shackles from the hands and feet of the mad. For I don't know if you are aware that at one time the 'standard' called for keeping the mentally ill in manacles. Later it put them in strait jackets and locked them in cells. At present the principle of 'no restraint' has come into effect. I hope that some day a stay in a hospital for the insane will be almost like freedom—that there the unhappy, sick mind will unfold its dreams without obstacles."

"Well, I'm not versed in these subtleties. But let's take another example: the upbringing of children. When I was in school, my greatest pleasure came from playing hooky. My delight was in fooling the teacher almost as a matter of honor, playing tricks, cribbing."

"Yes, yes. Upbringing. Not long ago Wincenty Pol, the poet, was sighing nostalgically, together with the readers of his 'Adventures of Benedykt Winnicki,' for the practice of educating grown men of good family with a heavy whip as an aid to memory—by flogging them as they lie on a carpet, according to ancient tradition. You would not agree with Pol's system?"

"He, no, but I—who knows?" sighed the director.

The young man looked at his father with a smile and a peculiar wink.

"You would not agree. We are a thousand miles closer than that to the bright meadow. The same in the upbringing of small children. We are a thousand miles from the cheders, one of which might be located in a house next door. The business of educating children is hurtling forward like a train. I've had a good look at schools in Switzerland—"

"Where school attendance is compulsory."

"Where a six-year-old child goes to a play school with the greatest pleasure. They tell him wonderful fairy tales. He makes the first friendships of his life and experiences the first mysterious delights of learning. But his mind advances from that school."

"Advances…But he never doubts that learning the alphabet, spelling, and calligraphic scrawling is torture."

"In the Hebrew school, God, yes. How hellish!"

"In other schools as well. And the child must be subjected to that torture. Every child who is born and lives to the proper age. Suffering! All work is suffering. What can we say? Hygiene is such an issue. How can they struggle with an epidemic in our villages? With mandates, of course. What can be done with highwaymen, with thugs?"

"Let's leave the highwaymen out of it. Whenever someone dwells too much on the subject of criminals, I think he is displacing the blame for something onto them."

"So what would you do with them?"

"I… I decline to answer that question."

As Korzecki said that, his eyes seemed to blaze with crystalline fire.

"Why?" Helena asked quietly.

"Because, madam…because…I don't know how to answer it."

"Because?" she insisted.

"I don't know how. My head hurts a little."

The young woman blushed. Her lips trembled and for a moment a look of humiliation distorted them. An uncomfortable silence prevailed. They heard the wail of the wind and the tapping of rain on the panes of the great windows. Korzecki seemed not to be conscious of it at all. A malevolent smile shimmered on his face. He began to speak without raising his eyes.

"You err when you say that all work is suffering. That's not so at all. I pass over the fact that we inherit from our forebears an addiction to work, which we can verify by pointing to the large number of wealthy people who work for whole days without compensation. Let's take—let's take something else. All renunciations, sacrifices, labors, heroic actions. Mickiewicz says—listen to these supremely wise words—'By the sacrifice of the spirit, I understand the act of a man who, having received the truth and identified himself with it, spreads it, manifests it, serves as its organ, its fortress and its army, not heeding the looks, the voices, and the countenance of the enemy.' Look here: is such 'sacrifice of the spirit' suffering, or can it be? He himself says that it is the most painful of all sacrifices, but it seems to me that he has in mind only its loftiness, its exalted nature. A man who identifies himself with the truth must feel joy, ecstasy, even when he is defeated, or so I assume. Even when he is overwhelmed—"

"That's surely a paradox," Judym interposed. "It seems to me that that really is the most painful of all sacrifices."

"I don't think so. Such a man experiences happiness in his action. He demonstrates the truth he receives; that means that he has an outlet for the happiness that's in him. There must be as much satisfaction in that as in a miser's schemes and shifts to save money or a stock market trickster's swindles."

As this conversation was going on, enormous thunderbolts roared and the rattle of the approaching storm shook the whole house. No one paid any attention to that except Helena, who glanced at the windows after each gust of the rising wind. The storm hit them like missiles; it beat them as if fists were trying to shatter the frames.

It was almost dark. A ruthless, somber, driving rain set it. Now and then a frightening glare lit the room, and then the bronzes, the trinkets, the metal fittings on doors and windows and other gleaming surfaces burst at the eye, only to dim suddenly as if they had been absorbed by a gasp, as hard fear took everyone's breath away.

"We've wandered from the subject," said the young man. His voice had an odd ring in the low rumble that filled the air.

"We haven't wandered from it at all," said Korzecki, who was evidently excited by the storm, for there was urgency in the way he spoke. "Do your 'standards' exist for a man who has received the truth? Can you make them an obstacle to such a man?"

"Certainly! Every citizen should be held back before undertaking anything so that society can inquire whether it will have a positive effect, can examine it to be sure it will not go against or undermine what the human race has laboriously built."

"Jesus Christ was nailed to the cross by the force of such principles. Men said, 'We have our law and according to that law He ought to die.'"

"That suffering saved the world."

"The power of salvation didn't lie in suffering, but in what He taught."

"So for you there are no fixed values? Do we not know for certain that infanticide, or the murder of elders, are bad things, and that the sense of solidarity among people is a good thing? That to speak truth is good and to lie is evil? And that whoever wants to propagate the idea of infanticide or destroy the sense of solidarity ought to be removed—"

"That to tell the truth is good and to lie is evil I, for example, who sit here in the same room with you, am not at all certain. Often to tell a lie, or even to profess it as a belief, is the highest virtue, merit, heroism, fully as much as speaking the truth is. I grant a man absolute freedom to speak either the truth or a lie. What can one man know of the truth or falseness of another man's soul? In the human heart there are oceans, deserts, mountains, wandering glaciers. Christ said, 'Judge not that ye be not judged.' That's everything. As for infanticide and slavery, you defeat me dialectically, for I can't equivocate about such questions. I'm at an impasse.

"In reality, we all know for certain that slapping a paralytic is a bad act, and whoever would do it should be restrained. That's a syllogism; that's all there is to it. But can you imagine the human nature we have in mind involved in such an act? The propagation of the concept of slavery is impossible among such people, just as it would be impossible for the two of us to go to a party where delicately brought up women were gathered and start a barroom conversation or, let's say, remove our clothes. It could be argued that such behavior is possible, but de facto it's impossible. Yet, after all, no written law forbids such freedom. It's one minuscule part of the all-pervading feeling of human connection that guides the flow of sensible, kind conversation that is pleasant to everyone.

"Only one thing is undoubtedly evil: injuring our neighbor. A human being is a holy thing that no one has the right to injure. With that exception, everyone is free to do as he likes."

"An idyll, sir! That's an idyll! That's Arcadia! Injure our neighbor—that's well enough! But what is an injury? What is its limit?"

"The limit of an injury lies in the conscience, in the human heart."

"Well, sir—aren't these jokes?"

"No. This is the thought of the greatest Creator of all. On it the world stands. Think what would happen to it if these words were expunged from memory: 'By this shall they know that you are My disciples, that you love one another.' Love between people should be sowed like golden grain, and the poisonous weeds of hate must be torn out and trodden underfoot. To hold man in the highest regard—that is the teaching."

"The speed of human progress depends on the demolition of the elements that block its path."

The director leaned toward Judym and said under his breath, "I confess, sir, that I don't in the least understand what those gentlemen are disputing about so fiercely."

Korzecki, still engaged in conversation with his opponent, turned quickly toward them and said, "Actually, about nothing much."

"It's so cold," the young woman whispered, looking apprehensively at the window.

"You're a little frightened. True? You're frightened," Korzecki said.

"Nonsense. Only a chill has come on so quickly! And the darkness!"

"Ah! The darkness." After a moment he added, "How unfortunate a person is who must now travel over an unfamiliar road! A man who rushes to an unknown destination, who keeps going, keeps going endlessly. That 'pilgrim who on his way toils by the glare of thunderstorms…'"

Hailstones mixed with rain began to strike the windowpanes. The talk died away. Judym rose from his seat and looked out the window. Amid the twilight and the downpour the fire of the great furnaces flared now and then.

The doctor was ill at ease. He thought of his fiancée. He was at the mercy of an illusion that when the storm was over, when the darkness dispersed, he would hear some news, some echo, some word. A silent sigh of something like consolation burst from him. He had already written a letter and addressed it. Who knew—perhaps some strange chance was bringing word from there, from those beloved places? Perhaps she was looking at the storm as well. Perhaps the same feelings, like nimble lightning, were illuminating the mournful dusk for her.

Out of nowhere the director put a question. "Doctor, you have just returned from Paris?"

"I returned two years ago."

Korzecki turned toward them with lively interest, only awaiting the moment to join their dialogue. At that very instant the butler drew aside a curtain and bowed to Helena. She rose and invited the others to tea. They passed to the next room and sat down at a very large table set with many plates and platters and much glistening glassware.

Young Kalinowicz seated himself by Judym. He informed the doctor that he had just finished the polytechnic in Charlottenburg near Berlin, that he was returning there to take a doctorate, and that in the meantime he was watching the drainpipe through which gold was flowing to France.

"Sir!" he exclaimed. "One's hair stands on end when one looks at what's happening here. I don't want to offend anyone, but medical help, for example, is given in a way that's like the mail. On the appointed day a doctor who has eight factories under him goes from place to place. Don't you find it painful sometimes to hear this?"

"No, God forbid. I'd like to find employment here, so I must get to know the conditions thoroughly and from all sides."

"Yes? You know, that's interesting. So you would like to settle here. And have you taken steps to that end?"

"Not at all."

"Do you have connections?"

"None."

"Ah, I see."

"Please don't take everything my son says about Zagłębie seriously," the director interposed. "He has a special disinclination, if you'll pardon me—"

"Yes, a disinclination, and really a special antipathy!" the young man said slowly. "These people murder those goodhearted physicians. A doctor's services are free, so everyone comes to him, sick or not, with delusions, with imaginary ailments. In the clinic at my place our doctor has sixty patients per hour. Just say whether there can be that many sick people in a small community! The fact is that in the country as a whole, forty-one percent of workers avail themselves of medical advice at the owner's expense, while fifty-nine percent do not."

"Where do those figures come from?"

"Of 856 enterprises examined, there was no medical assistance in 818. In ten that assistance simply existed, in twenty-four it was passable, and only in four was it up to standard."

Judym's eyes narrowed and he laughed deep in his heart. Memories of his struggles in Warsaw flashed before his eyes like a bad dream.

"Not only the conclusions but even the statistics are exaggerated," the elderly man said in the phlegmatic tone of a seasoned polemicist. "I understand profoundly the necessity for medical assistance. I am a supporter of it, a fanatical supporter, if I may say so, of hygiene and so on. But here is a fresh fact. Near the big furnaces there are scales for taking in ore. As a scale moves up and down, there is a heavy fine for anyone who sits on the scale and uses it, either to go up or to make a quick descent. Do you believe the statistic on the upward and downward movements of the elevator? That's also a statistic that you ought to note in some hemisphere of the brain—"

"There's no great need."

"Aha!"

"Most certainly."

"But there is something else. Between two furnaces is a shaft through which a scale passes. It hadn't occurred to anyone that it is possible to crawl in there. What do you gentlemen say? A man crept in and sat in a notch halfway up that shaft and whistled, staring down. The scales move silently. There was a roar in his skull on the very spot! The factory is responsible for that! There was no roof there, let it be noted, no roof!"

"There's a roof in this place, if I do say so myself!" said the young Kalino-wicz, helping himself to a very large portion of roast beef from a platter.

"Such a fellow working at the open-hearth furnaces, at the rollers, on the wire, earns a couple of rubles a day. How does he live, what does he do with the money?"

"Interesting question."

"He goes on a spree, he lives beyond his means and falls into debt. On Sunday you see a boor like that: stylish tie, handkerchief. He comes into a shop and orders: 'Collars, sir, only the most fashionable, the best.' They bring in special scented soap. Scented soap is in vogue just now."

"Isn't that offensive on the face of it?" the young man mumbled, eating like a hungry animal.

"Not so much offensive as sad."

"Why sad?"

"Everywhere excess, excess! In all layers of society, living beyond one's means, wastefulness."

"Soap—is that wastefulness?"

"No one saves anything. With earnings like this we still have a mob of bankrupts."

"Reduce the beasts' wages. Then they will behave more reasonably! There will be no soap or annoying neckties."

"On the contrary, the wages must be raised, and now! Raised! Let them get top hats from Paris and overcoats from Vienna."

The butler took the platter around and changed the plates.

It was evening when, after drinking tea, everyone except Helena left the dining room and gathered in the study. They smoked cigars: Korzecki, with a rather pompous look, held one as large as a carrot between his lips. Young Kalinowicz had just resumed his dispute with his father when the butler came in, cautiously approached Korzecki, and whispered something to him.

"Oh, to me. With a letter, surely?"

"I beg your pardon, engineer, sir, I don't know. It's something urgent, he says."

"Here?" Korzecki asked with a careless gesture. He followed the butler without taking the cigar from his mouth.

Judym wanted to end the visit soon, to leave right away. He linked his arm in the young Kalinowicz's and asked where Korzecki had gone.

"He's talking with some messenger who came here to find him."

A dream unfolded in Judym's heart: a letter from Joanna!

"Sir," he said quietly, "could I see this messenger? I expect some information that I am anxious about. Perhaps there is a letter for me."

"Please!" cried the student, pushing chairs aside as they exited the room.

They found themselves in an empty hall with a door that opened onto stairs. The stairs, which led from the second floor to the ground level, were not broken, but they stood steep as a ladder beside the wall.

Judym, standing in the doorway of the hall, saw a light down below. Korzecki was holding a candle in his hand; it flickered in a draft that rushed in through cracks in the timbers. The lower door was closed, but splashes of rain came in through every opening. The downpour rumbled on the roof of an outbuilding.

The messenger was standing beside that door with his back against the wall. He wore a cap with a visor, a capacious summer overcoat, and thick boots. His clothes were soaking wet. Water streamed from him and formed a puddle around his feet. Judym, who was looking at him attentively, noticed that he was shivering all over and that his head hung limp on his chest, as is often the case with people who are drenched to the skin. Korzecki was talking with him in a low voice that was drowned out by the hum of the wind.

"He's not here to see me," Judym thought. A vast grief wrung his heart.

Korzecki took the packet the dripping vagrant had brought and went up the stairs. When he saw Judym at the top, he bristled and asked harshly, "What are you doing here?"

"I thought some mail might have come for me."

"No, no. Nothing of the sort! It was that idiot, the courier."

"Courier?"

"A courier smuggling contraband textiles. Someone told him I was here. You see the state of my nerves! I didn't expect to find you here, and right away... A fine voice I spoke in! Don't say a word! I sounded ridiculous even to myself, let alone these well-bred friends."

"I'm sorry that I unnecessarily—"

"Nonsense. A smuggler..." he whispered. "I left a packet of corduroy for clothes in Katowice two weeks ago. I bought the corduroy in Krakow. I like that kind very much. Perhaps you'll take some for yourself. I don't want you to pay me. I told that rascal on the quiet to bring it to me one of these days. Today he had a propitious moment, so he tracked me down here."

"He's sick. I saw how he shivered."

"You think so?"

"I don't just think."

"He must have a glass of vodka. Quickly. The man is unwell!"

Korzecki walked quickly and overtook the butler in the doorway to the dining room. "My friend," he said, "be so kind as to bring out a glass of vodka to the man standing there. Give him two glasses. Even three."

"Let him have three glasses," Judym put in.

"Doctor—you know—be so good as to take them to him yourself. You'll see if he really has such a chill."

"I'll be glad to."

Judym took an ornate flask, a glass, and a candle from the butler and went down the stairs. The man was standing in the dark and appeared to be dozing. Judym put the candle on the ground and poured the vodka into the crystal glass. Then the courier raised his head and opened his large, pale blue eyes. The hand in which Judym was holding the glass went numb as if the air had suddenly grown cold.

The smuggler eagerly drank one glass, two, three. Then, without even nodding, he opened the door and vanished into the black chasm of night, into which the rain was still pouring.

Two hours later Judym was returning home in a carriage with Korzecki. The deluge had stopped. It was a dark night, foggy and unpleasantly chilly. In the impenetrable gloom, misty, whitish, decaying miasmas seemed to walk about with fleshless bodies. The roads were flooded; water flew from under the wheels in every direction with an ear-splitting hiss. When they had ridden out of the bystreets, Korzecki stood up and, holding the bar of the front seat, explained something to the driver. He sat down and said to Judym, "Would you like to take a little detour? Fine time! Wet…"

After a moment he added, "We can go to the tailor so I can give him this material for clothes right away. What do we have to keep it in the house for? Isn't that right? It only clutters up the place and nothing more."

"As you say. As for me, I'd be happy to take a detour."

"So plunge ahead, friend! Quickly! Quickly!" Korzecki called to the driver. "You'll get a ruble as big as your front wheel!"

The whip cracked and the horses stepped briskly forward. They rode for a long time in silence. In one place electric lamps appeared, surrounded by thick fog. The submerged light created a sad-looking circle around itself like the livid shadows around the eyes of the sick. Between that light and the road lay stagnant water. A bluish gleam played over the dark ripples in a shallow sinkhole. It moved with the motion of the carriage, ran with it like an arrow-shaped road marker coming out of the darkness.

"Where are we?"

"On top of the mine."

"And where is that water coming from?"

"The layer of coal is very thick here, but it's a couple of hundred meters deep. The coal is excellent. The ground sank into a void and its surface bent. The water collects in the basin."

He was silent, and again they rode some distance without speaking, this time through fields. Korzecki sat huddled in a corner, holding his packet on his knees. He began whispering something.

"What are you saying?" the doctor asked.

"Nothing. I often mutter to myself. Do you remember this poem:

That I hardly knew my native home,
That I was like a pilgrim who toils on the road
By the glare of thunderstorms..."

Judym did not answer.

"'I was...' What terrible words!"

In a moment beyond the power of words to describe, their hearts met.

Korzecki spoke first. "It must have seemed ridiculous," he said, "the show I made of myself tonight. I babbled like an old lady."

"To tell the truth—"

"Indeed. But it was necessary. I had a serious interest in what was being said. Didn't you understand what I was getting at?"

"There were moments when I had the impression that you were playing the devil's advocate."

"Nonsense! No."

"So you think crime is absolutely the same as virtue?"

"No. I only think that there are so-called crimes that should enjoy the same impunity as virtue."

"Ah!"

"The human spirit is as uncharted as an ocean. Look inside yourself. Don't you see dark abysses where no one has been, that no one knows of? What we call crime can't be extirpated by the force of coercion, or by any other force. I strongly believe that in that spirit to which we have not attained, there is a hundred thousand times more good—but what am I saying? In that spirit everything, almost everything, is good. Only let it be set free! Then evil will be seen to vanish."

"Is it possible to believe that?"

"I saw a picture somewhere. A criminal had been hung on a pole. A crowd of judges was coming down a hill. Their faces were full of joy, of victory. They were telling me that the man was guilty."

"But something proved to you that he was not. Perhaps he was a patricide? What made you believe otherwise?"

"Something spoke to me about it. Daimonion."

"Who?"

"Something divine in me spoke about it: the Daimonion of Socrates."

"What's that?"

"He speaks deep in my heart. There below the diurnal world I hear him. I would have gone and kissed the feet of that hanging man. And if a thousand credible witnesses had sworn that he had killed his father, his mother, I would have taken him down from his cross on the basis of that whisper. May he go in peace."

The driver stopped in front of a house. It was so dark that Judym could hardly distinguish the black mass of the building. Korzecki got out of the carriage and disappeared. For a moment only the swashing of his footsteps could be heard as he waded through puddles. Then a door opened. A dog barked.

CHAPTER XI

"Sprinkle Me, O Lord"

KORZECKI HAD acquaintances in one house in the neighborhood. Sometimes—once at Eastertime—he had visited there. They were the Daszkowskis, a family of aristocratic origin but no longer wealthy, almost impoverished. They had leased a farm of a few hundred acres on a poor, stony piece of ground. Their village could only be reached through forest, on the most impassable roads the world had ever seen.

Returning home for lunch after a ramble on foot one day, Judym found a middle school student in the lodgings he shared with Korzecki. The youngster alternately reddened and went pale as the engineer tried in vain to get him to throw off his shyness. When Judym came in, the student bowed to him repeatedly and lowered his eyes still more.

"Olek Daszkowski," Korzecki said by way of introduction. "He has come to ask if you, doctor, would be willing to visit his sick mother. I give you fair warning, though, that it's a two-mile trip. Isn't that right, Olek?"

"Yes, and the road…is very bad."

"Oh, you will put the doctor off coming! You must assure him that on the estate—"

"Ah, yes. A tree-lined avenue."

"Let him suffer a little discomfort!"

The schoolboy, not knowing what to say, only held his cap in his hand and shifted from one foot to the other.

"And what's wrong with your mother?" Judym asked in a very gentle tone. His voice was like a tender hand lifting a person with all its strength, a strength that came from deep in the soul.

"It's her lungs."

"She coughs?"

"Yes, doctor."

"Has this been going on for a long time?"

"A long time."

"Two years? Three?"

"Longer. As long as I can remember."

"Your mother has been ill for as long as you remember?"

"She coughed, but she didn't stay in bed."

"And now she does?"

"Yes. Now she's always in bed. She can't walk."

"Very well. We'll go. We can go right away."

"Doctor, if only—"

"Oh, we must eat first. No question about that!" Korzecki put in.

"But if the doctor—" the student said hastily. At that instant he realized that he was about to say something out of place, and he was confused.

"You see, the doctor must eat. And surely you are hungry, Olek?"

"I—oh, no! You are so kind…"

Soon lunch was served. The schoolboy was hesitant, picked at his food, and did not take his eyes from his plate even for a moment. Korzecki seemed cold; his tall frame was hunched over. He spoke with difficulty. When horses pulled up in front of the house and Judym walked toward them, he put his hand on the boy's neck and made his way haltingly down the steps with him. At the bottom he said, "Greet your mother and father for me. I would be happy to visit them, but something… By no means… So much work here. But tell your mother that—God willing, we will see each other soon."

Judym happened to glance at the man's face. He was gray. Two solitary tears ran from his eyes.

"God willing, we will see each other soon," he repeated in a cryptic way of his own.

The shabby, ramshackle wagon started up. It was pulled by two nags who were haggard and not well matched. One was a farm mare with a big lowered head; the other must have come from some livery stable. Now only her backbone, protruding like a saw, evidently impressed her companion from a lower echelon. On the box sat a man in a visored cap and highlander overcoat, who woke the horses from their stupor—horses that were transporting people of dignity in the same conveyance from which their driver had removed fertilizer or potatoes.

Judym's eyes wandered musingly over soft mosses and whitish-green bilberry leaves. Every stem of moss was composed of luminous stars, as if from sunbeams that came in contact with the earth and were transformed into tender plants. Amid this regal cushion of greenery, dear to lovers of woods, piles of large bluish-gray rocks were visible. Fir trunks with gray patches, overspread with dry moss, cut the distant horizon.

When the horses entered the deeper forest, under the shadow of spruce and fir, dark roots cut across the road like nests of snakes. Every minute the wagon creaked when its spokes sank up to the axle into the deep sloughs that had been stagnating in these places for ages. The mosses there could hardly push up through the thick reddish-yellow coating of dry needles. Cones and white, dried-out, broken branches lay everywhere. Here and there loomed black piles of rotting brush. Now and then from a distance came the cracking noise of a tree being cut down.

Sometimes the wagon slogged along in pure, deep yellow sand that hissed quietly as it sprinkled off the wheel rims. It was the only sound within earshot. Only once, somewhere in the distance, the crisp call of a bee eater sounded.

The sun crept stealthily into the interior of the forest. The shadows of trees and branches were so deep that, even at that time of day, dew still lay there. In one place a clearing met the eye, embraced on all sides by forest as if by a loving arm, for life and for death, for all time. Dark clumps of juniper rose from this green turf. Under a wall of spruce opposite, a solitary tree stump, cut close to the ground and stripped of its bark, gleamed white as a skull.

A white butterfly flew around in the silence. It landed on blades of the curling grass that hardly covered the barren earth. Among the gray stones, a low-growing yellow flower looked at the sun with wide-open eyes. In the deep hush, the quiet, tremulous chirp of crickets could be heard. A man could count the beats of his heart and feel the blood coursing through his veins.

Strange thoughts sprang to Judym's mind, thoughts not like a man's own but inspired by this magical, enchanted glade. It was clear that this patch of forest meadow was the only one in the world in which a person could live to immerse his soul and dream. To dream of things that lie in the deeps, in darkness, in closed places, things that do not pass or perish, that are as simple, naïve and mindless as this glade. To allow everything in his heart to flow out of it, all the holiness, all the ugliness.

All the while, the schoolboy said nothing. He turned respectfully toward Judym and answered all his questions only with yes or no.

Around four o'clock, the forest gave way to fields. In the distance, a clump of trees and a farm appeared.

"That's Zabrzezie," said the student. Soon they were driving into the farmyard.

This was a homestead that had seen better days. The manor house seemed even more deserted than the farm buildings, before which fertilizer rotted and violet dung-water glittered. It loomed white in the shade of four linden trees that grew in a row at its entrance. The sick woman lay there on a makeshift bed.

The appearance of the wagon evoked genuine panic on the property. People scurried around. A gentleman with graying hair and a weathered complexion came out to meet Judym and introduced himself as the patient's husband. Behind him came two homely young women who were alarmed and curious, for to them the doctor's arrival was undoubtedly an extraordinary event.

Judym immediately set about examining the ailing woman. She was a few years past forty, wizened as wood shavings. A brick-red flush in an elliptical shape blazed on her left cheek. The initial examination at once revealed consumption in the final stage. Only to help conceal the meaning of what he was seeing did Judym listen long and closely to those poor lungs as they labored with their remaining strength. When there was nothing left to do, he felt a peculiar sadness.

"What is there to say?" he thought. "Should one lie and pretend?"

"How do you find the state of my health, doctor?" the sick lady inquired when he sat down in a chair and meditated.

"Ah, madam… I won't conceal that this is a serious condition, but people do live with it, particularly in the country. I've known many cases of this type. I'll prescribe you a detailed treatment."

"Oh, I'll be grateful to you all my life, doctor," she whispered, looking into his face with burning eyes. "I so want to live, I so want…I have the children and the whole farm on my hands, and I'm lying here all the time. What would happen if I couldn't do—"

"Madam, you must forget about the farm altogether."

"Oh, if only I could, doctor. Those rascals, the peasants around here! If only it were possible to have good help! It's one thief after another."

"All right, all right. You must forget that they exist in this world. You must lie in the fresh air, you must eat—"

"I was drinking a preparation made by boiling pine bark."

"Boiling what?"

"Pine bark. It was dried on a baking tin—"

"From now on you won't take that. You must drink milk and cognac."

During the entire lecture on the treatment her case required, hurried footsteps, whispers and the clatter of plates could be heard in the house. Soon its master invited Judym to the table. After a moment his wife was to be taken to the bedroom, for night was coming on.

The sun arced down like a shield, a blood-red circle widening in a mist. Dark vapor spread over the earth and covered the red disc, which fell ponderously into vast depths that seemed full of ever-deepening sadness. A painful tumult stole into Judym's heart, and a sorrowful anxiety, as if that holy, flaming orb would never rise out of the darkness again. A mournful sigh came from deep within him; he could not understand what he was feeling. By chance his eyes fell on the sick woman.

She was sitting on her bed in a nightshirt, so poor, so emaciated, meager as a skeleton. Her lips whispered words of prayer. Her hands were folded and pressed tightly together. Silent tears trickled from her eyes. She was looking into the distance, at the sun, which was falling into the world beyond—into the unknown night, the everlasting road. For the first time in his life, Judym was listening intently to a human silence like the silence of the field and forest.

As the doctor sat intent on these meditations, a terrifying shriek tore into the stillness. It was an old peacock that sat on the housetop every night, emitting this wild, raw scream like rusting iron. Its echo flew through fields immersed in quiet, through the mists, through the surrounding woods. The sick woman shuddered and her thin hand touched the doctor's.

"I'm so afraid, doctor!"

"Of what, madam?"

"Of something like that…"

"It's nothing, nothing. Hold my hand tightly. What is there to fear here—"

"I hate it so when that old peacock cries. It seems to me that it's not him, but—"

"Oh, whoever saw such a thing!"

She lowered her head and fixed her smoldering eyes on his face.

"Doctor," she whispered, "have pity on me and help me live a little, just a little longer. I want to. I must! I want to know how things will be with Olek. I want to know what will happen to him."

Judym looked up and saw the boy standing by the woven fence. He was crying, hiding his face in his hands.

"He's my only son. Only he loves me. My daughters do, too, but he... One day our cook went to the fair, for these days each one does whatever he pleases, and Olek took a chicken and killed it and dressed it and roasted it for me on the spit. But he forgot to salt it. I ate the whole thing. I never said a word to him about not salting it. I salted those little bones with tears."

The sun went out of sight. It cast a sparse red afterglow that spread fear, not light.

"I'm so sorry that Mr. Korzecki can't come," the sick woman said. "He promised to visit us, but he hasn't been here for so long. When we see each other again—"

Olek spoke up. "Mr. Korzecki said he hoped he would see you again before long, mama."

Judym ate a great deal of chicken and lettuce with sour cream for dinner and left in the evening. The driver, who was not given to conversation, took him back by the same road.

It was dark. The moon did not shine. Only a lonely star scattered its quiet gleam here and there. The forest was submerged in blackness and in cool fog that spilled like water between the branches. Judym was closed into himself. Ideas awoke in his soul as if children who had been sleeping there were raising their miraculous little heads and revealing, without reserve, the thoughts that were flowing through their hearts. Strange thoughts...

The sick woman he could not help seemed the being to whom he was closest. There were moments when he felt that he himself was lying on that cot, looking into the waning sun, whispering a quiet prayer. With a drowsy eye he looked at that woman's whole life, saw it clearly, and lived through it vividly.

The wagon rolled into the clearing. A pale fog flooded the place like dreaming water. Motionless tops of spruces could hardly be seen against the dark sky. Below them stretched the forest night, impenetrable, stony.

Judym strained his eyes to find the white stump he had seen on the way

STEFAN ŻEROMSKI   299

to the farm—and was suddenly frightened to the core of his being. From far away over the dewy ground came the cry of the peacock.

The doctor closed his eyes, buried his head in his arm, bent over, and whispered something to himself with trembling lips.

CHAPTER XII

Daimonion

D R. JUDYM secured the position of factory doctor and took lodgings in the vicinity of the coal mine. The next phase of his life involved ordinary, run-of-the-mill work. Korzecki, who lived about a mile away, was his only friend. They met in the evening from time to time and passed a couple of hours in conversation.

It was not a healthy relationship. Korzecki was wearisome. When he appeared in the doctor's house, he brought anxiety and a painful sadness with him.

One afternoon in August, Judym received a letter by special messenger. It was a quote from Plato's *Apology of Socrates,* written in Korzecki's hand on a fragment of paper torn from a diagram made at work:

"Something that proceeds from God or a divinity manifests itself in me. This has happened to me from childhood. An inner voice speaks which, whenever I hear it, always leads me away from what I intend to do, but never drives me on to do anything.

"What has happened to me now has not happened by chance. On the contrary, it is clear to me that to die and free myself from the cares of this life is judged to be better for me. That is why this Daimonion, this prophetic voice, has nowhere offered me resistance."

Judym read this with no particular uneasiness. He was used to Korzecki's eccentricities and thought he was only looking at an invitation to visit, framed in the engineer's characteristic style. Nevertheless, he ordered horses.

He had hardly ridden out to the gate when he spied a carriage with a team galloping at full speed, racing down the side roads toward his house in a cloud of dust. He thought the horses were running away. He ordered his driver to stop and wait.

The carriage rolled onto the highway, still going full tilt. As it flew by his vehicle like a storm, Judym noticed that no one was in it except the driver in the box, who was shouting something.

The driver managed to stop his team about a furlong farther on. He turned back. Patches of foam fell from the horses' muzzles and a gray mass of dust covered the carriage. "The engineer—" the driver cried.

"Who?"

"The engineer!"

"Korzecki?"

"Yes! Mr.—Korzecki."

Judym got out of his carriage and quickly, instinctively, leaped into the other one. The horses flew like a hurricane again. Looking at their wet bodies gleaming through the dull brown dust, he only thought of what a glorious ride it was. It was good, pleasant, incredibly exhilarating that they had come just for him, driving with such fury. He lounged on the seat and stretched his legs.

Before his frame of mind changed, the carriage stood in front of Korzecki's lodgings. People were running in all directions. One person was pressing himself to the wall by the stairs so as not to block the way. The door was open.

In the second room, on the sofa that served as a guest bed, Korzecki lay in his clothes, covered from head to foot by a horrifying mass of blood.

His head was blown to pieces. Where the left side of his forehead should have been, and over all of his left cheek, lay a clump of cooling blood.

Judym lunged toward the body, but knew immediately that he had a corpse in front of him. There was no heartbeat. The outspread fingers of one hand were hard and black as iron.

He closed the door and, without thinking of what he was doing, fell onto a chair. There was a roar in his head and the crash of hooves galloping over hard stones… the crash of hooves galloping over hard stones…

His eyes moved sluggishly from one object to another. All the wardrobes and cabinets were gaping open and the clothes were dumped out. One drawer in the table was open. A large anatomical atlas lay there, open to the page with the likeness of the head. From the back of the skull to the front there was a thick red-penciled line running toward the left eye. Close beside it were several sets of handwritten letters and figures.

Judym threw the atlas aside and sat down in a corner, a kind of niche between two wardrobes.

He had seen death so many times. So many times he had examined it as a phenomenon. Today, for the first time in his life, he had seen its features and its soul. And he bowed to it, bowed deeply. The red line with an arrow on its tip seemed to come close to him; strangely, it reminded him of the arrow on the water rippling over the sinkhole that he had seen on the way home after the visit to the Kalinowicz family. A mysterious shudder ran through the deepest chamber of his heart, as if he were going to hear a bell tolling a cruel hour.

As he sat immersed in his thoughts, the door opened quietly and someone entered. It was a man, a tall blond with large, pale blue eyes. Judym recognized him.

The newcomer walked quickly into the room where the dead man lay. He did not notice Judym at all. His eyes went to the inanimate body with childlike astonishment. His face showed fright; he whispered something. He leaned over the remains and gently and carefully placed his hands under both sides of the lifeless head. He raised it as if he were trying to awaken a sleeping man.

Then he took the left hand in his palms. He tried to straighten the clenched fist, to flex the fingers. When the dead members resisted, he blew on the painful joints and warmed them with his lips. With motions like those of an old man, so great was his suffering, he tidied the dead man's hair and fastened the buttons of his coat. Only after a long time did he stop and stand without moving. He rubbed his forehead with an anxious hand. Judym saw into the depths of the man's soul, which was then seeing the stark reality of death.

The unknown man sat down beside Korzecki's feet and looked at him with wide eyes. His chest rose with a fitful, rattling moan as if a stream of blood were about to burst from it. His contorted mouth flung out short, broken words.

· CHAPTER XIII ·

The Torn Pine

IN THE MORNING, before eight, Judym was making his way on foot to the railroad station. It was early in September. The sun was still caressing the ground as dark, gloomy houses covered themselves with its bright robes.

The day before, Judym had received a letter from Joanna announcing her arrival. Together with Wanda and her grandmother, she was coming to Drezno, where the three women were going to meet the Karbowskis. The grandmother wanted to spend two days in Częstochowa. Joanna was going to devote one day to visiting a cousin who lived in a certain town in Zagłębie. She wrote that when she got off at the station she would like a few minutes with her cousin, but that she wanted to spend the whole "precious" day looking over the factory and other things worth seeing.

She underlined heavily the sentence expressing her decision not to visit anyone else. Reading what she wrote, Judym had the impression that the letters were oozing blood and contorted with pain. He walked to the station thinking only of what was involved in her wish to spend the day with him. The whistle of the locomotive at the station wrung his heart.

"Oh, if only she weren't coming today. Not today. If only it had already happened," he whispered with pale lips.

At the station he met several people who greeted him by raising their hats. That drained his self-confidence still more.

The signal sounded in the distance and soon, like a snake with colorful coils, the long body began to bend at the switches. In one of the windows the doctor saw Joanna. She was wearing a modest traveling hat and a gray dress. When she walked down the stairs from the car, beautiful as a joyful smile, somehow lovelier and more charming than ever, he shivered uncontrollably. He thought he would die of pain at her feet, the feet he loved.

For a moment they could not find words. Even the pressing of hands seemed strange to them, and being together and able to speak without witnesses, as they went down the street and away from the station, was an overwhelming novelty. Judym felt the delightful touch of a delicate, silky, warm glove on his right hand. With a slight movement, as if he were straightening the lapel of his coat, he held that hand to his chest as if it were inexpressibly precious; but the heart to which he pressed it had a writhing viper locked inside it.

They passed down a wide street, walking on a muddy pavement, speaking of neutral things. Joanna had to keep her dress from being soiled. Now and then she raised her glowing eyes, and at such times her luminous face reflected a touch of sadness at such a stiff reception—a sadness Judym did not fail to notice.

"Would you be so kind as to show me the factories here, Dr. Judym?" she asked a little flirtatiously.

"Gladly. We're just going—"

When he accepted the formal address without protesting, and immediately agreed to visit the factory, her face went pale for an instant.

They entered the factory yard and were surrounded by a wilderness of machines and workshops. In large open rooms, wire was coiled like golden serpents. The caves of open-hearth furnaces belched fire. Farther on they heard the groaning of steam hammers beating white steel beams.

Heaps of coal and scrap metal, ingots, and piles of rails got in their way. Judym had obtained permission to tour all the works, and had even gotten a technical specialist delegated to show him and his "cousin" around. The technician showed up quickly, clearly more inclined to serve as guide to the "cousin," even in the doctor's company, than to pore over a drawing in his office.

So the three of them walked together. The technician was a young fellow with elegant manners. The "cousin's" presence caused him visible distraction as he tried to organize his explanation of the percentage of iron in the local ore and the various types of ore that had to be brought in from elsewhere.

They went up stairs that led to a large furnace. They saw the cascade that cooled the heated wall; they saw the hose that brought hot air to its interior and that seemed to pulsate like an aorta. Joanna could not gaze long enough at the thin streak of slag that spurted like blood from the upper opening. The furnace was tapped near them and the fiery river spilled out onto the floor. Amazing sparks shot from that golden stream. Its waves flowed obediently to their troughs, which were opened for them by blackened people with mesh masks on their faces who wielded long poles. A glow still stood over that pool of flame when the three had to abandon it and go elsewhere.

They were led into a room where machines were pumping blasts of hot air. Gigantic wheels, a dozen or more meters in diameter, half buried in the ground, rolled in their places—rolled in silence and something like grandeur. In cylinders that glittered like mirrors something made a constant smacking sound, like the mouth of a sloppy monster chugging down a drink.

From another place came a blare not of this world: a short, abrupt, Satanic laugh. Joanna was deeply alarmed. She felt as if the laugh were directed at her, as if someone had seen her joyful dreams of happiness and her quiet love. She looked at Judym, seeking assurance to the contrary in his eyes, but that beloved face was impassive.

They looked at the open hearth furnaces, which produced steel that was poured out into ladles to make beams. The beams traveled from there to the rolling mill, where they were thrown into the bellies of the stoves again and heated to whiteness.

In large rooms lined with iron plates, all the doors stood open. Drafts blew along and across them, cooling foreheads, backs, and hands heated by white iron. There were no diseased lungs here, no nerves. Whoever got sick died.

A white steel beam sped through the room like a fireball on a handcart carried by people the visitors could not see. It fell on a grating that came out of the floor. The grating resembled a man's back a dozen or more meters in length, with something like vertebrae composed of elongated circles. It bent completely, like a spine.

Four enormous blackened people from one side and four from the other side of the rollers, wearing mesh masks, took the beam in their grip with long tongs. They pushed it hard between the lower rollers, which were wide open; the steel slipped in between them like a hunk of butter. The grating that rose from the floor waited for it on the other side. The workers' movements were fluid and rhythmic, almost like a dance.

When a white plate, crushed and bent like flatbread, appeared before them, they took it with their extended "hands" and pushed it in between the upper cylinders. Reduced to half its former thickness, it flowed out on the other side, where four men waited for it. They closed in with precise movements, like iron machines: one, two, three, four. They extended long hands armored in iron. They struck the plate and pushed it away. They immersed the hot tongs in water. They seized other tongs and waited like soldiers.

A ribbon of white metal, longer and longer like a flowing streak of fire, appeared above and then below, now here, now there. It floated in the air. It seemed to escape hurriedly, like a reptile in a fairy tale when angry children chase it. It hid in crevices and lost its vigor.

The gratings clanked and trembled. They rose to the height of the gaps between the upper rollers, then moved down to the lowest ones. High up, in silence, a man stood without moving from his place, turning a crank that pressed the rollers closer together. Near the gratings, steel snakes flew over the floor.

A white piece of a flaming bar, inserted into a tight opening, rushed out into the open every minute, making its way into narrower and narrower hiding places. Young men with short tongs stood there, seized the muzzle of the snake as it emerged, and carried it with easygoing movements to the hall. Only when the tail began to tap on the ground did they guide it to another crevice. The flexible body ran in at a mad pace; the tail, vanishing into the opening, fluttered left and right as if it were alive.

There was a deafening crash and a steel bar fell onto an anvil. A stationary steam hammer flew down onto it like a thunderclap, straight as the blow of a fist. The crushed "bloom" took on the form of a flat disc. Then in its center they set a tool that would beat out a perfectly round hole. A hammer beat furiously time after time, ringing with a powerful moan that resounded in the rooms, in the air, on the ground. The lion's roar of iron reverberated, groaning with the anger of mined metal defeated by the powerful arms of men.

The steel circle with the pierced hole would become the wheel of a locomotive. This heap of yellow clay extracted from below the earth would now travel the length and breadth of the world, reaching its remotest corners, carrying happiness and despair, violence and brotherhood, virtues and crimes. Before it would stand on the rails, it had fought with its master. It had eaten out his eyes and flooded his face with sweat. It had filled his lungs and his heart, which were exposed to heavy drafts, with the flames used to subjugate it. It had torn at his nerves in the very moment when the steam hammer tore at its particles and smashed them.

The steel was removed from the anvil, placed on curving forks, and pushed aside. Two people approached it: one with a sharp hammer like a mountaineer's hatchet, the other with a hammer on a long axe handle. The hatchet was put to the protruding edge of the wheel and the other hammer began to fall on its head. Not a single blow missed. The dry clank of iron on iron was heard. To Joanna it seemed like the singing that can be heard in a cathedral after the great roar of the organ: fearful, timid singing from the crowd.

The cooling wheel went farther on its way. Judym leaned toward her and asked, "Do you see the work these people are doing?"

"I see it," she said with amazement in her voice.

"Yes, yes! Watch them closely."

They said nothing more either in the rooms or in the big yards littered with mountains of dust, scrap, and sand. The wind sprang up, carrying dust and a strange airborne rust from one place to another. When they had said goodbye to their obliging guide, they passed the factory gates, left its walls far behind them, and walked beyond the town. It was almost noon.

The houses that stood by the road were smaller and smaller, shabbier and shabbier. The ditches beside it were polluted with poisonous runoff from the factory. Along that road at the end of the town stood shacks, the remains of country cottages, that aspired to look like town houses. The ground was swampy. Damp grasslands with loathsome water oozing over their dark bottoms lay all around. A little higher, clay pits were filled with rainwater. Pines that had survived the clearing of the forest rose here and there.

Judym went in with Joanna to the yard of one stinking homestead, opened the door uninvited, and motioned with his eyes to the people inside. There were children of laborers in the zinc works, abnormal specimens of humanity, prematurely old, with cadaverous faces and expressions that seemed to call on Heaven for revenge. Ugly, bad-tempered women looked at the visitors, as did sick people who might have thought the doorway to death was standing ajar at last.

They walked from house to house. Before they were able to get away from there, Judym asked without raising his eyes, "Where will we live?"

For a long time she did not answer, but her eyes brightened.

"Here?" he whispered, drawing something in the sand.

"Where you like."

"But would you like to be here?"

"Yes."

"Why here?"

"I'd like to help you with your work."

"Me... with my work..."

"Now you're thinking: 'Woman, is this your concern, or Mine?'"

Judym looked at her with fear in his eyes and said in a quiet, dreamy voice, "Where did you get that phrase?"

"We'll establish a hospital, like the one in Cisy. But, good Heavens! It will be completely different. I'll be your medical assistant."

"Good. But will you be able to manage the house? The house?"

"Ha, ha! I haven't been wasting time. I've been getting up early in the morning every day all this while and going to the housekeeper to learn to cook, do the washing, iron, fry."

"Make preserves?"

"You bet! If m'lord only knew what preserves!"

"Really?"

"Yes, really! I've put them all up from A to Z, the way it will be in our house."

"In our house..."

"In our own house. Don't think I want a large place, or furniture! Not at all! I can't stand furniture, polishes, lacquers. Curtains, carpets, I can't bear any of it! Wait, I'll tell you..."

"Joanna, dear—"

"Wait. Everything or almost everything that other people have too much of, we'll give up for the good of these people. You don't know how much happiness... With the leftovers that you'll give your wife, with those throwaways, you'll see what she will do."

"What she will do?"

"Before you look around, our house will be full of furniture as simple as that of the poorest people, but more beautiful than anyone's. We'll create a source of beauty here, a new sense of beauty, of art yet unknown that sleeps beside us like a princess under a spell. There will be pine stools, benches, tables, covered with simple kilims."

"Yes. Yes."

"A runner for the hall, woven in a peasant workshop from remnants of material, is just as nice as a Persian rug. Spruce walls are wonderfully lovely—"

"You're right!" Judym said, looking with wide eyes into her face, which was full of happiness. "That's true, undoubtedly. I thought so myself! A man becomes attached, must become attached, just as much to a simple kilim as to a Gobelin tapestry, to a stool as to an ottoman, to a print cut from a magazine as to a valuable painting."

"We'll love everything because it will be ours. We'll get it with our own blood and sweat, without harm to anyone. No, believe me! People who leave our house loving you will glance back and see the beauty in all our things. All the people you will heal, good doctor…Good doctor…"

A heavenly whisper of adoration came from her lips. She spoke on.

"Really, when you know everything, when you see it all closely! I'll love everything because it will come from you, from your clean hands. Those objects will become part of me, like my hands, my legs, perhaps even my head. Like my very heart. And if we have to throw it all away, to push it aside with one stroke…

"When a visitor or patient comes, that person will be amazed that people live so happily and in such a different style. Simple, clean furniture, wildflowers in a clay vase… What do we want with the cold glare of manufactured products? Why do we need clothes, carriages? I never felt greater delight than when my father took me to the woods in a cart with no springs, over a road cut by ruts and full of protruding tree roots. No spring could have bent so perfectly as the oaken ladders the carpenter carved to make the sides of the wagon. Ah, I lost my family home so long ago! I hardly ever had it. I was scarcely in my next-to-last year of primary school when my father died. I remember very little about my mother… Every creature has its hearth-fire, its roof. The little lark… he does, too. When I think that now that rootless life of mine is going to end!"

"And what will happen to those cottages that we saw a while ago?" Judym stammered out the words in a voice that was almost a growl. She stopped on the road and waited in astonishment. He looked at her but did not see her. His eyes had narrowed and gone white.

"What will we do with them?" he asked, standing still.

"With what?"

"With them! With these shacks!"

"I don't understand!"

"I must tear down these stinking dens. I can't watch these people live and die from zinc. Wild blossoms in a flowerpot, yes; that's fine. But is it possible?"

She took his hand because a premonition like cold steel was slowly permeating her heart. He jerked it away and said gruffly, rudely, looking straight ahead, "I must tell you everything, though it will be worse than death to me. I would truly, truly prefer to die like Korzecki—"

"Korzecki?"

"If only I had the word for this! I love you so! I never thought something like this could happen to a man. Those smiles of yours that reveal your heart as if they pulled a veil from it! Your soft black hair! I wake in the night and I can't sleep; I see you, I feel you on my heart. A long, pure, sacred moment passes before I realize that no one is there. And from the time I came here and began to look around, something in me has fanned the fire. It burns in me! I don't know what burns, I don't know what feeds that fire—"

"My God!"

"You see, dear—"

"My God! Your face!"

"You see, I come from the lower class, the lowest rabble. You can't image what that rabble is like. You don't have the slightest comprehension of what lies at its heart. You're from another caste. Anyone who comes from that underclass himself, who has lived through everything, knows everything. Here people die at thirty because they're old. Their children are mentally defective."

"But what does that have to do with us?"

"I have a responsibility for all of it, after all! I do!"

"You…a responsibility?"

"Yes! I'm responsible before my own soul, which cries inside me, 'I won't allow it!' If I don't do something, I, a doctor, who will? No one."

"Only you?"

"I was given everything I needed. I must give back what I took. That cursed debt! I can't have a father, a mother, a wife, anything I would press to my heart with love, until these miserable nightmares disappear from the face of the earth. I must renounce happiness. I must be alone. No one can be with me. I can't belong to anyone."

Joanna stood where she was. Her eyes were lowered. Her face showed no sign of life except for short gasps through her nose. She spoke a few quiet words that seemed drenched in the hot blood of shame:

"I won't hold you back."

"You wouldn't hold me back. It's I who wouldn't be able to pull myself away from you! The dried seeds of the parvenu are sprouting in me. I know myself. In any case—there's nothing more to say."

She trembled as if those words had pushed her backward. They walked side by side in silence, walked on and on. Wagons carrying zinc ore moved along beside them together with smaller wagons and carriages and many people on foot. They saw none of that. The highway led them to the forest and they sat down under a tree.

Joanna felt his arm against hers and saw that his head was hanging down. She could not move her hand. She sat as if she were fast asleep, like one who has imbibed a sea of pain and is too weak even for one sigh.

Judym heard her one burst of lonely weeping, as though she were weeping to God. He did not raise his head. He did not know what time it was when he heard her say quietly, from the depths of her tears, "God grant you success."

He could not answer, but some alien voice—as if it were the Daimonion of whom Korzecki wrote before his death—spoke from deep in his soul:

"God let it be so."

Joanna stood up. For a moment, from under heavy, listless, drooping eyelids, he saw her face, which was ravaged with pain. It was like a plaster death mask. Another minute and she was out of sight. She had gone along the highway toward the town, toward the railway station.

He sat there for a long time. When he looked at the road again, there was no one to be seen. There was only the wind, whipping up lime dust, sweeping it aloft like chaff: lime dust, rising like derisive laughter.

He hurried away.

He walked along the edge of the forest, then through the muddy grasslands. He wandered aimlessly. As evening came on he saw the skeletons of the mine buildings in a field. At the sight of them, terrible hatred and supercilious contempt opened in his heart like a muzzle with fangs. He walked on.

He stood on the bank of a wide body of water with a shallow overflow. In the low, scanty, yellowish grass, this black spillage of death was fermenting. It rippled above the chasm of the mine in filthy waves. The dark water seemed to be dreaming, waiting for the time when it would fall into the hollowed-out depths and fill the empty passageways, the alluring vacant spaces that pulled it, sucked it, called to it.

Judym recognized that water. That was it! He had seen it in the night.

That night… He searched the waves for a gleaming sign, a long moving needle that pierced like the finest Damascus steel. And he felt the point in himself.

Far, far beyond the forest a train whistle sobbed as if its sound were a mysterious word containing the meaning of life.

Just beside Judym's feet was a wide, dry rubble pit, a crater like a funnel with its narrow end down. The old, abandoned passages of the mine ran deep in the earth below it. Layers of sandstone and clay shale from the excavation for the building supporting the first floor had collapsed of their own weight and fallen; fragments of them filled the empty spaces that had contained seams of coal. The outside soil slipped down into the crater together with grass and bushes and formed a pit sixty feet deep. Where that soil had torn loose, streaks of gray and pale yellow sand could been seen.

Stunted, miserable pines stood all around. One of them grew on the edge of the pit. Because the ground under it was partially broken away, its roots on the right side were being pulled down toward the pit, while the roots on the left remained on solid ground; what had happened at the mine was tearing it in two. A part of its trunk reached up and another part went into the pit, as if the tree were a human being impaled. The lower part, pulled down along with lumps of soil, survived like parts of a body under torture. Its upper tentacles, deeply embedded in the earth, held on with all their might.

Judym stepped into the pit so no one would see him. He threw himself down on his back. From time to time he heard beneath him, deep in the earth, the sound of blasting with dynamite and powder. Above him he saw clouds moving over a blue sky: bright clouds, holy clouds, now reddening.

The ragged pine stood just over his head. From the pit he saw its split trunk, which leaked drops of resin like blood. He looked at the gash for a long time without turning his eyes away.

He saw every fiber, every sinew in the torn, suffering cortex. He heard lonely weeping around him, lonely as though someone were weeping to God. He did not know who was weeping.

Was it Joanna?

Or was it the passages like graves deep in the mine?

Or the ragged pine?

FINIS

A Translator's Note

I FIRST BECAME ACQUAINTED with Stefan Żeromski's writing in the 1990s, on a day when my Polish travel agent and I were driving out in Warsaw for lunch. As we passed the mid-city bookstore named for the great Bolesław Prus, the car stopped. I was informed that it would not move again until I had run into the store and bought Żeromski's *Popioły* (*Ashes*), a two-volume masterpiece about the Napoleonic wars.

I was hungry. The driver was adamant. I bought the book.

As I crawled through sentences whose author expected an incredible level of general awareness from his audience, it struck me that Żeromski was not the most reader-friendly of novelists. But in *Ashes*, as in *The Homeless*, his passion was incandescent, blazing through the barrier of language. He ruthlessly dissected the very souls of his characters. He abhorred platitudes, loved surprises, and posed enigmas fearlessly. Yet the position of his narrative in relation to the great questions was always clear.

Is war an evil, or a plow that prepares a moribund world for new life? That was the great question in *Ashes*. In *The Homeless*, Żeromski demanded:

Is health an amenity for the fortunate, or do all have a right to it?

What responsibility does each of us bear for the evils that happen to other people?

How do we relate to our families when we cannot accept their way of living, but we cannot forget or replace the sense of origin we share with them?

His answers, as they emerged word by word from the Polish, were often oblique, sometimes cryptic, never trite.

As a lexical exercise, translating *The Homeless* was neither very easy nor extremely difficult. At first both my modern dictionaries and much older ones offered me definitions that seemed an eighth of a tone off, but when I came across the *Dictionary of the Polish Language* edited by Witold Doroszewski (1958-1969), I found definitions that in most cases fit and illuminated Żeromski's text.

A larger difficulty was the author's refusal to disrupt his narrative with explanations, even when parts of his text were bound to be baffling, especially for readers from other times and places. For example, there were two rather puzzling mentions of fabric. In one, a man delivering a packet of corduroy for a suit to a friend was referred to as a "smuggler." In the other, the hero's sister-in-law, packing for a journey out of Poland, cut her best dresses apart at the seams to sidestep a law against bringing silk garments into Germany. Some research helped to connect and clarify these vignettes with a little information about the highly competitive European textile industry of the time and its tariffs—information not provided by the author.

A letter to the heroine from an unnamed country, written by her brother, opened a more perplexing information gap. The letter writer excitedly described taking a journey by reindeer-drawn sledge through a snowy landscape in deadly cold. Evidently he was in Siberia, but whether voluntarily or as punishment for some crime—and if so, what crime—was left unexplained in the novel. References to Siberia had to be veiled at the time Żeromski was writing because Russia occupied a part of Poland, and Russian censorship forbade mention of exile to the remote penal colonies. What other effects on the novel—what ambiguities, oblique references, or omissions—may have resulted from state-imposed censorship, or self-censorship as a secondary effect of it, are not fully known.

It is a special privilege to translate a novel written under such conditions. Even its gaps have their own eloquence. And the COVID epidemic, which set in not long before I started on the book, put its own stamp on the experience of translating the narrative. As I was working through Dr. Judym's fight with moneyed interests that refused to protect farm workers from malaria, news services were reporting that our meat packing companies would not adjust conditions in their plants to protect employees from the virus. In some quarters, physicians trying to control the epidemic were ignored, their warnings rationalized away, just as Dr. Judym's warnings were waved aside. Żeromski, it seemed, offered a penetrating view of the axes of human behavior—not only greed but nepotism, complacency, and class loyalty among the powerful—that cause history to repeat itself.

Contemporary reality resonated powerfully with the text, reinforcing its meaning and affirming its enduring value.

Stephanie Kraft
Amherst, Massachusetts
October, 2023

STEFAN ŻEROMSKI (1864-1925) was born near Kielce, Poland into a family that was aristocratic but not wealthy. He was a great lover of landscape; imagery from his home region, which included the Holy Cross Mountains, is prominent in his work. He was employed briefly in a famous spa town that was the model for the spa in *The Homeless* before he became a librarian. He led many social and educational movements that pushed back against restrictions imposed by the powers that occupied Poland before World War I. At one time he and his wife hosted an orphanage and an underground Polish school in their home. In the 1920s Żeromski was a leading contender for the Nobel Prize for Literature. Distinguished in his own time and known as "the conscience of Polish literature," he was deeply mourned on his death in 1925.

STEPHANIE KRAFT is the author of *No Castles on Main Street* and the translator of two Polish novels, *Stone Tablets* by Wojciech Żukrowski (Paul Dry Books, 2016) and *Marta* by Eliza Orzeszkowa (with co-translator Anna Gąsienica-Byrcyn). She was a newspaper reporter and freelance writer for forty years and travelled annually to Poland for more than thirty years.

JENNIFER CROFT is an author, critic, and translator. She won the Man Booker International Prize for her translation from Polish of Nobel laureate Olga Tokarczuk's *Flights* and a Guggenheim Fellowship for her novel *The Extinction of Irena Rey.*

BORIS DRALYUK is a poet, translator, and critic. He is the author of *My Hollywood and Other Poems* (Paul Dry Books, 2022) and won a National Book Critics Circle award for his translation of Andrey Kurkov's *Grey Bees.*